CLAIMED BY DARKNESS

CLAIMED BY DARKNESS

S.R. HARTLEY

CLAIMED BY DARKNESS
Broken Gods, Book 1

CITY OWL PRESS
www.cityowlpress.com

Cover Characters by Miroslava Hrebeňárová.
Cover Format by Tina Moss. All stock photos licensed appropriately.

Edited by Lisa Green.

For information on subsidiary rights, please contact the publisher at info@cityowlpress.com.

Paperback Edition ISBN: 978-1-64898-534-8

Digital Edition ISBN: 978-1-64898-535-5

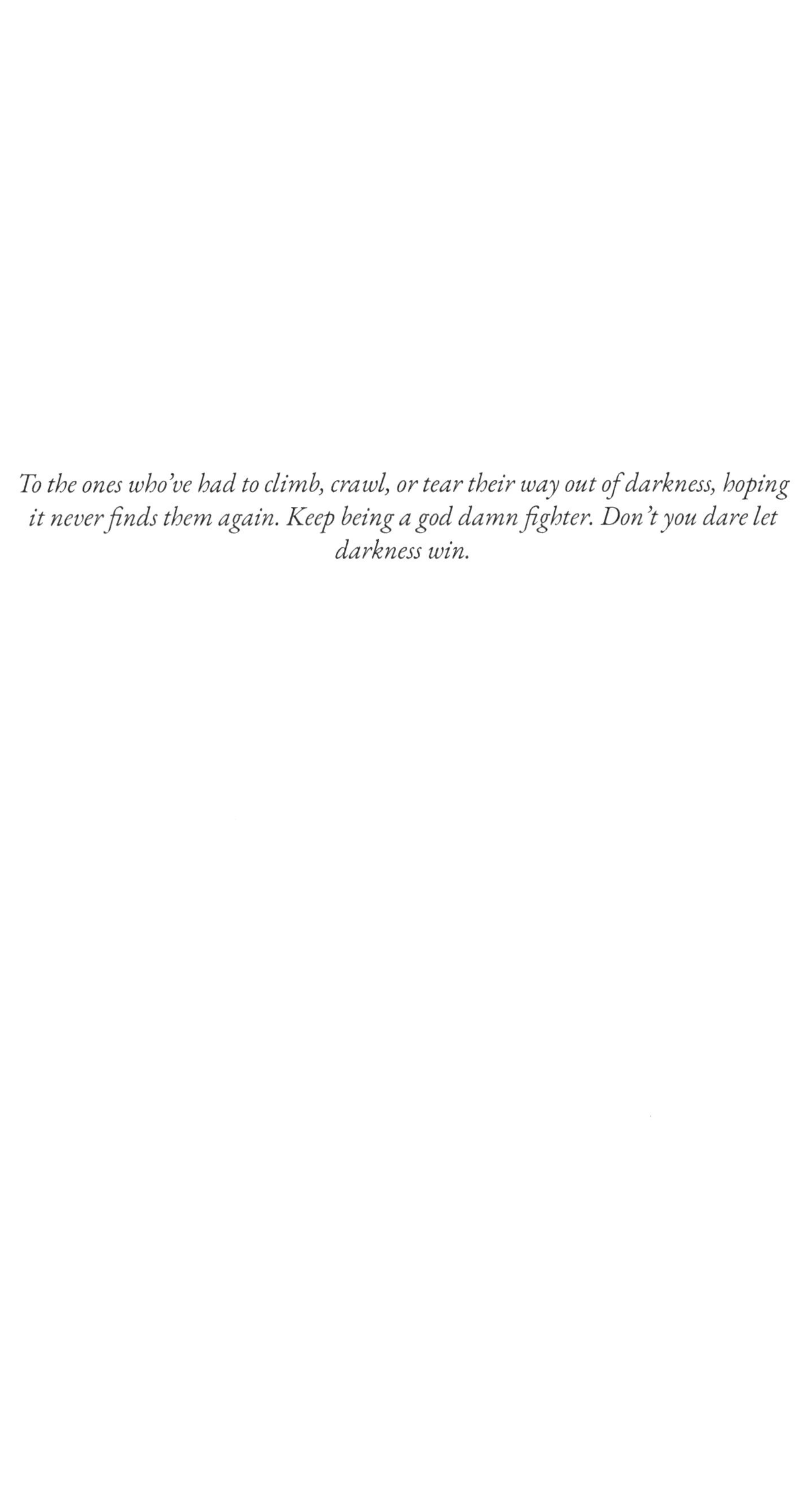

To the ones who've had to climb, crawl, or tear their way out of darkness, hoping it never finds them again. Keep being a god damn fighter. Don't you dare let darkness win.

PART ONE

HAUNTED

PROLOGUE

NORA

This can't be real.

My parents taught us to live and breathe like any day could be our last. The way they radiated joy and love and hope no matter what happened around us was something I've always admired.

Standing on the shore with Olivia's trembling hand in mine, I feel it happening almost in slow motion—my life falling apart. The light and happiness my parents embedded within me slowly drains away as darkness reaches out and wraps its tendrils of despair and suffering around my mind. There is no more light, only shadows and pain.

The frigid air against my skin sends goosebumps crawling up my spine, and the midnight hour lays a blanket of darkness across the scene. My sister and I huddle together, blurry-eyed and heartbroken as the rescue crew works on pulling our parents' car out of the lake beneath the lights of the Mackinac Bridge. Cars rush past overheard between Michigan's upper and lower peninsula oblivious to the horror unfolding before us.

I stare blankly as the paramedics perform chest compressions. The sound of cracking ribs splinters through my ears and a scream escapes my lips. My cries tear through the air as I let go of Olivia's hand and rush to their lifeless bodies, my voice breaking until it dissolves into desperate sobs. An officer wraps his warm arms around my middle and pulls me back, holding me as I kick and scream and try to escape his hold to be by their sides. When my body is too numb with shock and exhaustion to move, the man lets me go. I collapse to my knees. Tears burn my cheeks and my chest rips apart, knowing it's too late. They're already gone.

Shadows flicker and sway as the flashing red and blue lights bring the area around us to life. The paramedics are still now, as still as time seems. They stare down at my parents' pale bodies and then at me, their eyes solemn and depleted. It's over. Nothing will ever be the same.

As they die here, I die with them.

I can't pull my eyes away from my parents' bodies, their damp clothes clinging tightly to their pale skin, and the thick, black substance splattered and dripping across the visible parts of them I can see between the paramedics' bodies. What the hell is it? The officer helps me stand, leading me over to them as Olivia walks beside us. A moment to say goodbye. To identify them. To accept our fractured realities.

"What's all over them?" My voice is hoarse and weak as I point down at my parents. "That isn't blood. What is it?" I stare down at the paramedic kneeled beside their bodies, eyes wide and heart racing.

His eyebrows scrunch up as he gazes down at me blankly, as if the words I'm saying make no sense. "I'm so sorry," one of the paramedics tells us, shaking his head as he stands and finishes packing supplies into his bag before walking away.

"They made it to shore, but they were too far gone by then. I'm sorry, girls." The chief of police steps back, leaving us there to say our goodbyes.

Why aren't they answering me? I can't be the only one who sees it.

I can't speak as Olivia wraps her hand around mine and squeezes tightly. All I can do is stare down at them, the sound of waves crashing and police radio chatter becoming muffled and far away. Everything except for my parents and their cyanotic lips and their damp, wrinkly skin fades away. It's just them and nothing else. My body feels weightless and empty, like I'm just floating and lost in space, stuck in a nightmare that can't possibly be reality. None of this is real...

I'm not even real.

Something hangs in the air that I can't decipher, not the metallic scent of fresh blood from the gash on my mother's forehead, or the rising feeling of hopelessness that engulfs me. It's something else. Something wrong.

Something evil and dark, like ancient death and rot has been here lurking along the shoreline. Hazy tears trace lines down my cheeks, but I swipe them away and my vision clears. Now that the paramedics and the chief of police have walked away and I have a clear view of my parents, I gasp quietly, and I no longer know if what I see is real or imagined.

My hands shoot to my mouth as I take in the deep claw marks in jagged lines of three, and the bite marks like sharp needle points covering both of my parents' bodies. The thick, black ichor is everywhere. It stains their skin and drips from their limbs and blank faces onto the algae-covered rocks scattered around them. It can't be real, not when no one else seems to notice.

Olivia leans her head onto my shoulder, but the warmth of her touch and the affectionate, gentle reminder that she's here with me doesn't bring comfort the way it normally would. It feels suffocating. Everything does.

I pull away from her, gesturing down at their bodies. "This was no accident." I sob, unable to contain the heartbreak and confusion any longer. "What happened to them?" I whisper, my eyes darting around in the darkness, a sudden paranoia taking hold of my thoughts.

Whatever did this to my parents might still be nearby, and from the looks of the damage, it isn't something any of us have ever seen or experienced before. What the hell could it be? Doesn't she see what I do? It wasn't an accident. It can't be real. It's a fucking nightmare; it has to be.

"I know this is hard, Nora. I-I don't even know what to say or do. I'm a wreck. But they drowned. There's no other explanation." Olivia sniffles next to me. "They tried to make it back home to us." Her frantic sobs grow louder as I bend down and touch my mom's cheek, wanting to feel the blackness smeared angrily across her face, to feel that it's real.

It cannot be real.

I let out a hiss as I wince in pain, pulling my hand away instinctively. When the substance meets my fingertips it burns like molten lava—like acid that could rip and sear away flesh in an instant. My sister bends down beside me, her trembling hands gently closing our mom's eyes and then our dad's. As my world falls apart, my mind shattering to pieces, she stands, sniffling and wiping her flushed face with the sleeve of her sweatshirt.

Why can't she see the darkness splattered across their bodies, or feel it on her skin? Why hadn't the paramedics? God, why can't I just wake up?

She swallows thickly. "Are you okay, Nor?"

"No," my voice quivers. "Not even a little bit," I tell her, unable to tear my eyes away from my mom.

The necklace she always wore, the one she promised would be mine one day, is gone. She never went a day without wearing it, and yet her neck is bare now. The obsidian crystal always glowed with an otherworldly light, the purple, pink, and blue colors swirling and hypnotizing me whenever I gazed into it. It was a part of her. How the hell can I get through life without her? Without them?

No, no, no.

"Wake up! Wake up! Wake up!"

This nightmare needs to end, and though I scream at the top of my lungs, hoping to drag myself back to reality, nothing around me changes.

The black substance remains, and I want it gone. I want the memory of it erased and I want my memory of their faces to be untainted by this. Leaning forward onto my knees, I use my palms to frantically wipe at the thick, sticky, essence of evil, pushing past the burn as it sends jolts of scorching pain radiating from my fingertips up to my shoulders. I wipe at my mom's freckle covered cheeks first, then her neck and arms before wiping my hands on my jeans, whimpering as the pain shoots from my hips down to the tips of my toes. I need to see their faces. I need to remember them the way they were before. Not like this.

Olivia grips me roughly by the shoulders, forcing me to come to a stop. "What the hell are you doing, Nora? What has gotten into you?"

"Let me go! I can't leave them like this!" Pushing her away, I crawl across the ground to kneel before my dad, my trembling, aching hands wiping across his forehead, the thick, black venom setting every nerve ending in my body on fire. God, it hurts. It hurts and yet I continue to clean him, my vision blurring as my head begins to throb and feel heavy.

Thick, strong arms wrap around me, pulling me up and away from my parents, and I fight against them, scratching and clawing at their warm skin. This isn't real. None of this is real.

"Let me go! Please! Let go of me!"

"Can I get some help over here!?" A voice booms, and as the sound of boots crashing against rocks rushes toward me, my whole body begins to convulse.

The officer lowers me to the cold, damp ground as an empty numbness replaces the fiery burn within me. I gasp for air, but I can't breathe. I'm drowning. I've lost my mind. Something inside of me has snapped and I've gone completely mad. It's the only thing that makes sense.

Nausea sets in and I'm rolled to my side as bile burns its way up my throat and leaks from my trembling lips. Sobs escape as everything around me fades to black, my body stiffening and jerking as another wave of convulsions slam into me. I hear my sister repeating my name over and over, but it feels so far away, like I'm trapped in an alternate dimension that shouldn't exist, until finally I can no longer hear her at all. Until all I see is thick, smothering blackness and all I feel is the cold, icy touch of numbness taking hold of me. As my body stills at last and my limbs go flaccid, I roll onto my back, my mind slipping and fading into oblivion. The scent of death and rot pushes its way into my soul, but for a moment I don't feel afraid as a deep, comforting voice whispers into my mind.

Nora... my light... my flame... open your eyes.

But I can't open my eyes knowing the darkness surrounding me tonight has completely consumed me. Here, on this beach, with shadows closing in and numbness wrapped around my mind, my body and thoughts no longer feel like my own.

Darkness has claimed me.

CHAPTER ONE

CHAOS INSIDE

NORA

ONE YEAR LATER

Every day when I wake up, my first thought is how badly I want to die. My eyes flutter open and burn from the rays of sunlight pouring in through my lacy, sheer curtains, and I want to drift back off to sleep and never have to open my eyes again. The lake outside my window sends its waves rising and falling, crashing onto the shore in tumultuous chaos, mirroring the feelings I carry inside of me. I squint my eyes as I stand and peer out the window, the Mackinac bridge taunting me in the distance, like a ghost from my past life that will stand and haunt me forever. Every morning is the same.

I can't tell my therapist any of this. He'll send me back to the psych ward, a place where misery reigns and dreams go to die. I'm not like them, the people who dissociate from reality and can no longer decipher between reality and imagination. I know someday I might heal from my trauma, from the loss of the two greatest people I've ever known, and that someday I will move on. I know, and yet it changes nothing.

Life feels so meaningless.

As I pull on my cutest sundress and quickly smear make-up across my eyelids and lips, my limbs feel heavy and worn down. I have nothing left to give, but I must keep up the façade. Smile. Laugh. Tell them I'm alright. If the past year has taught me anything, it's that people see what they want to see. Grabbing my keys off the counter, I glance at the clock above the stove, the ticking sound ringing through the air and reminding me that time is still moving. Most days I forget.

I rush through town, savoring the quiet calm of the place now that tourists have left the island to avoid the isolation that comes when winter hits and the lake freezes over. They crave the peacefulness that comes from a town that prohibits cars and allows travel only by horse-drawn carriage, like some fairytale world where time moves slower and things are simpler. Yet, the thought of not being able to leave, of being stuck here with no way out terrifies them. I guess some fairytales aren't meant to last forever. I wouldn't want to live anywhere else.

The ferry ride takes twenty minutes, and I barely remember going from point A to point B. There are many times I struggle to remember what I've done or where I've been. Every day passes in a blur of faded colors and muted sounds. Jumping off the ferry and onto the dock in Mackinac City, I push my shoulders back and remind myself to appear normal as I stride toward Dr. Cooper's office.

Smile.

Laugh.

Everything is just fine.

As I sit in the dimly lit waiting room, the walls covered in sickly green wallpaper, I pick at the skin on the edge of my nails, impatiently waiting to be called back.

"Come on in, Nora." Dr. Cooper's bright smile radiates positivity as he holds the door open wide and watches me pass through. "How are you today?" We both sit down.

"Hi, Dr. Cooper! I'm doing good, thanks. How are you?" My voice is too high and too bright and too much like anyone but me.

"Good, good." Bradley shifts in his seat in front of me, crossing one leg over the other, and looks down his nose at me through his thick, black-rimmed glasses. "Tell me, Nora. How have you been, *really*?" His voice is silky and velvety, a sound that seems to caress deep into my mind and soul.

Dr. Cooper's voice is like a dark velvet dipped in honey, deep and comforting and sweet. It has always reminded me of my boyfriends voice in a way, and I'm pretty sure Ere's voice alone is enough to heal anyone in all the right places. His smile is small, but it's there. He truly wants the best for me, and I know it, but I can't trust him. I can't trust anyone around me anymore. I glance behind him at the cherry oak wood shelf lined with books from floor to ceiling and briefly picture him sitting at home with his favorite book and a glass of wine by the fireplace. It seems like a very Bradley thing to do after a long day of talking the crazy out of people like me. The thick curtains block out the sunlight, giving his office a cozy, relaxing atmosphere. If I try hard enough, I could maybe let my fucked-up thoughts and feelings seep out and leave them in the dark here in this place with him. But trying is hard. It's so tiring and I'm tired of being tired.

I give him my best *'I swear I'm not suicidal anymore* smile,' tucking my red locks behind my ears and fluttering my eyelashes up at him, attempting to convey innocence and a happy demeanor. I shrug my shoulders, my hands clasped in my lap, and my body relaxed and still. I will not let the truth show. I've practiced this so much now that it has gotten easy, fooling everyone into believing I'm fine. I will not cry. I will not let my hands shake or my mind spiral in front of him. I. Am. Healed. They will not lock me up again.

I take a deep breath before speaking, hoping to let the calm demeanor shine bright in the tone of my voice as well.

"Truly, I feel great," I giggle, shrugging my shoulders. "I've had a rough year. Like... really rough, I know. But I've learned a lot about myself and about life and the world around me. I know now how to handle challenging situations when they come my way. I'm so thankful for you. Thankful to be alive." I let my smile reach my eyes, and this time it is real. I appreciate everything Bradley has done to help me. He doesn't need to know that it was all for nothing.

He leans forward, placing his arms on his legs, and letting his hands hang freely. His facial hair is neat but scruffy, and his brown locks are messy yet stylish, making him look much younger than the forty-five-year-old man he is.

He sighs quietly and smiles in a way that immediately makes me feel awful for all the lies I've fed him these past few months. "Great. Hearing that makes me so happy."

He believes me. Every lie and every half-truth and every forced, fake-ass smile. I started coming in with my hair curled and golden eye shadow to brighten up my blue eyes, and the prettiest, brightest sundresses I could find, to fool him into seeing me as someone I'm not, and it fucking worked. How did it work so easily?

As I breathe in deep, the scent of leather and deception burns its way into my lungs and beats through my heart.

"I'm happy, too. For the first time in a long time, I am. I'm moving on. This is what my parents would want for me, and I know that now." I don't blink or move, keeping my eyes locked on his to show no signs that I'm attempting to deceive him.

"I'm so proud of you, Nor. You should be proud, too. Your mind tried to break you, you fought hard, and you won. You're a warrior." His leather chair creaks as he stands and makes his way over to his desk. "I'm writing you a one-month prescription for the medications I have you on. Increasing the dosage is no longer necessary with how well you're doing now." He leans on the edge of his desk, crossing his arms over his broad chest, smiling as if he feels so accomplished for healing me. For saving my life.

I'm an asshole. That's all there is to it. I'm a liar and a fraud and if God is looking down at me right now, he is surely shaking his head in disgust and disappointment. I don't care, though. I just want to be free.

I smooth the wrinkles out of my dress as I stand, tossing my curls over my shoulders and smiling over at him. "Does this mean our visits are over? Now that I'm... better?"

His smile vanishes, and he places his hands in front of him, palms facing toward me in a gesture to slow down. He shakes his head. "That's not what I'm saying. Not yet, at least. Let's see how you do with monthly visits instead of weekly. How does that sound?"

Horrible. Like a waste of time.

"Sounds great!" I beam, knowing it's what I should say and do. "I'll see you in a month, then?"

"See you in a month. Of course, if you need me at any time before then, please don't hesitate to call, okay?" He straightens up and walks to the door, then opens it and turns toward me. "Your prescriptions will be ready for pickup on your way home. Don't...forget it." He says sternly, probably remembering back to all the times I 'forgot' to pick them up after our visits before.

It doesn't matter. They'll end up down the drain where the rest of them have gone to die.

"I won't forget. Thank you, Dr. Cooper. For everything, really. I don't care what people say about you, you're not such a bad guy." I smile playfully and his deep, carefree laugh follows me out the door even as he shuts it behind me.

On my first day seeing him I told him the truth about what I'd heard from the others at the mental health facility. They'd all agreed he was an emotionless, abrasive jerk. I've never seen that side of him. He's not a bad guy at all, he is just slightly bad at reading people and picking up on emotions. Or maybe I'm just a really good actor. Too good, even. Standing in the waiting room, the receptionist scribbles my next appointment date on a business card, then slides it across the counter.

"September ninth at 10 o'clock, sweetie. See you then." Her smile doesn't meet her eyes. It's barely even a smile at all.

Her hazel eyes hold a sadness within them that she isn't very good at hiding. She isn't rude or unkind or bitter, she's just sad. Probably from a life full of pain and loss and heartbreak that never healed like she hoped it would. Looking at her feels like a glimpse into my future. She is me and I am her, and we both deserve much better.

The smile I give her is no longer the fake or forced one I show to Bradley, my sister Olivia, or my best friend Katie, and it's still far from the semi genuine one I save for my boyfriend Ere. I give her the real one. The one that's barely a smile at all, just like hers. As I walk out of the office and the sunlight hits my eyes, I block it with a hand and head toward the diner. It's almost dinner time and Liv will be waiting for me already. She'll be thrilled to hear the news that I'm healed.

Shattered glass and a high-pitched scream from behind the rough, beaten-up counter of Lake City Diner has me raising my eyebrows and smiling at the young waitress who giggles with the busboy passing by her. "That's the third one this week. Jenny is going to kill you." She rolls up the white towel she uses to wipe the counter with and playfully slaps his back with it. He pushes the squeaky swinging doors open and winks at her as he disappears into the kitchen.

They're probably only a few years younger than me, but somehow, they seem much younger and more alive. I'm twenty-three but Olivia and Katie tell me all the time that I might as well be ninety. They see an introvert who would rather read than go out. What they don't get is that my real hobbies the past year have been trying to fight off nightmares about monsters and simply making it through the day. Surviving is my main hobby. That's hard enough most of the time.

"Liv!" I squeal as my sister enters the diner, strutting toward me in her black dress and heels.

The old, faded paintings hanging on the walls, and the dated chandeliers hanging above our heads are not bright enough to distract from Olivia's entrance. She always looks stunning, and today is no different.

"Hey sis!" Her high-pitched sing-song voice echoes in my ear as she wraps her arms around me and squeezes tightly. "I've missed you so much." Pulling back and looking down at me, her blue eyes sparkle like sapphires as the sunlight dances across them.

She releases me and slides into the leather booth, her wavy dark hair bouncing as she takes a seat in front of me. The bright white smile she wears almost seems plastered to her face, like it couldn't possibly be real, but it is. She's always smiling, and I love that about her. She reaches across the table to take my hand in hers, and her bronze skin against mine makes my own look almost translucent. She resembles our dad, and everyone always called me my mom's little twin, my freckled cheeks and red hair reminding them of her. God, she was so beautiful.

"How did your appointment with Bradley go?" She smirks, raising her eyebrows up and down at the mention of his name.

She is obsessed with him. She saw him once and hasn't been able to shut up about him since. She thinks he has a thing for me, but I've never noticed or cared. I think she's just so eager for me to find happiness or to fall in love that she imagines it wherever we go. Also, there were whispers in town this past year of him having a relationship with a girl about my age, and Olivia always says I need an older man in my life to help level me out. It should be enough that I have a boyfriend at all, and technically, he is older. Only by a few years, but still, Ere helped me through my struggles these past five months. If it weren't for him, I'm not sure where I would be right now, or if I would be at all.

My sister doesn't agree with his choice in letting me sink into grief and darkness when I choose to. She believes I need someone who forces me into the light, to help guide me through my dark days. I never told her that I met him during my time at the local psychiatric hospital and that he understands the struggle with darkness as well as I do. She'd freak. She'd worry. She would convince herself he's even more of a bad influence on me, but Ere gives me exactly what I need. There's no need to pretend to be anything with him, I can just be. I consider myself lucky to have found someone as accepting and understanding as him.

"Dr. Cooper, you mean?" I correct her with a roll of my eyes and a smile. "He thinks I'm doing great. He said he's proud of the progress he's seeing in me and moved my sessions to once a month."

She nods once before taking a sip of the water the waitress places in front of her, and then we order our usual burgers and fries. It never changes, no matter how many times we've been here. I guess that makes us boring, but why change a good thing?

"I'm proud of you, too." Her eyes gloss over and I know she's about to cry before the first tear even falls.

"Liv. Don't. Don't you dare," I tell her, knowing that every time one of us cries the other one isn't far behind.

"I'm sorry." She dabs the tears away with a napkin. "I just... at one point I didn't know if I would ever get my sister back. I was so scared of losing you."

"Damn it, Olivia." My eyes sting as tears well up and warm my cheeks as they fall, and we both let out a laugh. "I'm sorry. That the past year has been a mess. That you've dealt with so much alone. That I couldn't be there for you like I should have been." I pick up my napkin and blot my tears away. "I've been such a shitty sister, haven't I?" I shake my head and look up at the ceiling, not wanting to face her and the truth.

My sister visited me every day for months while I was in the psych ward, whispering about a missing necklace holding secrets and monsters who are coming for me next. She was scared shitless, I could see it in her eyes even though I wasn't myself then. All she could do was tell me over and over that she believed me, but that I was safe for now and shouldn't worry. We haven't talked about those things since I got out, but I often wonder if a part of her did believe me. She has always had a strange obsession with supernatural occurrences, and there was nothing natural about the way our parents died. She has to wonder if maybe I was right. If maybe I did see things she didn't. I'm too afraid to bring it up again. I don't want the semblance of a normal life I have now to be ripped away.

I don't know how she has stayed so damn strong when she's the one who lost the most. A mom, a dad, and a sister. All gone in the blink of an eye. But

I'm here. She has been the strong, supportive big sister for long enough. I hate that I've made things harder for her than it needed to be. My heart hurts knowing she needed me and I couldn't be there to comfort her. Guilt eats at me still, even though at the time I was too broken to care. I was too lost then to know how much it'd torture me later on for not pulling myself together for her. All I can do is be here for her now that I can be.

"No, Nor, not at all." She reaches across the table and squeezes my hand. "Please don't think that even for a second." Her voice is calm and reassuring.

She will never just let me take the blame for things. She makes excuses and pretends there's hope for me even when there isn't, and sometimes I hate her for it. Other times, I want to prove her right and turn my life around, only I don't know how to anymore. I've tried everything.

I stare out the window and watch as cars and people pass by, wondering if they've ever felt even remotely the way I do right now. Lost and defeated. Alone yet not alone at all. Olivia never seems to feel this way. She always finds a way to see the light even when there is none to be found. I envy her for that.

"I'm going to do better, Liv. I promise. I'll be a better sister and friend. I'll do all the crazy things you and Katie beg me to do, no matter how badly I want to say no."

She rolls her eyes but smiles over at me as if hearing this makes her happier than I could ever imagine.

"I want to be better. I will be." I sit up straighter with my head held high, for a second believing I can will it into existence.

"You are better. So much better than you were before. Just promise me something, okay?" She leans forward, watching me carefully.

I nod my head, my eyes crinkling slightly, not knowing what she's about to ask of me and fearing I won't be able to keep the promise.

"Promise me that if you find yourself spiraling again. If you find yourself losing control or having thoughts of hurting yourself, promise you'll tell me. Don't keep it inside this time until... until it's too late." She swallows thickly, and I know why it's so hard for her to talk about what happened just six months ago.

Finding your sister pulseless on the floor surrounded by empty bottles of prescription pills probably isn't something you get over easily, if at all. A pang of guilt shudders through me at the thought of her there, panicked and alone. I'd never make the mistake of letting her be the one to find me if someday I chose to try again. She deserves better.

I take a deep breath in and out, just as Dr. Cooper taught me to do when I'm feeling overwhelmed. "I promise," I whisper, giving her a half smile that should give my lie away.

It doesn't, because she believes me, or at least she pretends to. She gets up to go to the bathroom, and when she does, I fumble with her key chain to find the card attached to it that leads in and out of the Mackinac Bridge. Our dad had special access because he worked for the city, and he used to take us to the top all the time. His card still works, surprisingly, I know because she still uses it at times. We used to go up there together until I became a suicidal mess who couldn't be trusted anywhere, let alone on a bridge three hundred and fifty feet above a large body of water. Olivia will be pissed that I stole his access card, but I haven't been there since our parents died, and haven't been to the top in years. I just want to enjoy the view of the city alone. There's a peacefulness up there away from the noise and lights that I've never been able to find anywhere else. Up there, all my scattered, broken thoughts slowly disappear.

After dinner and hugging my sister goodbye, I make my way down the street toward the bridge. I've been so afraid to face reality, to face my fear once and for all, but I will not let fear rule my life. I want to try for her, for Olivia. She deserves a sister who can always be there. A sister who she never again has to find lifeless on the floor. As badly as I want to take the ferry home, to just forget about healing and give up hope again, tonight hope calls to me. So just for tonight...

I will try.

CHAPTER TWO

GIVING IN TO DARKNESS

NORA

Darkness has settled into the city by the time I reach the elevator shaft of the bridge. With Olivia gone, it's as if darkness has taken over in my mind again, as well. My mouth is too dry and my breathing too fast as the elevator carries me higher and higher. I thought this might be good for me, to come to the place where my parents died and face it head-on once and for all. I fear I was wrong. Memories of black ooze, gaping wounds, and teeth marks push their way into my thoughts as soon as the elevator doors ding and close, nearly suffocating me in such a small space.

It wasn't real. It couldn't be real. God, I'll never be able to convince myself of that or that the darkness I felt surrounding me that night wasn't there. I felt it. It wanted me, too. It still does.

My hands shake and my stomach flip-flops as the elevator comes to a standstill and the doors slide open with a loud ding. The sound makes me jump as it pulls me out of my haunting memories. I feel it here, that darkness. I feel it everywhere. It's here on this bridge and in my mind, the sensation of being consumed and entangled with those shadows that lurked on the beach, relentless. I thought I could escape it for a moment here, but I was wrong. The darkness persists. I should go back. I shouldn't be here. I should know better by now than to trust my mind. It's not strong enough yet to be up here, in a place that makes it so easy to end the suffering once and for all.

Deep breath in... and out. I can do this. I'm okay. I'm more than okay. I. Am. Healed. Stepping off the elevator and onto the bridge, I remind myself why I came up here to begin with. The view. The peace. God, it's beautiful. The chill of the breeze cascades off the lake below, caressing my cheeks as I stand at the edge, gazing down at the picturesque scene laid out before me. Lake Michigan and Lake Huron on either side, the waves rising and crashing against rocks along their borders. The city lights shine brightly on the distant town, giving the false impression that we're all safe no matter how dark it might get. The full moon gleams overhead like a beacon above the city, whispering sweet promises of new beginnings and hope when daylight returns. Right now though, I cannot feel that hope.

The black depths of the water call to me... it calls to my soul. The deep, violent darkness within the lake can release me from the pain and torment at last. I can be free. My hair whips around me, the red streaks lashing against my face and reminding me I'm still here. That I'm real. I blink back tears as I gaze out at Mackinac Island, the city I grew up in. The city my parents adored until the cruelty that is life got in the way. Here on this bridge, life took everything from me.

Dr. Cooper reminds me often that there are stages of grief, and it changes from day to day. All I know for sure is the pain from it is endless and all-consuming. I've had to climb and claw and rip through thick, smothering clouds of darkness every day, and have rarely seen a tiny spark of light at the end of the tunnel. Every day is a new battle, and the darkness always has new tricks up its sleeve to try to break me...to end me for good. It takes so much and yet still wants more. I'll never truly be okay.

Closing my eyes, I lean into the breeze as another cold gust of air rushes past me, a sort of numbness wrapping its arms around me and caressing my skin like an old, familiar friend. The same numbness I felt on the beach that night. The same numbness that craved my surrender, that urged me to let go, to let it in. I don't know what's real anymore. The truth is, I'm no better than I was the day I voluntarily allowed myself to be put in the psych ward, no better than the day I hit rock bottom when my sister found me nearly dead. I am still no better. But here on this ledge, I don't feel so alone. I feel seen and understood. It would be so easy to just let it all go, to free myself from the nightmare of continuing on.

I miss my parents. I need to see them again. I need to feel their arms wrapped around me and the warmth and love they infused into my soul whenever they were around. I can't do life without them any longer. I've tried to move on, and I know everyone keeps reminding me that better days will come, but will they really? A year of misery has persisted, and it's all passed in a blur. I know I should fight these intrusive thoughts, if for nothing else, then for Olivia. She deserves better. Being up here makes it too hard to keep fighting for her. I should go.

With a racing heart, I take a step back toward the elevator, and then another. Icy, soothing numbness crashes into me again, the feel of it against my skin this time more commanding and forceful. I close my eyes and breathe it in. It's the scent of death and despair that has me freezing in place. Goosebumps climb across my skin as tendrils of evil coil around my mind, body, and soul, the comfort it brought slowly turning to icy emptiness. I open my eyes, gasping, wanting to remove the scent from the air and expel it from my lungs. I can't no matter how hard I try, the scent and feel of death pushes its way into me further, refusing to let me go. I knew it would come for me. I knew it wasn't over after all I'd seen that night on the beach. How could it let me live when I knew the truth? I fall to my knees, the hard metal sending shooting pains through my trembling legs. I need air. I'm suffocating. I reach for my throat, hoping to somehow force oxygen into my body, wishing the pain of being infiltrated and tormented by this darkness would end, but it's useless. I close my eyes, preparing for death here and now.

But death doesn't come. The pain ends and the air is no longer tinged with the scent of death and darkness. I feel nothing at all. My mind is numb. Opening my eyes, I rise from my knees and turn back toward the city lights and the temptation of the ledge.

I've always felt a fight within myself between the dark and the light. It doesn't feel like a fight any longer. Not anymore. Now, as I take a step up to the ledge, glancing three hundred and fifty feet down to the surface of the lake, the sound of the crashing waves is calling me home. Into the depths of nothingness. Into the unending darkness. Into the comfort of the unknown. Here, the never-ending suffering and aching of loss torment me. I don't want it anymore. I can't take it anymore. I won't. Taking a small step toward the ledge, I bite back tears that threaten to fall.

"*I belong to darkness...*" the whispered words forming and coming out of my mouth aren't my own.

I'm not in control. Darkness has won. Another step closer to the ledge has my breath catching in my throat. I close my eyes, holding my arms out wide.

"*I belong to darkness...*" I lean into the breeze and let it carry me away...

Down. Down. Down.

The rush of wind against my entire body feels like freedom, and the icy numbness feels like home. I feel nothing and yet I'm not afraid. The darkness whispers into my mind, promising me a life full of happiness and a love I never knew existed on the other side. It promises me everything. Opening my eyes, I smile as I free-fall toward my inevitable ending, imagining my parents with open arms welcoming me into the afterlife. This is how it has to be. There is no other option for me.

After all, I was born of darkness. In the end, into the darkness I shall return.

CHAPTER THREE

WINGS AND STARLIGHT

NORA

Fuck. Fuck. Fuck.

Suddenly, I'm snapped back into my body, and my stomach lurches and twists violently as my mind tries to piece together what led me here. Tears stream down my cheeks as I think of my sweet sister and Katie and how disappointed and heartbroken they'll soon be. The last thing I remember is appreciating the view from the bridge and then turning to leave. I should be on the ferry close to home by now. I shouldn't be here.

Thrashing in the air, screams force their way out, even knowing no one will hear me, that no one could save me now even if they wanted to. As I soar toward the surface of the rough lake below, I have no choice but to quickly accept my fate, whether I remember my decision to end my life or not, I know this is goodbye. Clamping my eyes closed tightly, I take in one last breath of the fresh, lake air, then accept my unfortunate ending. It was never a fight of darkness versus light for me. Darkness was always fated to win.

At the sound of flapping wings nearby, my eyes scan the darkness, my head jerking left and right but finding nothing in sight. Shock and fear course through me as suddenly something with large, feathery black wings crashes into me, swooping me out of the air and wrapping large, warm arms tightly around my waist. My gut-wrenching scream could shatter glass if there was anything but open skies and emptiness surrounding me. I fight against the force of whatever has a hold of me, but it's useless. It won't let go. I didn't want to die, but now I'm wondering if this might be worse, as the wings flap louder and I'm carried faster toward the rocky shore.

Maybe this is another nightmare, a new one to give me a break from the monsters that haunt me every time my eyes close. Maybe this monster is worse than the ones I'm certain murdered my parents that night a year ago on the same bridge that led me here to this one. Maybe I've finally just lost my mind completely.

The edge of the beach gets closer and closer, and I take a deep breath, preparing myself to run as quickly as I can as soon as my feet hit the ground. The trembling of my body does little to hide the fear that courses through me. A moment ago, I was okay with death. I welcomed it although it didn't feel like I was in control of my thoughts. But whatever it is that has a grip on me now, I have a feeling is much worse than death itself. I can't turn my head to look at it. I can't open my mouth to speak. I'm frozen in terror and wishing like hell I would have never come near the bridge tonight. I'm not ready to die, not this way, at least.

As soon as I hear the thud of boots hitting the ground, and feel the freedom of being released at last, I propel myself forward as swiftly as I can, using every ounce of strength within myself. I run without ever looking back. I don't want to see what it is that's sending its dark energy swirling around me. I'll never escape. It won't let me go; I can feel it. I push myself to run faster until my legs ache and I hold my side as the muscles there twitch painfully. I focus on the empty spaces between the trees as I race through the forest behind the beach, surrounded by nothing but complete darkness now. Maybe it won't see me. Maybe I'm safe. I hear nothing but the sound of my own shoes pounding against the dirt. Tripping over my wobbly feet, I stumble, falling face-first into a tree before collapsing onto the ground.

"Shit..." I mutter breathlessly, rubbing at the aching, burning sensation on my forehead.

Tucking my long strands of hair behind my ears, I place my back against the tree, crouching down in an attempt to stay hidden.

My breath is too fast, and my heartbeat thuds and echoes so loudly it might as well be screaming out my exact location. I close my eyes, hearing nothing but the leaves on the trees swaying softly in the wind. Deep breath in... and out. I force myself to count to ten, feeling the adrenaline subside and my racing heart slow. Opening my eyes to face the dark, I immediately regret the decision. Crouched before me is a man in a black robe with a hood pulled over his head. I can't see his face or even his eyes within the shadows of the robe. Maybe it doesn't have a face at all.

I open my mouth to scream, but nothing comes out except for a small, ragged whimper. The shock of the swords peeking out from behind his back, the daggers strapped to his legs, and the huge, black wings spread out wide behind him render me speechless and motionless. My eyes widen as I rake my eyes up and down as he slowly stands, hands hanging at his sides casually. He bows his head as if wanting to appear safe or even respectful in front of me.

What the fuck is he? Staring at him, it feels as if he's staring back at me, into my soul even, but I can't be sure. I need to see his face.

"Please let me go!" I beg, my voice cracking as sobs force their way through me. "What do you want from me?" I breathe out the words, feeling almost certain whatever this thing is wants to kill me.

Tilting his head to the side, he crouches down again, reaching a black gloved hand out toward my face. Instinctively I push his hand away and he stills, before slowly caressing my cheek with his thumb. My heart stops. I can't breathe. What the fuck is happening? When he pulls his hand away, he holds it in front of his face, and thick, red liquid drips from his gloved finger onto the grass between us. I reach up, wincing and hissing as I touch the wound near my temple, feeling the warm blood flowing down my face.

"You're hurt..."

I stiffen as his smooth, silky voice sends waves of déjà vu through my heart and into my soul.

"You should be dead." Ripping a piece of cloth from his cloak, he gently dabs at the blood dripping from my wound. "I'm glad you're alive."

I don't pull away, I simply watch him carefully, brows furrowed and eyes slanted, wondering why he doesn't just kill me. Is he responsible for my fall from the bridge? For my parents' deaths? Whatever he is, I want nothing to do with him. For the past year, I've wondered how true it might be that ghosts, monsters, or demons exist in this world, but here in this moment, I no longer have to wonder about any of it. It's true.

"What are you?" Blinking slowly up at him, I clench my teeth to stop the shivers that have my teeth rattling together, but the shaking isn't from the cold, it's from the fear racing through my body as he continues cleaning the wound on my head.

He appears too focused on getting the bleeding to stop to notice me watching him. I can't trust him. I don't even know what the hell he is. I need to go home. I need to get to Olivia. Quickly I reach for the sword behind his back, grabbing the hilt and standing as I pull it up and out of the holster. Pointing it toward him, I watch as he slowly—so terrifyingly slowly—turns his head to look at me. As he stands, he lets out a laugh that makes my heart race all over again. I feel his dark power pouring out of him in my direction, reaching and grasping at me to get closer. I can't let that happen.

As he takes a step toward me, I take a step back. Then another.

"Please!" I yell out, tightening my grip on the sword and preparing myself to use it if needed.

"You wanted to die." He prowls toward me slowly. "Now you want to live?" He asks, again tilting his head sideways as he watches me.

"I don't want to die. I... I don't even remember jumping! Please... don't kill me!" Lifting the sword up higher, I clumsily jab it in his direction.

"Believe me, Nora. I want nothing more than for you to live." The sadness in his tone distracts me, and my gaze shifts and settles on his face instead of his hands.

He sighs quietly, standing still as a statue before quickly lunging and grabbing the weapon from my hands. He doesn't even have to try hard. He overpowers me more easily than any human would. Pulling away from him, I stumble and fall, hearing the loud clunk of my head smashing against a rock as I land backward on the ground. I stare up at the man or monster or...angel before me, and everything around me blurs as I softly moan in pain. He pulls his hood back and reveals his face, and the last thing I remember before everything fades to black, is the look of pure panic and gut-wrenching torment in his bright green eyes when he scoops me up and into his arms.

"Darkness guide me. Gods save me." His voice is like a healing tincture to my wounds as he whispers into the wind.

He's so warm. His comforting energy shatters the iciness that wrapped around me before, making it feel wrong and unnatural and not okay. Somehow, his darkness seems to chase the other darkness away. His offers light. It's not suffocating or commanding like the energy I felt on the bridge, it's full of hope. Powerful and yet freeing. It's so many things, things I can't begin to explain or understand, but I don't need to understand it to tell the difference between the two. My head throbs in pain and I let it fall onto his muscular chest, unable to hold it up any longer.

We're back in the air in an instant, rushing up toward the puffs of white clouds far above. This can't be real. He can't be real. The sound of flapping wings thunders loudly around me as starlight shines brightly in my eyes, the clouds parting around us. Not even the closeness of the stars floating and twinkling around us tonight could outshine the beauty of him, whatever he may be. He is terrifyingly beautiful. Those haunting green eyes meet mine as he shifts me in his arms and opens his mouth to speak just as darkness pulls me under.

CHAPTER FOUR

SECRETS AND LIES

NORA

The sounds of beeping machines and hushed words awaken me from the deepest sleep I've had in a year. My throbbing head and fuzzy thoughts slip through as I force my eyes open and take in the room around me. The stark white walls and the scent of bleach scream sterilized hospital room. The white board with the name Nora Whitaker scribbled across it and the IV in my arm remind me that I'm the patient. I jolt upright, reaching my hand up to my head, feeling the thick gauze bandage wrapped all the way around it. I'm still alive. I'm miraculously alive. I might be for now, but Olivia is going to murder me for this later.

The scraping sound of a chair moving across the tiled floor is followed by my big sister rushing toward me then gripping my hand tightly. Ere sits in a chair right next to my bed, the warmth of his hand around mine bringing instant comfort, his relieved smile and soft golden eyes coming into focus. He leans forward and places a tender kiss to my forehead, brushing locks of hair away from my face.

"If you wanted me home early, all you had to do was ask." His deep, silky voice murmurs in my ear, and I smile weakly as I pull myself to a sitting position in bed.

"You didn't have to come all the way back here. I'm fine," I tell him, swaying slightly as a spinning wave of dizziness hits me.

"Sure you are." His long, dark hair brushes against his shoulders as he nods, scrunching his eyebrows and squeezing my hand tighter.

Katie finishes sending a text, smiles brightly at me, then comes over to stand next to Olivia.

I give her and my sister both a small smile because it's all I have the energy to give right now. Olivia's bright blue eyes have that glazed, glossy look that shows up after hours of being distraught and crying. I know that look all too well. I wear it often. Her dark brown hair is in a messy bun and her sweatshirt has mascara streaks on the sleeves from wiping her eyes. Pangs of guilt shoot through me seeing her this way.

"Hey sis." I squeeze her hand tightly in mine. "Hey Katie." Wavy white hair cascades over my shoulder as my best friend bends and hugs me tightly against her, squeezing just a little.

Her lips curve up as she pulls back to look at me, her striking icy eyes light and unbothered. "Hi, friend."

Olivia sniffles, wiping her tears, her bottom lip trembling slightly before she speaks. "Hey sis. I was worried to death about you!" The way she glares at me and then smiles softly after nearly breaks my heart

She's mad and I don't blame her. Constantly having to worry about me spiraling into a crushing, inescapable depression has to be exhausting. Here I am, disappointing her again. God, I'm an awful sister to have.

"I'm sorry, Liv. I'm fine, though. No need to worry anymore." Shrugging my shoulders hurts.

A sharp pain shoots up from my neck to the back of my head, and I hide it with a tight-lipped smile. Ere's eyes narrow into slits as I glance at him. He doesn't miss anything.

Slapping my arm playfully, Katie rolls her eyes. "What were you thinking being out there alone in the woods? You do realize you're much too clumsy to go on adventures without someone watching you, right?" She laughs, shaking her head and crossing her arms over her chest.

What? That's not what happened. My adventure was when I made my way up the bridge, and the nightmare was everything following which led to me ending up in the woods and ultimately here.

"You could have died out there, Nor." Olivia sighs, rubbing the back of my hand with her thumb.

She's the happiest person I've ever known. Her smiles and laughter are contagious and make it nearly impossible to be sad or down around her. She always knows what to do or say to make every situation better, or at least the best it could possibly be. Guilt eats away at me for putting her through so much already, and more so now seeing her pained expression full of worry for me all over again.

Tears trickle down my cheeks, and before I can reach my hand up to wipe them away Olivia's arms are around me and her head is on my chest. The wires connecting me to the heart monitor and the IV lines pumping fluids into me make it hard, but I carefully hug her back.

"I love you so much, Liv." Burying my head in her hair, sobs rack through my body, the guilt becoming too much to handle. "I'm so fucking sorry. I don't..."

Ere stands, the muscles in his chest flexing beneath his black button up shirt as he tenses. "Everything is fine, my love. Accidents happen." He lifts my hand, bringing it to his lips and presses a soft kiss against it. "I'll give you some time with them and then you should rest." His smile is full of sadness as he meets my eyes, then Olivia's and Katie's, before quietly slipping out of the room.

He doesn't like it when I feel guilty or bad about things I've done or mistakes I've made, even though I've made plenty. The past should remain in the past, he says, and guilt is the harbinger of pain. He tries his best to keep the pain away.

"Hey... it's okay." Olivia pulls away slightly to look at me, then brushes away her tears. "I'm glad you're safe. I can be mad at you later. I'll yell at you later. But right now, I am just so damn thankful you're alive."

Letting go of me, she stands up straight, glancing over at Katie. "I'm thankful that guy found you in the woods after you fell. You passed out and he just happened to come across you while hiking. You got so lucky." She places her hands on her hips, shifting her weight from one foot to the other and then shakes her head in disbelief.

I sit upright immediately at her words, and though my head throbs and the world starts to spin, I ignore it. There was a man... a man with wings, I remember. He saved me... I think.

"Did you meet this man, Liv? What did he tell you, exactly?" I scan the room then stretch my neck to peek into the hallway, wondering if the stranger is still nearby.

The cardiac monitor hanging on the wall begins to chime, loudly ringing out and it barely registers what's happening until a nurse comes rushing into the room.

"Honey, you need to relax. Your heart rate is extremely high right now, and you've been through a lot. Maybe it's time for your visitors to let you rest." Dark brown eyes narrow in Olivia and Katie's direction. The nurse's long braid sways behind her as she silences the monitor above my head, keeping her eyes locked on me.

"No! I need them here. Please? I'm fine, I promise." I lie, leaning back in the bed casually.

"Fine. Your pain medication is due around midnight, so maybe ask your visitors to leave soon so you can rest. I'll see you then."

As soon as she shuts the door behind her, I sit up, throwing my legs over the side of the bed to face Olivia. Katie comes around to stand next to her, placing a perfectly manicured hand on my shoulder to help steady me.

"Tell me everything you know about the man who brought me here."

I don't care if I look crazy or if they don't think I should concern myself with these things now, I need to know.

Olivia's lips form a thin line as she takes a seat in the emerald green recliner beside my bed. She looks me up and down once before glancing at Katie and then back at me. "I didn't see anyone. He used your phone to call the first number he could dial, which ended up being Katie. She got here first."

I'm fine. Everything is fine. I'm not falling apart.

"Okay then Katie, what did he look like? Does he have a name?"

She smiles, her pale blue eyes radiating only positivity my way. Her calm demeanor helps me relax a little. She doesn't seem scared of him at all. "His name is Kairos." She shrugs her shoulders, looking over my shoulder at the window behind me. "He was wearing all black. Black pants and black boots. He had tattoos… like… a lot of tattoos. I don't know what else I can say. Sound familiar at all?"

It doesn't because none of it's true. He was wearing a black robe and had unmistakable black wings, which apparently, she didn't see.

"Why does this matter right now?" Olivia stands, placing her hands on her hips and watching me carefully.

"What color were his eyes?" I whisper, remembering the mesmerizing bright green standing out in the darkness right before everything faded to black.

"Green. Your favorite color, right?" Katie smiles, twirling her hair between her fingers. "I think he was a blonde, too, but I was quite distraught when I got here and met him, so it's hard to say for sure really." Graceful as ever, she glides to the other side of the room as if she's walking on air, closing the blinds and keeping her back to me. "You need rest. That's all you should worry about doing right now, resting as much as you can."

"Yea, they thought you might have a concussion, and I think they're right. You're being a little weird." Olivia sits beside me in the too small bed, leaning her head on my shoulder.

Right now, I'm thankful she doesn't know the truth, that I threw myself off the bridge our parents crashed their car off of. It's the strangest thing, knowing you did something but not actually remembering the act of doing it. My mind went blank and something strange took over my body. Although the thought of this is terrifying, I'm thankful there isn't an obvious reason for Olivia to beg me to check myself back into the psychiatric hospital. I wasn't having visual or auditory hallucinations like last time or even dissociating and losing myself like before. This time felt different. I wasn't myself at all.

"I'm sorry I'm being weird. I think rest would do me good." I lift my head to look at her, and she smiles, brushing strands of red hair away from my face.

She nods. "Of course. Katie says you'll be fine. She claims the spirits beyond promised you'll be safe."

It's not surprising that Katie knew I'd be fine. Her intuition and the spirits she claims speak to her have never led her astray. She always seems to know everything.

"It's true. They did." Her smile is wide and bright, and my eyes drift down to the necklace she always wears, the pretty amulet wrapped in golden wire.

It always reminds me of my mom, of the obsidian one she always wore that went missing the night she died. I miss her. I know it was just a necklace, but she always promised it would belong to me one day. I wish I had that little piece of her to remember her by.

"Of course they did. I believe you." My laugh is hoarse and strained as I swing my legs back into bed and settle in. "Thank you both for being here for me. Now, go home. I'm fine."

Katie nods, rubbing my arm and smiling before leaving Olivia and I alone to say our goodbyes.

"I'll see you tomorrow, okay?" My sister gathers up her purse and keys before placing her hands on my cheeks and frowning down at me. "I'm sorry this happened, and that you're stuck here. If I could take your place, you know I would." Leaning down, she hugs me tightly, and I close my eyes feeling sleepiness crashing into me.

"You can. Just get in the bed and I'll leave," I tease, shooing her away with my hands. "I'll be fine. I love you."

"Love you too." She dims the lights as she leaves, shutting the door behind her.

Gripping my thin, white blanket in my hands, I pull it up to my shoulders, sleep already taking hold of me. I smile, feeling gratitude for having such a caring boyfriend, the most amazing sister, and the best friend a girl could ever ask for in my life. I'm also grateful to the man who kept my secret from them, but I'm terrified remembering the time with him in the woods. The beautiful wings and the multiple deadly weapons do little to make me feel safe. I push the thoughts away for now, focusing on getting the rest I so badly need.

When I get out of here, I need answers. I'm going to find him again. As much as I know I shouldn't go creeping around searching for darkness or welcoming it into my life, I know I will. I won't be able to stop the racing thoughts until I know the truth about what happened tonight, and possibly even the truth about what happened to my parents. If he's real, if supernatural creatures truly exist, then maybe he can explain what the hell happened the night they died. Maybe he understands the many things I can't explain. He should fear me, not the other way around. I won't be afraid. I refuse to let fear rule my life. I will not stop until I find this Kairos, if that's even his real name, and I will demand the answers I deserve.

If he doesn't kill me first, that is.

CHAPTER FIVE

ANGEL OF DEATH

KAIROS

The streetlights are all that are left in the city as Mio and I keep watch in town. Shops are closed and people are finally off the streets and safe at home. It's just the two of us in our fighting leathers and armor strolling through the sleepy little town of Mackinac Island, long swords strapped to our backs and celestial daggers in each of our hands. The quiet streets are what I prefer, but even if the streets were still crowded with tourists and residents, they wouldn't see us, not really. They'd see two men in their mid-twenties, fierce and a bit rugged to them, maybe, but our wings, weapons, and magic would go unseen through their oblivious mortal eyes.

I open my palm, letting little bursts of lightening dance along my skin, the cracking and popping of thunder overhead following seconds after. I like a good thunderstorm, and the city could use a little rain. With the recent uptake in evil that's been creeping in, black venom stains the streets and the sulfuric scent of the Underworld and the demons who continue to crawl out of it, permeates the air. It needs a good cleansing. The stench of them is so intense I can almost taste it. There could only be one reason Nyx is sending her minions here, of all places, when there are much bigger cities full of people she could easily torment or torture and enslave, but I am not ready to face that truth yet. She couldn't possibly know Nora is here, could she? The attacks are getting more violent and happening more often. It's taking away from my time of guarding Nora, and I don't much like it, especially after what happened tonight on the bridge. It leaves me with no choice but to rely on Katie's wards of protection she places around Nora wherever she goes, and as much as Katie cares for her and tries her best to keep her safe, those witchy wards aren't full proof. They can't save her from herself. Nora needs me, and yet here I am, hunting demons again instead of being there for her. I should be there.

"Kairos, I know you've had a rough day, but you have got to stop sulking. You're killin' my vibe, here, man." Mio turns to face me while continuing to walk backwards down the cracked, uneven sidewalk.

His dark hair cascades over his eyes, but even with the dim lights shining overhead, I can see the green glinting with amusement. I hope he fucking falls. I hope he trips and lands on his ass simply for talking like that.

"Really, Mio? You are one hundred and thirty years old. Only young, hip kids say things like *'killin' my vibe,'* and I'm sorry to tell you this, but you are neither of those things. I'm embarrassed for you."

My first in command flashes his pearly whites as he comes around to walk beside me, slapping me on the back as he does.

"There he is. I know your mood is improving when you revert back to making fun of me." He glances up at the dark clouds and the flashes of blue and white streaking across the sky then striking on the ground around us. He shakes his head. "Letting your frustration out in the sky always helps, too."

"You know giving you shit is my favorite hobby. Next to killing demons, of course."

His burst of laughter is short, as he tells me, "That I do." He slows his walking down to a crawl. "You know she's going to be okay, right? We will all do whatever it takes to protect her."

"Thank you. I know she will be, because I will make sure of it." I stop, twirling my dagger in my hand and keep my gaze pinned on him.

He nods once before continuing forward, letting the conversation end. Mio and I have known each other for over a century, and one thing I enjoy about our friendship is the way we both know when to let conversations die. We say what we need to. Nothing more and nothing less. Nora is a tough subject for me, and Mio respects that.

I want to believe Nora is my fated mate reincarnated—the one who built my army from the ground up to fight against Nyx and her demon hoard a century ago. Being with Hemera felt like fate. Like a destiny I never dreamed could be real. If I was to be king one day, she would have stood by my side as queen. No one else existed when it was her and I. Ever since her death, I've barely existed at all. The gods wrote prophecies that promised her return, but that was over a century ago. I'm still alone. I'm still burdened by memories of the day she died and how the gods allowed her to be taken from me. Maybe the gods lie. Or maybe Nora truly is her. Gods, I'd give anything for that to be true.

"Let me ask you something, Mio." I pause as he glances back at me, nodding and furrowing his brows. "Do you think we could have more than one fated mate? If one dies, do you..." I swallow thickly, shrugging my shoulders and averting my gaze. "What if she isn't Mera? What if Gaia is wrong?"

He steps forward, placing his hands on my shoulders, his eyes softening in a way that only happens when he's using his power to calm my spiraling emotions. "Listen, Ro. I know this is hard for you. I know it has to be hard to accept what Gaia has said to be true, but... the celestial prophecies never lie, man. Nora is the one. Why do you think our queen above has me tagging along with you day and night?" His lips curve up at the corners just slightly as his emotional manipulation continues to swirl and sparkle in golden rays around me, easing my anxiety ridden mind. "Someone will need to take your place as head Guardian and commander of the Dark Legion of warriors. You will be king soon. Your fated mate, your queen has risen."

My weak, unsure smile comes out lopsided, but it's the best I can offer him. He's right. Nora is my fated mate and will be my queen when I choose to accept the crown in the Realm of Darkness. Fear holds me back from fully accepting the truth because I am terrified of losing her again. The moment I laid eyes on Nora it felt like a part of my soul had left my body, like it knew it must make more room for her soul within me. Every part of me screams that she's my fated mate the same way it did for Mera, though Nora's soul doesn't seem to recognize me. I would sense it if it did. Telling her the truth would solidify the bond for us both and she wouldn't be able to deny her soul of what it craves, what it was born to love, but I haven't gathered the courage yet to tell her about us or celestials or any of it. Fuck, her human boyfriend will be a problem for us, I can feel it. He's not going to let her go easily. I don't blame him, but she is not his to claim.

"What if I don't want to give up my position as commander of the army? I can do both."

"No. You can't. Your queen will need you by her side, not out here on the streets fighting demons while she rules the realm. Leave that to us lowly norms who weren't birthed by royalty and destined to rule. He throws his huge, muscular arm over my shoulder, glancing over at me. "You will be a great king."

"Sure. If you say so." I push his arm off me. "If you're to learn how to be head guardian and commander, then we should keep practicing."

"It'll be an honor and a privilege to replace you, my king." He bows his head low, crossing one ankle behind the other in a sort of curtsey that has me rolling my eyes and shaking my head.

I sigh heavily, stopping and gazing into the heavens, up to the gods and goddesses hidden away on Mount Othrys or wherever the hell they are, begging for them to look past Mio's bullshit to see him for who he truly is. A damned good leader and the most trustworthy celestial I know. There's no one who'd be better for this role than him.

"Tapping in on the future celestials emotions here on Earth isn't easy. It takes a lot of concentration and patience to focus on only one of them when there are so many. You'll fail many times while learning to block out all but the one you're assigned to. Once you hone in and sharpen your skills, it's easy. Sometimes, in cases like Nora, where depression and grief have taken over their every waking and sleeping thought, it hurts." I shoot him a quick, comforting smile, slapping him on the back. "Luckily for you, you're the master of emotional manipulation. It'll hurt much less if you use that to your advantage on either them or yourself."

He nods. "In cases like those, I've learned, it's nearly impossible to help them. Even my power can't fix the kind of broken that comes from grief. Their hearts aren't open to healing quite yet." He strolls away, then leans his back against the brick wall of a coffee shop, crossing his arms over his chest. "You want me to check in on her? I can try, but you're much better at connecting with her than I am."

It's not that I'm better at it, he simply doesn't enjoy doing it. Her thoughts are dark, and her feelings are messy, and her pain has a way of clinging to you even after you disconnect. I get it.

Depression is a bitch. I wish I could take it away and absorb it into the depths of my own corrupted mind instead. It wouldn't survive there. That darkness would run away screaming in fear rather quickly, I think. I'm a much scarier monster than it could ever pretend to be.

"Just try, Mio. You need all the practice you can get if this will be your life soon. Your simple days of being merely a warrior for the realm are coming to an end. You'll be a leader soon. A guardian. The mortals will rely on you. I'm almost certain Nora will not be the worst case you encounter in your life." Taking a deep breath, I focus on the flashes of color in the sky, my power a constant wave of humming energy that calms my nerves. "How is she feeling after everything tonight?"

He sighs, uncrossing his arms and closing his eyes. A swirl of bright white light glistens in the darkness, his power reaching out to connect with Nora's soul. In my case, if I focused only briefly, I would immediately decipher what she was feeling or going through, but for him it'll take some time. It's not easy swimming through endless streams of information to get to the core of one specific mortal's feelings or emotions.

Securing my daggers to the straps on my thighs, I lean my head back against the wall, my mind being invaded by Nora's face the way it has for the past year since I began guarding her. Feeling her break as she crouched in front of me in the woods, fearing I would kill her almost broke me, and I don't... *break*. I trained my mind to act as steel to be a shield against enemies, but *her*... her grief and pain, it shatters me, and it fractures those impenetrable shields I've created.

I could never hurt her.

Mio's eyes open, and I already know what he'll say before he says it.

"Nightmares again. But at least she's sleeping, right?" His careful smile is followed by him sliding his daggers into the holsters on his hips and turning toward me. "You'd like me to go to her, wouldn't you? To calm the nightmares that plague her."

I put away my own weapons, leaning helplessly against the wall. "Yes. Please?" I keep my eyes pinned to the raging sky, the thunder and lightning growing fiercer. "I can't tonight. I'm just..." Sighing loudly, I run my hands through my rain-soaked hair, brushing it away from my face. "I need to kill something. That's what I need."

"Fine. You do that, then. I'll go, but only if you end this storm. Do you want her to sleep peacefully tonight, or to be woken up endlessly by your raging storm between her fits of nightmares?" His jaw clenches as he watches me, as he feels me slowly crumbling from the inside out.

Guilt is eating me alive. I watched her climb to the top of that bridge, and she chose to give up on life. She let herself fall. Even if she could have miraculously survived, she never would have made it back to the shore, not alive at least. I watched from above her in the sky and I knew I could save her if she fell, but it didn't hurt any less watching her willingly step off the bridge. Gods, I didn't know things had gotten so bad. I should have fucking been there before she even considered ending her life.

I nod. He's right. Still leaning casually against the wall, pretending I'm not seconds from falling apart, I open my palms and watch as lightning strikes down against them. The storm instantly dies, taking my rage and fury with it. I'm no longer angry. I'm numb. I'm broken. I'm pissed at myself for not seeing the signs, that as much as she pretends around everyone to be okay, that she's still hurting. An eerie silence seeps into the town now that the storm within me has passed, and I welcome it. I need the silence so I can deal with my own shit instead of letting my power do it for me. Looking to Mio, he tips his head, then with a blink he's gone. I wish I could go to her, but one of us needs to keep watch over the city. Besides, I need time alone to gather my thoughts.

Pushing off the wall, I head toward Main Street, sensing an evil presence growing closer. I pull out my daggers, letting the celestial light of the weapons lead the way.

I need to face Nora and tell her the truth. Tonight, she wanted peace. She's searching for an escape from the pain of her mortal existence, but death will not bring the release she craves. It will only be the beginning for her. How will she feel when she wakes up from death and realizes she's just like me?

Forever lurking in the darkness, I stand ready to fly in and save the day, over and over again. It's exhausting, really. It's also exhilarating and thrilling, but so gods damned lonely. If it wasn't for the eternal loneliness, it'd be a beautiful immortal existence. One that those from both the Realm of Darkness and Realm of Light will forever be grateful for. I hope she can learn to feel the same way.

I stalk into the shadows of the alley, the dark power of Nyx's minions pulsating against my senses. As much as I enjoy guiding and guarding celestials both before they ascend and after, I enjoy the slaughtering of demons much more. If they're nearby, I will not give them the satisfaction of continuing to live. They will all fall and become nothing more than scattered, ancient ash in the wind.

"Well, well, well..." I say into the darkness, smelling the stench of sulfur and death oozing out of the demons' bodies. "Haven't I made it clear by now that entering this realm is a death sentence? Your queen will never learn, will she?" I ask, tilting my head and observing Nyx's hell hounds.

The three demons stand and stare, their twisted forms casting an eerie shadow on the ground as they tower over me. Each of them are nearly eight feet tall, their muscular frames unmatched by any demon I've ever encountered. There is never an end to the Queen of Demons little experiments; there is always a more menacing demon waiting just around the corner.

I step under the single streetlight here, allowing them to catch a glimpse of my face. The face of an unrelenting demon killer, that's the face they see right now. Tonight, like any other night that I encounter vile creatures in the dark, I'm no longer a guardian or a guide. I'm simply the angel of death. I spread my wings out, their darkness eclipsing all the surrounding city lights, the velvety black becoming a backdrop for their doom.

"Our queen is sick and tired of you getting in her way. You are always in the way." The demons' words are more like a guttural growl than anything. The deep, otherworldly sound makes my skin crawl.

"Oh? Well, that's funny, because I was thinking the same about her. She will never fucking learn that I will not stop until her whole realm one day crumbles and none of you exist." Stepping toward them, my smile promises death and relentless pain.

"You are the one who must learn, Kairos..." the sound of my name crawling out of its wide mouth, the black venom dripping from sharp, gnarly teeth and onto the pavement, sends a shiver through me. "The girl belongs to Nyx. She always has. You will not save her. Just like you could not save her last time. She will rot alone in darkness just as you tossed Nyx in that cave and left her to rot when you allowed your parents to banish her." The three demons' deep, roaring laughter echoes off the brick walls on both sides of us. "And she thought you were friends. One day you will pay with your life, boy." The deep laughter grows and I stiffen.

I feel dizzy. Not from fear, but from the bullshit spouting from their mouths. The lies. They'll say anything to get a reaction from me. My hands shake with the desire to slice their throats here and now for even speaking of Nora, but I force myself to wait. I stand in place, tightening my grip on my weapons and willing myself to hold back from ending them, at least for a moment.

"What would Nyx want with Nora? She's useless to her. Just a celestial and nothing more." I swallow, keeping my eyes pinned to the one in front, the one who takes a staggered step forward. The ground shakes and crumbles beneath its feet.

"Nyx, too, was once just a celestial. Now she is the most powerful queen to ever exist. Those who are unfortunate enough to look into her eyes end up writhing in pain, begging to be put out of their misery. She cannot wait to watch you writhe, Kairos. She cannot wait to take her away from you all over again." A wide smile slowly creeps across its face.

I've had enough of their mind games. I want them dead.

"If I allowed you another day to live, I'd tell you to pass along that I feel the same. I can't wait to hear her beg for her life one day." Tucking my wings behind my back, I raise my daggers, preparing to slowly end them. "Unfortunately for you, I've had a shit day and watching the blood drain from your hideous bodies will be much more satisfying than having you pass along that message to your queen." I smile as their red eyes glow even brighter.

As the first winged demon steps toward me, I tighten my grip on my weapons and strike.

My daggers find their mark in the demon's neck, and my laughter rings out as its black blood sprays in all directions. It cascades down around me, covering my face and neck in the sticky, warm substance that clings to my skin and sets it ablaze. The pain is worth the kill. As the demon slumps to the ground, it shatters and disintegrates into dust.

The second hell hound approaches, its enormous jaws unhinging inches from my face. The thunderous roar it releases makes my skin prickle with the reminder that it could easily kill me. The demons teeth alone can swiftly end the life of both mortals and immortals, the sharp points resembling three-inch razor blades that gleam and drip with their deadly, dark venom.

With a deafening growl, it stretches out its leathery wings, ready to rip my face off where I stand. I clutch its thick, scaly neck and hurl myself onto its spiky back. As it begins to roll, it takes me down with it, but I refuse to release my grip. Even as my daggers fly through the air and my body meets the pavement, I hold tight to the scales, digging my fingers deep into its flesh and letting it know that it will not win. The demon scratches and claws against the hard cement as it rolls, the horrendous sound like clinging metal against unbreakable stone. As soon as the demon death roll ends, I grip the spike on its head and unsheathe my sword, plunging it deep into the beast's evil brain.

Then it is nothing and I am death itself.

Nyx's demons seem to think that all celestials are as forgiving as the ones from the Realm of Light, but that assumption is wrong. I'm the harbinger of death, the future King of the Realm of Darkness, and the guardian of the mortals on the Earth Realm. Ourahnus and his realm can cage them and attempt to tame them all they want, but within my realms I deny them a second chance.

The second demon turns to dust, and I spit on its remains before using the back of my hand to wipe blood from my face. With the wave of a hand, I call my celestial daggers back to me, smiling as their bright lights flash to life in my palms. Red eyes slant as the third demon glares my way, lurking and hiding in the shadows. They come here seeking to hunt, torture, and murder mortals and celestials who lack the same training and power as me, but now it cowers in the corner like the spineless pathetic prey it knows it has become. I stalk toward it, taunting it with the sound of metal slicing through air as I toss my dagger up and expertly catch it.

I want to feel its fear, a dark and poisonous presence coursing through its veins. I want to drink it all in, to bathe in it and fucking savor it until the end.

Quickly, it turns to flee. The impact of its long, spiky tail against my body sends me stumbling backward. I quickly recover and secure my weapons to the straps on my thighs, and with one small leap, I'm airborne, wings beating rapidly behind me as I soar through the night. The scent of adrenaline and desperation permeates the air as my prey realizes its fate. It cries out, its panicked roars pushing me faster and faster.

It's focused only on making it to the open portal at the end of the alley, and the icy breath of evil that slithers around it as I get closer turns my blood cold. The Underworld is a place of nothing but darkness and despair, a place where the worst nightmares imaginable are brought to life. Nyx is deranged and the demons will do whatever pleases her because they're even more so.

I push myself faster, the wind against my wings letting me feel weightless and free. As I descend, I tuck them in and allow myself to freefall, the pull of gravity helping get me quickly to the ground. I land in a crouch as my boots hit the pavement, locking eyes with the hell hound and giving it my best 'fuck you' grin while spreading my wings out wide behind me. My fist connects with the pavement and the ground splinters and trembles as my power spreads through the cracks, sending lightning racing toward its still shocked face. I focus my unwavering gaze on the monster, and the lightning bolt obediently follows my line of sight, delivering a powerful blow that leaves it stunned. The moment my lightning connects, it coils around the scales and flesh, the cracking and snapping and stench of burning electricity filling the air. As the demon convulses on the ground, there's a pure, undiluted fear brimming in its eyes. A wave of satisfaction washes over me.

With a wave of a hand, I close the portal the hell hounds ripped open. It won't matter. There will be another one opened tomorrow and the day after that. They never fucking learn. Staring down at the pathetic demon, I punch a hole through its hard, scaly chest, ripping its heart out with my hand in one swift movement. Holding the lifeless organ in my fist, feeling the burn of the black blood as it drips from my fingers and runs down my arm, I keep my eyes locked on the demon as its life drains away. I enjoy watching the darkness in their eyes disappear. I revel in knowing the realms are one demon closer to being rid of evil for good.

The heart and the body dissolve to dust, but the blackness still clings to my skin.

"Ashes to ashes, dust to dust..." I whisper into the gust of wind I create, scattering the powdery remains around me.

All that remains now is the steady rhythm of my heartbeat, the sound of my breath, and an unwavering determination to hunt down every vile creature across all realms, ensuring their ultimate demise.

"I missed all the fun, I see. What a bummer." Mio towers over me, shaking his head and clicking his tongue. "You're a mess, man.

"Always killin' the vibe, bro. I was having fun." Smiling up at him, I use my shirt to wipe blood from my scraped-up hands and face.

His laughter is immediate and overdramatic. "Gods, you're right. That's awful. I'm embarrassed for you that you just said that. I'll never say it again."

"Good. Thank you." Putting my weapons away, I crack my neck and stretch out my fingers. "Nyx's demons somehow keep getting stronger... and faster."

"You getting too old for this, Kairos? Maybe it is time for you to bow out. Old man can't hang anymore."

I roll my eyes. "I can hang just fine, thank you. I was just pointing it out. Her creations are getting worse and worse. I fear what they'll someday become if we don't end her for good."

"I know. And we will. I promise. She has had it coming for a while. With the recent increase in demon activity, Gaia and Ouranos, or hell, even the gods themselves might come out of retirement to do something. Either way, something must be done. It can't go on this way forever." He turns and we head toward the deserted streets, and I welcome the bright overhead lights as they come into view.

Being in darkness for too long can make you want to live there. It has a way of sucking the life out of you slowly and tempting you to never leave.

"The demons know, Mio. Nyx knows Mera has returned and that she's here. How the hell did she find out?"

The shops and the streets fade away as my thoughts spiral on what the hell I'm supposed to do now.

He stops walking but doesn't turn to look at me. "Maybe they're bluffing. Trying to get a reaction out of you."

I don't buy it. Neither does he, but there isn't much else to say, so we let it die for now. We saw this coming. It shouldn't be a surprise to either of us.

"How is she?"

"Better. She was sleeping peacefully by the time I got there. *He* was there. The mortal man." He smiles but it doesn't reach his eyes, there's a sadness within them that he's trying to hide. "It's going to be okay. Nyx will not get to her. The Gods are on our side." He squeezes my shoulder as we make our way back through town, neither of us speaking.

Which Gods are on our side? I fear our gods abandoned us long ago. The moment Nyx's darkness stained our white wings, they let us fall from the Realm of Light. Even Ourahnus won't visit our realm since the heavens fractured in two. We are no longer celestial beings of any god, though my realm doesn't believe that to be true. Maybe the others are right and they're hiding on Mount Othrys and observing, writing new prophecies, and consulting with oracles, but we haven't seen them in a century. For all we know they're dead. All we have is each other.

Something feels off, but it's not Nora whose energy clings to me. It's Mio's soul now that needs healing, the unspoken anxiety is hard to ignore. He's more worried than he's letting on. He is afraid we will not be able to save her and that it will be my downfall. It nearly was last time, so I don't blame him for worrying.

"Why don't you go home for the night? Get some rest." Waving my hand in front of us, I open a portal to the Realm of Darkness to send him home.

I will not be going with him, not while Nora is here helpless and alone. Katie's wards of protection can only stop so much from entering, and with the demons now threatening her life, aware of her emergence, I won't be going home anytime soon.

"You need rest too, you know. You've had a long day. A long year actually, since you've started guarding her. The way you protect and care for others is inspiring, but don't forget to take care of yourself, too." He steps through the portal, turning to nod as he closes it behind him.

Unfurling my wings from behind my back, they launch me into the air on pure instinct. I let go of my glamours and enchantments once I'm airborne, the shadows are my friend. As I soar through the sky, making my way to Nora, I whisper my realms mantra over and over...

Darkness guide me, gods save me....

Not her. *Not fucking again.*

CHAPTER SIX

BLESSED BE

NYX

THE REALM OF LIGHT: APRIL 10TH, 1848

White puffs of clouds pass by. I reach up to try to grab them, smiling as they slip through my fingers. Being so high in the sky with the Earth realm so far below is something that still brings me comfort. Most days I'm thankful to have been saved as an infant by Queen Gaia and King Ourahnus and brought here, even if I am being used as an experiment. They're aware of the witch and demon blood that runs thick through my veins, even thicker than the celestial blood I was born with, but even so, they want to believe there is hope for me. For most of my years, they've taught me about celestial laws and the ways of the Realm of Light but now begins my training to wield my power as a witch.

They hope the darkness I have within can be blinded by light from my celestial and witch power, until darkness is forced out of me like it never existed. I believe the darkness cannot be avoided, unlike the clouds here in the Realm of Light that part ways and slip through my fingers, never wanting to be felt against my skin. Darkness makes itself known because it wants to be felt. It wants to reign. It demands attention.

It makes sure I feel it slithering beneath my skin whether I want it there or not.

"Are you Nyx?" A sweet voice asks. A woman steps into the meadow with long, white hair glistening as rays of sunlight shower over her.

I'm not sure whether it's the beauty of her alone or the path of bright pink and purple wildflowers that come alive and sprout before my eyes as she comes toward me that leaves me breathless. Gods is she beautiful. Her stunning blue eyes shimmer as she stops before me and extends her hand. Hesitating, I smile and shake it nervously. The feel of her soft skin against mine makes my heart race.

"You must be Hekate. I'm delighted to finally meet you. Gaia raved about your power and your ability to teach. What an honor it is to be in your presence." Clasping my hands together in front of me, I smile as I fully take her in.

Her white, flowing dress is elegant and feminine, highlighting all her best features, yet still modest enough to fit in here where we all wear white robes. The obsidian amulet around her neck is wrapped in golden wire, and there are colors within the crystal that swirl and change by the second. The crown of thorns and roses across her forehead appears to be made of pure gold and is adorned with a crescent moon followed by a full moon, and then a waning crescent with radiant blue jewels outlining each of them. She looks much more exquisite than I ever imagined the Queen of the witch covens would be.

She steps toward me and bows her head. "Please. It is truly an honor to meet you, Nyx. Your power is like nothing I have felt before. I am thrilled to have the opportunity to train you." Opening her palms, she smiles as she summons her glowing blue power, never taking her eyes off me.

My wings have a touch of this same witch given power, glowing with a soft blue light in the darkness. There's never a dark day here in the Heavens, though, so the glimmer of light enshrouding me is only visible when I visit the Earth Realm. Most agree my wings are beautiful, despite what else they might think of me. Everyone besides the deities here believe I am evil or cursed because of the darkness that runs through my veins. Why the fearless rulers of this realm trust me to be here, I will never understand. I'm glad they do. I hope to stay here and earn the others' trust, too.

In the celestials' eyes, beyond the rulers here, if I did not have my stunning white wings, I'd be nothing more than another demon for them to vanquish

—another thing to protect the mortals from. They wouldn't hesitate in killing me even for a second.

Hekate's blue light glimmers so bright that it's impossible to look directly into but much harder to look away from. It's magnificent. Her magic pulsates out around us as she invokes a circle of light, creating a dome of privacy just for her and I. The color blue has never looked so beautiful, but still, it does not compare to the beauty of her eyes. The sun vanishes as if someone plucked it from the sky, and a full moon the color of crimson takes its place. I huff out a quiet laugh as I take in the beauty of the darkness she conjured while barely having enough time to blink.

"How did you...?"

"Being a skilled witch takes years of practice, Nyx. It will not be easy at first, but I promise if you stick with me, it will be worth it." She sits in the grass a few feet from me and gestures for me to do the same.

I don't hesitate. I immediately sit, crossing my legs in front of me. Here with her I've never felt more like myself or more alive, and I've also never felt so...*free*.

"Does the blood moon have special significance to our power?" I keep my eyes pinned to her.

I don't think I could look away even if I tried. Hekate is like a bright star in a night sky, a flaming torch at the end of a dark and suffocating tunnel, the one who will lead me where I belong. She is the brightest star I've ever seen.

After summoning black candles in a circle around us, she waves her hand and brings them to life. The blue shield around us grows brighter and brighter as thorns and roses climb up the walls and close us in, creating a perfect garden of privacy. Only the curved arch at the top is left open to allow the red glow of the moon to shine down upon us.

She doesn't look at me as she speaks, busy setting up for our lesson. "Every element and celestial object is one we worship. They all hold a power within which we can wield to make us stronger and fiercer. Some can help us heal others or even raise the dead if we have the ability within us." Her lips turn up at the corners as she summons two golden cups in her hands. "The *selini aimatos* in particular is important for opening portals to new and higher levels of consciousness. It is also great for blood magic." As she smiles her eyes flash with excitement and candlelight flickers across her features.

"Blood magic," I breathe in a hushed whisper, afraid for the punishment of even speaking of the dark magic might bring. "It is forbidden." It has been for centuries, and I enjoy my place in the realm here, though others surely wouldn't mind my absence. I do not want to be forced to leave or worse if the others were to find out about my use of dark magic.

"What we do in the shadows is between you and I, Nyx. The Gods and Goddesses of the realms cannot even see us now." Her steely eyes pierce into mine as I smooth out the wrinkles in my robe and readjust my legs beneath me.

The witch laughs and my eyes dart back to her. The sound is like music to my ears, a whisper in the wind that calls to my soul. I can't help but smile though fear runs rampant in my mind.

"Fear not, my dear.. Magic is neither good nor bad. It is neither dark nor light. The one who wields it chooses which side they are on. Blood magic has many great purposes for a witch."

"What great purposes could dark magic have?" As I gaze up at the moon, I feel a familiar sense of churning within my soul, like the darkness within me is ready to combust and set the world ablaze. I grit my teeth, fisting my dress and praying to whichever God might still care for me to push the darkness down deep, to never let it make its way to the surface.

Darkness guide me. Gods save me.

My question hangs in the air as she retrieves a small, elegant dagger from the front of her dress. "It can be used to form everlasting bonds between our people. On the other hand, it can be used to break bonds, weakening our enemies. I have seen it wielded to create love and to create life." Glancing at me, her eyes soften as she sends waves of energy my way, pushing thoughts into my mind of my mother and how I was born.

I don't want to remember. She was a fool for accepting a blood bond with a dark God, the very bond which brought me into existence. She was a powerful witch who let a celestial impregnate her and then allowed dark blood to run through the both of us, a bond and a scar on my soul that I too will forever bear. The same dark god she bound herself to eventually killed her. The celestials could have slaughtered me for being what I am, and I would not have blamed them. No one else exists like me. No one ever should.

"The main purpose for bringing forth the blood moon is to harness ancestral power. To open doors which are normally hidden. Simply ask for that which you desire and open your vein as an offering to her. You shall receive what you wish for." Shadows dance across her face and there is not so much as a glimmer of a lie hiding there.

What she says is true. I can feel it. The power shining down upon both of us feels electric and alive. The moon is a radiating sphere of magic waiting for us to make an offer. I can learn to use my darkness for good. I have so much power within me, if only I could learn to use it. Hekate is a blessing sent to me by the gods and goddesses themselves. Dark power and maybe even darkness itself is not something I should fear. As Hekate said, it is the one who wields the power who ultimately chooses which side they are on. I choose light, always.

"What shall we ask for tonight? What shall we offer her?" I swallow nervously.

I'm unsure if I can be trusted with knowledge of such power. This darkness at times seems to have a mind and choices of its own. But I am sure of how I feel around Hekate. I trust her. She will teach me to be good. With her near, my body vibrates with power in a way that has me convinced I could have everything I have ever desired. With her I no longer feel out of place, like a mixed breed creature who must be watched carefully or treated with special care. I just feel like me. Not Nyx the dark one or Nyx the cursed. I am Nyx the celestial witch whose darkness is a gift as much as the light.

She gives me a half smile before raising her dagger up and pointing it directly toward the moon, her icy hair falling behind her shoulders as she tilts her head back. "Mother Moon, Goddess of Earth. Hear us. We ask of you to bless us with your power, under the guidance of the blood moon and with darkness as witness to our pleas. Let Nyx become one with myself and my covens. Let her share my blood and share our ancestor's wisdom from this day forward. Forgive her for the selfishness, the greed, and the vanity which came before this day. Accept her as one of your own and one of mine. Hear me mother moon and goddess of earth and let her power rise!"

She keeps the dagger raised, and her eyes do not flick open as the clouds roll in, not even when thunder rolls overhead or as lightning strikes the ground all around us. As the wind swirls rapidly within the dome and our hair blows wildly, she still holds the dagger toward the moon without flinching. Even as whispered words from unseen strangers echo all around us, strangers who I cannot see but feel as though they're right next to me, she simply smiles. Their power brushes against my skin softly. They whisper my name into the shadows. They circle around me again and again, tiny speckles of blue light and surges of power. I hold my breath and refuse to blink, too stunned to look away.

Hekate lowers the dagger into her lap and locks eyes with me. She glances around as if she can see them, the ones who whisper in the dark. With a single nod to the ethereal forces, she runs the dagger across her palm, letting blood drain into her golden chalice. The warmth from the powerful forces hums like electricity buzzing through the air. Still, the storm rages on as she sends the dagger floating my way, and I gladly retrieve it from the air. My trembling hand does not hesitate or flinch as I slice open my vein, letting it spill into the cup in front of me. My offering to the moon if she will accept me.

Hekate holds her cup up above her head, eyes locked to the sky, so I do the same. Prickly, warm power radiates in the palm of my hand. Love, light and darkness combine to form acceptance of all that I am and who I am meant to be. Intense power spreads from my hand and tingles as it climbs down my arm and pushes its way into my blood stream. It weaves through every part of me, attaching to every fiber of my being. It does not leave a single cell unaffected, and there's a distant, gentle murmur of acceptance by the powers that be.

I am no longer just a witch who can wield an unimaginable amount of power. I am power.

The contents in our cups bubble and splatter out as they boil. My hand is warm, and my heart is full as I watch the liquid from Hekate's cup rise to meet the blood from my own. It is no longer my blood or her blood, or the power from the blood moon above. It is our blood. Our power. The union of our souls. My heart thuds loudly in my chest and my lips curl up into a wide smile as the liquid contents slowly descend back into the cups in our waiting hands.

Blood magic cannot possibly be evil when it holds such beauty. Not when it feels so right.

Hekate's bright smile puts the glow of the moon to shame, even as it appears now like a spotlight above our heads, watching and waiting for what happens next.

"Nyx, will you accept this offer from our ancestors and from the Mother Moon? They offer you to join us. To be one of us. They offer to guide you in the journey of becoming a witch, so long as you take heed to this warning: do not let your power lead you down a dark, winding path, for you may get lost in the darkness and never find your way back." The witches' eyes glow now with a bright blue hue, the color swirling and holding me captive.

I want to be like her. I want to strengthen my power and use it only for good, to prove I am worthy of this. To prove to Gaia and Ourahnus that they made the right choice in saving me and letting me live with their people. Most importantly, I would like to prove to myself that I am worthy of living. The ancestors' words of warning replay in my head, but even in times when all hope felt lost, I have never been tempted to give in to darkness. I despise it more than anything.

It is light that will always guide me home.

"I accept their offer and will heed their warning." Glancing up at the moon nervously, I pray I've said the right thing.

I have no idea what I am doing or where I will go from here, but I want this more than anything. I would love to spend more time with my new queen.

"Here, here." Hekate raises her glass to the moon then brings it to her lips.

"Here, here." I smile, drinking the thick, sweet contents down in one gulp.

As she lowers the cup from her lips, I do the same. She slams the cup into the grass in front of her and her glowing barrier of power disappears. "Blessed be!" She yells, smiling up at the welcoming sun.

"Blessed be!" I echo, sitting the cup down beside me.

The sun is too bright. The clouds are too close, and the air is too thick. I yearn to be back within her dome of darkness. There, everything felt right. For the first time, so did I. At times it feels like oxygen does not exist. Like my lungs might collapse and my heart might die from lack of feeling. Today, with the Queen of Witches in front of me and the moon cutting through the darkness, I felt everything.

Hekate stands, and with a slight wave of her hand the candles and cups disappear. I stare up at her in awe as she braids her hair, her delicate fingers completing it so effortlessly. I cannot bring myself to stand just yet. I feel as though I'm one with my realm, but also one with each realm in existence. I would hate to break the connection. I'd hate it even more so to stand and break the connection I feel looking at her. Like a magnet she tempts me to come closer. If I am Earth, she is my gravity. If she is the moon then I am the darkness that will gladly fade into oblivion, becoming nothing more than a backdrop for her beauty to shine.

She crouches down, plucking two sad, shriveled-up flowers from the dirt, then motions for me to come closer. "Watch. Magic truly is the most wonderful, beautiful gift in the world." As she opens her palms with the flowers inside, I watch as the brown stems slowly brighten to green. I gasp as the petals rise and return to life, their purple hues blossoming more vibrant and lively than the ones scattered on the ground.

Watching her breathe life into that which was dead does something within my heart that I cannot explain. My mind feels at ease. Suddenly, my future looks so bright.

I meet her eyes with my own, tears obscuring my vision. "That was beautiful," I whisper. "You...are beautiful," I sniffle, wiping away tears and forcing a smile.

"Your turn, Nyx." She watches me patiently as I gaze at the beautiful flowers at our feet.

I pluck one flower and then another, pinching them gently between my fingers. She believes in me and somehow that seems like enough, though I have never used magic before. I close my eyes, feeling my power rise to the surface. I do not push it away and suppress it like times before. The familiar tingle of magic reaching my fingertips quickly ends as Hekate gasps and my eyes flutter open.

Quickly I stand, my hands covering my mouth, and my body spinning in small circles as I take in the damage. Gods, what have I done? I should not be trusted with this kind of power. I drop the shriveled-up stems on the ground, my breathing fast and uneven. Dead flowers smile up at me, their crumpled, hopeless bodies stripped of all life. Not only the ones in my hands—a circle of death replaces the ones which were thriving around us before. My power killed them all. I killed them.

"Nyx, it's okay." Hekate says, placing her hands on my shoulders. "One thing you must remember, is that you possess great darkness within you, a darkness I do not yet understand. You might only touch one thing, but that darkness can quickly spread like wildfire until you learn to control it. We must always be careful."

"I... I did not even touch them. They should have been safe." I back away from her, letting her hands fall from my shoulders to her sides, putting distance between us to keep her safe. "Please... stay back!" I lower my trembling hands from my mouth, eyes wide and full of terror.

I cannot let myself hurt her. I would never forgive myself for such an act. She is not safe with me, wherever I go only darkness will follow.

"I do not fear you, my dear Nyx." Her laugh rings out around me, stunning me where I stand. "Your heart is more pure than any I have ever encountered. I am intrigued by you. You are magnificent." Her words are barely a whisper. "Come," she says, placing one reincarnated flower behind her ear and then carefully tucking the other one behind mine. "There is much more to show you." A simple glance at the field of wildflowers by her, and they are once again blooming with life. "We are a team now, you and I, and your darkness simply needs to be tamed." Leaning forward, she whispers softly, "Let me be the one to tame you."

As she heads out of the meadow toward the thick, green forest, I brush my fingertips against the spot where her hand gracefully skimmed across my ear. I wish I could hold that touch within my heart and feel it endlessly. I have never met anyone as accepting or as gentle as her. My darkness fades. It curls up and hides, fearing what Hekate might be capable of.

She turns, glancing over her shoulder with an encouraging smile, and as she disappears beyond the trees, I pick up the bottom of my white robe, tuck my wings behind me tightly, and follow after her.

I will follow her anywhere.

CHAPTER SEVEN

THE STRANGER

NORA

The hospital staff observed me overnight to rule out a concussion, and although I truly believe there's something wrong in my brain, I'm happy to be going home. The terror from the night before hasn't worn off yet, the feeling of suddenly being hundreds of feet in the air soaring to sure and permanent death still scares the shit out of me. What terrifies me most is not remembering how I ended up falling to begin with. Did I jump? Did I fall? And why the hell can't I remember? There's definitely something wrong with my brain. It's broken.

I'm broken.

Olivia and I sit side by side on the ferry as we make our way back to Mackinac Island, and I can't pull my eyes away from the blue waves of Lake Michigan—the ripple and rise of them before they crash back to the surface. The waves have a way of hypnotizing me, but today they hypnotize me in a new way as flashbacks from the night before replay in my mind. I almost died. I should have died. Shutting my eyes tightly, I breathe in the fresh, soothing lake air. It brings a sense of peace straight to my soul. I enjoy living in such a small town, this tiny island surrounded by water and lush trees. I'll never leave. My parents always said the same.

Olivia would much rather live in a big city, but she chose to stay here to be close to me. She doesn't trust me to be alone, and honestly, I don't blame her. I have a way of spiraling into dark places that lurk in the corners of my mind and struggling to find my way back. She has saved me from myself countless times while Ere has been there to numb the pain. Without either of them I'm not sure I'd still be here today.

"You okay, sis?" Olivia asks, looking me up and down and giving me a small smile when my eyes lock with hers.

I smile back as her dark hair whips around us in the breeze, taking in the scent of her citrus shampoo. She's so happy and carefree. Even after our parents' sudden deaths she found a way to smile through the pain and grieve quietly.

There was nothing quiet about my grieving.

The many suicide attempts and random men I hooked up with to try to mask the pain before meeting Ere are living proof. I never knew true darkness until I lost my parents. I've only been pretending to feel better.. After last night, I think it's safe to say pretending isn't working.

"I'm okay. I'll be okay, I mean," I tell her, grabbing my red locks in my hand and securing them in a ponytail with the scrunchy I pull from my wrist. "My head is just killing me and... " I swallow thickly, closing my eyes and trying to find the right words. "I miss Mom and Dad so much, Liv. Every single day. I'm starting to wonder if it'll ever get easier." Warmth slides down my cheeks, and I quickly wipe it away.

Olivia's bright blue eyes shine with a layer of tears just waiting to fall. "I know, Nor. I miss them, too. I don't know if it'll ever get easier, but all we can do is try to be okay." She wraps her arm around me and lays her head on my shoulder. "Do you want to go see them today?" Peering up at me, she sniffles.

"Yes. Can we, please? Maybe that's exactly what I need." I lean my head on hers, sliding my arms around her and squeezing tightly. "I love you, sis," I whisper as the ferry slows and the horn blares to announce our arrival to the docks.

"Love you too." She lifts her head up, wipes away her tears, then flashes me a bright wide smile.

That's how she grieves. She feels the pain in small bursts and then it passes, much like most do, and then she's right back to her happy, carefree self. I will never grieve or feel pain that way. My pain festers and wraps around my heart and soul until nothing but darkness remains. Then, once the soul crushing darkness creeps in, my emotions and thoughts drown in endless, tormenting agony.

I don't know what the hell is wrong with me.

As the ferry reaches the dock and people line up and swiftly exit, a wave of dizziness hits me. I clench my teeth and smile as Katie glances my way, hoping it isn't obvious that I'm teetering because she'll force me to go home. She doesn't notice, thankfully.

Walking down the brick road that leads to St. Anns Cemetery, Olivia and I loop our arms together and I remind myself to breathe. The sun sets behind the trees and shadows dance across the graves, and a part of me fears the ghostly mother who haunts this place might appear. People often come here for fun, then leave sharing stories of spotting her weeping above her child's grave before screeching and vanishing into thin air. I understand the pain of losing someone who holds every piece of your heart.

That kind of pain never heals, and more often than not, I'd like to scream, too.

Olivia releases my arm and takes a seat near my parents' headstone. I kick off my flip flops and lay down on my back, staring up at the sky the way my mom and I did when I was little. Twirling pieces of grass between my fingers at the spot they were laid to rest makes me feel more connected to them, to the reality that they're gone. I try to make myself forget until memories of them come flooding back and I let them drown me.

"What are you thinking about?" Olivia lays down next to me and interlocks our fingers.

"How hard life is without them." I close my eyes, trying to remember their faces and smiles and how they lit up any room they walked into.

Most of the time when I picture their faces all I see are black smears and claw marks, and I get so goddamn mad about remembering them that way. I take a deep breath, forcing the images away.

"We really had the best parents anyone could ever ask for, didn't we?" Her words are a soft whisper, but I can still make out the quivering of her voice.

I nod in response, but her gaze is focused on the sky, her thoughts far away. "We were so lucky to have them. I would give anything to have them back." I open my eyes, noting how the rays of sunlight have vanished, letting the stars now twinkle brightly above us.

The air is frigid against my skin, and the shadows are gone now that darkness has taken over. The darkness in my mind took over long ago. I wish I could fight it. I'd love nothing more than to suffocate it, to chain it up in the back of my mind so I never feel it or think of it again. I'm not strong enough. Fighting feels hopeless.

"Mom and Dad would want you to be happy. They would want you to move on, Nor, to live your life fully. They wouldn't want you to stay frozen in time the way you have been." She leans up on her elbow, staring down at me.

The wind tousles her hair, and it brushes against my cheek as she watches me, her eyes clear and full of wisdom. I'm only two years younger than her but she seems much older. She's definitely much smarter. I'm a college dropout. I left Florida State University's psychology program to come home for the funeral and never went back. Maybe one day I will. Olivia's degree in early childhood education, and her joy of helping those around her serve her well at the elementary school she works at. Kids love her, their parents love her, and a lot of it has to do with how much she takes after our parents. Their joy and love for life, their way of staying positive in any situation, and the way they never gave up hope that better days were on the horizon. I don't know where all my negativity comes from, but it isn't from them. I guess I'm a different breed.

I sigh, sitting up and crossing my legs in front of me, facing the forest that lines the cemetery on all sides. "I know, Liv. I know they'd want me to be happy. I'm trying," I tell her. "It might not look like it some days, but I try so hard every day to be better. To do better." I glance at her, shooting her a half-ass smile before turning back toward the trees.

She knows I try. She also knows I fail spectacularly when I do. Even before our parents' deaths I struggled to find happiness. It's like it has always been just out of reach, and no matter how hard I try to grip onto it and claim it as mine, it eludes me and always will.

Darkness always wins in the end.

"I know you try. Someday you'll have everything you could ever wish for; I just know it." She stands and brushes dirt off the front of her jeans before throwing me a mischievous smile. "I'm going grave hunting. I guess there's one here that dates back to the early eighteen hundreds. I want to find it. Apparently, it's cursed." She raises her eyebrows up and down as she extends her hand to help me stand.

She has always been into things that are dark, creepy or just plain weird, so adventuring out to find the cursed tombstone doesn't surprise me. I can't say for sure how many times I've heard her claim that ghosts and witches most likely exist, even vampires, at times. She's obsessed with 'uncovering the truth and secrets of the world,' as she says, refusing to admit that life might just be this. Mundane. Boring. Although, after all I've seen and experienced this past year, I'm finally on her side with this. There are definitely secrets that need uncovering. I wonder again if Olivia believes all the crazy things I told her about our parents' deaths more than she cares to admit. If anyone would, it'd be her. Her and Katie both tend to run toward that which most people would run from. They go on antique runs all over the state, hunting for cursed objects and antique artifacts. The first thing Katie does is check the jewelry section for my mom's amulet. She knows how much it meant to me. I don't believe I'll ever see it again.

"Give me a minute. I want to stay with them a little bit longer."

It's the truth, but also, I refuse to risk bringing any more doom or gloom into my life with cursed objects. I have enough of that going on already.

I watch her mindlessly roam around, brushing dirt off random grave markers and kneeling to get a closer look. My eyes wander back to the woods, and my heart leaps out of my chest. I grip the grass at my sides with both hands, hoping the touch against the earth will ground me and bring me back to reality. In the shadows I make out a figure standing there watching me. It wears all black. What stands out most are the huge, feathery black wings peeking out from behind its back and the bright green eyes that pierce into my soul.

Darkness has such a tight hold on me that no matter where I go or who I'm with, it will surely follow. What does it want from me? I stand up slowly, taking a small step forward to get a closer look. It takes two steps back. My hands tremble and my eyes widen as the fear of what this thing might want with me takes over my thoughts. Is it an angel or something sinister disguised as one? Olivia steps up beside me, first gazing at me and then letting her eyes drift to the spot mine are locked on in the darkness between the swaying trees.

"What are we looking at?" She asks, squinting her eyes in the direction of the lurker.

I raise my hand, pointing a finger in the direction of the figure. "That. Don't you see him? He's just watching me. Him or it, I-I don't know." My voice is slow and hushed, not wanting the stranger to hear me.

She looks at me and then back at the trees before settling back on me for good. "There's nothing there. Just... a whole lot of trees." She gently places her hand on my shoulder. "We should get you home. You need rest."

"Who are you?" I whisper, more to myself than for my sister.

"Nora, who the hell are you talking to? There's literally no one there."

I take a step forward and then another, before deciding to throw all caution to the wind as I full on run toward the dark figure. I don't care what happens when I reach him. I don't care if my mind is playing tricks on me or deceiving me. I need to face him. The wind whips across my face and everything around me fades away. Each time my bare feet meet the cold grass, I push myself forward with more urgency. I sprint toward the man or thing or angel, refusing to let him get away. I need to know what he is. I need to know why he keeps showing up and why he's watching me.

"Nora! Stop!" Olivia yells, and her heavy breathing follows close behind me.

All I can focus on is the stranger. On his dark hood and the dark wings and the dark aura that emanates around him. He isn't hiding. He wants me to see; I can feel it. As I reach the tree line, bright green eyes glisten from within the shadows. White teeth come into view, as a smile made of temptation and secrets flashes across his face. He's enjoying this, seeing me desperate to find out the truth.

Right before I reach him, so close I could almost touch the feathery wings, the creature nods once before leaping into the air and disappearing somewhere within the glimmers of starlight.

I'm left standing alone, spinning in circles within the trees as I stare up at the sky. The sound of flapping wings drowns out the frantic screams of Olivia as she races over to me. I can't tear my eyes away from the canopy of trees above us, hoping to get a glimpse of him between them so I can beg him to come back. To not run or hide. All I want is for him to talk to me, to prove that he's real. I need him to explain why the hell he's here and what he wants with me. To tell me how I ended up on top of that bridge and why the hell he swooped in to save me. I need to know what he is.

As terrified as a part of me feels whenever I'm in his presence, there's also a part of me that's intrigued and left in awe. Knowing something so beautiful can exist within the darkness leaves me wanting to know more.

To know him.

CHAPTER EIGHT

DROWNING IN SILENCE

NORA

Sipping my glass of wine, I shift in my chair. I smile at the family pictures hanging on the walls. Candlelight flickers across happy faces and silly poses, reminding me of what I've lost. A year ago, I couldn't tolerate looking at these. Pain would consume me and before I knew it, I'd be curled up on my parents' bed sobbing and unable to move for days. I could barely breathe then. Olivia would wrap me up tightly in her arms and hold me until I had no more tears left to cry.

I'm glad she moved in here with me. I wouldn't have made it through the last year without her. Her friend with benefits, a military guy who's rarely free is home for the weekend, so she's at his place tonight leaving me alone here to drink my wine and deal with my thoughts. Those thoughts are surprisingly quiet tonight and have been since I was released from the hospital a week ago--since feeling like darkness was closing in on me, watching from the shadows and waiting for me to follow it into the unknown. This peace is exactly what I need right now.

Rain trickles down the window, and I watch as a solitary drop slowly makes its way to the bottom of the pane, merging with the puddle forming on the ledge outside. There's something so peaceful about rain, about the way it comes hurling toward earth before it's stopped in its tracks and laid to rest.

But it never really dies. The cycle of life for this single, fallen rain drop carries on. What a beautiful thing to witness, rebirth. If only people could be the same.

Finishing what's left in my glass, I stand and make my way to the dimly lit kitchen, the flames from my candles dancing and swaying, leaving moving shadows on the walls. The new, plush carpet beneath my feet is a comforting reminder that it's okay to move on and necessary to heal. Remodeling the house my parents left to me felt wrong. At first it hurt. But I'm trying to move past it, and I know this is what they would want.

The medications Dr. Cooper ordered for me glare in my direction from the marble counter. After what happened on the bridge, the dissociation and attempted suicide, you'd think that would be enough to convince me to take them, but it's not. I turn on the water at the sink, followed by the garbage disposal, then open the lids and pour them all down the drain. It's the same thing every month, but I have to pretend I'm trying. I have to pretend I'm taking the meds and that they're working, too, which is the hardest part of it all. Dumping money down the drain feels like it should be a crime, but I have no choice.

I will not let prescription medications numb me more than my depression already has.

Standing at the kitchen window, I watch as the waves rise and crash to the shore, beckoning me outside to rise and fall with them. It has been so long since I've enjoyed our private little beach. The memories that come with it are like little daggers straight to my heart.

Memories of my dad fishing and cursing the wind for ruining the perfect toss of his line into the water. The laughter of my mom and the twinkle in her bright blue eyes as she watched me chase after seagulls, mimicking their panicked squawking as they ran from me. The sighs and squeals of Olivia sunbathing on her favorite pink towel, swatting away bugs and mosquitoes.

Those days were the best days of my life. I would give anything to have them back, to have that pure, unfiltered happiness in my life again.

I rinse my glass out in the sink, then head to my bedroom, pulling my sundress up and over my head as I enter the room. I quickly change into my red and white flowery bikini, then throw a towel over my shoulder and head to the sliding glass doors leading out to the beach. Stepping outside is like stepping into a time capsule. The chilly lake breeze rushes into me and I close my eyes and smile, breathing in the long-forgotten scent of joy and laughter.

As I walk toward the edge of the water, the grainy sand beneath my feet makes the memories feel much more real. Sometimes they feel so far away, so lost to time and darkness that I wonder if they ever happened at all.

Gazing up at the twinkling stars made brighter from the dark clouds hiding the moon, I admire their beauty. There has always been something about the stars that sends hope into my heart.

Without darkness we would never appreciate the light.

I toss my towel on the ground as I slowly make my way into the water, walking further and further away from the shore. It's freezing cold as it reaches my waist and then my neck, but I don't care, I push off the floor of the lake and swim anyway. I fight against the icy waves, propelling myself through the water until the chill disappears and I feel nothing. Something far below the surface, or deep within my mind, whispers to me to continue swimming and not look back. It feels right letting the waves carry me away, giving them the power to drag me out of my thoughts. I don't stop swimming even when I know I should, even when it dawns on me that I've never been out this far before.

Like a siren, the depths of the lake sing to me, calling out so I can follow it into eternal darkness. I don't want to stop. I don't want to go back. I want to stay here forever floating with the waves, forever one with the lake and the darkness or the siren who whispers that I should stay. I dive underwater, swimming deeper and deeper toward the vast, empty floor. I can't see the bottom, but I want to feel it beneath my feet. Down there, no one will ever find me.

I'd like to stay here in the darkness where it's quiet and I'm free. In this place where pain and heartbreak no longer haunt me. I can find myself again, here within the darkness.

I smile as I swim faster. I'm so far away but so close to being one with the waves, eternally bound to them and them to me. The whispers surround me, caressing the broken, painful pieces of my soul.

Nora... Nora... soon you shall be free...

I kick harder and swim faster. I push the last of the oxygen in my lungs out, preparing my body to never need it again. I will need nothing else as I drift along with waves and darkness wrapped around me.

Ouch. Something grips my arm tightly and I scream, though there is no air in my lungs and nowhere for the water to go except for down my throat and into my airway. Screaming, choking, and spitting out water, my lungs burn and my heart quivers in fear.

No. No, I can't go back.

I resist the hold of whatever grips my arm, even as it drags me quickly through the water and toward the shore. It doesn't let go even as I beg for it to set me free. It clutches onto me tighter. My vision blurs as tears cascade down my cheeks, but the waves crashing around me wipe them away. They tug at me, forcefully attempting to pull me back to where I belong, but the grip on my arm is stronger, refusing to let me follow the whispers from the darkness. The voice, the siren or the darkness, screams my name now, the sound haunted and tortured and pained. She's broken just like me. Her voice fades away as my head rises above the water, but her screams fill my mind like claws scraping down my subconscious, begging, urging me to follow her, the sound muffled and far away.

Hands grip underneath my shoulders and carefully drag me to shore. The sand beneath my damp skin brings awareness to my surroundings, and I make out a dark figure standing above me. The darkness in the lake still calls for me. The screaming continues, but now it's only my screaming cutting through the silence on the beach as I crouch over, coughing and spitting out the taste of bitter water as it bursts from my lungs. The flap of wings thunders loudly above me, but I see nothing in the sky or here on the beach, though I felt him here for a moment, the one who watches... the one who seems to be determined not to let me die. He saved me. For the second time now, he has protected me. The whispered voice releases me from its grip, and the dark pull toward the depths of the lake fades away. It's gone. And he's gone. I wish he were still here, because I'm absolutely terrified to be out here alone.

That was real. It was so damn real and this time I remember everything. The night on the bridge, though I can't remember how it happened, was similar to what happened here tonight. Something took control of my mind, and my thoughts and actions weren't my own. It wants me dead. It's not going to stop until I'm gone.

Trembling from the cold, chest heaving out of hopelessness and fear, I dig my fingers into the sand, taking a deep breath in and out... everything is fine. Maybe I'm just spiraling again. Maybe I'm hallucinating. No. I can feel the darkness inside of me, running deeper than I probably know. It will wrap its claws around me tighter and tighter until I have no choice but to give in. I gather the courage to stand, brushing sand off my legs as I steady myself and catch my breath. I don't want to look behind me at the lake or the waves or the darkness that has its sights set on me, for fear of what might happen if I do. It controls me. My mind is not my own.

I need serious help, and I'm almost certain it's not the kind I'd get from prescription pills or therapy. Deep down I'm afraid I might need a priest to cleanse my soul, because this darkness I've struggled with for so long suddenly feels like a possession over my mind.

This is no longer a struggle with depression or grief, it feels more like a haunting.

I need Ere. I need his comforting voice to calm my nerves and tell me I'm alright, but I can't tell him about this. He'd think I've lost my mind. I should wait to talk to him tomorrow when I've had time to recover from whatever the hell this was. What I need is to talk to Katie immediately. Maybe she has some witchy tincture or potion that can help me. If nothing else, maybe she'll reassure me that I'm just going completely insane. At this point I would accept it over the alternative. At least that would mean there is hope for me in the end, that I can fight whatever this is.

CHAPTER NINE

SEEING THE LIGHT

NORA

As I enter *Coffee Oasis*, I take in the comforting scent of freshly baked pastries and the gentle hum of conversation. I'm relieved to see Katie hasn't shown up yet. I could really use a minute to sit alone and let the warmth of my coffee soothe my nerves. I'm a complete wreck emotionally. I texted my beloved witchy friend last night as soon as I was back inside the safety of my house and away from the tempting call from the depths of the lake. She agreed to meet me here this afternoon on her lunch break if I promised to stay inside for the rest of the night and rest. I agreed. Going back out there wasn't something I considered, not after the realization of how close I came to death.

I know it was him... my shadow, my stranger with the wings is the one who saved me. He refuses to let me go. I'll thank him if he shows himself to me again one day, but not before asking a million questions. I glance around the brightly lit room, at the unfamiliar faces busy reading the paper or sending emails before they start their long day, a part of me hoping emerald eyes will meet mine. Now that I know the truth, I can admit to myself that deep down I always knew something about him felt safe. He doesn't want to hurt me. Then again, I don't know anything anymore. My thoughts and my mind can't be trusted.

The bell above the door rings, and Katie strides in gracefully. Her white dress flows down to her feet and the deep cut in the front steals all the attention. She pulls her sunglasses off and tucks them into her designer bag as she smiles and opens her arms wide, stepping toward me.

"I've missed you," she says, bending and wrapping her arms around me.

"I've missed you, too. Where have you been?" I sip on my coffee as she takes a seat in front of me.

She sighs. "Work has been crazy. You know how the end of summer is. The endless tourists dying for a glimpse into their future cleaned me out. I'm working on a massive restock for next season." She combs her fingers through her wavy white hair, her blue eyes sparkling like rays of sunlight exist within them.

Katie is beautiful. Not only is she beautiful, but she's also smart and kind and the best friend anyone could ever ask for. She has been here for Olivia and me through so much over the years, and I don't know where I'd be without her. Simply being near her calms my nerves and brings peace to my soul.

The waitress stops at our table and Katie orders her coffee the same way she always does. Black like her soul, or so she says, but her soul is one of the purest in the world. She has a light within her that reflects and shines, spreading positivity to those around her.

"I know. I might need to make a visit to your shop soon. I think I need a tarot reading or a blessing or... an exorcism, possibly." I wrap my hands around my warm mug, my eyes wide and pleading for help.

She sips from her mug as her eyes search mine. "What exactly happened last night that has you so shaken up today?"

I stare at my hands, afraid of admitting the truth and hearing her tell me I've lost my mind. Maybe it's what I need to hear to help sanity find its way back to me.

I look up, deciding I have nothing left to lose. "I went for a swim. At first it was fine. It was fun." I tuck my hair behind my ears, glancing around to make sure no one is listening. "I felt this pull to swim deeper and further away from shore until I could reach the floor of the lake and never resurface. Something, and I don't know what, had a hold of my thoughts and actions. It controlled my every move. I couldn't escape, Katie, it was terrifying," I whisper, averting my gaze and focusing on the dark liquid within my mug.

She leans forward, placing her warm hand on mine, and gives me a small, sad smile. She looks at me like she thinks I'm crazy. I probably am. "You're not crazy, if that's what you're thinking. I believe you, Nor. But if you felt as though you had no way to break free, how did you?" She leans back in her chair, her eyes calm and unreadable.

I give her a half smile, unsure of how I should answer. If she doesn't already think I'm crazy, she will now.

"*Someone*... or *something* pulled me back to the beach. I felt their hands wrap around me and I fought against them. I didn't want to be saved. Once I was out of the water, I heard... wings flapping above me and that was all. There was no one there, but I was glad to be free, to have my mind back again. While I was out there, I was not in control... I-I don't know *who* or *what* was, but it was *not* me." I shake my head back and forth to clear my thoughts. "I'm scared, Katie. I don't understand what's happening to me." My vision blurs as my eyes fill with tears.

She smiles as I sniffle and wipe them away. "I know this seems bad, and it is. I don't blame you for feeling the way you do. But the good news is, it seems you may have a guardian on your side, and that is a blessing." She clasps her hands together in front of her, looking down at her freshly painted nails. "He saved you from the bridge, too, I hear."

My eyes dart to hers immediately. "How did you know the truth about the bridge?" I lean toward her, and in a hushed tone I beg, "please don't tell Olivia. She'll worry herself to death if she finds out about the *multiple* strange suicide attempts I've experienced this past week. *Please* just don't."

She huffs a laugh and shakes her head. "Of course not. Her hysteria would drive us both mad, especially if she found out I was aware and kept it from her. There's no need to tell her." She waves her hand nonchalantly, smiling as if my life isn't falling apart. "You're going to be fine, Nora. I promise." She pulls out her phone and glances at the time. "I have to get back. I have a tarot reading scheduled for one o'clock, but we'll talk more later." She stands, grabbing her purse and putting her sunglasses back on.

"Wait! How do you know him? You said at the hospital his name is Kairos and just now that I have a guardian on my side. You mean...like, an angel? I know you believe in the strangest things, but seriously? *Angels* on Mackinac Island??" I shake my head in disbelief as she tilts her head down, peeking at me over her glasses.

"He might pull out his dagger if you call him an angel, but yea, something like that." She smiles and winks. "Oh, Nora. You have no idea yet of the unbelievable things that exist in the world, but I guess we can't keep it from you for much longer." She smiles, pushing her glasses back up to cover her eyes. "Later. I promise, okay?"

I sigh. "Fine. I'm meeting Ere at home and he's staying with me tonight, so I'll call you tomorrow as soon as he leaves."

She nods, turning and waving over her shoulder as she glides through the coffee shop and leaves.

Things just keep getting stranger. Guardian angels might exist and my best friend acts like it's no big deal. Maybe she understands what the hell is happening to me. She doesn't seem surprised by the terrifying things I've told her, that's for sure. What else does she know and why the hell hasn't she told me? I never knew Katie was one to keep secrets, and honestly, I'm a little hurt that she's been keeping things from me. We're best friends. We don't lie or keep secrets, it's just not who we are. The thinking and wondering will have to wait until later. I need to head home before I'm late.

Being with Ere, the comfort of his arms around me and his calming energy, always makes everything better. He's exactly what I need right now.

A knock at the door has me on my feet and smoothing out the wrinkles on my red dress in seconds. I hide my romance novel in a drawer of the coffee table before rushing to let Ere in. Last time he saw me reading one of my books, he laughed and said love in novels is written unrealistically, giving women false expectations of men. For me they've always been an escape. A way to disconnect from the real world and get lost in another. He doesn't get it. Now, those romance novels are my dirty little secret.

I swing open the door and he smiles like I'm his favorite person in the world, the way he always does. Before I can even lock the door, he pulls me into his arms, lifting my feet off the floor and swinging me in a circle as I giggle and wrap my arms around his neck.

"I've missed you." His hands settle on my waist as warm golden eyes melt into mine and every part of me forgets about everything except for him. "I'm sorry I had to leave after I spent that night at the hospital with you. Work has been particularly busy lately. Too much going on at once."

When my feet are back on solid ground, I run my hands down the smooth muscles of his biceps all the way down to his forearms. I pull back slightly, admiring the look of his tan skin in the black tank top he wears.

"I've missed you, too." I smile as he leans down, his soft lips brushing against mine as he kisses me. "I get it. Bosses are busy. You always come back to me, and that's what matters."

Ere lives and works an hour away in St. Ignace, but he used to come here often to party with his contractor work friends. It's how we met. How he ended up at the same psychiatric hospital as me. Too many late-night bingers for him and a downward spiral into drugs which led to his mental collapse. He checked himself into the hospital. He knew he needed to get better. Hooking up with him was meant to be a one-time thing, but after that first night together I couldn't get him out of my mind. I pushed him away at first, but he was persistent and sweet and ultimately, I couldn't resist him.

Now his island visits are just for me.

Leaning his forehead against mine, he stares into my eyes and breathes in deep. "Let's see," he says, and my breath catches in my throat as swirls of gold hypnotize me. "You want me to make pancakes again. Really?" He laughs softly.

That sound is something I'll never get tired of hearing. The muscles in his arms flex as he places his hands on my shoulders and pulls me in for a quick kiss, before turning and heading to the kitchen. I do want pancakes, but I always do when he's here. No one makes them better than Ere.

He rummages through my cabinets while I set the table and then lean my elbows on the island and admire him as he whips up the most delicious pancakes in the world. As he sets our plates down, I choose my seat and then he slides into the one in front of me, the chair now looking minuscule compared to his large frame.

"You have no idea how beautiful you truly are, do you?" Reaching across the table, he intertwines our fingers and looks at me as if he's seeing me for the first time.

This is why I care about him as much as I do. It doesn't matter what darkness lingers in the back of my mind, with him it's hard to feel it there. All I think about or feel is him. Nothing else exists.

"Thanks, Ere. You have no idea how sweet you are, do you?" I smile, biting my lip and enjoying the thrill of seeing his eyes drift down to my mouth as he watches me.

"How've you been, my love?" His eyebrows scrunch up in that way they do when he knows something is wrong but also knows I'm trying to hide it. His shaggy black locks flow like a curtain over his eyes and he brushes it back away from his face. The way his eyes melt into pools of liquid gold as he watches me makes it hard to look away.

I can never escape the trance he seems to put me in.

"I'm okay, Ere. I've been better, but I'm happy you're here to distract me. How have you been?" I swallow thickly, hoping he'll let it go and not expect more than I'm willing to tell him.

How can I tell him I believe something or someone has been fucking with my mind and wanting me to off myself? I can't. He'll panic and worry that I've snapped again and that I'll end up back in the psych ward any day now. There's no point in dragging anyone else into this. I'll figure it out.

Freeing my hands, he relaxes into his chair, throwing one arm over the back. "I wish you trusted me more, Nora. I've known you long enough to sense when something is wrong. Why don't you just tell me what it is?" He shakes his head, glancing up at the ceiling. "We can't make this work if there are secrets..." The muscles in his face twitch as he forces his mouth to stop moving.

I'm sure he has much more he'd like to say, but he tends to keep things inside to spare my feelings. To not make me feel bad even when I should. He's not wrong, though. Secrets and lies wrap around a relationship and slowly squeeze the life out of it until there's nothing left. Still... there are things I can't tell him yet, mostly because I don't understand them myself.

I sigh, crossing one leg over the other and sitting up straighter. "I'm... I still struggle some days, Ere. Sometimes I wonder if I'm too much for you. If you might be better off without me in your life. I don't know how you deal with me." My eyes burn and my throat is too dry, and suddenly I feel like I'm drowning all over again.

Ere is perfect and I'm anything but. I tried hard to push him away in the beginning for that reason. I was scared I'd drag him down into my darkness alongside me. He helps me accept all the broken, messed up parts of myself, but at times it's hard for me to appreciate all the beauty and kindness he has within him, because I'm so messed up. Most of the time I truly believe he deserves better.

"No," he growls, leaning closer and placing his elbows on the table. "I'm a better man *because* of you, Nora. I love you. I know you refuse to say it because you're scared, but I know you love me, too. All I want is for you to accept every damaged, dark piece of yourself for what they are, and to feel your feelings for me fully, but you refuse. I *deal* with you, my love, because I can't live without you. I won't do it." He brushes his hair out of his face with one hand, and I watch as it falls back down, framing his perfect jaw line.

I shake my head at his words. They're not true. There's so much wrong with me. Too many things to name. Every time he tells me he loves me it breaks my heart, because although I know how I feel about him, my mind is chaotic and unstable, and I need to heal before I fully let him in. I need to know how I feel with a sane mind and a heart that's not locked up for fear of losing someone again.

I can't lose him too.

"I'm not trying to pretend my feelings don't exist, Ere. What I can say for sure is you make my pain fade away and I don't feel scared or alone with you. You make me feel less... damaged, and I'm thankful you accept me just the way I am. It's not fair to drag you into my self-pitying bullshit, and I'm sorry." I gaze down at my hands to avoid meeting his eyes.

He reaches across the table, pulling my chin up with his fingers and forcing me to look at him. The warmth and comfort of his touch spreads through me, slowly calming my mind.

Everything goes quiet when he's near and especially when he touches me. A sort of comforting numbness takes over to replace the constant pain.

"You never drag me down, Nora. Your love lifts me up. It gives me hope," he whispers, caressing my cheek with his thumb. "No matter what you go through, I want to be there however you need me to be. I want you to use me. To abuse me however you please. All I want is you." His jaw clenches and my heart races as his eyes drift from mine and linger on my lips.

I can't breathe. If I breathe now, the tension between us might shatter and force him to stop touching me. I don't want him to stop. What I want is for him to pull me closer, to feel his breath on my lips and taste the honesty of his words on my tongue.

"Ere..." I whisper, not knowing what to say or how to feel with him so close. With him watching me as if he'd kill or be killed just to have me in his arms, or to kiss me just once.

He takes a deep breath, closes his eyes, and then rests his arms on the table between us. My face feels cold without his touch. My soul feels empty without him near. My heart thuds loudly wanting to jump out of my chest to follow after his. I want him more than I've ever wanted anything before.

"You know I can read you like a book, right?" He flashes that crooked smile I've always adored. It renders me incapable of coherent thoughts or speech. He shakes his head in amusement as my silence lingers on.

I clear my throat and focus on steadying my voice before speaking. "Yea. You always have a way of knowing my thoughts and emotions before I even have time to voice them. How?"

"I don't know," he whispers. "When you look at me, your eyes reveal everything. They always have and always will."

"Well, I'll have you know, sir, that your eyes reveal more than you think. I can read your thoughts," I lean in closer, my voice barely a whisper, "right at this very moment," a flirty smile takes over my lips

I know what will happen, and though he made us this delicious meal that neither of us have touched, all I can think about is how badly I want him. There's plenty of time for pancakes later. My need for him in this moment can't wait.

"What am I thinking, Nor?" His eyes burn into mine. "Tell me."

"You're thinking that I look sexy in this little red dress, and that you'd love to bend me over this table and have your way with me... *right... now.*" I lick my lips, savoring the moment his eyes follow the motion of my tongue.

He swallows, a nervous smile tugging at his lips. "No, actually. I wasn't thinking that at all." His smile vanishes and his pupils dilate, lending an air of darkness to his eyes. "I was thinking," he says, his voice dripping with desire. "How tempting it is to carry you over my shoulder to the bedroom and use my teeth to tease and undress you while I take pleasure in hearing you beg and scream my name." The way he licks his lips triggers an immediate, intoxicating sense of arousal. "But you were shockingly close. I'll give you that." He winks at me and my cheeks flush, the burn causing me to shift uncomfortably in my seat.

Fuck my damaged heart and broken mind. Fuck my head for screaming at my heart that I'm not good enough for the irresistible temptation that dangles within reach. I need him.

The shock on my face is met with laughter from him, and electricity dances along my spine at the sound of it. My body is weak and my head spins and now I doubt my ability to hold myself up in this chair. The words he spoke and the way he looks at me ignites a rush of arousal that has me clenching my thighs. He knows me too well. Slowly, his eyes rake down my body, settling on my exposed thighs, his expression turning predatory. My body pulsates with an intense need that only he can satisfy.

I force a smile, my voice turning low and sultry. “I don’t scream men’s names, Ere. I make men scream *my* name.” I return his wink, and a thrill runs through me as I watch his mouth pop open.

With a feral glint in his eyes, he brushes his fingertips across my flushed cheek, before quickly standing and throwing me over his shoulder, with me giggling the whole way to the bedroom. Suddenly it feels like the dark clouds have parted just a little, swallowing us both up and allowing us to get lost in them together.

Darkness always returns, but Ere is there each time to welcome it with me. With him, I will never have to suffer alone.

CHAPTER TEN

DARKNESS RISING

NORA

"You've come a long way from that good girl you used to be when I first met you," Ere croons, his fingers absentmindedly tracing patterns on the soft sheets of my bed.

With a playful smile, I look up at him, leaning my head in my hands. "Well, you've certainly changed too, haven't you? You used to seem so gentle and sweet, but now... you act like you want to devour me whole. What changed?"

His smile makes my heart ache. It's a reminder of how good he is to me, how he always wipes my tears and reminds me that someday things will be better.

"Nothing changed," he says, his voice strained with emotion as he swallows. "I just... realized what it is you need, and it isn't the innocent, soft version of me." His caramel eyes search mine as he continues. "What you've always needed is someone to help you see yourself for who you truly are. Someone who can teach you to love every little flaw within, so you can become the best version of yourself. You need someone who can understand and accept you without trying to change a thing, even the darkest corners of your mind and soul that may scare others. It doesn't scare me." I involuntarily lean into his touch, as he brushes a strand of hair away from my cheek.

"Maybe I should scare you. Have you been inside my head? It's pretty scary in there sometimes, Ere." The brush of his hand against my cheek stills me.

His touch sends tingles of love and acceptance, his energy a shelter from all the pain.

"I enjoy the darkness. In the dark is where I feel most alive. It's where you do, too, or are you too afraid to admit it?" His eyes burn into mine, and it feels like the blood in my veins is now boiling. The temperature in the room has gone up way too fast, and it's suddenly so damn hot.

I swallow, feeling sweat bead on my forehead and fire still coursing through me all the way to my core. The desire and need I feel for him is unreal. "I... I'm afraid of the darkness. Sometimes it feels like it'll swallow me whole. Like I'll lose myself completely once I give into it. But I do feel more alive when there's darkness surrounding me. The light is too... blindingly real." I shake my head and avert my gaze, not wanting to admit anymore truths.

His crooked smile has me biting my lip and forcing myself to fight the urge to pull him closer to bring his lips to mine. "Own the darkness within, and you no longer have to fear it. Own it. Claim it. Give yourself to it completely, and you will hold all the power instead. You have no reason to fear or run from that which you control," he tells me, his eyebrows crinkling together and his hand wrapping around the back of my neck softly. "Sometimes running toward the thing that scares you the most is exactly how you take back your power."

He's right. I know he's right, but I've never known how to take back control. To teach my mind it doesn't have to fear an invisible force that wants to take over. As his words ring true and my mind grapples with the idea of what it all means, I relinquish all control. I have no reason to fight who I am or who I want to be, or what I want, for that matter. And right now, all I can think about is how badly I want him.

I look up at him under my lashes, forcing my eyes to stay locked on his. "I'm afraid of you. I'm afraid of what I feel whenever I'm with you. I want to run. My heart tells me to push you away so I never have to lose you." I close my eyes, leaning my forehead against his.

He lifts his head and gazes down at me, his own eyes filled with a need that must mirror my own. "You are never going to lose me. I promise you that. You can run or hide or force yourself to not let me in, but I will always be here reminding you of the truth." As he speaks, his voice is filled with darkness and unsettling promises. "The truth is, I'm the one who sets your soul on fire. The one who reminds you to breathe when the world is suffocating." His finger traces a path from my breasts to my belly button.

"Promise me again. That I'll never lose you." My eyes are focused on his fingertips, still lingering below my belly button, just inches away from where I want them to be.

"Never. I promise I am yours." He smiles as he notices my eyes focused on only his fingers. "And... I promise to fuck you until every last breath escapes you. Until your screaming ends because you no longer remember my name or even your own." With a wicked grin he threatens, "I will make you beg over and over again, until your voice ceases to exist at all." His eyes scan my chest, my erect nipples, and my trembling thighs. "I will take... *everything*, Nor." His voice drips with a mix of confidence and greed. "And you will gladly give it to me. Do you understand?" With his final words I'm rendered speechless as I gasp for air, nodding my head in agreement.

He gently teases me with his fingertips, dragging them up and down my body until they become an irresistible distraction, tracing a path across my neck, my breasts, and down to my belly button. I crave so much more. I close my eyes, savoring the electrifying arousal that courses through every inch of my body. God, he's sexy. He is going to ruin me and my entire existence one day, I can feel it. As he tugs at the fabric of my panties, the forceful snap back against my flesh pushes me over the edge, and I crack. Whatever ruin my relationship with Ere brings or whatever hell I might have to crawl through after because good things never come easy, it'll be worth it.

I briefly open my eyes and the searing passion in his gaze is too much for me to handle. Gripping his face in my hands, I force our lips together. His soft lips and hot breath fuel an overwhelming desperation inside me. I will die here and now if I can't have him. I fist his hair in my hands tightly, pulling him closer as I explore his mouth with my tongue. He kisses me softly at first, then it's as if something snaps within him as well. His kiss turns needier and hungrier as he sucks my tongue into his mouth, drawing out a moan from deep within me.

Rolling on top of me, his body weight presses down against me as he firmly restrains my hands above my head with one hand, while the other violently rips my dress apart. With a flick of his wrist, he removes it entirely, nonchalantly tossing it onto the floor as if he didn't shred it to pieces. His grin is predatory as he uses his teeth to remove my panties, tearing and biting at them without mercy. The bastard.

As he sinks his teeth into my neck and moves on to my breasts, shivers ripple across my skin. Our eyes meet, and a taunting smile creeps across his face right before he latches onto my nipple, eliciting a sharp cry and then a soft moan from me as pain slowly turns to pleasure. Moving on to the other nipple, his teeth clamp down harder this time. I scream, and a rush of hot air brushes against my skin as he laughs. I lift my head up off the bed to glare at him, but he places his massive hand on my face, forcefully pinning me back down. He applies just enough pressure to keep me immobile and avoiding eye contact.

With each bite, he smiles and laughs at my shocked cries and satisfied moans, and the twisted pleasure I derive from it only deepens. I know if he touches me at the exact spot I crave, I'd be drenched like I never have been before. With a firm grip, he bends my legs, pushing my knees against my chest and keeping them locked in place. With his hands distracted, I lift my head, catching sight of the fierce, animalistic look in his eyes as he observes me, and my heart stops.

He lowers his head down too slowly, a sexy grin playing on his lips as he drags his tongue across my skin, avoiding my clit with each tantalizing lick. My eyes are glued to him, and my breath comes out in uneven bursts. Watching him taste me is the most beautiful sight I've ever seen. I lift my hips up toward him, impatiently urging him to lick the spot I'm desperate for him to.

"Ahh... ahh... ahh... stay still," he commands, his tone leaving no room for disobedience.

It only makes me wetter. I cry out in frustration, my plea filled with an overwhelming need, but he remains stubborn and unwilling to give me what I crave. He licks every inch of me except for the spot where I ache for him the most. It's absolute torture.

"Are you ready to beg? Hmmm?" His voice, deep and husky, fills the air as he playfully teases me with his tongue. "I want to hear you beg." Another lick and then another. "Beg or I won't do it," he taunts, inflicting a stinging slap on each breast.

A cry of pain followed by a moan escapes my lips. I don't know who I am anymore.

"Please," I whisper, my voice full of desperation as I meet his gaze. "Please make me come. I can't..." His tongue on my clit renders me speechless, thoughtless, and nameless.

He alternates between gentle circles and rough, demanding strokes as I moan his name uncontrollably. The perfection of pleasure he delivers is too much. I'm screaming now as I get closer to falling over the edge.

He was right. I'm screaming his name. The bastard was right about all of it.

"Beg for it," he demands, his eyes locked on mine, daring me to submit. "Fucking beg..." he growls, and I can't watch him any longer.

It's too much and it's too good, yet somehow, it's not enough and I need more. "Please, Ere, please? I need you to make me come," I cry out, my voice cracking and quivering, unrecognizable even to myself.

I'm questioning my own identity. Who the fuck am I and who the fuck is he? The only thing that's clear is how much I ache for every part of him, desperately needing it all.

"Good girl," he praises, his voice dripping with satisfaction as his thick fingers slip inside me.

With each thrust of his fingers, he brushes his thumb against my clit and my pleasure intensifies. I reach down to grip his hair, but he abruptly pushes my hand away. As he pinches my sensitive nipple, a jolt of pain sends me spiraling, making it difficult to see clearly. Each moan and cry of his name leaves my voice growing more ragged and fragmented, the ecstasy overwhelming me as I come undone on his mouth and fingers. The aftershocks of the orgasm leave me breathless, moans pouring from me in a continuous stream.

His eyes melt into mine as my body trembles with waves of pleasure, my moans slowly fading away. Standing before me, he undresses slowly, his gaze never leaving mine. His tongue glides across his lips as he advances toward me, his demeanor resembling a predator who's ready to pounce.

Fuck. I'm done for.

"Roll over," he orders, so I do.

I'm too slow. My body is too weak. He grips my hips tightly and maneuvers me himself, positioning my ass in the air before him. With one hand he firmly holds my face down, my cheek sinking into the plushness of the mattress. For a moment I don't think I can take anymore, until my clit is in his mouth again and I whimper as I grind against his tongue, another orgasm building up inside me.

"Fuck. Just look at you," he whispers, and I shiver as his warm breath grazes my skin. "What do you want now? Tell me..." he demands.

Faint sounds bring my attention to him, but I can only see that he's kneeling behind me, unable to move from my place. He moans softly as his body gently rocks and he presses his hand against my back to steady himself. He's stroking himself and I can't see. I'm dying to catch a glimpse, but as I move, he presses his hand against my back harder. The desire to touch it, to taste it, to witness his rhythmic strokes up and down his length, consumes me.

"God, *please*...give me your dick," my voice is weak and my body trembles with an aching need.

The bed shifts as he walks around to the side of it, positioning himself directly in front of me. So I can watch. So I can be tortured. So my body can burn alive with the desire to feel him inside of me.

"What would you do for it, Nora?" he asks, a slight smile playing at the corners of his lips. "What would you *give* for it?" The sight of his golden eyes shimmering with intensity, and his teasing, crooked smile as he strokes himself makes my pussy convulse on sight.

"Anything... *everything*," I confess, as I stare up at him like the sex God that he is. With my head still down on the mattress and him standing before me, I'm bowing to him in this very moment.

I would bow over and over again for this man.

His smile widens, and then he's behind me, leaving my world in ruins. With him inside of me, everything else fades away. Pain and heartbreak and fear no longer exist and my hopes and dreams that died, their remnants crumbling like ashes in the wind... they no longer matter. Ere exceeds the beauty of any sunset, any book, or any beach I've ever seen.

I'd sacrifice all the joys of life, the warmth of the sun, and my freedom, even... all in exchange for this. For *him*. It would be worth it. He's all I'd ever need.

"Don't hold back. Let yourself go." I detect a smile in his voice, even as he thrusts so deep inside of me that I can't form words.

He grips my hair in his hands, pulling my head back as I scream out his name. Every time I think he can't possibly thrust any harder, he proves me wrong. Tears roll down my face, but not from the pain of how rough he pulls my hair, from the intense release pulsating and building in my core. Over and over, I moan his name, his grip on my hair tightening with each plea.

Every powerful thrust and painful throb sends a part of me escaping into the universe to be lost forever.

Thrust. Goodbye pain.

Thrust. Goodbye sadness and anger.

Thrust. Goodbye grief.

Tears continue to fall, but feeling so goddamn free from it all feels so good. I'm numb, yet every fiber of my being feels more alive than ever. Here with Ere, I've never felt more in touch with my true self.

Wrapping my hair around his hand, he continues to push in and out of me as his fingers stroke my clit, setting all my senses ablaze. He traces a path up my back with his tongue, and as he brushes his lips against my neck, all I can think about is how I wish this could last forever.

"I want to make you come so hard that your mind erases every other man from existence," he whispers breathlessly into my ear.

He relentlessly caresses my clit while his thrusts leave me gasping for air. I can't hold on any longer.

"Please...please...let me come..." I beg, my voice filled with desperation and submission, exactly the way this new, untamed Ere likes it.

His grip on my hair tightens and he sinks his teeth into my neck. With each stroke of his fingers on my clit my world is dismantled, leaving only pleasure in its wake. Wrapping an arm around my waist, he tries to keep me still, but I thrash as the orgasm shreds the last part of my reality away. The sounds forcing their way out are wild and untamed, unlike anything I've ever heard from myself before. Waves of convulsions ripple through me as his release pushes mine on for longer. Gasping for air, his grip on my waist tightens, our bodies slowly relaxing as the electrifying jolts of pleasure subside.

The rush is relentless. I can't catch my breath, let alone remember my own name. Collapsing onto my bed in a naked heap, drenched in sweat and satisfaction, I laugh to myself at how right he was about everything he promised me. I couldn't even remember my own name. There is nothing I crave more than him, and though he does scare me, he always delivers on his promises. I can trust him.

As I drift off to sleep with the warmth of Ere's body tangled up with mine, I smile knowing things have changed between us. I don't need to run or push him away or ever feel like he's too good for me. He's not going anywhere because he truly does love me. My mindset of our relationship is forever altered, and although I have lots to work through and figure out, I have hope that I won't mess up what we have.

He's right... sometimes running toward the thing that scares you the most is the best thing, because he scares the shit out of me, but only in all the best ways.

I'll keep running toward him, always.

CHAPTER ELEVEN

FALLING HARD

KAIROS

This man defiling Nora will be the death of me if it doesn't end soon. The sound of skin against skin and the breathy words escaping her lips feel like daggers slicing through every aching, throbbing artery in my heart. There is no hiding from or denying the truth any longer. I love this woman. Nora is my fated mate. The gods were right. Mera has returned. Anytime I'm near her I feel whole again, and every time *he* touches her it breaks me a little more.

"Bastard," I whisper, turning my back to the window and facing the old, faded wooden dock instead. The glow from the red hued sky, the colors dancing across the glistening lake and burning into my eyes hurts much less than what's happening behind me.

The crimson burnt skyline matches the color of my now bleeding heart.

Gods, I miss the feel of her. The taste of her. The pleasure filled cries of my name slipping off her tongue so beautifully, like it is the only word she cares to know. This is absolute fucking torture.

"I'll take your place if you want, Ro. I don't mind watching, really." Mio steps up beside me, his smile wide and proud as he slaps me on the back.

I shake his hand off and face him. He thinks he's hilarious. What I wouldn't give to watch him sink and drown in my sorrow.

"Fuck off, Mio," I spit, crossing my arms over my heaving chest and narrowing my eyes on his smug face. "How good it must feel to have no heart."

"Dramatic much? I was only kidding. Come on, man." Sliding his hands into his pockets, he looks down, kicking the sand and avoiding looking anywhere near the window.

Normally I can handle him, badly timed jokes and all, but tonight I'm not in the mood. Seeing Nora laid out before this unworthy man, begging for him and giving herself to him freely, has me tempted to rip open the skies and let my power tear the world apart. She deserves the eternal love she's fated to have—a thing no simple, mortal man can give. Only I can offer that to her. Not him. *Me.*

Fate, though, can be a fickle and disappointing thing at times. I've seen it happen before. Some celestials, Mio himself even, refuse their fated mate, too stubborn and set on choosing who to love for themselves. Maybe Nora too will choose love over fate. With her I'd undeniably have both. The mortal can't live forever. He'll leave.

I'll stay forever in her arms if she'll let me.

"You okay?" Mio keeps his back facing me, staring off blankly at the fading sunset over the lake. "We can leave, you know? Katie is nearby and her wards and ours will protect Nora. She's safe."

"I'm not leaving her," I tell him as he turns his head slightly to glance back at me. "But you're free to leave whenever you wish, of course."

I unzip my leather jacket, the long sleeves and thick material suddenly so tight that I feel like I'm suffocating. Tossing it on the ground at my feet, I shake out the sweat from my hair, smoothing the damp locks away from my face with my hands. Even with removing part of my fighting leathers, I still can't breathe. It's like the walls are closing in, the sky falling and pressing down upon my shoulders, the gods whispering from their mountain top in the highest part of heaven that I've failed. I don't know how much more of this torture I can take.

After Nora's jump from the bridge, I didn't think it could get much worse. Not until she swam out to the middle of the lake and let herself sink to the bottom. Both of those things have Nyx and her mind games written all over them. It was her. She tried this same type of shit when Mera was alive last time. Katie was on guard that night while I trained with my soldiers in the Realm of Darkness, and she said she'd simply gone out for a swim, but Nora can't be trusted if Nyx is taking the reins at times. Neither can Katie's judgement. I rushed back as soon as Katie's glowing message reached me in the sky, urging me to get to Nora immediately. That's one thing I hate about being away while she's here—the fact that she's untraceable by me and left vulnerable to attacks, even the ones on herself. I need her to be safe. I'm not leaving her again, no matter how much it hurts to be here and witness this.

Mio sighs, pulling out his dagger and turning to face me. "You want me to kill this Ere guy? Say the word and I will." He pretends to slice his weapon across his own throat.

I smile, watching as he spins the weapon in his hand, knowing if I asked him to, he truly would do it. Unfortunately, the celestial laws forbid killing innocents, so if the king and queen were to find out then it would be bad for both of us.

Is this mortal truly innocent? In my eyes he's not. There is nothing pure or innocent about him because he is fucking the love of my life.

"Nah. I'd rather kill him myself." I huff a laugh, and he nods, stretching his wings out and strapping his dagger back in place.

Honestly, I'd enjoy doing it. I'd revel in his misery and pain. The dark part of my soul longs to remove this fools' hands so he cannot be lucky enough to touch her ever again. As he smiles and commands her to beg for her pleasure, my hand tingles with the desire to grip my dagger and jam it firmly into his vocal cords, rendering him speechless for good. Fuck this guy.

I flex my hands at my sides, facing the window and forcing myself to keep my eyes locked on the two of them, though all I want is to disappear. I'm not one who has ever been good at reading peoples' souls or auras, not the way Katie and the witches can, but there's something I've always found to be off about Ere. Maybe it's just the way he looks at her like she's a scattered puzzle that needs to be put back together. Like she's broken. Or maybe it's the way he says her name, like she belongs to him whether she wants to or not.

Either way, I fucking hate the guy. Can't stand him. I wish only death and unhappiness upon him. Fuck, I'm not okay.

Nora's silky red hair and bright eyes are all I focus on as I glance back through the window, the light from the lamp on her nightstand casting their moving, writhing shadows on the pale walls. If I were to see her bare body again one day, tangled up in the sheets with mine, it would be an honor and a privilege. It can't be this way. I want it to happen because she wants me to see, not because I'm creeping around outside her window, stalking and watching her like some gods damn pathetic lunatic. For now, it's simply what must be done to keep her safe, because after centuries alive I've learned to trust no one. Trust is a careless thing.

Even those who appear innocent enough sometimes have secrets they'd do anything to keep in shadow.

"Kairos, when are you going to talk to her? Do you normally wait this long to talk to the ones you're guarding, or are you just nervous because she's your mate?" Mio holds his celestial sword in his hand, and as he spins and slices through air, the sound of it drags my attention away from Nora and back to him.

I conjure a whirlwind that rips through the air and knocks the heavy sword out of his hand. "Worry less about me and more about your shitty sword fighting skills. Your stance is awful. Even without my power I could have easily knocked that weapon out of your hand."

I laugh as he smiles, his dark hair falling into his eyes as he uses his booted toe to kick the hilt of his sword, sending it flying up and back into his waiting hand, expertly. I can't lie and say I'm not impressed. He's the best fighter I know, with and without a weapon. I trust him with my life more than anyone else. His only true celestial power is his ability to manipulate emotions, which all celestials have to some degree, but his is like nothing I've ever felt. He doesn't simply make one feel what he wants them to feel, he sends them spiraling into the emotion, deep and unwavering and relentless until they no longer know what's real. It's a hell of a skill to have on your side during battles.

I prefer the raw, intense, real emotions no matter how good or bad they may be. I'd rather they carve out a hole and leave me festering in a pit of my own agony than to feel nothing at all. I wouldn't know about happiness and how it might feel. It has been too long since I've felt anything like it. Not since Mera.

"You're just jealous. You wish you looked half as good as I do while swinging a sword, commander." He salutes me mockingly with his middle finger while bowing at the waist.

Shaking my head I turn away. He's right about one thing. I need to introduce myself to Nora. I need her to know me, to see me and not be afraid. Mostly though, I want to introduce myself selfishly, not wanting to spend another day without her knowing I exist. I'm tired of using glamours and magic to hide from her. I want her to know that the only thing I care about now and forever is her safety. Whatever may come her way, I'll be in the front lines providing a shield from harm, a shelter for her to curl up within to remain safe. She deserves to know there are celestials on her side. That I am on her side.

The tense muscles in my neck relax as the act between her and the bastard ends, and the quiet stillness of the night takes over. I breathe in deeply, awareness that I was holding my breath slamming into me as oxygen at last soothes the burn in my lungs. I couldn't stand to smell his arousal any longer or taste his scent in the air. As I watch Nora's breathing, the rise and fall of her delicate chest beneath the silky covers, I wish for nothing more than the chance to caress her forehead until she falls asleep the way I used to. To whisper goodnight against her ear and hold her until the sun rises again. The man, Ere, has a sloppy, satisfied grin plastered to his face as he wraps his overly muscular arms around her. I would give anything to be him in this moment. I'd kill to take his place.

Until the day she becomes a celestial, until she knows the truth of what we are to one another, I have no choice but to let her live out her human existence and be with whoever the hell she chooses to be with, even if it kills me. I'll continue letting my own fragile heart break, as long as she's happy. Raising my palms, I send a new wave of light around the home to shield her from any harm, the old shield dimming away. Katie is supposed to be here soon to do the same, sending up protective wards of shimmering blue. Anyone or anything who wishes Nora harm and passes through our barriers will alert our senses immediately as long as we remain in the same realm.

Stepping back, I gaze at the white light surrounding her house, then smile as Katie's blue dome of protection goes up around it, the glittering colors blending to become one. Glancing over my shoulder, I nod and she does the same. She wiggles her fingers in a small wave, her magic glowing on her fingertips and stretching across the beach, wrapping me up in comforting waves of positivity and peace. She's sending me a message. Everything will be okay.

She knows I'm hurting. She senses the struggle simmering deep inside of me, ready to burst into sparks of electricity and chaotic waves. I close my eyes and let her power wash over me, allowing the anger and frustration to fade away. Focusing on the waves crashing along the shore, I force them to slow and die out until the water is unnaturally calm and still. I smile as she clasps her hands together in front of her, her white cloud of hair wild and untamed in the breeze until I compel the wind to subside, letting her hair fall still behind her back. It's my way of telling her I'm okay. My emotions do not rule me. Fear does not rule me. I'm thankful for her calming presence in this moment. Mio would send me into a blissful, never-ending pit of false happiness if it were up to him.

Katie teleports to my side and places her tiny hand on my shoulder. "Everything will be okay soon, Kairos. I think you should talk to her. We both should." Her glowing eyes swirl to life.

"What if she never loves me, Katie? What if she loves him too much to let him go?" I sigh, closing my eyes and breathing in her calming, warm energy. "She might never remember what I meant to her."

"Well, you will never know if you don't try." Her voice goes up an octave as her lips curve into a smile. "Someone I once loved made the mistake of holding in words they wanted to speak and letting hope die before it ever had the chance to bloom. Do not let the hope in your heart die, Kairos. Let it live. She will remember everything one day, and she will love you even more because you never gave up on her. Whatever she has with him will feel like nothing. It *is* nothing."

Katie was asked to protect Nora by the rulers of the realms because a new queen rising must be safeguarded at all costs. She's the only one from the realms who is trusted by each realm leader, even Ourahnus who hasn't spoken to any of my people since the day we fell from his realm. Her ability to bring unity and peace is like nothing I've seen before. She has a way of making everyone adore her. There's a magic in that ability alone. I haven't known her for long, but I see why Nora loves her. She always knows what to say, even when everything feels like it's falling apart.

"I'm sure you're right. Just... a bad night to be me, that's all. I'll be fine." I straighten my shoulders and hold my head high.

Mio is right. I'm being dramatic.

"Hey, Katie!"

Speak of the devil and the devil shall come.

"Mio, please. Not tonight. Let Katie have a moment of peace." I give him a stern look of warning, but I know it won't matter.

"How's it going, little witch? Want to get out of here and grab a drink?? Or dinner or even breakfast tomorrow, if that works better for you? I am all yours if you'll have me." He runs a hand through his hair, smiling as he adjusts his wings and puts one hand on his hip and one on her bicep, pretending he has any semblance of swagger.

She removes his hand with two fingers, letting it fall to his side. "I will not be having anything with you, Bromios, not now or ever. Thank you, though." She tilts her head and her nose crinkles as she gives him a forced smile. "Let me know if you or Nora need me, Kairos."

She's gone before I can even blink. Turning to Mio, I slap his chest with the back of my hand as laughter spills out of me. For a moment I'm thankful to have a distraction from the heartbreak and pain of my own life, instead focusing on the embarrassment of his.

"That was good, bro. Almost as good as the last fifteen times you've tried and failed at flirting with her." Shaking my head, I walk away, still laughing under my breath.

"All it takes is one yes. She's just playing hard to get, man. One day she'll surprise us both and give me a chance. You'll see." He jogs to me as I open a portal to send him home.

"It's late. Check on our soldiers and let me know if there's anything at all they need. I'll meet up with you tomorrow."

"Try not to cry too much, Ro. You'll have permanent eye bags soon if you aren't careful." He laughs as he faces the portal.

"Ha-ha. You're hilarious. *Go.*" I wave a hand, sending a heavy breeze hurtling toward him, helping him along.

"Fate is on your side, Kairos. Remember that. It's all going to be okay." The portal closes and he's gone, thank the gods.

I'll stay a little longer. I know I should rest, especially after the heaviness today brought with it, the feelings stirring within my soul that I can no longer ignore or pretend aren't real. I know the truth. My heart is no longer my own. It belongs to Nora. It always has. As difficult and painful as all of this is, I know I must be patient.

One day, Nora will be the most beautiful queen to ever exist in the celestial realms, but more importantly...

It will be me who stands beside her at the throne, because she *will* be mine. She is mine. She just doesn't know it yet.

CHAPTER TWELVE

DEATH AND THE TOWER

NORA

The scent of sage lingers in the air from Katie cleansing the house of negativity and evil earlier today. Now the flickering candles cast shadows across her features as she lays out her tarot cards on the coffee table with Olivia and I sitting across from her on the floor. Olivia giggles and snorts next to me so I elbow her in the ribs.

"Shhh... this is serious stuff. Grow up," I whisper, then we both giggle as we take another swig of our sweet wine.

As soon as Ere left this morning, I called Katie and begged her to make time to give me a tarot reading today. She happily agreed after I promised her lots of wine. Last night I had a breakthrough with Ere, and I woke up in good spirits, but I know this feeling won't last forever. If I want to hold onto happiness and make it work with him, then conquering the darkness once and for all has to be a priority. I can't allow it to keep dragging me down. But I need answers and the truth, and more than anything, to find out if something dark truly is after me.

Katie's eyes flutter open, and she peers across the table at us with an amused look on her face. "Both of you grow up." Her smile fades as she snaps her eyelids shut and lets her hands hover above the cards. Slowly she moves them back and forth, her usual way of infusing energy into each one.

Olivia and I share a quick glance just as the air around us stills, and warm, electrical currents brush against my skin. The hairs on my arms and the back of my neck rise as the flames from Katie's candles do the same, swaying and reaching up toward the energy that floats around us. I can't see any change, but I feel the sudden shift in the air, the charged power wrapping itself around not only me, but possibly the entire world. I've never been given a reason to believe in magic or witchcraft, but with the strange and terrifying things I've experienced in the past year, nothing would surprise me anymore. My friend is a witch. I no longer question it at all as her pale, icy eyes explore mine. My thoughts relax as my mind opens to let her in. It's like she unlocked some deep, hidden part of me that was closed off before, letting me melt into the belief that magic exists.

"You want me to pick three cards." My voice is a soft breath of exhaled energy, my nerve endings tingling and dancing in delight.

How I knew what she wanted me to do, I'm not sure, but I can't pull my eyes away from hers as I reach down and slowly slide one card from the sprawled-out deck, after another. Those blue irises swirl and glow in a hypnotizing way, and though it should be unsettling, it brings me only comfort. I couldn't look away even if I wanted to. Without her saying a word, I know what this means, her showing me these parts of her. There will be no more lies. No more secrets with her. Only the truth.

Olivia squeals next to me as she leans up against the table, kneeling and clapping her hands as she watches. Her voice and movements are blurred and muffled like she's barely with us at all. "This is so exciting! I can't wait to see what your future has in store for you, Nor. It'll be amazing, I just know it!"

My heart beats slower than I'm used to, and my breathing is non-existent. Katie's white hair sways side to side as she shakes her head and clicks her tongue at the cards she scoops up into her palms. I feel strange, but not in a bad way exactly, just in a way that leaves me slightly out of touch with reality or like I'm disconnected from my body. Am I even here? Is any of this real?

Katie clears her throat as she places the first card down on the table, pushing it toward me. She sits up straighter and rolls her shoulders. I'm a soul floating above my body, living without the constraints of mortal existence. I'm not only surrounded by magic, I *am* magic.

"Tell me, Katie. What shall my future bring?"

She glances at me briefly before speaking. "First you chose the ace of pentacles. It urges you to say yes to any of life's opportunities that present themselves to you, even when it may not be what you think you want or need. Even when your soul whispers within that it might end badly, a yes is sometimes how the most difficult battles are won." Her eyes flick to Olivia, who leans forward with interest.

Katie sighs softly watching Olivia tilt her head, her full lips curving downward as she picks up the card and studies it. "That's it? Will she get her happily ever after or not? I'm dying, here."

Katie ignores her completely. "Your second card is the tower. Something will soon happen that shatters everything you thought you knew about yourself and your life. Things must first fall apart to be rebuilt even stronger. Do not fear the changes that are coming." Her lips curve up at the corners as she reaches across the table and gently squeezes my hand.

A wave of dizziness hits me. I feel like a part of me resonates with what she's saying, like deep down I understand some hidden meaning of her words or forgotten thoughts that are buried somewhere in my mind just out of reach.

"What about the last card? What does it want to tell me?" Even as I speak the words, it sounds strangely unlike me. My voice thrums with an ethereal sense of power.

Magic truly exists. And if magic, the kind that radiates light and positivity like Katie's is real, then that means magic must exist within darkness as well. Like the dark energy I felt on the beach the night of my parents' deaths. It was different from this magic, the swirls of hidden light that caress my mind and breathe truth into my soul. A magic as dark and cruel as what wrapped itself around their bodies that night came straight from hell. I don't know how to feel about any of this.

"Your last card is death." Katie pushes the card toward me, tapping it with her black, coffin shaped nail.

The shirtless devil with horns does little to bring me comfort. I immediately push the card away.

Olivia picks it up and studies it carefully, her eyebrows scrunching together in concentration. "It doesn't signify death or even that something terrible will happen."

Katie smooths back her hair and smiles wide as her blue eyes swim with excitement. "Exactly. It doesn't mean what most would think. To achieve rebirth one must first experience death. It can be a major aspect of your life ending or letting go of something that has been holding you back. You must move on from the past to find renewal and transformation, and letting go of all that you fear is the only way to receive all life has to offer." She pats my hand then stacks the deck of cards into a neat pile.

All I can think about is grief and pain and loss and the fact that I know I need to let those things go. But it feels impossible to move on. I have to find out the truth of what happened that night, and why my parents were victims to such darkness. I read books on dark magic and ancient evil, scoured the internet and watched countless paranormal documentaries, but all of it led me nowhere or worse, back to the possibility that I'd lost my mind. Someone somewhere knows the truth.

As Katie blows out the black candle on the table and waves her hand in the air, the magic in the room vanishes as if it was never there to begin with.

"Thank you, Katie." I stand, grabbing our glasses off the table and heading to the kitchen to replenish the wine.

Flicking on the bright lights, the white marbled counter comes to life, no longer lost in shadows and illusion. I need the light right now to snap me back to reality. Life gets stranger by the day and I'm not sure what to make of it.

Tossing the empty bottle of wine in the trash, I rinse our glasses and set them on the counter next to the sink. Turning to face Katie and Olivia, I cross my arms over my chest. "We're officially out of wine. Now what?"

They make their way into the kitchen, both leaning their elbows on the island as they smile up at me, their fluttering eyelashes giving their plotting and scheming away.

I groan. "What do you two want from me?"

"We were thinking that maybe, just maybe, you'd possibly want to go out with us?" Olivia's eyes drift to Katie, who nods her head in agreement.

"Let's get some real drinks. The good stuff. It has been quite some time since we've had a proper girl's night." Katie stands up straight, placing her hands on her hips and looking me up and down. "You could ditch those hideous sweatpants for something a little more..."

She clamps her lips together as I roll my eyes and tug at my loose t-shirt, offended that she pointed out my poor fashion choices, but knowing she's right.

"Please, Nor? How could you tell us no? Look at us," Olivia says as the two of them lean into each other, placing their bottom lips over their top like spoiled children do when they don't get their way.

As they burst into laughter, I can't help but join them, shaking my head as they throw their heads back and sway unsteadily on their feet, the wine taking hold of us all. They're ridiculous and at times a bit irritating, but I love them more than anything. Turning and heading to my bedroom I don't glance back, knowing they've already won. They've dealt with a year of being forced into a life of solitude here with me. If they want us to spend time together, I owe them a night of fun. More than that, they deserve for me to be there for them the way they're always here for me.

"I'm going to need your help getting ready. I'm not nearly as good at doing make-up or curling my hair as I used to be." Glancing back with a smile, they perk up and run toward my room, both of them grabbing one of my hands and dragging me along with them.

"Maybe we can find you a cute boy to bring home!" Olivia squeals, pushing open my closet doors and peering inside. "Ere is nice, don't get me wrong, but maybe he isn't the one. You can't seem to make up your mind about him." She runs her hands along the fabric of my worn, old clothes, scrunching her nose up as she promptly closes the doors and turns her back to them. "You won't attract any guys worthy of your attention wearing that. I'll grab something from my closet for you." She saunters off, hips swaying, and humming to herself happily as she heads for her room.

There's nothing wrong with Ere. I'm the problem. So many times he has tried to turn our situationship into a real relationship. He's shown up with red roses and taken me on romantic dates and picnics under the stars. He did all the things women adore and long for, yet I still couldn't help but push him away. The truth is, he deserves better than I can give him, because I'm a work in progress. I'm incomplete. After last night though, I believe that one day, I might be better for him.

Shooting Katie a half smile, I admire her beauty as she applies a fresh layer of nude lipstick before running a hand through her perfect wavy hair. Her eyes meet mine in the mirror and she spins on the stool to face me.

"Don't listen to your sister. Tonight is about having fun, okay? We miss you." She stands and plops down at the edge of my bed, crossing one bare leg over the other.

She's always dressed and ready for a night on the town, so beautiful and elegant in every way. I wish I had the confidence she does. She could have anything she wants with just a look or a smile. Katie doesn't use her beauty, though, not the way some do. There's so much more to her than that.

Sitting beside her, I pull one leg up leaving the other planted firmly on the floor. "Magic is real, isn't it? I sort of believed in it before, but after tonight there's no denying it. I felt your power, Katie. It was beautiful. There's much more I don't know about, isn't there? I mean, besides the existence of guardians and witches?"

She watches me pull and twist at the fabric of my shirt nervously, shifting my eyes around the room. I've joked many times about her being a witch because she owns a crystal shop and does tarot readings, but until tonight I was only humoring her. I've always only believed in what I could see with my own eyes, but I didn't need to see Katie's power to know it was real. Every part of me recognized what I felt as something otherworldly and magical. She's more amazing than I realized.

Patting my knee, she nudges her shoulder against mine, and I bring my eyes back to hers. "Does it scare you? Knowing there are many things you don't yet understand and much more you have yet to see?"

"No. What scares me is the thought that guardians, witches, and magic exist and yet darkness somehow always seems to win. What's the point of magic if not to make the world a better place? To end suffering and death?" Swallowing thickly, memories and thoughts of the unfairness of my parents' deaths swarm in, stinging and lashing at me as I swat them away.

"Maybe they try, Nor. Maybe trying sometimes just isn't enough. Sometimes darkness is stronger and more powerful than even the celestial guardians are capable of handling. But it's what they were created for, to fight darkness. If witches and celestial beings exist in the world, you would assume they try to make the world better. Wouldn't you?" Her pale, smooth face doesn't twitch or yield as I keep my eyes pinned on her, searching for any sign that what she says is untrue.

If every witch is as pure as Katie, then I know they could do no wrong. She's too good for this world. I hate the sadness that lingers in her eyes, the deep sorrow she thinks she hides so well.

"You told me tonight I need to let go of the past to welcome the future. I'll try. What about you Katie, will you try as well?" I pause as she shifts uncomfortably, staring at a spot on the floor. "You told me you've had your heart broken, and I get being scared of being hurt again, but you deserve happiness and love more than any of us. There's someone out there waiting for someone exactly like you. Maybe it's time you open your heart and stop holding onto your pain."

Glancing over at me, her eyes are hopeless and devoid of light. "I fell madly in love once, Nora. I will never choose to put myself through that kind of heartbreak again. To me, it's not worth it. I'd rather die a thousand times and live a thousand lives alone than to ever suffer that kind of loss again." She stands, making her way to the window on the far side of my room, peeking out the curtains and losing herself in her thoughts.

It kills me to see her this way. Her pain is a wound even I can feel, still gaping and bleeding while salt is poured in, never having a chance to heal.

"I'm so sorry for whatever happened to you. For whatever pain you've been through." Pushing off the bed, I make my way to her, wrapping an arm around her shoulder and leaning my head against hers. "If you need a friend, I'm here. Whether it's for a shoulder to cry on or to release the secrets and pain you're holding inside, I'll always be here."

Her eyes glisten with tears as she looks at me then quickly looks away. "Thank you, friend."

She says nothing else and neither do I. We lean against each other as we gaze outside, both our hearts aching for different reasons. Hers for a love lost and mine for a pain I don't understand but wish I could heal.

CHAPTER THIRTEEN

SUNSHINE AND TANGERINES

NYX

MAY 18TH, 1848

The scent of sunshine and tangerines brings instant peace to my soul as Hekate's white hair flows around me, brushing against my cheeks while she giggles quietly and kisses me. My once forgotten heart screams at me to tell her how I truly feel, how deeply her love has planted itself within me, forcefully giving meaning to life for the first time. She has no idea what she means to me.

Rays of light from the large bay windows in my room dance across her pale skin, the white sheets rumpled and wrinkled from our long day of enjoying each other's company in the Realm of Light.

"I'm proud of you for who you're becoming, Nyx. For the progress you've made lately. You should be proud, too." Her glowing sky-blue eyes lock with mine as she brings her face closer, so close I can taste the air she breathes.

Straddling me, she wraps her soft thighs around my waist, guiding my hands beneath her lacy dress until I'm firmly gripping her hips. Gods, she is like a warm breath of fresh air, so inviting and intoxicating and more perfect than anything or anyone should be. I feel the heat building between my thighs as she gazes down at me.

"Should I be proud? How might the gods and my king and queen feel when they discover all you have really been teaching me this past year, Hekate? Like... how to kiss," I croon, leaning up and brushing my lips softly against hers. "Or how to make love." Wrapping an arm around her waist, I flip her onto her back, pressing my body into hers as I roll with her. Heat flares in her eyes and my heartbeat quickens at the squeal of shock and delight that rushes past her lips, breathing life into me. Lowering my head slightly, I drag my tongue across her lips and shiver with pleasure over her suffering, a soft moan humming within as she realizes I won't yet give her the satisfaction of kissing me. "Or how to fuck." I lick my lips and give her a teasing smile and then she can't take anymore, gripping the sides of my face and pulling my lips to hers. She suffocates me with her kiss, with the desire pulsing through her until I no longer remember how to breathe.

Pulling away slightly, her eyes are contemplative and sure as she brushes strands of my dark hair away from my face. "I do not care what the gods or anyone else thinks," she whispers, teasing the sensitive skin along my spine, her fingertips dancing slow and torturous strokes against me. She smiles with satisfaction as the pleasure of her touch makes my body shiver in response. "I only meant to be a mentor and a friend, someone to teach you how to wield your power. They can be angry if they wish, Nyx, but I never meant to fall in love with you. I do not believe either of us could have stopped this."

Her words send a thrill through me like I have never felt before. No one has ever loved me. Not even my own mother who was so desperate that she sacrificed my soul and my future for a manipulative demon. He promised her everlasting love so long as she promised him a child who would one day be powerful enough to free him from the fiery pits of the Underworld for good. She never loved me. She was insane. The king and queen pitied me when they took me in as a newborn babe, discovering that my mother had been slaughtered by the same demon she went to bed with to birth me, but they, too, will never love me. I am simply a tool, a weapon, a mixed-breed fool who wanders through life with no one who truly cares, thanks to my mother. My demon blood makes me unlovable.

"You cannot love me." I shake my head, averting my gaze. It does not matter how many times I might hear her say it, a hundred times, a million times, even, I still would not believe it.

I have never felt worthy of love. I never will. Despite that, I refuse to let someone as perfect as Hekate slip through my fingers. I will be better for her.

One day I will accept her love and find a way to give it back to her times a hundred. I will do whatever it takes to keep her forever.

"Well, I do." The sun begins to set outside my window and the darkness settling in is illuminated by the blue glow in her eyes. "Not only do I love you, Nyx. I know you love me, too." She nibbles at my neck playfully, smiling at the look of shock written across my features as her words wash over me.

Grabbing her wrists and pinning them above her head, I slowly and torturously drag my tongue across her lips, burning on the inside as her eyes roll back and then snap shut, allowing herself to get lost in the pleasure. Her body shivers beneath me as she presses her hips into mine.

"Let me show you exactly how I feel about you, Hekate. Let me taste your desire on my tongue. Let me hear the desperation escaping your lips as you call out my name again and again." Pulling her bottom lip into my mouth, I suck on it gently, savoring her quiet moan that vibrates against me. "I cannot bring myself to tell you how I feel, not yet... so let me show you instead."

I grip the fabric of her dress, pulling it up and over her head. She eagerly wiggles free of it and carelessly tosses it onto the floor. As I kiss her from her neck to her collarbone, the warmth of her chips away at the walls of ice I have kept my heart locked within for far too long.

I will let it shatter to pieces for her.

Her body trembles and blue specks of her magic swirl around the white light of my flames, the colors glittering and dancing and filling the entire room with our power. I make my way down to her breasts and her magic brushes against my skin, so desperate and hungry and needy for more. Pulling her nipple into my mouth, I graze my teeth lightly against it, my clit tingling as she grips the nape of my neck, holding me there and arching into the warmth of my tongue. Her sweet cry of pleasure pushes me over the edge. I need to touch her, to feel her, to taste her like it could be the last time. I cannot wait any longer.

My magic surges as I gather it in my fingertips, using the vibrating thrum of a small flame to trace small circles around her belly button and across her chest. My arousal floods my senses so fast and hard I am nearly burning from the inside out, watching her glow with celestial light as she whimpers and begs and writhes against my power, her legs spreading wide as my magic teases the spot right above her clit. It's too much. She lets out a breathless moan, sucks her bottom lip into her mouth, and as her eyes firmly lock on mine, the fire inside me cannot be contained. I must refocus in order to put out the flame, to avoid letting my newly found magic consume us both.

"Say it again, Hekate. Tell me how you feel for me..."

I refuse to touch her, removing my hands from her skin until she utters those beautiful words once more. My flames persist, though, the gentle, warm tingle of them climbing up her legs and settling at her hips.

"I love you, Nyx. I will always love you." Her words are merely pants of breathless, desperate need.

"You are perfect," I whisper into the skin at her hip, then lazily drag my tongue up her ribcage and bring one nipple and then the other into the warmth of my mouth.

I let her fully kiss me at last and she loses all control, our lips crashing together and our tongues silently expressing exactly what I am too scared to admit. Our kiss is deep and passionate enough to merge our souls together for eternity, binding us together as if we are fated to be. In this moment I know exactly how I feel for her. I know what she is to me. She is everything. One day I will be strong enough to tell her. I will no longer be afraid One day I will be everything she needs me to be.

As she moans against my tongue it makes me wetter, and as she grips the sides of my face to kiss me deeper, the ice around my heart shatters completely. I always knew she would be the one to set my heart free.

Sliding my fingers across the slickness between her legs, she loses all control, grinding her hips hungrily against my skin.

"Nyx..." Her whimper is barely audible, but my lips curve up at the corners as I watch her fall apart so beautifully.

The need to taste her consumes me as she gives in to her pleasure, succumbing to my touch and relinquishing control of her body over to me. Lying down on my stomach in front of her trembling, spread legs, I push two fingers deep inside of her wetness knowing she cannot take much more. She is too easy to please. Too easy to push over the edge and send spiraling into an oblivion of pleasure. I know she is close already. Her muscles tighten around my fingers harder with each thrust, so eager to fall apart around me. I flick my tongue across her sensitive clit and her back arches as she begins to grind into me, gripping the silky sheets between her fingers.

She savors every second of my tongue against her skin, moving her hips in small, slow circles as she comes closer and closer to the release her body craves.

I will never tire of her. I will never tire of this.

Pushing my fingers into her deeper and faster I bring her clit into my mouth, sucking on it like the delicacy it is, like the sweet blessing that she is. The desire between my legs builds and burns and tingles, each second of pleasuring her making my need for her grow. I need her now even more than she needs me.

As she falls apart against me, I grip her hips, forcing her against my tongue even harder, tasting her more thoroughly, and pushing my fingers inside of her until she is screaming my name. I let her whimpers and the pleasure that leaks onto my tongue quench my unbridled thirst for her. Even as her moans die out and her body trembles, I do not let her pull away from me. I want to feel every last drop of her pleasure trickling across my tongue. I want to ravish her until she can no longer move or breathe or imagine life without me ever again.

Her breathless laugh rushes out in a quiet huff of air as I pull myself up to hover over her. I moan softly, letting her taste the love we made with a kiss, pulling her tongue into my mouth and sucking it in greedily.

"Let me taste you, Nyx. I need you," she whispers, removing my thin dress and gripping my thighs as she slides down and positions me above her. I straddle her mouth eagerly, and the warmth of her tongue is against my skin immediately. Leaning forward, I grip her breasts, enjoying the fullness of them in my hands. I caress her and feel her and allow my thoughts to fade away and focus on nothing but my pleasure. She pulls my clit into her mouth and the soft touch of her hands stroking my thighs sends shockwaves of pleasure along every burning nerve ending in my body. When she gives my nipples the soft little pinch she knows drives me wild, I feel my wetness leak and settle in her pretty little mouth. It makes me hungrier for her. I grind my hips in slow circles, and her tongue does the same as she ravishes me, sending her shimmering blue power swirling around us. Each brush of it against my skin brings new sensations, a passionate lick or a gentle lash or a persistent touch that begs me to fall apart for her.

"Please... say it again, Hekate. Convince me this is real."

"I will love you forever, Nyx."

As the words ring out around me, her name pours out in whimpers and the most beautiful orgasm rips through me, shattering the ice around my heart and my soul and every truth I try to hide when she is near crumbles to nothing. Every inch of my body is electric and alive with her in this moment. In every moment with her. I know the truth as well as she does... I love her.

My heart thuds against my chest and my breathing catches in my throat with words I want to say, but cannot yet, burning at the back of my throat unspoken. I collapse on the plush mattress next to her, knowing nothing has ever or will ever feel as good as being with her does. I would kill for this woman. Die for her. Take on any celestial, demon, or god known to man for her.

Anything for her.

"Say it, Nyx. Say what it is you're thinking in that pretty little head of yours. Say how we both know you feel already." She turns to her side, dragging a fingertip softly up my arm as I pull the sheet up around us.

Her blue eyes sparkle and glow brighter than ever as I roll over to face her and smile. "You know the truth. Why must I say it?" I try and fail to swallow back the fear of what might happen once I admit the truth.

Good things never last. In the blink of an eye everything disappears. Love dies faster than it takes for it to bloom, withering away to nothing but dust and death and disappointment. I cannot lose her. Once I say it, I fear fate or destiny will take it all away.

Her voice is firm but understanding as the bright glow in her eyes sparks and fades away. "I need to know I'm not in this alone. That you're in this with me as much as I am with you. I just need..."

"To believe. To have faith in the future. That is all you need, my love. If we are truly meant to be, then we have all the time in the world to figure it out. We are immortal, after all." Bringing her hand to my lips, I kiss her palm, and she glances down, avoiding my gaze.

"I don't want to lose you. I'm scared of how life felt before you walked into it. How lonely it all was before I found you. I can't bear feeling that way ever again. So sad. So lost. So empty," she sighs, glancing up at me as her lip quivers slightly.

Cupping her chin in my hand, I caress her cheek with my thumb and smile over at her. "I will never let you feel that way ever again, do you understand me? I will not let you. I am not going anywhere, my love. I am yours. There is no one else for me, not now or ever. It is you and I against the world from here on out," I promise, leaning forward and brushing my lips against hers.

Someday I will be brave. I will tell her what my heart yearns for her to know so badly. I will tell her the truth, that I am a coward, and that I am even more scared of life and of her than she could ever imagine.

"You and I against whatever may come our way." She places a kiss to my forehead. "I'll never stop telling you how much I love you. I'll tell you until you get so tired of hearing it that you finally admit the truth. That you, Nyx, love me, too."

Shaking my head, I laugh as she lays her head on my chest. I run my fingers through her silky hair, caressing her worries away. As her breathing slows and her eyes remain closed, I hold her while she sleeps and do not let go. Here, with Hekate's head resting on my chest and my arms wrapped around her tightly, there is no other place I ever wish to be.

I will never again let her wander through life alone unless she asks me to.

CHAPTER FOURTEEN
WICKED THING

NORA

"No... I'm not ready to go. Let's sing one more song. Have one more drink with me, come on. You guys are no fun!" Katie and Olivia head toward the exit of *Lunar Waves*, dragging me along with them.

This nightclub has always been our favorite, with its neon lights and karaoke lasting until the bar closes, so many of our nights spent bonding happened here. We've been here for hours but I'm not ready to leave. The air around me is electric and alive, and surprisingly healing to the soul, once you get past the stuffy scent of musky bodies and cheap bourbon.

The strobe lights flash across Olivia's face, shining a spotlight on her flushed cheeks and sweat drenched hair from our endless dancing. "I'm sorry, sis. I work in the morning, but we'll have to do this again soon!" The thumping music drowns out her words, but from what I can hear, her voice is clear and focused, severely contrasting my drunken haze.

"Boo!" Rolling my eyes dramatically, I pull her into my arms.

Red locks of hair stick to her cheek when I pull away, and we giggle as I untangle myself from her, tucking the loose strands behind my ears.

"Fine, Olivia. You go and I'll stay." Katie sighs, her voice hoarse from all the singing and struggling to be heard over the noise. "I'll stay for just a little longer while you wait for Ere, Nora. If he's not here in thirty minutes, then we're out of here. I mean it!" The smile she offers shows a hint of annoyance, but her eyes light up as I squeal with excitement.

"He had to stay late at work, but he'll be here. How could he say no to this?" With a playful smirk, I twirl and flip my hair in their faces and both girls burst into laughter. Adjusting the pink, sparkly crown I somehow convinced a bride-to-be to give me earlier, I take a deep breath. "Come on! The night is young, Katie, dance with me." Grabbing her hand, I tug her toward the infectious energy of the dance floor.

Olivia waves goodbye and heads to the exit. I blow her a kiss as Katie and I dance and laugh and twirl each other without a care. I jump and spin and sing at the top of my lungs until I forget about everything except for what's happening here in this moment. I can't remember the last time I felt so happy and carefree. When the song ends, we make our way over to the bar, and out of the corner of my eye I spot a pair of bright green eyes focused only on me. I order a drink and bring it to my lips. The man behind those eyes watches my every move.

"That's Kairos," Katie says. "The man who brought you to the hospital. Look familiar?" She brushes her hair behind her shoulders and waves across the bar at him.

Of course he looks familiar. I've thought of those eyes often. Only every night since that night in the woods. Something about his messy blonde hair, the intense gaze, and the tattoos that swirl down both arms and cover even his hands and fingers makes my eyes widen in response. I have to force them to relax and return to normal. My boyfriend is hot, but I can't lie and say Kairos isn't.

I can't stop staring. "So you trust this guy?"

My heart races and a rush of arousal slams into me as a crooked smile slashes across his features.

"We like Kairos, Nora. Most of the time, that is. Let's go say hi." She grins, grabbing her drink and heading to the other side of the bar.

I'm not sure I can do this. I should leave. I've wanted to meet him, but now that my head spins from tequila and I take a step forward, I contemplate leaving both Katie and him here without saying a word. I should go home. Sitting my drink on the bar, I pin my eyes on the exit as I turn to make my way to it.

"Excuse me," a smooth, velvety voice sends shivers down my spine, and I freeze.

Fuck. For a split second I consider making a run for the door, but I'm honestly unsure if I can even force my body to move. I was so close. Am I ready to meet the dark stranger who has been watching me? I have no choice now.

Slowly, I turn and face him. "Hi, how can I help you?"

Dear Lord, why did I say that? I can feel the burn as it creeps across my cheeks, the crimson color drawing his attention. His eyes shift from my cheeks back up to my eyes, and his crooked smile remains. There's no doubt in my mind now that I should have run for the exit while I still had a chance.

"Kairos," Katie greets him with a smile and a nod, looping her arm through mine.

"Katie," he replies, dipping his head slightly but keeping his gaze pinned to me.

"So, you two are friends, then?" My eyes widen as they glance at each other and then back at me.

Katie shrugs. "We've known each other for a while, yes."

"We've bonded through sharing the same goals. You could call us besties at this point, wouldn't you agree?" That crooked smile sets my soul on fire.

"Are...celestials more powerful than witches?" I place my hands on my hips, tilting my head to the side as I wait for him to respond.

Both Kairos and Katie laugh, but I don't. It was a serious question, albeit one I was only brave enough to ask thanks to the alcohol coursing through my veins.

"He wishes." Katie's wide smile is followed by him brushing his hair back from his face and shaking his head.

His eyes narrow, but a smile dances across his lips. "So, you've told her a thing or two, I see. I thought maybe Nora and I could talk... alone. Or were you leaving?"

"We were actually heading out soon. It's too bad, really." Katie sighs. "Maybe now isn't the best time for the conversation you're wanting to have with her, anyway. It can wait." Her voice is firm and unwavering, even as his smile fades and his jaw clenches.

"I've waited long enough. It's time. You told me yourself we need to talk to her, and it seems you've already had the chance to." Crossing his arms over his muscular chest, his eyes burn into mine with the intensity and heat of a thousand suns. "Maybe you should let Nora decide for herself what she wants. It's not your choice to make, Katie."

I want answers. I told myself I would find this man and get them, so running away from him now doesn't feel right. Although he scared me a little the night I fell from the bridge, I didn't feel fear when I saw him at the cemetery. I feel a lot of things here with him now, and not one of them is fear. I'm drawn to him. I feel safe.

"Nora, we can go. You don't need to stay unless you truly want to. There will be plenty of time for discussions when she hasn't chugged half a bottle of tequila." Katie glares at Kairos. "We only came over here to say hello and leave."

I tuck my hair behind my ears and turn to face her. "I'd like to stay and talk. You can stay at my house with Olivia, and I'll meet you there later. I'm waiting for Ere, anyway. He'll be here soon and can get me home safely."

I can't leave. What if he can tell me the truth about what happened to my parents? Or has useful information about the darkness that keeps invading my mind? I'm not going anywhere.

Katie glares at Kairos and he glares right back. "Fine. If you think this is for the best, then be my guest. I hope you know what you're doing."

"Don't worry about us. We'll be fine." He winks at her, and she groans loudly, her shoulders sagging as she gives up the fight.

Giving me a quick but too tight hug, Katie turns and leaves without another word. My gaze lingers on her back as she hastily makes her way out the door.

A part of me wants to leave with her. I'm scared. Not of Kairos. Only of what he might be here to tell me. I'm not sure I'm ready for the truth, or that I can handle much more after my conversation with Katie earlier. But if there's a chance he can shine some light onto my current situation, the forgotten suicide attempt on the bridge or the one I too clearly remember in the lake, then I have no choice but to listen.

"Would you like to sit?" He gestures to the back of the club where tables and booths line the walls.

"Sure. Yea, that'd be great. I have a friend meeting me here soon, but we have plenty of time. He's running late."

Heading toward the booth in the back corner, he stops walking and glances back at me. "Your *friend*, as in your boyfriend? Great. I hope I get a chance to say hello." He forces a tight-lipped smile and then continues on, leading us through the crowd.

In the corner of the club where the music fades to a distant hum, he leans in close. "By the way, I'm Kairos," he says, flashing one of those crooked smiles I've already learned to expect. "What shall I call you?"

"You know my name. I heard you say it already." I shake my head, raking my eyes up and down him as I continue. "It's Nora, but you can call me Nor if you'd like. It's what my friends and family have always called me." I lean back against the velvety booth. "It seems you already know a thing or two about me. How?" I take a sip from the drink in front of me, not remembering ordering it, only that it wasn't here before and yet now here it sits.

I'm drunk. I'm not in the stumbling-and-falling-down stage, just the my-mind-is-mush-and-I-can-barely-register-what's-happening stage, but I sip on the sweet drink anyway.

"As much as I love your given name, I think I'll call you princess instead," he gestures to the crown on my head, and I immediately regret ever putting the damn thing on.

I yank it off, untangling my hair from the pointy bristles meant to keep it in place, then toss it onto the glossy, burned wood table between us. I glare at him. "If you want to live, please never call me that again."

My cheeks burn as I smooth out my hair, pretending his words didn't bother me, but I'm not okay. I'm mortified. I'll literally never recover.

Hearing my threat, his smile widens, his shoulders shaking briefly, a laugh I'm sure that I can't hear past the music blaring behind me. "Would you believe me if I told you I've been stalking you?" He arches an eyebrow up and leans his elbows on the table, resting his chin on his clasped hands. The little daggers tattooed on his fingers remind me how dangerous he might be despite my gut urging me that I'm safe.

I chew on my bottom lip, staring into my glass and considering his words. "Have you? Can I ask why the hell you'd be doing that?"

I'm not surprised. I know it was him who swooped in to save me after the fall from the bridge, and the one who watched me from the tree line at the cemetery. I'm almost positive he saved me from the lake the night I nearly drowned, too. As I meet his gaze, his eyes hold me captive and I don't want to look away, the bright green now revealing swirls of light blue as I look at them closer. I force myself to focus on anything other than his eyes, instead focusing on his fingers now wrapped around his cup and tapping on the thick glass. The fact he has been watching me might creep out someone whose sanity was still intact, but I'm quite certain mine shattered to pieces a while ago. It has the opposite effect instead, sending waves of guilty excitement pulsing through me.

Wearing that charming smile, his lips hovering over his glass, he takes a swig of his whiskey. "I tell you I'm stalking you and it gets you excited. You are just full of surprises, aren't you?"

A strange power thrums to life around him, and instantly I recognize it as magic, though it's much different than how Katie's felt earlier. His is a bit darker. A bit more chaotic. But still, an underlying light similar to hers exists within it. As our eyes meet this time, I couldn't look away even if I wanted to. His power holds me in place, caressing my soul in a gentle whisper of recognition. It's as if live wires dance between us and through us, sparking and burning me alive. I can sense my soul reaching out for him, screaming at me to remember something that seems too foreign and far away to grip onto. I feel only light and love as his gentle eyes rake over me, a look that somehow makes me whole again after so long of being broken.

The magic fades away, and with it my shattered sanity returns. I remind myself to think of Ere and his warm, golden eyes and how much he adores me and takes away the pain. Kairos is a stranger. One with magic that apparently can make me lose myself for brief moments. But now that it's gone, I feel like myself again.

I laugh, pushing my shoulders back and pretending I felt nothing out of the ordinary. "I'm not...excited about the idea of you stalking me. But what could a mere mortal really do to stop you even if she wanted to?"

His emerald eyes swirl with specks of sapphires, the colors spinning and entrancing me to the point of no words. The motion and even the hues are reminiscent of the lake's waves and how they steal my attention; the way they endlessly rise and fall.

Soothing magic wraps around me, brushing against my skin and my mind and I shiver at the intimate feeling of it—the feeling of him, in a way—touching me. I lower my eyes back to my drink, feeling too exposed and too vulnerable to look at him.

"You're lying, princess," he says, tilting his head and narrowing his eyes. "I can sense everything you feel as you feel it." He smiles and my heart flutters. "But you're right. There's nothing you can do. I won't stop. It's not an option."

The fact that he can sense what I'm feeling has me shifting. If his magic can sense everything, then I need to focus. I can't let myself get lost in his eyes and let the beauty of them distract me from the important questions.

Placing my elbows on the table, I lower my voice as I lean forward. "Do you know anything about my parents' deaths? What the hell happened to them? And also, what the hell is happening to me?"

It's time for the important questions. The reason I wanted to meet him in the first place was to find out what he knows, and that's all that should matter right now. I need answers.

Lowering his voice to a quiet, smooth timber, he places his hands flat on the table, leaning in closer. "Will you believe me if I tell you the truth about why I'm here, or will you believe you've lost your mind completely?" His voice softens and the energy radiating off him relaxes. "Maybe you're just imagining that I'm here. Maybe I'm not even real."

I shake my head, crossing my arms over my chest as I fume on the inside. "Unbelievable. Is my life and my mental health a joke to you?"

He sighs, guilt flashing behind his eyes. "Nothing about you is a joke to me."

"I know you're real. I can see you just fine." I roll my shoulders back, narrowing my eyes. "I've never hallucinated anything."

"Oh? Well, you could have fooled me. You let your therapist lock you up and throw away the key. You let your sister convince you that you'd imagined what you knew deep down was real. You've never believed you were truly mentally unstable at all, did you, Nora?" He relaxes, throwing his muscular, tattooed arm across the back of his booth.

"What is it you want me to say? That monsters are real..." I gesture toward him, "and that angels exist, because that's what you are, right? You're an angel?" A huff of laughter escapes from my trembling lips. "Something dark and evil murdered my parents whether people believe me or not. I'm not crazy. What I can't understand is why. Why them?" I sigh, my shoulders sagging as I finally let it all out, feeling both drained and relieved by admitting the truth.

I can't speak of these things with Dr. Cooper or Olivia. For months I've had to hold it all in, pretending what I saw was a figment of my imagination. A psychotic break. A trauma response to losing my parents. It feels good to have Kairos acknowledge that what I saw was real, as terrifying as it all might be.

"Sometimes there is no answer for why. What matters now is that you believe. That you trust yourself and your instincts more than anything or anyone else. What you saw is real, Nora. I see the monsters myself. I kill them myself, too, and happily so." He tilts his head to the side, watching me carefully as he continues. "And yes. Celestials are in fact real. That's the term we prefer."

A glimmer of magic flashes, and briefly he allows me a glimpse of the feathery black wings spread wide behind his back. God, they're beautiful. He is beautiful. I blink once and a veil of magic reappears, his wings replaced by shadows cast on the wall from strobe lights and dancing people behind me. I knew I hadn't lost my mind. I knew it the night my parents died and the following months I spent at the psychiatric hospital. It was fear that kept me from admitting it to myself. Knowing the truth is one thing, but admitting the fact that monsters killed my parents out loud? It's fucking terrifying.

"I don't know what to believe sometimes. My whole life feels like a lie. Some days it's... hard to *breathe*. To even... *exist*." The last part comes out in a whisper as warmth spills from my eyes and falls down my cheeks.

Kairos clears his throat, his eyebrows scrunching together as he reaches out to me. "Nora, I'm sorry. Katie was right. You're not ready. I'll answer any question you have later. That's enough for tonight." Slowly, he reaches to brush away the tear tracing a path down my cheek, his hand hovering near my face momentarily. Then he swiftly draws back, grabbing his drink and emptying the glass.

The sound of my uneven breath fills the silence, tearing through the emptiness left in the air from him pulling away. "No, it's fine. I'm okay."

His concerned gaze pierces through me as if he carries the weight of my pain in his own heart, longing to ease it but not knowing how to. "You're not, and I hate it. I wish I could heal your heartbreak and end your pain. I would take it on myself if I could."

"Thank you. It's getting better," I lie, knowing it's what everyone around me wants to hear. "Or maybe it'll get better eventually. I'm sitting here with you now, so maybe this is the beginning of something good. My very own stalker. What a dream," I tease, raising my eyebrows playfully and flashing him a smile.

I just want to break the tension. To push away the pain and the dark thoughts before I go tumbling into a suffocating abyss I can't escape from.

His laughter fills the air and my heart catches. The sound sends goosebumps racing across my arms and prickling against my neck, the melody of it warming my soul and sending me into a fit of laughter of my own. Waves of peace and comfort thrum around me, wrapping me in a soothing embrace. Despite my world being flipped on its head and my life sort of being in shambles, being with him does something to me that I can't understand.

The light within Kairos reminds me to breathe.

"I'm happy to be of service. For now, I should get you home safely. It's getting late. Katie is going to kill me." His eyes search mine and then subtly drift from my eyes down to my lips, a blush appearing across his chiseled jawline. The intensity of his stare tears me open, exposing every wounded, broken part of myself that I try so hard to hide.

He looks at me like if he exists somewhere in heaven, then I'm every cloud and each star and all the tiny molecules that keep him in place there, preventing him from crashing down to earth. His lopsided smile takes my breath away. God, what is it about Kairos that has me suddenly questioning everything? He's right. I need to go.

"Witches aren't prone to murder, are they? I've made her mad many times and the worst she's ever done is force a sage cleanse and a moon water bath on me to clear my aura of any negative energy. You'll be just fine." My shoulders shake as I tilt my head back and laughter pours out of me.

Leaning forward, he rests his arms on the table, bringing his hands closer to mine. "I enjoy watching you laugh. It's intoxicating."

The heat from his skin radiates toward me, and I try and fail at not imagining how good it might feel to have those tatted hands all over me, like a forbidden touch I know I should resist. I fail again at not thinking about how exhilarating it might be to have them wound in my hair as his lips ravage my own. Crossing my legs to calm the rising tide of arousal pulsating between them, the small amount of friction against the sensitive area has me closing my eyes and letting out an internal sigh of pleasure. Damn, he's hot. If only I were single...

"You are one wicked little thing, aren't you?" His fingers twitch slightly, stealing my attention, the little daggers and the letters M-E-R-A tattooed across the skin there stealing my attention..

I force my eyes away from the letters, looking back up at him. "What?"

"Never mind." He looks down and shakes his head as his lips twitch at the corners.

Our eyes meet and embarrassment washes over me as I remember what he said about sensing what I'm feeling. Shit. He felt that. I'm sure of it. I'm almost certain by the amused look written across his features that he knows exactly what I was trying and failing miserably at not thinking about. I should get home before I embarrass myself any further.

Tearing my eyes away from him, I break free from the alluring thoughts that infiltrated my vulnerable, drunk mind. I'm attracted to guys besides Ere often, but sitting here with Kairos feels different. It feels dangerous, like a wildfire building up inside me that has only just begun. It doesn't make sense. He's a celestial being, someone who couldn't possibly be feeling the things I do right now, could he?

"I'll walk you home." He slides out of the booth, offering his hand to help me up.

I stand and face him. "Why are you doing this? I mean...why are you here, Kairos?"

His throat bobs, then he blinks slowly before answering. "To protect you. I vowed to keep you safe."

"Vowed to who? Or what?"

"The celestial queen in my realm. Gaia asked me to guard you. As soon as I laid eyes on you, I knew I couldn't refuse. I knew you were special." He lowers our hands down but doesn't let go, staring at them absentmindedly.

"A... *queen* asked you to protect little ol' *me*? Do you realize how insane that sounds? All of this is insane." I sigh. "I'm not special, Kairos. You're wrong. Besides, I don't need anyone to protect me. I have plenty of people who care and plenty of people who I disappoint already. Do yourself a favor, and don't add your name to the list."

His eyes are a serene sea of confidence as they meet my own. "You're much more special than you know. I'm not going anywhere. Not until I can be sure you're safe."

"Keep me safe from what? Or who? What the hell aren't you telling me?" I pull my hand out of his, suddenly wanting to put distance between us. "If my life is in danger then I deserve to know the truth." I take a step back.

He steps forward. "Nora, I'll tell you everything. Whatever you want to know. It's a lot to take in, so trust me when I tell you, you need sleep before anything else." He reaches up, tucking my hair behind my ears as he smiles at me.

"I need to get some air. I'm sorry. Please don't follow me." I turn and head toward the exit, ignoring the groans and complaints from the blurry, faceless people as I push past anyone who stands in my way.

I need out. I need to breathe for just a moment.

Most of what I've learned tonight isn't surprising. I knew I hadn't lost my mind and that something evil had attacked my parents. I know something is after me now, too. But Kairos and celestials and kings and queens is all too much to handle in my current state. I just want to go home and sink into bed where I can process it all before my mind spirals out of control.

Pushing the heavy metal door open, I step into the dark alley and lean into the crumbling, brick wall. The rough rock digs into my skin as I slide down it, pressing my face between my knees and forcing deep breaths in and out of my lungs. A beer bottle rolls down the alley and clinks against the wall as a breeze whips past. I welcome the silence that follows. The club is too loud and it's all too much. I'm happy to be free of the chaos.

A loud shriek is followed by a guttural growl, and I'm on my feet in seconds, searching the shadows for any movement. *What the fuck was that?* I stumble forward, squinting into the darkness, but I see nothing.

"Nora! Run!"

That voice, the one that soothes my pain and calms my fears, is panicked and familiar. Ere. Oh god... it's Ere.

CHAPTER FIFTEEN
YOU TERRIFY ME

NORA

I take a step forward, eyes wide and voice unsteady. "Ere?"

He screams, the sound pained and hopeless and absolutely terrified. My heart shatters.

"Ere! Where are you!?" My words are hoarse as I yell out for him, the scent of death and decay lingering in the air.

Keeping my hand pressed firmly against the wall is all that keeps me steady as I hobble down the alley to search for him. "Ere... oh god. Please be okay. Please be okay."

The sound of flapping wings thunders overhead and then Kairos drops down from the sky, landing on the pavement in a defensive crouch. His black wings are spread wide, and his bright green eyes are pinned on me. "Run. *Now.*"

I back away as he pulls out a dagger and it lights up in his hand, the glowing weapon chasing away the shadows around us. I turn to run. A loud thud sounds out behind me, and slowly I turn back toward Kairos to face it. My unsteady legs shake and my heart trembles within my chest, hoping and praying that Ere is okay.

He's not okay.

A scream tears out of my throat, my knees throbbing and aching as I collapse on the unforgiving cement. My throat burns from the screams I can't contain, but the tears that fall burn even hotter. I take in the thick, black substance splattered across his torso, exposed by the t-shirt that's now ripped to shreds and barely hanging onto his body at all. The blackness drips from him, meeting the pavement with a hiss as it sizzles and steams and then evaporates into nothing.

"Please, just breathe," I whimper, sobs escaping my quivering lips.

I place my hand on his chest, the slight rise and fall of it giving me hope that he can still be okay. He's alive. Kissing his forehead, I wipe my tears and push myself to my feet. Four sets of red eyes are locked on Kairos as he spins and leaps and slices at large, scaly bodies. He admitted that monsters are real, and that he kills them, but this is not at all what I imagined. Their pointy teeth drip with the black substance that stained my parents' skin, the same substance that now stains Ere's skin, too. They tower over Kairos who is at least six foot two, their spiked tails thrashing and their claws lashing out at him as he fights them all at once.

I hate them. I want them all dead. In fact, I'd like to slaughter them all myself.

"Nora... *please... go*," Kairos begs, only glancing my way briefly before jabbing his dagger into one of the thick, scaly heads.

The dagger glows brighter as he drags it across another monster's throat, its black blood dripping until suddenly the body shatters into pieces and turns to ash. I won't let them hurt anyone else I love. They will fucking pay for what they've done, even if it kills me. I run to Kairos, stealing the other dagger from the strap on his thigh, pointing it at the beasts who now focus on me. They taunt me, their glowing eyes narrowing into slants and their jaws widening as they let out a menacing growl, then snap their sharp, needle-like teeth together.

The sound is like shattering glass, but I ignore the terror that spikes my heart rate. I clumsily stab at one of the monster's hearts and it leaps away, rolling across the ground and sending chunks of cement flying.

"What the hell do you think you're doing, Nora!? I told you to run!" Kairos waves a hand, and a whirlwind of air pushes the monster back who advances toward me, then he leaps on it and tackles it to the ground. Black blood splatters as he jams his dagger straight through its heart.

It shatters and scatters in the wind. He's slightly more viscous and terrifying than the beasts are.

"I refuse to be a coward, Kairos." I step forward, slicing at the monster whose wide mouth curves up into a disturbing smile. It lets out a deep roar and slaps my hand away. "I'll never sit back and not at least try to protect the ones I love."

I lunge for the scaly body, using one hand to hold onto it as I stab it over and over in the abdomen. It growls and I growl back, screaming and stabbing, its black blood dripping down my fingers and searing my skin. I smile as its crimson eyes burn into mine, and just as I lift my dagger to meet its face, Kairos glares at me as he raises a sword and slices its head from its shoulders. The bloody, wide-eyed head rolls across the pavement, and I watch with satisfaction as it shatters to bits.

"Do you enjoy coming close to death? Is that what this is?" Kairo's palms spark with electricity and he gathers a large orb of lightning between his hands, sending it flying through the air.

It hits its mark. Lightning surrounds one of the two remaining beasts and stuns it so it can't move. It falls to the ground in a fit of seizures. My eyes widen as I realize the extent of his power.

"No, Kairos, as you know, I've had plenty of brushes with death lately, and none of them were particularly enjoyable," I grunt, charging at the last monster. I clench my teeth and prepare for the impact of my dagger against its heart. "But I do enjoy watching these things die."

I reach the beast, and it stretches its arm out to grip me by the throat. Claws tear at my skin, its hold tightening around my neck. I gasp and choke, kicking and scratching at it as the monster lifts me into the air and tosses me into the brick wall. I'm not sure whether the sound that echoes in my ears is from the brick or my bones cracking, but pain shoots up and down my spine as I slam into the wall and my shoulder aches as I land on the ground in a heap. It happens too fast to even scream, let alone to try to gather up the strength and run. It leans down and clamps its mouth around my thigh, the pointy teeth digging in and sending a hot, prickly pain through my entire body as they slice and tear through my flesh. I scream, scratching at its head with my nails as it bites down harder, refusing to let me go. Everything hurts. The fiery pain courses through my body like poison, spreading and latching onto every nerve and fiber of my being until all I feel and all I can think of is that pain. My vision blurs and I feel myself slipping into oblivion, a comforting numbness caressing my skin and slowly replacing the pain. Ashes rain down on my skin as Kairos ends the creatures life.

"Mio!" He yells, and then hushed words that follow are all I hear.

I'm paralyzed. I can't move or blink or control even a single muscle in my body. I'm surprised I'm even still breathing. All I see is darkness as the black poison invades my senses. Kairos was right. Today is the day I die.

My only hope is that Ere makes it out of this alive.

I'm lifted off the ground, and the warmth of strong arms holding me tight to a muscular chest brings peace and comfort to my mind. I drift in and out of consciousness until Olivia shrieks my name, jolting me awake as I'm placed on something soft and familiar. My couch. I'm home. I'm alive. A large hand grips mine. A tingly sensation starts in my fingers and spreads from there to the rest of my body. I can move again. I wiggle only my toes and fingers at first, too afraid to move anything else and feel the searing pain again. But it's gone.

Opening my eyes, I groan as my temples throb and my throat burns from so much screaming. Olivia paces back and forth in the kitchen, running her hands through her wavy hair as Katie talks to her and she nods every now and again.

"Ere!" I jump to my feet, swaying slightly and Kairos reaches out, placing his hands on my hips to steady me.

"Look at me, Nora." He swallows, searching my eyes, pain flashing within his own. "Are you okay?"

I nod, taking a deep breath and forcing myself to not look away. I'm not okay. I won't be until I know Ere is okay, but I allow him a moment to assess me and take in the damage. "I'm fine, thank you. I feel infinitely better than I did before, thanks to you, I assume?" I give him a small smile.

He nods toward the larger sofa against the wall. "He's fine, okay? Please relax. You've been through a lot yourself."

I rush to Ere's side and kneel in front of him, his breathing steady and his skin no longer covered in the dripping, black poison. "Thank you for helping him." I glance over my shoulder at Kairos, and he simply nods and then takes a seat on the other couch.

"I feared you'd use my own weapon against me if I didn't." He leans back, glancing at Katie who is glaring at him and not at all trying to hide it.

"Is he going to be okay?" I brush Ere's hair away from his eyes as I lean forward and kiss his cheek.

Olivia pulls me to my feet, wrapping her arms around me and holding my head against her chest, squeezing me tight. "What the hell is going on, Nor? I'm sort of freaking out right now. Katie gave me a quick rundown when you guys just appeared in the middle of the living room out of nowhere, but—*what the actual fuck*? Do those two men have *wings*?" Her voice is high-pitched and frantic and her eyes dart around the room like she doesn't know who or what to focus on.

"Sounds like you're all caught up. This is your dream come true, Liv. You've always wished for magic and monsters to exist, and well...they do." I shrug, gripping her shoulders and forcing her to sit.

Wait, two celestials?

"Your boyfriend will live to see another day, Nora. My man Ro always saves the day." A stranger plops down between Olivia and Kairos, tucking his wings in tight and wearing a bright, wide smile.

"Who are you?" I glance at the man and then at Katie, who doesn't seem surprised to see him here.

Katie takes a seat in the recliner on the opposite side of the room. "You haven't had the pleasure yet of meeting Bromios." Her nose scrunches up as she gives him one of her fake, forced smiles.

I get the feeling she doesn't like him, but I'm not sure why.

The man leans forward and extends his hand. Katie rolls her eyes but smiles as I slowly offer my hand to him, assuming he's just going to shake it.

"Call me Mio." He lifts my hand to his lips and kisses it once, just a soft quick brush of his lips before leaning back and throwing his arm over Kairos' shoulder.

"Olivia, this is Kairos. Kairos, my sister Olivia, which I'm sure you already know." I shake my head, glancing at Ere and hoping he'll wake up soon.

"If you want me to wake him I can." Mio stands and comes to my side as I take a seat on the edge of the couch where Ere lays, staring down at his still body. "We weren't sure how much you wanted him to know of this... of *us*. But it's your choice."

If this is a part of my life now, these creatures and magic and monsters, then I need Ere to be a part of it. I don't want us to keep secrets from each other.

"Please wake him. I have a million questions, but I'd prefer he be here with me. I need him to be." My vision blurs as tears prickle at the corners of my eyes.

Kairos stands and makes his way over to me, placing his hands on my shoulders. "If it's what you think is best. But we have a lot to share with you." His eyes shift to Katie, and she nods. "If you think he can handle it then I'll wake him myself. If he freaks out, though, I give Mio full permission to knock him back out so you aren't pissed at me. You terrify me a little." His crooked grin makes me smile, even with all the madness that's happened tonight.

He's so close to me, and as I look up at him his eyes swirl and hypnotize me in a way that makes me never want to look away.

I need to look away.

"Wake him. He can handle it. He loves me and will accept anything that'll be a part of my life." I turn away and he sighs behind me.

"As you wish, princess." Bright, white light pulsates in his hand, swirling around his fingertips as he places them to Ere's temple.

Olivia jumps up, covering her mouth with her hands as she steps up closer. "Holy shit. I can't believe this is real," she breathes. "I always hoped the world was a magical place, but seeing all of this... it's unbelievable." She huffs a laugh.

I shouldn't be surprised that Olivia is taking all of this new information about the world we live in so well, considering her love of all things creepy and strange. But she's handling it better than I am. I'm freaking out on the inside, just hiding the fear and confusion running rampant in my mind. But this is what she has always dreamed of. She hoped to one day stumble upon something weird and magical, and she has. I get why she's thrilled. Ere on the other hand, I'm not sure how this will play out. All I can do is hope for the best and believe in us always. I'm not even sure how the hell *I'm* taking all of this without the comfort of tequila or the rush of adrenaline in my system.

It's going to be okay. Everything will be just fine. It has to be.

PART TWO

FATED

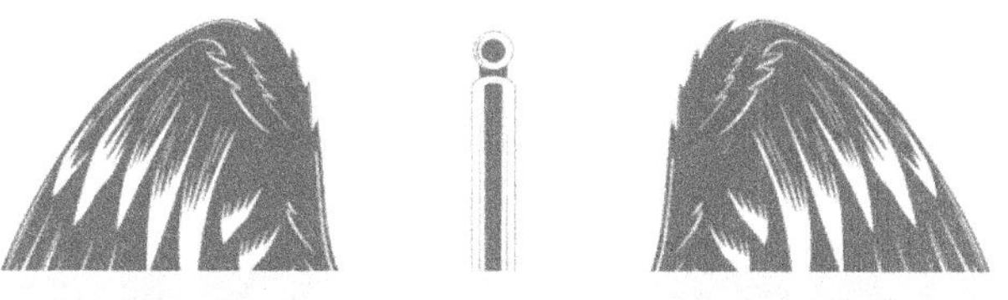

CHAPTER SIXTEEN

TRUTHS AND LIES

KAIROS

I should have let him die in that alley. I should have jammed the dagger into his throat while I had the chance. Mio shouldn't have offered to wake him. *Bastard*. I planned on letting him sleep until my magic wore off, letting him drift in a sea of nothingness so I could spend more time with Nora without him in the way. For her, I guess I'll let him live... for now.

"What do you remember happening in the alley outside of the club?" Nora turns to *him*, placing her hand on his knee as his eyes shift around the room.

"I remember it all. What were they and why did they attack me?" His eyes meet mine and drift up to my wings. "What the hell are you two?" He swallows, putting his arm around Nora and pulling her in close as Mio gives him a wide, proud smile.

I wish I didn't hate him, but I do. I'm playing nice for her only, but gods is it hard to ignore the looks and the touches between them, knowing she's fated for me. I want him gone. Fuck Nyx for sending her demons to attack him and dragging him into this. I know this is a message. A threat. Next it will be Nora.

I lean my elbows on my knees. "They were demons from the Underworld, and there are plenty more where they came from. They're after Nora and they were simply using you to hurt her." I clench my fists as Nora caresses his knee with her thumb. "Mio and I are celestials from the Realm of Darkness. I was ordered to protect Nora here on the Earth Realm. I'm her guardian."

The bastard touching my fated mate huffs. "Celestials and demons? Realms? I feel like I'm losing my mind." Running his hands through his thick hair, he stands and paces in front of the couch.

Nora's eyes follow him. She's scared this is all too much for him, I can sense it. She's afraid he'll leave. If only I could be so lucky.

"I'm a witch." Katie waves. "There are lots of witches here on this realm, just so you're aware. The world is not at all what it seems." Katie's blue eyes glow as she smiles over at him.

Olivia gasps quietly and then leans in to get a closer look. "You people just keep getting weirder. I love it."

The sister approves. At least that's one less person Mio will have to place in a magically induced coma for a bit for not taking it well. There's still a slight chance Ere will have a meltdown and we'll have no choice but to send him back to dreamland. Here's to hoping.

"Which one of you are going to tell Nora what *she* is?" Mio chimes in, standing and making his way to the kitchen. He leans against the island, looking first to Katie and then at me as he waits.

That's why he walked away. He was afraid I'd murder him. *Godsdamn him to hell.* Why is he like this? I'm trying to ease her into it all, not give her every bit of information all at once. It'll be too much. I almost hate him as much as I hate Ere right now, though watching him clasp his hand around Nora's, I truly don't believe I will ever despise someone more.

"What does he mean, Katie?" Nora's high-pitched tone reveals her panic.

Katie says nothing.

"Kairos? One of you tell me what he's talking about, *now*. What... am I?"

Katie stands, removing her heels and tossing them beside the recliner. "I have a confession first, one that ties into all of this. I suppose I might as well get it out of the way." She sighs. "Kairos, I need you to stay calm and save all your questions for later." She glares at me, and I hesitate for a moment before nodding back and leaning in closer.

Her energy has shifted. It's no longer calm and full of peace like it usually is. Instead it's a nest of turmoil and anxiety. *Shit. What is she keeping from me?*

"My name isn't Katie. I'm... Hekate. The Queen of Witches and Magic."

A glowing crown appears around her head, one wrapped in thorns and roses that disappears just as quickly as it appeared. "I'm here to protect Nora for many reasons, but mostly because we were friends in a past life. I helped create her. I faked my death and switched up my name to keep hidden from Nyx." She crosses her arms and peers into my eyes, her own glowing as her power reaches into my mind.

Suddenly memories of Mera and Hekate push their way in. Memories of the two of them laughing and dancing at the balls in the Realm of Light. The two of them fighting together against Nyx's army, never leaving each other's sides. *Her...* Nyx's lover before she was banished from the Realm of Light.

"Why can't I remember you, Hekate? If you were friends with her, I should have remembered without you having to show me. What the hell is going on?" Positioning my elbows on my knees, I lean forward, tilting my head as I watch her.

She raises her eyebrows and then sighs, her shoulders falling and her face going flat. "I told you to save all questions for later. We'll get to it, I promise, but basically the gods came to me with a message. Sort of. For now, this is about explaining to Nora who she is and why we're here. We'll talk later." I give her a stiff nod, but keep my eyes pinned to her as she focuses her gaze on Nora. What the hell does she mean the gods came to her with a message? We thought all the gods who remained after the war with Nyx were in hiding, or worse, dead and in the Elysian Fields in the Underworld. Their names and faces are all a mystery. We cannot remember them, and we sure as shit don't see them or hear from them. We no longer feel them here in the world. They came to her. They exist still. I'm not sure whether I should be thrilled they aren't dead or pissed they refuse to show themselves, but I'll work through that later. As I look at Hekate now, it's as if somewhere deep down I always knew she was a queen, and I can't make sense of why I had forgotten until now. I sense her power taking up more space in this room than would ever be possible for a mere witch, because she is letting me feel it for the first time. Holy shit. It's true.

"Helped create me? What do you mean?" Nora stands as Ere leans back against the couch and stares blankly at nothing. He looks as lost as I feel.

My eyes follow Nora as she paces the living room, hands running through her hair and her breathing too heavy. It takes every ounce of restraint in my body to keep myself pinned to this seat, to keep from taking her into my arms and holding her against me. I believed she was Mera before, but seeing Hekate's memory more than confirmed what I already knew had to be true. I'm suddenly a man gone mad who can't think or feel anything except for her soul and how it's connected to mine. She is more than just mine. More than just my fated mate.

She is my entire heart that was for so long lost, now living and breathing here in front of me.

I sit quietly, waiting for Hekate to respond as she steps up to Nora and takes her hands. "You were created, Nora, in 1851, by myself, the Queen of Celestials, Gaia, and the Queen of Darkness, Nyx. We called you the Divine One because you held so much light within your soul, A divine light that no one else has the power to possess or wield. You are so special. One of a kind, truly. We were best friends instantly." She smiles but Nora suddenly pulls away, her hands trembling as she sits down next to Ere.

"Why are the demons attacking people I love and coming after me? And if what you're saying is true, why don't I remember any of this? Who I am or this... power you say I have." She leans her elbows on her knees, running her hands through her hair and then grasping it tightly between her fingers as she stares only at the floor.

Taking a deep breath as I decide where to start, I glance at Hekate and she nods, leaning back in her chair and crossing her legs. "I believe they're once again after your power. It's like watching history repeat itself. Nyx has done this before." Shaking my head, I meet Nora's gaze as she finally looks at me. "At first, I thought your grief was sending you spiraling. I thought it was the reason for your jump from the bridge, but I'm assuming you weren't in control. It was all her."

Olivia jumps to her feet then, anger and pain reflecting in her eyes. Finally, a reaction that makes sense with everything she's learning. "What the hell do you mean, the reason for her jump from the bridge? Nora, you jumped from a bridge and didn't tell me!?"

Hekate reaches out and places a hand on her arm, blue light sparkling across her skin. "She's fine, Liv. That's all that matters now."

Olivia takes a deep breath, and then sits, saying nothing else.

Nora's eyes glaze over, and her features contort in anger, no longer stunned to silence. "It was her who forced me off the bridge? Her who haunted my thoughts? Her who nearly drowned me in the lake!? Was it all her, then!? What about our parents?" She spits through clenched teeth. "Please tell me the reason they're dead isn't because of me. Because of *her*."

Hekate's power flashes as she sends sparkling waves of blue toward Nora, wrapping it around her in a comforting embrace. Nora calms slightly, closing her eyes and allowing the magic to ease her worried mind.

"Let's start with why you don't remember your past. It ties into your parents and why they are not here now, though I can't say I completely understand it all myself." Uncrossing her legs, she reaches up and runs her fingers along the obsidian necklace around her neck, the blue, purple, and pink colors swirling within it and stealing my attention. "The necklace your mom cherished. The one that looks similar to mine, I believe it was once yours, though for the life of me I cannot remember for sure. Bits and pieces of my past are fuzzy still. Like something is blocking me from knowing the full truth." Her eyes shift to me for only a second, but long enough for me to understand it's something we'll need to discuss later. "But they came to me once, your parents, and had a message for me from the gods," she shrugs, smiling softly at Nora. "I didn't believe them at first. Two mortals speaking to divine beings seemed unbelievable, but then they spoke my real name. They called me not Katie, but Queen Hekate, and suddenly I remembered who I was. I remembered who you were, too. Your mother placed my hand on her swollen belly, and I knew it was you. I knew I had to do whatever I could to protect my friend."

Nora's tears slide down her cheek, and I wish I could sit by her side and wipe them away. Ere does not. He sees them but does nothing, almost looking at her incredulously like he's shocked she believes any of what we're saying. He doesn't have to believe it now. He will one day when she's out of his life for good thanks to fate.

"What was the message, Katie? What did they tell you?" Nora breathes, tilting her head slightly to the side.

Hekate smiles and then leans forward. "Truth is more powerful than even fate, and that remembering who I truly am will lead me closer to fulfilling my destiny. The message was not just for me, but for you, too. I believe your memories are tied to that amulet your mother loved. She insisted that you would need it one day to remember your past. She told me the truth would be twisted if you couldn't remember it for yourself. That fate itself might never recover." Clasping her hands in her lap, her eyes glow for a moment before fading back to their normal icy blue. "They knew their time here would be cut short, Nora. They knew their fate, and they were not afraid. They believed they had served their purpose. The purpose the gods themselves sent them here to set into motion."

Nora and Olivia gaze at each other, tears streaming down both of their cheeks. Guilt pulsates off of Nora, but her sister does not blame her for the loss of their parents. All I feel from her is love and understanding. Acceptance. She wishes she could protect Nora, too.

Olivia smiles. "Our parents were the purest and kindest souls I have ever known. Of course they could speak to the gods," she huffs a laugh, wiping away her tears. "They were brave for putting themselves in the middle of this. I don't know if I would want to." She glances at Nora nervously, fear at last swirling behind those dark blue eyes.

She's scared for Nora. I am, too. I wish my mother would have told me about her being on the Earth Realm before her parents were killed. I could have protected them. Maybe even saved them. I could have fucking done *something*, though if fate had any say in it, it happened exactly as it was meant to. There is no fighting fate. It's set in stone. It is irreversible and unbreakable, and not without purpose.

Fate is an unwavering force that cannot be untethered.

I look to Ere and his eyes are wide, still lost in space and refusing to look at even Nora, though he has no problem glaring in my direction. Olivia has her legs tucked underneath her, a fuzzy blanket thrown over her lap and looking drowsy but determined to stay awake and be here for her sister. And Mio... if I could smite him right now I would. His eyes meet mine and then dart to Ere, a question lingering in his eyes that I know too well. *Do you want me to kill him now?* His eyes ask, and *yes*... more than ever, yes, I do. But I'll settle for just ruining his night with the truth.

I stand and reposition my wings, shrugging out of my leather jacket and tossing it on the back of the couch. "I don't want to keep secrets from you any longer. If you want the whole truth, Nora, then it's what I'll give you." Taking a deep breath, I kneel in front of her, taking one of her hands in mine.

She doesn't pull away. She doesn't even flinch. A part of her feels the connection, too, I'm almost certain. "What is it, Kairos? Tell me," she whispers.

"Hekate was not the only one who knew you back then, Nor. I did, too." I blink back tears as my heart pounds against my chest, begging for her to recognize the truth. "We are so much more than any of this. More than any mortal connection you might find here." I glance at Ere and he's no longer lost in thought, he's solely focused in on me. Ignoring the burning look of hatred, I smile up at his girlfriend. "We are fated mates. We were created for one another," I tell her, a lump forming in my throat as I swallow back all the other words I'd love to say.

She stares at me, tilting her head to the side and searching my face for something, for what, I don't know, but she doesn't speak. I let her search. I let her feel into her soul and her heart to find the right words while I kneel before her and wait.

Ere laughs beside her, only for a brief moment before yanking me up by my shirt and pulling me to my feet. He says nothing as he releases me and then swings hard with his right fist and slams it into my face. I don't move or flinch or hiss in pain, not because I want to play it cool or pretend I'm fine, but because a mortal punch truly is barely a hit at all against our bodies. I should laugh. I should swing back. I should fucking rage and tear his heart straight from his chest and shove it down his throat, but I won't. Not here and not now, not with Nora watching and deciding whether she can trust me.

I close my eyes, I take a deep breath, and I let it fucking go, because if I were him, I'd be pissed, too. I simply smile at him, not a wide, cocky smile, but one that promises that if he touches me again his hand will return to him a little more broken, or possibly not be returned at all.

Nora jumps to her feet and puts herself between the two of us, her palms on his chest as she pushes him back and away from me. "Ere, what the hell? That is not okay!"

Throwing his arms up, he glares at me and then at everyone else in the room before looking down at her. "None of this is okay! He's fucking lying, and I won't just sit here and pretend to be okay with it." He relaxes, cracking his neck and clenching his jaw. "I love you and you know that, Nor, but I won't listen to this any longer. If you truly believe that bastard is your fated mate after everything you and I have been through together, then what the hell am I even doing here?" He sighs, taking her hands into his and gazing at her with a look of a man scorned a hundred times. "I can't do this, Nor. I'm sorry, but I just...I can't." He shrugs, shaking his head as he lets go of her and slowly backs away.

"Ere, wait. Please, let's just talk about this..." she follows him to the door and then it slams behind him as he leaves.

No glance back at her. No hesitation. Just gone without as much as a second thought, leaving her crying in the doorway all alone. I clench my fists and resist the urge to drag him down the darkest alley I can find and tear him to pieces with nothing but my teeth like a bloodthirsty hellhound.

Olivia jumps to her feet and rushes across the room, pulling her into her arms. "I'm so sorry, Nor. I'm so fucking sorry."

The woman I love, my fated mate and future queen, slides to the floor and falls apart before my eyes and I can do nothing. I can watch. I can let my own heart break for her. I can let her pain shatter me to pieces and tear me apart, but I can do nothing to comfort her. I feel guilty. I feel lost. She fucking loves him, and I just tore that love away. I should be glad he's gone, but as Olivia helps her stand and leads her into her bedroom, the sound of her sobs fading as the door clicks closed behind them leaves me regretting my decision to tell her the truth. She's hurting because of me and now I'll have to live with this guilt, and her with this reminder, of how selfish I am until the end of our days.

"Ro, you okay?" Mio comes to my side, squeezing my shoulder once before letting his hand fall away.

"No," I growl, my fingers twitching at my sides as Noras pain becomes my own, the fated bond fully snapping into place now that both of us are aware of the truth.

Her pain will always be my pain and mine will be hers, and godsdamnit does this pain hurt. The stabbing, twisting knife lodged in her heart, the burning of her lungs as she struggles to catch her breath, and the churning in her stomach as she tries not to vomit on the bathroom floor—I feel every ounce of it. I want to go to her. I want to hold her and tell her it'll be alright, but I know it's not what she wants or needs. She needs to be alone. She needs her sister and her best friend, not the stranger who claims to be something she'd never even heard of before today. Not the selfish prick who caused this pain.

"I'll make sure she's okay, Kairos," Hekate stands and gives me a small, pained smile. "You two will be fine. Just remember this is only a mere blip in your long lives together. Try not to let it get to you. She *will* love you again one day." She walks past and I meet her gaze and give her a small tip of my head.

A half-ass bow for a lost queen who has risen. It's the best I can do for the time being.

"I'm going to stay, Mio, but you should head home. I'll call on you if I need anything." I open a portal to our realm, to my home and Nora's home... *Mera's* home... and Mio says nothing as he steps through.

He knows I need the silence. The time to think or feel however the hell I need to so I can get over my brooding. Depending on Nora's mood, this may take a while. Our feelings are so entangled together now that I have no way of knowing when either of us will be okay. I'll stay for tonight. For however long I need to so I can speak to her again.

I'll stay until she asks me to leave.

CHAPTER SEVENTEEN

WATCH HER BURN

KAIROS

Hekate watches me without speaking as I run my hands through my hair and pace back and forth in Nora's kitchen. All I can think about is Nyx and who she will consider the next roadblock in getting what she wants. I'm a big, tattooed, demon slaughtering roadblock, so I know I need to take Nora away soon. Although, I do wish she would come after me. I wouldn't hesitate for a second in jamming my dagger into her cold, icy heart.

Nyx is the only monster all other monsters fear, and I'd love nothing more than to be the one to put her down.

Her power and mind games are a poison that once fully set in slowly eats you alive. I'm not even sure what to say or do at this point.

"What the fuck?" I'm nothing if not simple with my words.

We both stand and stare into oblivion as the clock near the stove *tick, tick, ticks* annoyingly above our heads. Grabbing two empty wine glasses off the counter, I push them toward her. "Do the witch thing where you fill these up with only the best wine. The strongest there is."

She waves a hand above them, making a glowing white liquid appear in the glasses, and I know it's Holy Chardonnay before it even touches my lips. I savor the numbing sensation that ensues shortly after. Better than the Saintly Rosé most celestials enjoy. That wine will have me dancing, singing, and staying awake for days. I'm not much in the mood for dancing today.

"In Vino Veritas," she mutters, clinking her glass against mine.

"What truths, Hekate? I'm not so sure I can handle anymore confessions today." I bring the wine to my lips, gulping it all down quickly. I need to numb the pain, to calm the raging storm rising within me. She just stares at me unblinking, and I sigh heavily. "Fine. Start talking."

She refills my glass then turns on her heels and heads for the living room. I follow behind her and slump into the recliner, clutching the armrest with my free hand as she gracefully takes a seat on the oversized couch. She crosses her legs. "Ask anything you'd like Kairos. I'm an open book. You deserve to know the truth."

I take a small sip of my wine knowing if I drink this one too quickly, I'll be passed out near the waves with seagulls pecking at my wings within the hour. I wave a hand in her direction. "A fucking queen in the flesh. I still can't believe it." I flash her a crooked smile and shake my head. "All it took for you to remember was someone simply speaking your name," I breathe. "Do you think it's the same for the gods? We speak their names and suddenly they just exist again in our minds? They got a message to you, and called themselves gods to Nora's parents, which means they haven't forgotten who they are. I can't understand why they don't want us to remember. What the hell are they hiding from?"

She smiles, her eyes crinkling at the corners as she glances up, pondering my words, and then her smile fades. "What are they hiding from, or what are they hiding *from us*, is what I wonder. I also wonder why I was forgotten. What else we might be forgetting. I remember a whole life where I was known as the Queen of Witchcraft, and yet, I cannot remember any god or goddess from before. Not one. Kings and queens were always known for having close ties with them, and yet, nothing." She taps her temple and then shakes her head. "There are glitches in my memory, in all our memories, and once I remembered who I was it's all I can seem to think about." Her shoulders lift slightly and then she brings her glass to her lips, her gaze far away and lost in a distant time. "Who or what is powerful enough to make us all forget? But *why* is the question that has been driving me mad for a couple of decades. Allas, I cannot find any gods or goddesses who exist in any of the realms, so maybe it'll be another couple of decades before we know the truth. Or centuries, who knows?" She throws herself back against the couch and sighs heavily.

Nyx's hellhounds in the alley told me things I assumed were lies because I don't remember them, but what if Hekate is right and there are many things I've forgotten? Things other than the lost gods who we've all forgotten somehow. No, that monster and I were never friends or anything like it. It was likely just more of her mind games, fucking with me to see if she could get a rise out of me. I can't lie and say Hekate isn't right, though. There are definite glitches in my memory. Not during my time with Mera, but of whatever came before. It's almost like nothing existed until a few years before she was created, but maybe that's just what love does. It makes everything before feel meaningless and unimportant, like nothing was real until love took hold of your life.

"I'm sorry," I tell her, leaning forward and clasping my hands around my glass. "I guess I've always just told myself the truth will reveal itself one day. That when they're ready they'll show themselves again." I gaze into my glass, spinning the liquid within in a small circle. "I always assumed it was because of us. Because of my people. We disgraced them and they needed time away." I clench my jaw and look up at her. "We were never meant to be this way," I whisper, raising my wings up for emphasis.

Hekate's eyes soften and she straightens, setting her glass on the floor near her feet. "No, Kairos. You believe in fate. In destiny. Things happen as they're meant to. You are not less of a celestial than the others because your wings have turned. It's not your fault." She smiles over at me, a kind and compassionate curve of her lips, one that says she takes pity on me.

"No, it's not my fault or my soldiers or Mera's fault. Nyx ruined the peace of the realms. She pitted us against each other. Mera and I led our army into a battle against darkness, and in doing so, this is what we became. We let the darkness seep in. We went against my father's wishes thinking we were protecting the Realm of Light, and the gods, I believe, could not forgive us. There is no one to blame for this other than your Queen of Darkness," I spit, anger coursing through me. "Speaking of that vile creature, how the hell could you ever love her?"

This time she's the one to tip her glass all the way back, sucking down every drop of the glowing substance. It might as well be Novocain. "We did love each other once." She sits her cup down, inhaling deep as she rolls her shoulders. "It was before she was banished from the Realm of Light. Long before your people were cast out." Her eyes soften as they move up to my black wings, the constant reminder of being shunned by the Gods. "She wasn't always bad, Kairos. I let her down. She needed me and I failed her. Sometimes, I don't blame her for being so hellbent on getting vengeance. I would be pissed, too."

I lean forward, resting my elbows on my knees. "You trained Nyx to use her power, if I remember correctly? Then you betrayed her by going to the king and queen and informing them she had fallen a bit too deep into darkness." I swallow, clenching my jaw and averting my gaze. "The punishment which led to the mutilation of her wings and her vengeance against the realms. I couldn't remember before what happened, but ever since you showed your true self to me, I remember everything. You chose trying to save innocent people over your love for her. I can't even begin to imagine how hard that must have been."

She nods, wiping her cheeks with trembling fingers and leaning back against the plushness of the couch. "I didn't know they would hurt her. I just..." she shakes her head, shrugging her shoulders weakly. "I only wanted to save her from herself. She had no idea what harm she put herself in by diving headfirst into darkness. I never should have trained her to wield that kind of power, knowing the kind of darkness she held within her."

Nyx got what she deserved. She turned evil and corrupt as soon as she began playing with dark magic. I feel no pity for her, not after everything she has taken from me and my people. Though, a part of me understands her hatred or desire for revenge. Our wings are sacred.

At least when the celestials fell from grace the gods allowed us to keep our wings.

"You still love her. Despite everything she has done and everything she has taken from us... you're still in love with her." It's not a question. I can see it in her eyes. There's no denying her love for Nyx.

She sniffles, pulling her legs up and wrapping her arms around them. "I do."

"You think you can help her." I stand, pacing in front of the sliding glass doors, the sheer curtains blowing as a breeze whips in through the crack Hekate left open earlier to banish the negative energy.

It felt stuffy in here then and even more so now. The air is stale and hot and suffocating.

She doesn't look at me. She stares past me as if lost in her own thoughts, disconnected from reality. "I do." Her whispered words are hoarse and faint, the feel of her aura as weak as she now looks.

"Hekate, I need you to know that I will rip her heart straight out of her chest the moment I get the chance to." My words are harsh and true, and I'm still pacing, not even looking at her.

I won't sugar coat shit for her just because she loves the bitch. My hatred runs thick and deep. It's much deeper than the abyss that lies below the flaming Pit in the Underworld, the one Nyx and her little monsters crawl out of each morning. My words set her soul on fire.

She jumps up, glaring at me with glowing eyes and her blue power glimmering to life around her. "You will do no such thing," she spits, her hands clenched into small fists at her sides. "You have no idea what you're talking about. No idea what she has been through."

I come to a stand still, lightning dancing at my fingertips and sparking along the outline of thick veins on my forearms as I step toward her. "Whose side are you on, Hekate? There is no grey area when it comes to darkness vs. light. There is no in between. You either stand with the witches and celestials... or fall victim to Nyx and the demons." Lightning flashes across my vision, the anger raging deep within me.

I trusted the witch before, the way she cares for Nora and protects her is admirable, but if my fated mate's life is at risk because of her being here, then it's time for her to leave.

"I am on Nora's side. She comes first no matter what." Her words are stiff and forced, but her eyes soften as her power fades. "Sit down, Kairos. There's more we must discuss. It's important you understand the entire situation." She tips her head toward the chair, her golden crown appearing and reminding me she is not just a witch, but a queen commanding me to take a seat.

Fine. Only because I care for Nora. I don't care about the rest of this shit, not the unrequited love of Hekate and Nyx, and especially not her desire to keep the evil bitch queen alive. I will show no mercy as I turn her to ash one day.

Inhaling deeply, I shut my eyes and force my magic away for the moment. Anger can wait.

"What else is there for me to understand?" My eyes burn into hers and hers burn right back.

"I don't believe Nyx is herself." She leans forward, filling her glass back up with sweet Novocain and bringing it to her lips. "I believe there must be a way to purge the darkness from her soul. With the help of King Ourahnus I've been experimenting on her demons in the Realm of Light. I think whatever force it is that controls them has its claws embedded deep in her as well." She nonchalantly sips her wine.

Her words crash into me like the rising waves climbing higher and higher outside the bay windows from the storm headed our way.

"You can't be serious. My *father* is helping you with this?" I throw my hands up, lightning striking the sand outside the window from the pent-up anger I'm trying to hold in. "There is no darkness plaguing her, Hekate. She *is* darkness."

"Believe what you want, Kairos. Mera comes first, but what if I could save both of them? I have to try. You would do the same for Mera and you can't deny it. You would never let me or anyone else kill her." Smiling, she tips her glass back, emptying it again.

Nyx isn't a victim. She's a predator. She will haunt and torment Mera until there is nothing left to take from her. Nothing left to take from me.

Until the Underworlds sky shines bright.
Until celestial' wings are neither black nor white.
Until the realms are shattered and made anew...
You belong to me, and I belong to you.

The promises we made at our claiming ceremony play over and over in my head, Mera's voice tearful and full of joy before it all came crashing down. Nyx cannot have her. The part of my divine soul which is still full of light wants to tell Hekate I will spare Nyx so long as Mera is safe, but the dark part of my soul... there is no stopping it from burning her realm to the ground with her in it if it means my fated mate lives a long, happy life with me.

I will enjoy watching her burn.

CHAPTER EIGHTEEN

RIVER OF RED

NYX

SEPTEMBER 4TH, 1848

"Why are we here, Hekate? What is so special about this damp, bug filled forest, and this river, anyway?" Stepping over sticks and mud, I grimace as a snake slithers past my foot and disappears beneath the berry bush beside me.

Hekate's white hair falls nearly to her waist, captivating me like freshly fallen snow that sparkles under the light of the moon. Her pale blue eyes are the stars that guide me through the night as she turns and gives me a mischievous smile. She has been talking about bringing me here for weeks, proclaiming this place possesses magic beyond my imagination. It looks like any other forest to me. The greenery is beautiful, yet rather ordinary, but she swears we must travel just a little further. If it weren't for her beauty and charm, I would have gone back home already. I despise hiking.

"Trust me, Nyx. You've seen nothing like this place before." Continuing down the path, her dress follows behind her in the mud, her magic keeping it perfectly pristine. "The gods allow me entrance because I have earned their trust as queen, but they would not be happy with me for bringing you along.

Let's keep this between us." She stops and turns to face me, her golden crown sparkling above her brow.

"Of course. I will never tell. I promise." I step forward, brushing my lips against hers as I press my palms against her lower back and pull her in close. "I enjoy our little secrets very much."

I give her a delighted smile as her eyes begin to glow, the blue light within them growing brighter and brighter until it is impossible to look away. I adore her. Having her as a teacher has been a blessing and a curse. A blessing because she has taught me how to be the best witch I can be, and a curse because if the king and queen were to find out how deeply I care for her, they might make her leave. Being part witch, celestial, and demon at times has its perks, but being blessed by Hekate's presence is the biggest perk of all.

"Close your eyes." Her voice is enchanting and ethereal as it flows around me, gusty currents of wind swirling around us like a gentle, yet powerful cyclone.

As the air turns frigid and the scent of wet earth is replaced by frosted pine, her laughter floats through the wind. The quiet of the forest becomes a gentle whisper in my ear. Beneath my heels the ground is no longer squishy from mud and rain, it is firm yet softer than a cloud.

"Open your eyes, Nyx." Her heated breath against my ear sends chills down my spine.

As I open my eyes, I gasp. This place is much different than the Realm of Light. The greenery is gone, replaced by pearlescent, puffs of glistening leaves that resemble snow, but as I reach out to touch one, it feels nothing like snow. Butterflies zip past, their bright pink and purple wings gleaming like torches in the night. Wildflowers line the path we traveled as far as the eye can see, blanketing the ground in a kaleidoscope of colors that glow like the butterflies' wings. Where darkness and stars once were, the sky illuminates our surroundings, the shimmering fuscia, lavender, and cerulean so bright the stars are hidden within the colors.

"Where are we, Hekate? What is this place? It is the most beautiful place I have ever seen." Stepping forward, I bend and touch the bushes of white and the flowers covering the ground.

Holding my hand out in front of me, I smile as a glowing butterfly lands upon it, fluttering its iridescent wings.

Hekate steps forward and takes my free hand in hers. "Come, Nyx. There is more here to see."

She leads me deeper into the magical forest, the chilly breeze brushing against my skin as if it is alive and urging me forward. Everything here has life within it, like it is all living and breathing with a heartbeat just like mine.

"I never want to leave here," I whisper, gazing up at the tall trees as they sway to and fro, reaching up toward the colorful sky and waving hello.

Hekate comes to a stop, the river in front of us sparkling and shining brilliantly. It mirrors the sky, those same colors swirling and dancing like magic runs through its veins. I could stare at it forever. The way it glistens is like diamonds in the sun, like the stars were plucked right from the sky and placed within it.

"What is it?" My words are hushed, not wanting to disturb the endless peace around us.

"This place is called Mount Othrys and this is the River Oceanus. It's a sacred place the gods visit at times to discover and scribe new prophecies. The water here is said to make dreams come true. It is believed to be a mirror into the future, if you gaze into it long enough."

"I believe it. There is more magic here than I ever thought could exist. It is truly like a dream." Kneeling before the river, I peer into the water as it ripples and swirls in front of me.

"Would you want to see your future? If you could, would you like to see if the dreams in your heart might come true?" She kneels beside me on the plush, white ground. "I've seen my future already, parts of it, anyway. I know you question your place here with the celestials. You believe you belong on the Earth Realm with my coven of witches, but I believe they can offer you much more than we can, Nyx. I believe you're capable of guiding those who may be lost into the light. I believe you possess the power to heal and to give hope to others who have none left." Peering into the river, her eyes shine brighter than the sky. "You must believe in yourself the way I do." As she turns to me, she brushes a strand of hair away from my eyes, securing it behind my ear.

I lean into the warmth of her touch. "I believe in you," I whisper, my heart racing and my breath coming out too fast. "I believe anything is possible as long as I have you with me." My smile is small but genuine as I hold onto so many words that try to claw and rip their way out of my heart and into the emptiness.

I love you, my heart screams. I love you and I hate that I do not know how to admit it. It kills me that I have been so unloved myself that I fear those three words will be my undoing. She is all I have, and love is pain. Love is loss. Love is giving someone the power to hurt you, to leave, to rip your heart out and break you, and I can't... I cannot be anymore broken.

Nodding once, she turns back to the river which now churns faster, the bright hues blurring and becoming one. "Peer into the river and shut off your mind. Let the energy wrap around you like a comforting embrace. Become one with it and allow it to become one with you. It will not harm you. It will free you from any doubts you have of the path you're on. It will assure you that you're exactly where you're meant to be."

She focuses her glowing eyes on the water, raising her hands up and sending it spinning into a whirlpool of colors. The lights shine brighter and though they are hard to look directly into, I force myself to stay focused. I gaze at my reflection, my dark hair cascading to my waist in waves. The deep mahogany of my eyes blends into the pupil, becoming orbs of vast obsidian. My smooth, pale skin peeking out beneath my white robe is flawless in the reflection.

Magic surges, vibrating through the air, the river and forest wrapping around me like a gentle embrace. Warmth courses through my veins, the power latching on and becoming one with my soul. I am it and it is me. We are the same. In my mind's eye, a vision of myself in all white appears, the usual attire here in the celestial realm. Then I'm kneeling on the floor of my bedroom and an old, faded grimoire sits in front of me. Candles lit in a circle around me are the only light. A black cloud appears, like a shadowy figure made of smoke and darkness and nothing else, and it breaks through the protective circle of magic I casted out around me. The shadow grips me by the throat and forces its dark energy into my body, attaching to my mind and corrupting my soul.

My body shakes violently, and I want the vision to end. I try and try to force the wicked power out, but it is useless. The darkness persists no matter how hard I fight it. It latches on, sinking its teeth in and crawling deeper into the crevices of my soul where it cannot be found or contained or controlled by even me, refusing to let me go. The vision ends and a new one begins. I stand before the gods in the hall of justice. Crumbling to my knees, I beg for forgiveness and understanding as tears stream down my hopeless face. Metal clangs and air whips past my ears as a punishment by the gods is served. The sword slices and severs my beautiful white wings, mutilating the most sacred part of me. Fighting this, too, is useless. I scream and beg as the gods abandon me, casting me out for good, the realm opening and spitting me into an abyss of darkness and pain. I'm left with nothing. No one to turn to. Alone for eternity.

The vision of one day being disowned feels too real, like fate announcing itself before suddenly crashing into me. Screaming so loud the ground shakes beneath Hekate and I, the river stills, but even so, it does not release me from its grips. I try but cannot look away. It is not done with me yet. The reflection I gaze down at now is no longer my own. My smile turns wicked and vengeful, far from the innocent celestial witch I am here today. Black horns protrude from my head as snakes slither and crawl around my shoulders as if they too are a part of me.

The water darkens before my eyes, bubbling and steaming as it turns to the crimson color of fresh blood. Hekate gasps beside me but I am frozen in place, unable to blink or breathe or force myself to look away. She roughly grips me by the shoulders and screams my name.

"Look away, Nyx. Please look away!"

Her breathing is labored and panicked as she pushes herself off the ground, still sobbing and watching the red river flow and ripple in front of us. The crimson fades as darkness swirls in, and the water rages angrily as it becomes blacker than the night and blacker than my soul is destined to become. I cannot breathe as I collapse to the ground, my knees trembling too hard to hold myself up. A knot of dread coils in my stomach and I gasp for air as warmth trickles down my face. The once pure white ground is ruined and stained red from the river, stained like my hands will surely someday be. I knew I never belonged here. I felt it the day of my death as I transformed into a celestial and have felt it every day since. There is something devouring any light I have within me, suckling away at anything good I have left. A thing more dark and evil than I have ever felt lurks within, just waiting for the perfect moment to rear its head and strike.

Hekate, still struggling to command the elements with her magic, at last waves her hands and with a blast of her glowing blue magic, the forest and river disappear. My tears continue to fall. The silvery moon casts a brightness across the dark sky that feels wrong, as if the cosmos are smiling down at me and taunting me for facing my haunting, bleak future. The twinkling stars remind me how broken and dark my future will be, how lost I will become buried within darkness. Even as Hekate grips my shoulders and teleports us back to my bedroom, the sobs still rack my fatigued body.

She tucks me into bed and curls up next to me while I stare off into space.

I feel nothing and everything all at once. If that is to be my fate, then there is no escaping it. Fate does not lie. The celestial prophecies do not lie. Life as I knew it is over.

Hekate presses her lips to my forehead and runs her fingers through my tear-soaked hair. "What did the river show you, my love? It matters not. I will protect you with my life." Her gentle whispered words bring the sobs boiling back to the surface, but I force them down deep.

"I feel it, Hekate. I can feel the darkness within me already. I always have," I croak, my voice hoarse from the crying and the blood curdling screams. "There is nothing you or anyone else can do to stop it. I will only disappoint you if you believe there is hope for my soul...or hope for us. Something dark is coming. It is here already."

I cannot face her as I admit the truth. I turn away, knowing I must move on from the one I love, the one who deserves love more than anyone. I must accept that I have lost her already, and that in the end, I will only hurt her.

"Please leave. I no longer want you to teach me magic. I have no interest in being a witch or a celestial. I would like to disappear and never return." Tears glide down my cheeks, but I am numb. I ignore them, pretending they are not real, that none of this is real. She appears in front of me, kneeling and kissing them away.

Her eyes lack their usual luster and radiance. They are red-rimmed, dull and hopeless. She feels it, too, the truth in my words, that there is no hope left for me. She will never admit it out loud. She will pretend until pretending is no longer possible. I am tired of pretending.

"I don't care what darkness may come or what may try to corrupt your soul. I will fight for you until the day I die. I love you, Nyx. I am never leaving your side." Her bottom lip trembles and the air tastes of her tears, the salty aroma making my own vision blur watching her break in front of me.

I do not wipe her tears away. Gods do I want to hold her and kiss her until my head spins and my heart no longer aches and I forget everything that happened today. I let her cry alone instead. I let her heart shatter like glass because I have to. It is the only way this can end.

She must learn that loving me is as painful as every slice and gash from the glass pieces she will now have to force back together.

"I do not love you and I never will." My voice is flat and emotionless as I hold myself together, staring at her blankly. It kills me to lie. To hold in the truth and pretend I am not dying on the inside. "Just... let me go, Hekate.

Find someone who cares and live a happy life without me. I will do the same."

The ice around my heart that I once let shatter for her wraps around the now lifeless thing within my chest once more. Every piece of my soul untethers and shreds to pieces as I attempt to rip the part of me that cares for her out of my body. As I let her go, darkness clings to me tighter, the shadows smothering out my light and wrapping around my mind. I let it. Without her, I am nothing.

She wipes at the silvery streaks on her cheeks as she stands and shakes her head, her eyes full of disbelief. "You're lying. We are meant for each other. We knew it the day we first laid eyes on each other. Our love was written in the stars, Nyx. There is no escaping fate." Her voice is no longer gentle and sweet, it is laced with a rage I have never seen from her before.

Good. I need her to be angry. I want her to hate me. To despise me and want nothing more than to end me to keep our realms from any suffering or chaos I may cause in the future.

Throwing the thick, suffocating covers off me, I sit up, laughing wildly. "Our love was not written in the stars, Hekate! Our love was a lie. Not a moment of it was real. You just wanted it so badly you convinced yourself we were perfect. I wish I had never met you. The darkness within me cannot be fixed or contained no matter how badly you want to believe it can be. Neither you nor the gods can save me. My fate is sealed. There is no hope for me, Hekate. *Leave*," I spit the words at her like venom, letting it permeate the air with my false hatred.

She is hopeless. Her shoulders sag and her eyes darken and even the aura around her is faded and weak. She is giving up. As she glances at the door, she hesitates briefly before turning to leave. A part of me crumbles as I watch her take one step and then another away from me, a part of me that I fear might never be repaired. I feel the loss of her already, the emptiness in my soul that slams into me and leaves me numb. I will never forgive myself for hurting her. I will never heal from letting her leave.

The door creaks open and she doesn't face me as she speaks. "I will never give up on you, Nyx. Even if your darkness reigns down upon the *entire* world, there will always be hope in my heart. One day I will save you."

The moment the door closes and I am alone, I cover my mouth with my trembling hands to stifle the sound of the sobs that rack my body. I cannot imagine facing this darkness alone, but I know pushing her away was for the best. My limbs shake and my rib cage burns as tears force their way out. Once my body relaxes into the heaviness of despair and the well of tears within is dry, numbness takes over completely.

I had to let her go. I must let everyone go. My future is darker than I ever imagined, and I do not want to drag anyone down this dark path with me. The warning written in that grimoire was right, the grimoire I saw myself with in that terrifying vision. I should have never opened that door to darkness. I only wanted to peek inside, to get a glimpse of the power I might learn to wield, the power that surges through my veins. Now I fear I might need that dark power to fight whatever is coming for me. My feet hit the cold, wooden floor as I make my way to my dresser and pull out the grimoire of the dead from the top drawer. Taking a deep breath, I run my fingertips across the material, tracing the stars and the moon and the large owl imprinted on the leather cover. I never told Hekate what I had done, how I had stolen the book from the arsenal of forbidden items in the weapons room, but it called to me. It whispered my name each time I passed by, and I believed it was meant to be mine. She never would have agreed to letting me steal it. She would have feared what the punishment would have been for me."

I sit on the floor and place the grimoire in front of me. I should not open it. I should burn it or tear it apart or toss it from this realm and into any other, but I cannot help but feel like things are playing out exactly how they are meant to. Maybe it is the darkness playing tricks on me. Maybe my mind is too far gone to see how catastrophic this might be. But I cannot let it win. While I can still fight it, I must try.

Closing my eyes and praying to the gods to save me, I slowly open the book. With a quick flick of my wrist, the black candles on my alter and dresser flash to life. I must train my mind to fight against this darkness that is coming for me. I can win. There is a small part of me that believes there may be hope, but this is a battle I must fight on my own. I will become darker. Crueler. More wicked and vile than it can be prepared for, and only then will I turn it to nothing.

I am Nyx. I am night and starlight and darkness entwined, and this truth is what will keep the shadows from suffocating me.

Darkness cannot have me. Not if I become the darkness instead.

CHAPTER NINETEEN
YOU ARE NOT ALONE

NORA

The sunlight trickles in through the curtains, so I clamp my eyes closed, wishing today they hadn't opened at all. Thoughts of crimson eyes, black blood and glowing daggers pierce through the foggy haze of the night before. I should be waking up with Ere wrapped around me, his warm arms keeping me safe. Instead, my sister and best friend are taking up most of the bed and leaving me with nothing to keep me warm, not even my thin top sheet.

I miss him. The way he smells in the morning and the way his lips curve up the moment our eyes meet. I roll onto my side and grab my phone off the nightstand. No missed calls. Not one text from him. He always texts me good morning when he's away. God, what the hell am I supposed to do now? He keeps me together when I'm on the verge of falling apart and reminds me that if I do, it'll be okay. My fingers hover over the keyboard as I pull up our texts and then slowly I type the only thing I can think of to say.

Please just tell me you're okay. I miss you.

I hit the side button and let the screen die, putting my phone face down on my nightstand. I'm sure I'll hear from him soon. We have to be okay. I refuse to lose another person I love.

The smell of cinnamon, warm maple syrup and fresh bacon hits me and my stomach growls. After all the craziness that happened last night and never having a chance to eat, I'm starving.

"Who is cooking breakfast so early? It smells delicious." Olivia inhales deep and smiles, then meets my gaze and sadness flashes behind her glossy eyes. "Morning, sis. You okay?" She sits up and pushes the covers down past her feet, nudging Hekate awake.

Hekate groans dramatically and tugs the blanket over her head. "That would be Kairos. He wants to talk to you this morning, Nor. I told him Liv and I would make ourselves busy." She tosses the blanket off and stands, her icy hair still wavy and perfect.

"Hekate, you're making the rest of us look bad. We just woke up and we drank a shit ton of alcohol last night. Liv and I look like complete shit, and you," I wave my hands in her direction, grimacing as I do. "You always look so god damn perfect. It's really not fair."

Olivia smacks me in the head with one of my feathery, plush pillows, and I nearly sway right out of bed. Hekate and her both fall into fits of laughter immediately after. "Speak for yourself, Nor. Besides, she's a witch and a queen. I bet she uses her power to stay this beautiful. She's hundreds of years old. An old crone probably lives under all that magic." My sister dodges and rolls out of bed as Hekate's mouth pops open and she attempts to smack her dead in the face with a pillow.

We laugh, but it doesn't last long. Once we're all out of bed and facing the reality of the day, the momentary joy quickly fades.

"Have you heard from Ere?" Liv stands by my side as I rummage through my dresser and pull out a pair of black leggings and a faded grey band t-shirt.

I shake my head. "Nope. I texted him when I woke up, but..." I shrug, having nothing else to say.

Olivia lays her head against mine and wraps both arms around my shoulders. "It'll all work itself out. Everything Hekate and Kairos told you is insane. I'm having a hard time accepting it all myself, so I can't imagine how you're feeling. I'm sorry I didn't believe you before. About mom and dad, I mean. I should have believed you." Sighing, she lifts her head to look at me. "I'm here if you need to talk, okay?"

I swallow thickly, taking a deep breath as I loop my arm around her waist.

"Thank you," I smile up at her, searching her too calm eyes. "Does any of this scare you as much as it does me?"

She huffs a laugh, her eyes widening. "It scares the shit out of me, Nor. Not the magic or the immortals or even the monsters that apparently haunt the island, just the thought of something happening to you is what scares me." Her arms drop to her sides, and her bright blue eyes glisten. "All we can do is believe everything will be okay." She shrugs, forcing a smile and turning away.

Hekate pushes the bathroom door open and looks at me and then my sister. "Bromios is waiting for us, Liv. I finally accepted his invitation to have breakfast together after fifty times of being asked, but to his shock and disappointment, I'll be bringing you along." She smiles wide and proud, clasping her hands behind her back and swaying side to side, brimming with excitement.

Olivia shakes her head but laughs. "That's cruel. Hilarious, but cruel. This will one hundred percent ruin his day, and possibly destroy his confidence," she says, opening the bedroom door and stepping into the hall.

Hekate winks at her and follows close at her heels. "I'm counting on that, friend. I truly hope you're right."

Their laughter echoes down the hall, and as much as I love to see them enjoying themselves the best they can, I close the door and press my back against it. Gazing off into nothing, I force deep breaths in and out of my lungs, slowly counting to ten. What would Dr. Cooper say now if he knew of my current situation? If I told him a dark queen had plagued my mind and was responsible for all the dark thoughts and suicide attempts this past year?

I laugh to myself imagining the way he'd look at me, his thick eyebrows slanting in concern, his black glasses falling down his nose as he leans forward to tell me I've gone mad. Shaking the thoughts away, I quickly clean up in the bathroom and change, brushing my teeth vigorously to get the taste of tequila from my tongue.

I put on a brave face and open my bedroom door, holding my head high as I scan the hall and then the living room for any winged immortals. I walk past the kitchen to my right, and no one is there. Then I check Olivia's room and Hekate and her are already gone. I shut her door and then turn around slowly, slamming into something large and hard in the process. My eyes drift up, hesitant and slow, and bright green eyes meet mine. That crooked smile sends my treacherous little heart fluttering.

"H-Hi." My stuttering only makes his smile grow wider, the crooked edges curving into a full-on grin.

"Good morning, princess," he replies, bowing his head and placing the sparkly pink crown on my head from the night before.

Fuck. He's hot *and* funny? If it were any other time and I hadn't just had my heart crushed to pieces, I'd say I'm done for. But I'm not in the mood.

"Ha-ha. Very funny." I roll my eyes, pressing my palms against his chest and pushing past him to inspect what's happening in my kitchen. "You made all of this for me?" I glance his way and his deliberate, slow steps are like that of an animal stalking its prey.

Fuck. I don't hate it. The hairs on the back of my neck stand on end as he approaches behind me.

His warm breath tickles my ear. "Who said I made you breakfast, princess? This is all for me."

There are piles of pancakes, omelets, and bacon on plates along the counter, and bowls of fruit piled so high they're nearly toppling over. I shake my head and move past him, leaning against the island as I watch him flip the bubbly pancake in the pan. He glances over his shoulder to wink in my direction, then faces me fully and leans against the marble counter.

"You had a rough night. I wanted to do something nice, that's all." He shrugs, his knuckles turning white as he grips the counter behind him.

"Where are your wings?"

"Your sister just couldn't resist trying to touch them, so I glamoured them." He leans forward and whispers, "I think she likes me."

I roll my eyes. "She is obsessed with magical, weird things, so that tracks." I look him up and down and give him a teasing smile.

"How are you feeling about all of this, Nora?" His eyes pierce mine. "Knowing you are to be like me one day? You'll have wings of your own, though mine are nothing compared to yours. Yours will be amazing," he breathes, his smile returning.

How do I *feel*? Confused. Terrified. So absolutely lost that I don't know where to begin with all the questions I have for him. It's unbelievable. A part of me wonders if I've fully lost my mind and spiraled into a long-term hallucination. How can I be a divine, powerful being with my depression and pain and darkness?

"I'm not sure how I feel. It's a lot to take in." I push off the counter and straighten, but my body sways side to side. My vision blurs and my head spins as dizziness crashes into me.

Weightlessness hits me and I feel myself beginning to fall. Kairos disappears and then reappears by my side, wrapping a steady arm around my waist as he guides me to my favorite plush couch. He sits right next to me, his face only inches away. His arm supports my back as he waits for me to recover.

"That was unbelievable. You disappeared into thin air like you were never even there. How did you..."

"If you stick around long enough, you'll see many more unbelievable things. There is so much magic in the world. So much beauty you've yet to uncover. You have more magic and light within you than you can imagine. I am nothing compared to what you will be. You, Nora, are destined to bring an end to darkness. You'll be the savior of the realms." His blonde locks of hair cascade over his eyes, and I fight the urge to reach out and brush them away.

Beauty like his should never be hidden.

"That's a lot to ask from someone who has no power," I breathe, smiling despite the heaviness of his words.

Reaching out, he tucks a loose strand of hair behind my ear. "There's no need to worry yourself over it now."

I tilt my head to the side, my eyes drifting up and down his body. "If what you told me is true, that you are my..."

"Fated mate?" He smiles, taking a seat on the coffee table right across from me. "It is true."

I nod. I can't bring myself to say it or admit it might be true, but if that type of connection exists in the world, Kairos wouldn't be the worst person to be fated for. I can allow myself to admit that much.

"Why can't I remember you? A part of me feels like I should remember something. And what if my memories never return? Then you're just left without a fated mate?" I whisper, searching his face, his eyes, his lips for any miniscule reminder of the past.

Leaning his elbows on his knees, he clasps his hands together and stares only at them. "Not only me. You, too, Nora." His eyes meet mine, electricity sparking and flashing within them. "If you never remember then it isn't only me who is cheated out of the best love of my life, it will be you, too. We are finding that amulet. We believe Nyx stole it from your mother, but one way or another, we're getting it back. And then, you will remember me and if I have any say in it, she will be dead."

I can't speak or blink or look away as he stands and makes his way to the kitchen. I'm a mess. My heart beats so fast, out of fear or excitement, I'm not sure. It's dying to remember him. I am, too.

"Let's eat. You need to gather your strength." He moves around my kitchen like he owns the place, and I settle into the cushions to quietly observe.

All of this is crazy. There are so many questions spinning endlessly in my head, but all I can focus on is him. The way he moves so gracefully, his black leather such a contrast to my white kitchen. How his eyes linger on my face as he delicately places pancakes on plates. No matter what he does, his eyes always return to me. This man, this immortal celestial being, has saved me. He comes to the rescue again and again, as if my death means his own heart might stop beating. There's so much light around Kairos, the kind that makes me feel like I have light within me, too. Like we all do.

He sets two plates full of food and coffee that smells divine on the table and sits in the recliner across from me. His lips twitch at the edges as he notices my eyes tracking his every move. "Please, eat," he says, gesturing to my plate.

"Why do I need to gather my strength?" I take a bite of bacon then wrap my hands around my warm mug and take a sip, still watching him the whole time.

"Because we are leaving." Cutting into his pancake he doesn't look up.

"Leaving to go where? What if I don't want to? Will you force me leave?"

"You're no longer safe here. I won't force you to do anything, but I think you should come home." Pausing with his fork and knife in his hands, he glances up, his wings finally appearing for emphasis. "To my realm. To *your* realm."

"What the hell does that mean? *My* realm. *This* is my home, Kairos." I set my cup down, glaring at him as he refuses to meet my gaze.

"I would have no realm if it weren't for you. I would have nothing. It is most certainly *your* realm." His wings ruffle behind his back as he glances down at my plate. "Maybe you'll be a bit less grumpy after you eat. It certainly used to do the trick." His crooked, taunting smile is followed by him shoving another bite of pancakes into his mouth.

I shake my head, forcing bites of food into my mouth and choosing to take the high road by pretending he isn't here instead of arguing. It's not him I'm upset with, it's the situation at hand, but it's hard. I don't want to leave Olivia or Hekate. Ere isn't speaking to me yet, but I don't want to leave him, either. Maybe he just needs time. I don't want to be alone in a whole new realm.

Kairos' fork clangs against his plate, and then I feel a gentle thrum of light and warmth wrapping around me. "I know you're scared, Nora. It's okay. But you are not in this alone." He leans his elbows on his knees as I meet his gaze. "I'm with you and I'm not going anywhere."

"How do you always know what I'm feeling? It's creepy," I groan, crossing my legs and leaning away.

Something like pain flashes within his eyes and then he's running his hands through his hair nervously. "As your guardian I could sense what you were feeling, but once a fated bond snaps into place, it's different." He sighs heavily. "I feel your fear now. Your pain. Your grief. You're no longer alone in any of it. When you remember what I am to you, you won't be able to ignore my feelings either. It does feel a bit like reading each other's minds." His smile is forced.

"When exactly did it snap into place?"

"Last night. When I told you the truth. That was all it took for fate to take the reins. It's no longer just a possibility, it's our destiny. It *will* happen." There's a truth in his eyes that I can't ignore and a hope in his words he can't hide.

He felt it all then as my boyfriend left and ripped my heart in two. Every jab of pain, every teardrop, and every gut-wrenching pang of loss as I fell apart in my bedroom. I keep quiet. I don't want to crush his building hope, not without knowing the truth myself. For all I know he's right and we really are fated to be. At this point, nothing would shock me.

"Kairos, Nyx will find me wherever I go. I won't be safe anywhere, and neither will you if you keep protecting me." I push my plate away and lean back into the plushness of the couch.

Shaking his head, there's a dangerous glint in his eyes that makes my heart lurch. "The moment she comes anywhere near you, Nora, will be the day she regrets every decision leading up to it. I will be there ready and waiting to end her pathetic life. You have no reason to be afraid. In fact, she should be the one trembling in fear." His smile is wicked and dark, all light around him drifting away.

Life as I knew it before is over. Everything I know about the world I live in is a lie. He's right, I *am* scared. Terrified actually. I'm scared about my future and of him and I'm scared that the darkness creeping around in my mind will take over completely. *Her* darkness. I'm terrified I'll lose myself and never find my way back.

Maybe I need an escape. If I run so far away that I can't hear Nyx's whispers in my mind, too far for her dark power to reach me, maybe I can feel like myself again. The girl who smiled and laughed without guilt eating away at her mind for being alive while her parents are gone. The girl who was free of darkness and pain. Kairos said I'm meant to bring an end to darkness, to be a savior of the realms, but how can I save anyone when I can't even save myself?

I just want to be free.

The air is heavy, like I'm submerged under water and can't take a breath. I fear the moment I'll have to face Nyx; the moment everyone realizes I can't fight the darkness that's entangled with my soul. She'll win this game like she did before. Deep down in my core I can already feel it.

She will fucking win.

"I can't do this. I can't face any of this yet, I just can't." I stand and rush toward my bedroom, but his arms slip around my waist and turn me to face him.

I'm frozen in silence as waves of green and blue rise and fall, hypnotizing me in his arms. I can't look away. I can't run or hide no matter how badly my mind begs me to escape him. In this moment, I don't want to. Some hidden piece of my soul doesn't want to.

"I promise to keep you safe. I won't let her hurt you. Just *please*… trust me."

My heart melts and my thoughts scramble to find the right words. "What if I can't fight the darkness? What if I disappoint everyone? I'm afraid it's too late for me." I swallow back the tears, refusing to let him see how weak and lost I truly am.

No one can see. I have to pretend to be strong until I believe it myself. Until everyone else believes it, too. I'm fine.

Taking my hand in his, he brings my palm to his chest and holds it there. The steady thumping of his heart calms my own. "Feel how my heart beats for you. Feel it with everything inside of you, that I'm just as afraid as you are. It's okay to be scared. Let's be scared together. Let's fight this together the way we always have." His gentle words caress my soul, the sensation like licking a wound I didn't realize even existed.

He's afraid? This man, with his multiple swords and daggers — who's capable of taking down whole ass demons — is afraid?

"What are you afraid of?"

"Everything. Losing you again. Losing my people and my home. I'm scared of you refusing to let me protect you when it's the only thing I want to do." His eyes snap closed and he shakes his head.

He's scared of Nyx taking me away from him again, too. She killed me before. He lost me. He has had to live with that pain for a century and to live through it again would be torture. God, no wonder he's so persistent on taking me away. I would be, too. Hiding out in his realm might be good for me. Maybe I'll remember something, anything, that could connect me to my past... to *him*. If we loved each other once and are fated to be, then he deserves for me to at least be open to the possibility. I want to go. I need to know everything.

"I'd like to see your home. I want to see what it is you're so afraid of losing." I smile as he lowers my hand from his chest, his eyes flashing with excitement.

Standing here with Kairos, suddenly I'm not ready to die. Those dark thoughts fade away. I want to live. Not only do I want to live, but I want to thrive, and I want to fight until my lungs burst and my heart gives out.

Death cannot take me — not if I take it first.

"*Our* home, Nora." He smiles, wide and untamed, and my breath hitches.

I should protest his words, tell him it's not my home and never will be, but I can't. Seeing his power, his *happiness,* radiate around us in glimmering white speckles of light makes me happy *for* him. Even if I never love this man, there's something that tells me he has suffered more than he's willing to show, and for that alone he deserves to be happy.

I smile up at him. "Your magic is beautiful. It soothes my worries. I feel safe with you."

"Don't let the celestial light fool you." He leans in closer. "My power is a rageful beast." His lips quirk up as I tip my head back and laugh. "Thank you for trusting me." Brushing his fingertips along my cheekbone, he tucks loose locks of hair behind my ears then wraps his hand around mine and leads me to my bedroom. "There's something you should probably do before we leave."

As he comes to a stop at the foot of my bed, he waves a hand and celestial light glimmers across the covers. My mouth pops open and my eyes widen in surprise as I take in what's laid out before me. Black fighting leathers appear like the ones he's wearing now. They have the intricate buttons and zippers and the insane amount of loops for holding weapons, just like his. But this set has a long lacey skirt that fans out from the back of the pants, giving it a girly flair. It's the most beautiful outfit I've ever seen. I run my hands across the butter smooth material and something about it feels right. Like it was made just for me. I look up at Kairos and joy lights up his face, and something about that also feels right.

"Thank you," I whisper, unable to take my eyes off him. "Is this what I used to wear? Is this hers? *Mine*?" Thinking about who I might have been in a past life, how I dressed and acted and felt, sends a wave of exhilaration spiraling through me, like a connection to my past has been made. It's not much, but it's enough for now.

I feel her within me. I feel...*me*.

"It came straight from your closet and there are many more where that came from." Perched on the edge of my bed, he trails his fingertips across the material. He scoops the clothes up into his arms and smiles. "After you get dressed, we'll leave if you're ready." Shifting his attention to the bathroom in the corner of the room, he pushes the clothes into my arms.

"I'll call Hekate and Olivia so they can meet us here, and then I'm ready. I want to see them before we leave. Liv is going to be so jealous." I laugh, turning and heading toward the dim light filtering in from the light above the bathroom sink.

I feel stronger with Kairos. I feel brave and powerful with him close by. I think it's the way he believes in me, like he sees a light within my soul that lies dormant and waiting to spark to life.

Stopping as I push the bathroom door open, I glance at him over my shoulder, not meeting his eyes. "Please don't leave. I don't trust myself being alone with everything that's happened."

I hate admitting that I'm vulnerable or that I'm scared of Nyx's power taking over my thoughts again, but I am. Right now, I don't feel her darkness clinging to me the way it did the night on the bridge or when I went for a swim, for the moment I feel like I've escaped its clutches. But I know it's here, watching and waiting. It always is.

He shifts on the bed, his wings peeking out from behind him. He doesn't even blink. He doesn't hesitate or look away. He says what's in his heart, always. "I've waited a century to be by your side again. I'd stay right here forever if you asked me to. I'm not going anywhere. I'm here." His white light shimmers my way, and I smile as his power nearly drowns me in a colossal amount of positivity and hope.

"Thank you, Kairos."

For now, I'll trust his judgement to leave. I'll let my safety be a priority even though I'd rather we fight to get my memories back. He wants me to remember him. If he thought we stood a chance right now, I'm positive he'd do whatever it would take to make it happen. I'm grateful he's willing to do what he believes is best for me, even if I don't agree. Having him near is like seeing the world for the first time with my eyes truly open.

With Kairos near, I can't imagine a battle darkness will win, not when only light exists around him.

CHAPTER TWENTY

REALM OF DARKNESS

KAIROS

Gods save me. She'll be the reason for my untimely death. It's her beauty that will have my heart giving out, stuck frozen and unable to beat. My gods, it hurts. To touch her without being able to drown her in my love, and to gaze into those sapphire orbs of light and feel no love in return...how the hell am I going to keep surviving without her remembering me? I've spent a century trying not to forget a single moment of the time we spent together. Like the nights we spent falling in love under the twinkle of the stars, or the moment fate crashed into us and we made love beneath those stars for the first time. The night she first told me she loved me was the best night of my entire existence.

She is my flame within the darkness, and without her, light for me has ceased to exist. She is my *reason*—for breathing—for fighting against darkness—my entire reason for living.

Her. My everything.

"Take my hand." I pin my gaze to the atrocious pink walls of her bedroom, needing a distraction from how tempting she looks in her leather fighting gear. As much as I want to, it's not polite to stare. "Are you ready?"

She smiles and places her tiny hand in mine, and there is not an ounce of fear in her eyes when she looks at me. Stepping toward me, for the first time since I started guarding her, I sense no fear in her heart either. Knowing she feels safe with me makes me want nothing more than to lay my own life on the line. I'd rather die than have to live through watching her be ripped away from me again.

"I'm ready. I trust you. I know you'll keep me safe. You've proven yourself a time or two already." Pulling our interlocked fingers into her chest, she whispers, "I know you told me I should close my eyes, but I don't want to. I want to see everything."

The intense trust in her eyes and the way her heart races every time she looks at me fucking kills me. She doesn't look away and it kills me to not be able to do a thing about it. To not be able to hold her against my chest and bury her so deeply within it that she can never again be taken from me. I want to run my fingers through her hair and bring her lips to mine, to let her feel the fire and electricity that ignites every time our mouths meet. Nothing has changed. She is still mine and I am hers whether she believes it yet or not. She will. She has to. No one can escape fate. In the end it will be us who fulfil the divine prophecy of putting an end to darkness.

Together, we will.

Flashing the crooked smile I've sensed drives her crazy, I place my palm out in front of us and the portal opens. The swirls of black with shimmering blue and purple invite us home. Each time I pass through the portal, it's like stepping through a radiant cloud made of starlight, but tonight I don't notice. Not when I have the brightest star of them all standing next to me. She steps in closer, resting her head on my shoulder and she squeals, her eyebrows lifting as she squeezes my hand tighter. We step through the glowing lights together and the portal closes, engulfing us in a flash of bright white light.

She isn't scared of any of it, not with me by her side. The wind howls and whips past, the colors fading as the portal gently drops us into the Realm of Darkness. Her explosive laughter echoes into the vastness of the empty field near my house and seeing her this way is contagious. I'm not sure why exactly we're laughing, but I laugh, too. My ribs ache from laughing so hard, but seeing the joy flood through her, a joy I haven't seen her experience in so long, is thrilling. We used to laugh together like this often before she was taken from me. The memory of all I've lost slices through my heart and soul, but I push it away. I fight against the pain. I will not lose her again.

"This is amazing, Kairos," she breathes, releasing my hand as she spins in slow circles and then stops and gasps at the towering points and sharp lines of the grey washed city below. "This isn't at all how I imagined the celestial realm would be. It's so dark and gloomy." She frowns for a moment and then her lips curve up. "But god is it beautiful."

Gentle, kind eyes glance my way, eyes that drift up and down my body and stop at each weapon strapped to my back and thighs. She tenses but her energy doesn't radiate fear. I sense that she feels safer here with me than she does anywhere else or with anyone else, and a part of her is angry with herself for feeling that way, because of *him*. Ere. I wonder how long it'll take for her to no longer miss him, and for me to no longer be stuck feeling the pain of it alongside her. Though, I am thankful for this pain. Her pain means she's alive. That she's here with me again. I'll suffer every day for the rest of my life if it means her heart is beating.

"I've learned to appreciate it. I didn't always," I admit, stepping up to the edge of the sloping hill, the grass slick beneath my boots.

Gazing out at the city skyline, I admire the sunset as it slowly settles in. From up here the whole place looks like it could have been plucked right out of one of Nora's beloved gothic fairytales. The dark, thick clouds never allow us any direct sunlight, but at least we do have night and day. The Underworld is a constant pitch-black abyss whereas The Realm of Light was at times too blinding. The Realm of Darkness is somewhere in between, the perfect balance that offers rest for my mind and my eyes.

She steps up beside me and gazes out at the city. "Why didn't you appreciate it before? What changed?"

"My whole world changed in an instant being sent here. Life wasn't always like this. I was surrounded by light. Surrounded by sun and beauty." I sigh. "It was all taken from us in one last battle with Nyx and her demons. But *you*—your power gave us this place to call home when the gods banished us from the Realm of Light." I stretch out my fingers before tightening them into fists, forcing the anger away. "You gave us this last gift as you died in my arms. It took a while to get there, but eventually I realized that anything touched or created by your hands deserves to be cherished. Until now it was all I had to remember you by. It became this constant, welcome reminder that you were real. That *we* were." I don't look at her as I smile, but I feel her watching me, feel the energy within her ignite as she catches that smile, wishing she could remember me.

She doesn't need to admit that she feels that way. She wouldn't admit it even if I asked her, I'm sure of it, but she can't hide the truth, that she feels *something* for me. A part of her does. I'm still angry and bitter about the war, and over the anguish I felt for a century after she was taken from me, but I reign it all in for her. Now is not the time for anger. All that matters is she learns the history of our people and how we've managed to heal since she gave us this beautiful gift, one not even she or the gods were aware she possessed the power to give. Not until the moment her anger surged, her flames raged, and the sky cracked open as we were cast down to Earth. It is a power that I still don't fully understand, but from what I've seen, it's not one any of us want Nyx to have her clawed fingers wrapped around. When she saw Nora's power rise that day it only made her want her more.

And oh, how the entire world would suffer if the demon queen were to possess or control such a power.

"You have hope for me. You believe I'll be free of her darkness one day. What do your people believe?" Red streaks glisten in my peripheral vision as she moves in closer, her hair blowing wildly in the breeze.

Adjusting my wings and considering her words, I notice her fidgeting nervously with the golden bands on her fingers. She's not as relaxed or as fearless as she's pretending to be. Even being here now, she's still nervous, understandably. Though, she is handling it much better than I would. I wouldn't believe a single word anyone said until I remembered the truth for myself. Hopefully it won't be much longer before the amulet is returned to Nora safe and sound, but I fear Nyx won't give it over easily, if at all. She stole it for a reason. Getting it back is going to be hell, which is why she's here now. Nyx expects us to come after it, to come after her, so we did the thing she'd least expect me to do. We ran. I hate it but she's safe and for now, it's the only thing that matters.

Taking a seat in the damp grass, I shrug out of my leather jacket and toss it down next to me. I meet her eyes and then offer my hand to help her sit. Her half-smile is followed by a vibrant bloom of pink spreading across her cheeks as she clutches my palm. She keeps her eyes on me, even as she sways and stumbles and I grip her waist, slowly lowering her to the ground next to me. We sit shoulder to shoulder, her looking at me with a dazed smile, and me looking at her like she's the only thing that matters, just as hundreds of pairs of wings begin to thunder overhead. Her eyes widen as she tips her head back to watch the celestials fly past, and a shocked giggle escapes her lips.

I gaze up at them, the warmth of her shoulder pressed into me, until I can't stand not looking at her any longer. I fear she'll vanish for another hundred years if I look away for too long. "They believe in you the way I do, Nora. Not one of them has ever given up hope that you will return and shine light back into the world."

She looks at me for a moment, her eyes softening as they meet mine, then she leans back on her hands and kicks her legs out in front of her, enjoying the show above us. "Where are they going? God, they're beautiful." Her words are a breathless whisper that grips my heart and brings my eyes straight back to her.

"So beautiful," I whisper, not bothering to avert my gaze as she catches me watching her and not my people, instead smiling in confirmation as realization flashes in her eyes. "When the sun goes down everyone goes home. We never lived in darkness before. There was only light. Ever since that light was taken, people feel uneasy staying out past sunset. I guess it feels wrong in a way, to imagine thriving in darkness. It's what we're taught to fear more than anything."

"They're terrified of their own home. How sad." She looks back up and then closes her eyes, crossing one ankle over the other as the celestials make their way out of the city. "But you aren't afraid, Kairos?" Her chest slowly rises and falls, her shoulders relaxed and unbothered though her heart suddenly races.

I shake my head but my breath catches because denying that I'm afraid is a godsdamned lie. I might not fear darkness the same way the other celestials do, but I'm terrified of it ripping us apart again. Mostly, I fear only what it might do to her.

"I live and breathe to fight darkness. To extinguish it not only here, but everywhere." I run a hand through my hair to push the tousled waves out of my eyes, but the wind sweeps it right back into my face. "I am the son of the rulers of the celestial realms. The commander of the Dark Legion of Warriors. For my realm, I've had to learn to be strong. To show no fear. To be brave no matter what." Gazing down at the city streets, I focus on my soldiers as they change shifts, some of them preparing for a long night ahead of guarding our people. "If I show fear, the whole realm will. If I panic, so will they. I have no choice but to control my emotions and lock my feelings away," I admit as the celestial light from the streetlamps below flicker on. "Pain and fear won't keep a realm from crumbling. Only strength and courage will."

She turns toward me, her sapphire eyes locking with mine and refusing to let me go. "Kairos, no one should have to always pretend to be strong and fearless. It's okay to be scared. I'm sure they would understand if you told them you were. That's a lot of pressure you put on yourself to be perfect, but it's okay to not be."

I can't admit the truth, how every moment is tainted by my fear of what her future might hold.

I huff a laugh, shaking my head. "I am far from perfect, Nora. I spiraled after the war. When you died, I…" Pulling my knees up, I lean my elbows across them, closing my eyes and forcing the pain down deep. "I nearly destroyed cities and realms along with the trust of the Realm of Light because my power raged from all the anger and fear I let consume me. I almost ruined everything. I chose to never let fear rule me again."

She straightens and her eyebrows slant, her energy swirling with too many emotions to decipher. "What happened after the war with Nyx? Why did I need to create this realm for you? Why can't everyone just live together in peace?"

I hate talking about this. Thinking about these impossible things. Peace. Unity. It was the reason she was created, a piece of each realm to unite them all, and it all royally went to shit as soon as Nyx set her sights on her power. There's no hope for unity now, not after what The Queen of The Underworld has done.

"No one truly knows what happened that day. Only that as we fell to Earth, the light faded from our wings." Clenching my jaw, I pull myself to my feet, helping her up with me. "All I know for sure is the gods turned their backs on us that day and then abandoned us entirely. We can't even remember their names now. It's as if they never even existed. Some believe it was destiny, something that was always bound to happen." I stand and turn my back to the city, then pause, glancing back at her. "I believe it was Nyx who did this to us."

She shakes her head as she rises and then comes to my side. "Nyx? How could she do that? She isn't a god. And what would be the purpose of changing your wings?"

I shrug weakly. "We wanted unity more than anything. We wanted the war with darkness to end. She saw it as an opportunity to divide us." I reach for her hand, and she comes to me, slipping her silky palm into mine. "I believe as her dark power surged that day on the battlefield, it corrupted us. How much it damaged us, I'm unsure of, but I felt something change within myself as darkness wrapped around me. The icy numbness crawled along my skin, and the stench of evil forced its way into my soul, and there was nothing I could do to stop it. That moment is when the Gods cast us out of the Realm of Light. We could never go home. She broke us. Maybe even more than we know."

Her fingers twitch, a tremor running through her as she grips my hand tighter. "That's how I felt the night on the bridge. And in the lake, I felt it all, too. The darkness, the cold touch of numbness, the stench of evil—oh my god. I'm so sorry if it's true, that Nyx did this to you. To your people. All because of me. Because of her hunger for my power."

Her guilt kills me. My bleeding heart cries out for her to understand that it was all worth it, because even if my soul wound up withered and tormented, if it had been lost to eternal darkness or shot into oblivion instead, at least it would have died protecting her. It would have still been worth it.

I can't tell her that, though, the intensity of that truth too much to admit yet without her remembering how deep and passionate our love was, so I simply smile and send waves of warm light and comfort into her heart. "None of this is your fault. The Dark Legion and I *chose* to protect you. All of it was *for you*, Nora, not *because of you*."

Tucking wind tossed strands of hair behind her ears, she smiles and then chews on her bottom lip. "So, what do we do now? Now that I'm here and safe from Nyx for the time being, what's the plan?" Her eyes roam over the city, admiring the dreary but beautiful landscape now engulfed by darkness and starlight.

"For now," I tell her, stepping closer and brushing her hair behind her shoulders. "All you need to worry about is getting rest."

"And where exactly will we be resting?" She stiffens.

"My home." Smiling, I wrap my arms around her waist and she gasps as I pull her against me.

It could be our home one day. If we find a way out of this mess and a way for her to remember me, we could spend countless happy centuries in it together. I would never want to leave.

"What are you doing?" Her eyes glimmer with nervous excitement as they linger on my lips.

"It's easier to fly." Spreading my wings out wide, I crouch and prepare to take flight. "We don't have vehicles here because we—"

"Have wings, right." She nods, taking in the height of the sprawling hills surrounding us and the city far below. I can only assume she's imagining falling to her death. "I won't let fear rule me." Taking a deep breath, she pins her eyes to me. “I’m not afraid. Not with you.” She wraps her arms around me and then rests her head on my chest. “Is this okay?”

Her warmth encases me in a way that lets me pretend for a moment she’s mine, and I am whole again at last. I’ve missed this. Gods, I’ve missed her.

“This is perfect,” I whisper, savoring the feel of her against me. “As long as you feel safe.”

She doesn’t lift her head, but she squeezes me even tighter. “I would feel safer if you carried me. Can you, please?”

Her heartbeat is as wild and erratic as mine, hers from mostly fear, and mine from the thrill of holding my long-lost love again. Swooping her up, I gently cradle her in my arms, and she smiles and relaxes against me.

“Better?” I ask nervously, afraid I’ve gone too far.

“Yes. Better,” she whispers, burying her face in my shoulder, her palms pressed firmly against my back.

I want nothing more than for Nora to feel safe with me but holding her now isn’t only about her. It’s about my safety, too. Leaping into the air, the thunderous clap of my wings is nothing compared to the roar of my heart that at last feels safe again. I have hope that we’ll get her memories back to her and hope that she will love me. In this moment, I want to scream into the heavens so the whole world can hear how my love for her has never and will never die.

I will always have hope for her and I.

CHAPTER TWENTY-ONE

CHASING HAPPINESS

NORA

Light spills through the crack under the door as Kairos showers, and I can't help but stare. I'm not sure what the hell I'm even watching for. The door is made of solid marble, black with intricate lines of gold, but I can't help but wish it was made only of glass. To see him drenched in water and foamy bubbles, to get just a glimpse of his slick skin and the thick muscles beneath every tattoo covering his arms and chest would be a dream. I know I shouldn't think this way. I know this, and yet still, I can't deny my attraction to him. I've felt it since the night I officially met him at the club. There's something about his soul that refuses to let me pretend I feel nothing. I try and fail. I blame it on the fact that I'm being haunted and possessed and need a distraction from the chaos that is my life. It has to be that.

Kairos gave me a thorough tour of his home as soon as we got here. The black marble covers every surface, and though the gold accents are stunning, the coved ceilings that form a dome above each room is my favorite part. Even the outside of the homes here are carved from thick marble, all of them with spires stretching up toward the starlit sky, each its own little temple or sanctuary of peace jutting into the cosmos. Kairos said stars are made of celestial light, but not the ones here. They're made of divine light. Even with the bright blue diamonds twinkling in the sky, it's dark and moody here and I love it.

The darkness that has tormented my mind for the past year feels weak in the Realm of Darkness. In a weird way, it's like a part of myself is missing after carrying it with me for so long. One thing I've learned about those of us who have darkness in our veins, is as much as we want it gone, sometimes it's sad to see it go. We're left with these gaping holes from all the things it takes when it leaves. How do we refill those empty spaces? I suppose we should feel lucky that it left at all, even if it is fleeing and will return. Some of us aren't so lucky.

A part of me wishes I could stay here and be free of the darkness forever, but I know this is only temporary. I miss Olivia and Hekate so much already. And Ere. I miss him, too. I understand that all of this is a lot to deal with but refusing to call or even respond to my texts is low. Shouldn't he care how I'm doing? Shouldn't he want to make sure I'm okay? I can only assume he has officially bailed. He finally reached his limit on the level of madness he can deal with from me.

My thoughts drift away as Kairos begins to sing, his deep voice warm and gentle and comforting. I can't help but smile. His baritone singing is off key and far from being good, but my soul sings along just the same. The shower handle squeaks and the water abruptly shuts off, so I quickly pull the black t-shirt he let me borrow over my head, inhaling the rich, leather and amber scent of him deep into my lungs. I toss my towel into the shimmery hamper by the door, for a moment wondering if it's possible that it's made of pure gold. From the looks of it, it might very well be. Having his intoxicating scent wrapped around me sends excited shivers through my body. I leap into bed, pull the covers up to my chin, and then fix my eyes to the wide-open balcony doors and the orbs of celestial light hovering around outside, just as he enters the room.

According to Kairos, the Realm of Light is powered by celestial light, and without the existence of it, the realm could no longer exist. Divine light, which is even stronger and more powerful, he says, only existed within me before I created the Realm of Darkness and planted it here. The celestials believe that without the existence of divine light, all light would cease to exist. Something about that thought terrifies me, that my life, my power alone, keeps the realms from crumbling to nothing. It shouldn't be me. It should be anyone but me who holds that power.

"You look comfortable."

His voice pulls me away from my thoughts, my eyes widening at the sight of him. I force my face to relax, giving him a neutral, unaffected smile, though it's difficult as he leans against the door frame, shirtless with only a thin towel wrapped snuggly around his waist. Good god, he's a work of art. I rake my eyes up and down his body, admiring the smooth muscles and the intricate black ink that does in fact cover his entire abdomen, chest, and arms.

He. Is. Perfection.

"Nice towel," I blurt, closing my eyes for a moment and fighting the urge to scream for committing the crime of not thinking before speaking. *It's fine. Just... be cool.* "You look pretty comfy yourself. I mean I doubt you could get much more comfortable unless you lost the towel completely. Nothing beats lounging around completely nude, am I right?"

Nailed it.

His slow, crooked smile tells me that I did not, in fact, nail it. Crossing his arms over his muscular chest, shoulder still pressed against the door frame, his green eyes shine brighter than the celestial light outside the balcony.

"Are you asking me to get naked for you, princess?" His teasing smile grows as my cheeks blaze from his words. "You could at least spend a little time getting to know me first. What's my favorite color? My favorite flower?" Straightening and letting his hands fall to his sides, he tucks his wings in tight and prowls toward me. "My last name, even, what is it?" His head tilts slightly and he's still wearing that annoying, amused smile that taunts me.

He thinks he's being funny, but he's not. I can't laugh right now, not when I'm so thoroughly humiliated. He's too hot for me to be able to form coherent sentences, and it doesn't help that he can sense everything I feel whether I try to hide it or not. I'm an awkward mess with him. Not that I've met a winged, immortal man before, but even without that, Kairos is like no one I've ever encountered. His claiming to be my fated mate doesn't help the situation either. I don't know how the hell to act.

Brushing his wet blond locks back, his emerald eyes sparkle and penetrate my soul. My heart thuds loudly in my chest. He refuses to look away and I find myself not wanting him to, wanting him to dive deeper into my soul instead, to find and capture the part of me he says used to exist with him and bring her back. I panic as his hands clench the towel at his waist, hoping he doesn't actually plan on removing it, but also really wishing he would.

"What is your last name, then?" Breathless words somehow find their way out, his body suddenly feeling too close and yet too far away.

"Kairos Davenshire is my full name. My favorite color is red. My favorite flowers are roses." The corners of his lips twitch, but not with a smile, with an unspoken sadness. "Roses have a special meaning to me." His throat bobs as his eyes drift from mine to my lips and back up again. "I want you to know everything, Nora. About me. About this realm. About you and... *us*."

It drives me wild, the way he looks at me as if I'm the only thing he sees. Like I'm the only thing he has ever or will ever be able to see. I want to know everything about him.

Sitting up in bed, I tuck the silky blanket around my waist, leaning my back against the leather headboard. "How old are you? How long have you been a guardian and the commander of your army? Was I happy before? Were we happy together?" I tilt my head, noting the way his spine stiffens and then the muscles across his chest flex and unflex as he shifts on his feet.

I should have asked one question at a time. That was a lot to bombard him with all at once. I'm sure this is hard for him to handle, having to worry about protecting me from evil while also teaching me about things I should already know. There's just so much I still don't understand.

Taking a seat on the edge of the bed and facing me, he stares down at the floor. "I'm young compared to most of the celestials. I'll be two hundred years old on July thirteenth." He looks at me and smiles. "Don't worry. You can skip getting me a gift next year, considering you feel you barely know me."

I smile but roll my eyes dramatically and we both laugh.

"I spent my whole life training to be a guardian and a fighter before I met you. Unlike you who was created out of magic, I always knew what I would become because I was born and raised here with my parents."

"Your parents. The ones who rule the celestial realms," I breathe, shaking my head in disbelief.

I can't imagine the pressure someone would feel being a son or daughter of such high-ranking rulers. It couldn't have been easy for him. Especially now being separated from his father.

He nods once, rubbing his hands down the front of his towel. "Being a celestial is my whole life. I just want peace in the realms. So do my parents. So did you, and we fought for it every day once you formed the Dark Legion of Warriors. I joined and became your first in command and we were inseparable after." Meeting my eyes, his smile is weak and his voice cracks as he continues. "You were happy. We both were."

I wish I could climb into his mind and experience the past the way he remembers it. I'd love to remember us. I hate that I can't.

"You're amazing at what you do, Kairos. You saved me from myself when no one else could. If everything you've told me is true, then the gods allowed me to reincarnate for a reason. We're together right now for a reason. Maybe this time we'll finish what we set out to do. We can demolish darkness for good." I lean forward, placing my hand on his. "I hope one day I can be as happy as you say I was before. For so long I've thought it was impossible for me, even though some days are better than others. I'm starting to wonder if maybe I was wrong." Taking a deep breath, I close my eyes, inhaling the swirling power full of light and comfort that he carries around with him. "I swear I can already feel my soul changing since I stepped into this realm."

If I was being completely honest with him, I'd admit that I felt something stirring within my soul the moment he crashed into my life, something that urges me to open my heart to him, but I won't say that. I can't admit the truth just yet.

"I believe you have a way of bringing out the light within me." I pull away from him, running my hands over the velvety blanket draped over my lap. "Maybe out of anyone," I say for good measure, not wanting to sound too sure or to give him too much hope that I might believe we're truly fated to be, because I don't know what I believe yet.

And I definitely don't know what I want. All of this gets much more complicated by adding Ere into the mix. What if he does reach out to me? What if he decides he still wants to try? Do I just forget about what we had together? Forget about the love that was starting to blossom between us?

Standing, Kairos makes his way to the dresser in the corner of the room, the golden handles glistening as he pulls a drawer open. "Does your boyfriend not bring out your light? Does he not make you happy? You seem pretty damn happy in his presence, to me," he grumbles, pulling clothes out of drawers that he then slams closed.

He slips into the bathroom for just a moment, long enough to throw on the black t-shirt and grey sweatpants that fit him so deliciously that I try not to drool. When he comes back out, he smooths out the waves of his hair and his shoulders sag as he sighs heavily.

He must have sensed my thoughts drifting off to Ere and what the hell I'm supposed to do. There's no use pretending with him. He senses it all anyway. It's a nice change after pretending with everyone else for so long. Ere is special, yes, but he doesn't push away the darkness. Instead, he helps me accept it as a part of me. There's a power in that as well, but I'd rather it be drowned out by blinding light until it no longer exists in me at all. If I had a choice in the matter, the dark parts of myself would be gone.

"I'm happy with Ere. He helps me accept the good and the bad things within. My broken, messy pieces have never scared him. He loves me for who I am." I shrug, staring at my hands as he watches me.

Stepping forward, he softly runs his fingertips along my cheekbone, then lets his hand fall weakly to his side. "You are not broken, Nora. There's not one thing bad about you. Don't you dare let anyone make you feel otherwise." As he looks into my eyes, the stars exist within them, a wide-open galaxy full of hope and promise and wonder, and I can't breathe.

He sees me. He understands me. It's as if Ere helps numb my wounds and forces them back together, and Kairos, he rips my heart open allowing my lost soul to breathe life again. I don't know how I feel about this revelation of truth, but I know I shouldn't voice it or consider it to mean more than it does. I don't know Kairos yet, and Ere is good to me...*was* good to me. But as I unravel the layers of Kairos, I'm learning that there's so much to like about him. His heart is pure and beautiful.

"Are you planning on sharing my bed with me, or should I sleep on the couch again?"

"Hey, I didn't make you sleep on my couch last night. You could have went home."

He shoots me a look that says, *I would never*, or something much more intense like *you're my fated mate and I refuse to let you suffer alone*, but says nothing.

Biting my lip, I look over at the leather couch, the gold blanket and pillows scattered across it. It looks comfortable enough.

"Fine. Only if you're a gentleman. If you try anything I'll scream. The gods will hear my cries of destress and smite you where you lay." Laughing, I scoot to the opposite side of the bed, giving him room to slide in beside me.

"You wouldn't." His eyes slant as he climbs under the covers and then waves a hand nonchalantly to shut off the orbs of celestial light floating high above us.

"Oh, but I will. Don't say I didn't warn you." Turning toward him, I raise my eyebrows up and down, daring him to try.

His eyes soften as his crooked grin grows, then he turns to his side, shifting his wings until he's comfortable. "I respect you. I respect your feelings for Ere. My only concern right now is making sure you're safe. Everything else we can figure out later." His smile now is sleepy and weak, but his eyes dance with light as he tucks hair behind my ear. Then he curls his arm under his head to use it as a pillow as he gazes over at me.

Smiling up at him, I rest my arm under my head just like him, then, cuddle in a bit closer. We aren't touching. There's space between us. But still, the warmth of him near is enough to calm any worry I might have had before. "I feel very safe with you, Kairos," I whisper.

I do. I also feel happier than I have in a while which scares the shit out of me. Back home I gave up on fighting my dark thoughts and depression for the most part. I chose to pretend I was fine instead of actually *trying* to be fine. The desire to rid myself of darkness and pain for good grows by the second here with Kairos. Fighting for happiness sounds better than pretending. Fighting for my mind to be free sounds invigorating. I will not sit back and be used or abused by Nyx or anyone else any longer, and I refuse to let any more harm come to Kairos or his people. They've all suffered enough. I have too, and I'm tired of suffering. We'll all be free one day and I will chase the promise of happiness until I can't any longer.

Death will have to take me.

CHAPTER TWENTY-TWO

LET IT BURN

NORA

The wind caresses my face, my red hair swirling around me like a gleam of light against the thick, dark clouds rolling past overhead. The distant bleakness of the towering temple and city skyline in the distance steals my attention, even with the commotion on the ground. The clang of metal reaches my ears as the Dark Legion in their fighting leathers begin training far below. Hundreds of men and women with ebony wings pair up and swing and slice toward the others weapon with deadly precision. I find it both amazing and terrifying.

Kairos believes they'll be prepared this time if Nyx and her demon army were to ever attack here. Their celestial wards, he says, will alert them far in advance, giving them the upper hand. Apparently, Queen Gaia's wards are impenetrable. I hope he's right. I hope we never have to see if it's true. Nyx found her way into the Realm of Light once, after all. The thought of her here sends chills creeping along my skin, not out of fear of what she'll do to me, but a deep terror of what she might do to these people. To *him*.

Kairos steps out onto the balcony and hands me a warm mug, clinking it against mine in a silent 'cheers.' I snort as he brings the cup to his lips and winks at me before taking a long sip. "Sorry. Fresh out of tequila. I hope coffee will suffice." A crooked smirk and aquamarine eyes envelop me in warmth.

Tilting my head to the side, I roll my eyes overdramatically. "I only loved tequila so much that night with you at the club because it helped me escape the nightmare of having to talk to you. You're a real bore, you know?" I laugh but he does not.

He bumps his shoulder into mine playfully. "Please. You felt anything but bored that night," he says, leaning his elbows on the railing, his face now close to mine.

"Oh yeah?" Leaning in closer, my lips inches from his, I whisper, "tell me then, Kairos, what *did* I feel?"

"You felt exhilarated. The excitement rolled off you in waves. I make you feel alive." His smile is wide, but I can sense the questions in his eyes. Despite his proclamation, he's unsure how I really feel.

Looking into his eyes is like staring straight into the eye of a storm, the calming sensation right before thunder claps.

"What you sensed that night, Kairos, was the repulsion I felt from your over-the-top flirting. And also...boredom." I shrug, keeping my eyes on him.

I try to play it off, hiding the sarcasm in my tone, but then laughter slips out and a smile creeps across his lips as I explode into a fit of giggles. He laughs and shakes his head, knowing my words are all lies. Everything about Kairos is beautiful, but his carefree laugh, his playful mind, and his selfless, open heart are quickly becoming my favorite things.

"Okay, little liar. Finish your coffee and get dressed. You've got an army to reintroduce yourself to." He winks before chugging the last bit of his coffee and then heads into his bedroom without looking back.

"God, you're bossy," I tease, following close behind him.

Too close, apparently, because when he comes to a sudden stop and faces me, I crash into his hard chest, splashing the contents of my mug all over his shirt. Gripping me by the shoulders, he gently peels our bodies apart as I mutter curse words under my breath and wipe at his shirt with my bare hands. Not surprisingly, his lips twitch as he holds back a smile.

"What I meant to say, princess," he waves his hand and bows low before continuing. "Is please can you get dressed and ready so as not to leave the immortal army who is expecting us waiting. They've only been hoping for your return for over a century, after all."

His smile is cocky. I roll my eyes as I push past him and make my way to the closet. He is bossy. I was only stating a fact. Rummaging through clothes in the closet, I decide on one of the signature black robes of the realm. The emblem on the front features golden wings with a sword pointing down between them, just like almost everything else in the closet. I glance again at the wall of leather before sliding the closet closed. It's sexy and I can tell Kairos prefers it, but it feels unnecessary today. I won't be training or fighting, and I like the breeziness of the robes better. Running a golden brush through my hair, I turn toward Kairos, opening my mouth to speak.

Instead, I gasp. In his robe with the hood drawn up, flashes of the night on the bridge push their way into my thoughts. A shudder runs through me remembering the fear I felt plummeting toward the lake and then again when I faced him. I thought he wanted to hurt me. I know now that couldn't be further from the truth. There isn't the tiniest piece of Kairos that would enjoy hurting me. As he smiles and offers up his arm, I loop mine through it and we descend the spiraling marble staircase together.

Out on the training field, we keep our distance as the celestials continue fighting, paying no mind to the two of us standing here. Mio, the dark-haired green-eyed friend of Kairos' who I met at my house last week smiles brightly as he spots us together quietly watching. The celestials' fierceness is hard to ignore. In their black leather, their wings furrow and unfurrow as they twist and dive and roll across the ground, gleaming weapons in hand and strapped to their bodies everywhere imaginable. But god are they beautiful.

The celestial runs toward us, and Kairos leans down, whispering in my ear. "Try not to stare or gawk too much over his looks. Mio is already overflowing with an abundance of confidence. He needs no more." He laughs quietly and then straightens.

Is the big bad celestial jealous of what I might think of his friend? I shake my head at him and click my tongue as I turn back to Mio, avoiding a conversation about his possible jealousy. His first in command is without question a specimen to admire, for sure. As he smiles, the little dimples on his cheeks deepen and Mio always seems to be smiling. I think if I spent more time with him, we'd be good friends in no time. He radiates joy. He reminds me of Olivia and my heart aches thinking of how much I miss her.

"Hey Commander!" His voice is silky smooth and brimming with warmth, and excitement. He slaps Kairos on the back and then turns to me.

"Nora. Looking as beautiful as ever, I see." He winks, gently placing his hand on my shoulder and nodding toward the army. "We're almost finished running through drills and then I can introduce you to everyone. I'm sure you're dying to be free of conversation with this bore." He motions toward Kairos with his eyes.

I can't help but laugh. "That's funny, I just told him earlier what a bore he is." Placing my hands on my hips, I abruptly put on a serious face. "Please, Mio. Help me."

He laughs and the sound is wild and carefree, and I laugh with him, ignoring the annoyance in Kairos' eyes as he glares at us.

He clears his throat. "Forgetting your manners, Mio?"

"Shit. Right." Mio bows his head immediately, all humor fading away. "Darkness guide me." As he straightens, he flashes another wide smile my way. "See you soon, Nor."

"Gods save me, *prick*." Kairos spits, smiling after him as he walks away.

"What the hell was that?" A huff of confusion escapes my lips.

"Are you referring to the celestial mantra or that man child you just encountered?" He crosses his arms and his eyes light up as swords clang and soldiers spin through the air in circles, dropping to the ground faster than my mortal eyes can track.

"The thing you said to each other. What was that?" My eyes are glued to the celestials, admiring how stunning they are even as they fight.

I step forward to get a better look, mouth hanging open in awe.

"Darkness guide me. Gods save me. It's our mantra." He moves in closer, ignoring the soldiers and focusing only on me.

"What does it mean?" I clasp my hands in front of me, giving him my full attention as I wait.

"It means to follow darkness wherever it leads in order to conquer it. If we do just that, gods and goddesses will save us in the end." He swallows, his fingers twitching at his sides.

"But you believe the gods have turned their backs on your people. That they abandoned you after casting you down to Earth. Do you believe they'll still save you if a time ever comes where you need their help?" My heart races as I consider the possibility that maybe they wouldn't save them. That maybe they would again let them fall.

He inhales deeply. "We have no choice but to believe. Faith. Fate. Destiny.

All of it is what keeps the celestial realms going." Looping his arms around my waist, he leaps into the sky without warning, and I scream.

His laughter is short as he peers down at the celestials. "Look at them. Look how amazing they are. They're determined and devoted to their faith even with all we've been through. After all we've lost. I won't ever be the one to take that away from them no matter what I might believe."

I gasp in awe as the soldiers suddenly get into a new formation. Their wings are spread wide as they form a circle of protection around those in the center while some of them stay outside the barrier acting as the enemy trying to push through. They don't get through. Their wings shield the ones in the center so fiercely I can't even see them there at all. A shield of darkness made of wings. It's beautiful.

"What if their wings were hurt during battle? Or worse, what if they lost them completely?" My mouth hangs open as I watch the rows and rows of celestials practice the move, barreling toward the enemy as one to force them back or knocking them on the ground.

Kairos' wings shift and flap and then we drop down lower, giving him a better view while he floats on air and watches his Dark Legion in action. "Our wings typically heal as quickly as our bodies." He takes a deep breath. "Celestial daggers will kill us no matter where we're harmed, but holy fire on our wings mutilates us. It keeps a celestial alive to suffer an eternity of feeling the loss. It's like losing a limb in a traumatic way. I'm not sure mentally one could ever truly heal." Noticing the horrified look on my face and my loss for words, he gives me a small, reassuring smile. "As far as any of us know, there was only one who possessed that kind of power. A god or goddess. Like all the others, we don't remember what they look like or even their name, only that they existed. They could be dead for all we know. Holy fire isn't a power anyone else has ever wielded."

"It has happened before..." I murmur more to myself than him, but he nods his head anyway.

"Only once. To Nyx," he replies, and as my boots hit the ground a wave of nausea crashes into me at the mention of her name.

My body feels weightless, like a shell of a person stands here as my mind drifts somewhere far away. The saying 'hell hath no fury like a woman scorned' seems fitting for what the gods did to Nyx. She isn't going to just give up on me. She's going to do whatever it takes to get me under her spell, to use my power against the ones she feels wronged her. The ones who stood by as the gods took her wings. Her coming after me can't only be about some crazed thirst for power, it must be about much more. It's about vengeance and destroying the realms like they destroyed her. Being here makes me a danger to this entire realm. She'll find a way in. She'll find a way to hurt the ones I care about until I have no one left. Until there is nothing left.

Celestial warriors shake my hand and greet me one after the other. They all say *'darkness guide me,'* so I reply with *'gods save me,'* the way I've learned I should. One after another after another. As soon as one of them step away, I forget their name. There's so many of them. I repeat the few names that stood out in my mind, hoping to at least remember a couple. Josephine. Bailey. Ananthe. Fuck, I'll forget those too as soon as the next wave steps forward to greet me. The emblem on their chests, the wings with the sword down the center, glistens and mocks me as they stoop to bow at my feet and welcome the Divine One home. The Divine One who will one day undoubtedly be their undoing once Nyx gets ahold of me.

I want to go home. To my real home. This is all suddenly too much. I have no energy left and my head is throbbing by the time we finally head back to Kairos's home.

"Why are we not flying? It would be so much faster," I groan as we make our way up the grey brick path leading to his house at the top of the hill.

His pace is slow and steady, unrushed and unworried, as he loops my arm through his and places his warm hand on top of mine. "It would be faster, yes. I thought you might like the fresh air and the silence after so much stimulation. I know it was a lot meeting each of your soldiers. I felt your anxiety and fear, but you held it together so well."

I freeze, forcing us to a standstill as I process his words. "Kairos, what if I can never be her again," I breathe out, unlooping my arm from his. "We don't know if I'll ever have my memories back. I might never remember these soldiers or this realm or even myself."

He takes my hand, caressing the top of it with his thumb. "I know you're struggling to believe any of this without your memories. I can't even begin to imagine being in your shoes, but as soon as you stepped into the Realm of Darkness, we all felt the rush of divine light entering and your soul coming home. You *are* Hemera." He brushes the back of his fingertips across my temple and then down my cheek and smiles. "Nora and Mera are not two separate people or beings. You are one and the same. All you're missing are your memories, and they will be returned to you one day. We just need to have a little faith."

He's right. I am struggling. I don't feel like some magical divine being like everyone believes I am. I just feel like *me*. Nora. No one else. I'm not only missing my memories, I'm missing the power I had before that makes everyone so sure I'm something special. Right now, I'm just a mortal. Until I die, apparently, which means for now and while I'm here I'm useless to Nyx. That, at least, brings me a little comfort. I push back my shoulders, willing hope and happiness into my heart, knowing now isn't the time for doubt or fear. I'll be strong and brave for him. For Kairos, I'll do many things, because I know he'll do anything for me. The man is a saint.

"I'm sorry. It's just been a long day. A long week." I sigh. "I'll be okay," I nod, remembering what he told me that first day here about fear.

I will not let fear of failure or fear of the future rule my mind.

"It's just a lot of pressure and I don't want to disappoint anyone," I whisper, facing forward and putting one foot in front of the other as he follows my lead.

My whispered words carry so much more meaning than he realizes. It's not just the soldiers I worry about disappointing, I fear disappointing this entire realm and everyone in it. I worry that I've already disappointed Ere by being who I am, and it won't be long before I disappoint Hekate and Olivia, too. If someday I have to permanently leave them to live out my life here, I'm not sure how they'd feel. And then there's Kairos, looking at me with hope in his eyes and trust in his heart, even knowing Nyx can use me as a weapon against them all if she one day chooses to. How the hell do I not let everyone down?

Kairos offers a tight-lipped smile. "You have never disappointed us, Nora. You never could. Trust me." His wings shift behind his back and the feathers glisten as the blue stars made of my divine light peek out from behind dark clouds.

The torches imbued with celestial light that line the pathway here and surround each house flash to life as the last of the sunlight fades away. Darkness was not allowed to exist here even for a second. It sensed it. It felt it. It immediately chased it away.

"I trust you, Kairos. It's myself I don't trust," I admit, pinning my eyes on the marble steps coming into view.

"You'll learn to trust yourself." Clasping his hand around mine, he pulls me to a stop in front of the steep steps leading up to the front door.

"I was created with darkness and it's not going anywhere. I'm fated to carry it with me until I no longer exist. How could anyone trust me? Why would anyone even create me? Nyx was born with the same darkness within her and look what became of her."

He pauses, turning to look at me with furrowed brows. "Sometimes being so close to something gives you an advantage—a way to learn it's weaknesses and eventually control it. I believe you're better equipped to take it down than any of us since it runs in your blood." His eyes drift away to the celestial orbs of light that have taken over completely now that the day has come and gone. "Darkness believes you belong to it, but I believe your fate is dependent on what you choose. Whether ultimately you let it win or choose to let it burn."

Making our way up the steps, a tight knot of fear coils in my gut, because as soon as he says those words, I feel the darkness within trying to push its way back up to the surface. I had convinced myself it couldn't reach me here, that I was safe, but I'm not. Maybe none of us are. I take a deep breath and hide the shock and terror with a smile. I don't want him to know that I feel it returning. Or that it suddenly feels like the light here is only a temporary shield that will soon be useless against it. The shield is cracking. It'll soon splinter to pieces, letting darkness completely consume me.

Even with Kairos next to me in this realm so far away from Nyx or The Underworld, I feel darkness calling my soul back home. Although, it is much easier to ignore with Kairos' endless positivity and his shield of light that he keeps around me. But darkness hasn't given up on me yet, and I don't believe it will.

"I choose to let it burn," I tell him as he opens the door, and we step through together.

Something deep within smiles wickedly at the lie I tell him and at the lie I tell myself. I feel her dark power creeping closer, hissing and unfurling as it pulls back to strike. I will never escape her. I shake my head, trying to clear the thoughts that I'm not sure are even my own.

This is not your home. You do not belong here. You should be where darkness reigns and shadows chase the light.

I shouldn't be here. I led the celestials straight to darkness once and their black wings are proof of that. The reality, whether Kairos wants to admit it or not, is that I could very well become just like the Queen of Darkness. Just an evil, vile creature who haunts and tortures for fun. If Nyx takes full control of my mind and my power, then there's no hope for me left.

Maybe one day my wings too shall burn with holy fire.

CHAPTER TWENTY-THREE

GODS SAVE ME

NYX

OCTOBER 6TH, 1848

I cannot fight it any longer. The darkness I let in the moment I first opened that wretched grimoire has seeped into every thought and broken fiber of my being. I was a fool for ever believing I could wield such darkness and not let it drag me deep into the pit where it was born from. It wanted this. It knew I would try anything to prepare for it to come for me, and now it's too late. It owns me. The moment I was born I felt it within, clashing against my light, but now…now it is all I feel raging inside, scraping and clawing at my mind. My light is unreachable now. The celestial parts of my soul have vanished. And my wings, the shimmering ivory feathers replaced by silky onyx are proof that I have nearly lost myself entirely to whatever lurks and waits deep in The Underworld. The scent of brimstone fills my room as eyes made of blood on a silhouette of thick shadows haunts me from the forgotten realm below. He is ready. He has been waiting for so long.

I haven't left this room in days, or maybe it has been weeks. Partly out of shame for what I know I am becoming, and partly out of fear of what I might do if I were to leave. For days now after drifting off to sleep I awoke in the middle of doing something I cannot remember beginning to do. The lurking shadow is playing games with my mind. I cannot even trust myself any longer. The bright white walls I once loved burn my eyes now that darkness has made its home here. It is like my body and soul are repulsed by the same blinding light that once brought such comfort. The dim flicker of candles and the creeping shadows they cast along the walls are all that soothe my blighted soul.

Books are scattered around me on the floor, pages upon pages of ancient spells and cleansing rituals that have all proved to be useless. There is no healing me. The celestials sense a change in the Realm of Light, a change within the one most of them believed would inevitably succumb to her dark power, and they have begun plotting what they might do when the celestial part of me slips away completely. They do not know I can sense their every feeling and hear every thought that passes through their minds now that I have let darkness in. Even from here within this cave of isolation I have created so far away from the others, still I hear their minds hoping and praying for the gods to end me before I end them. I do not blame them.

They do not even know about *him*, the one who lies in wait in the fiery, gaping pit of The Underworld. The way he has patiently waited for his chance to devour the light out of each one of them. Or how he drags his claws down my subconscious, informing me of these things and pleading to allow him to seize control of me. I am a danger to this realm if he succeeds. I am a danger to everyone.

Conjuring my bright orange flames in my trembling hands, the darkness pushes its way in, suffocating my light. Flashes of ebony replace color for brief moments, a constant fight of light versus the absence of it entirely in the palms of my hands. My power grows dimmer by the day. Soon all light left in my magic and even my soul will be siphoned out and fade away as it follows the shadows into oblivion. I shift my hate and my anger to the grimoire on the floor, the book full of promises of death, rebirth, and power greater than any being should ever possess. I send my flames spiraling toward it. I need it gone. I need for it to disappear before I disappear instead. My power is useless against it. A barrier of protection on the cursed pages sends my flames surging back toward my face, barely missing their target as I duck to avoid them.

It opens back up to the page. The same vile page it always opens to, the one it will not let me avoid looking at no matter how hard I try. There are words scrawled on the weathered paper in blood that speak of unlocking the

Abyss, the flaming pit in the Underworld where a cruel and vengeful death god lives trapped and secluded from the realms. The gods of light and the witches joined forces and banished him there centuries ago, sealing the pit with magic after my birth. Doing so ended the dark gods reign of terror over the realms for good.

My mother knew him. She not only knew him but was foolish enough to bind herself to him for eternity. All of it is written in the book. This evil, wretched book. I am his daughter, what is left of the bond he severed with my mother the day he slaughtered her. They called him the devourer of light. He feeds on light, devouring it to make himself stronger until the one he drains is nothing but an empty shell of a person. The darkness calls to me, whispering my name and urging me to do what it asks or risk everyone I love being slaughtered. The celestials who were kind enough to take me in. Hekate, who returned to the Earth Realm to be with her coven. I cannot let it get to them. I must unlock the Abyss which holds demons, despair, and a dark god who wishes to use me, beneath it. I have no choice.

The darkness will slaughter everyone I love.

I try and fail again to burn the evil book as it whispers my name louder.

Nyx, Queen of Darkness, Goddess of Night, this is your fate.

I burn it. I burn and burn and burn it, my lungs aching as I scream, my magic fighting against the flames that spiral back toward me from whatever ungodly magic protects the grimoire. As I scream, my magic turns darker, the black flames surging back toward the book, and this time the leather and pages turn to ash. I crawl across the cold floor, picking up the pieces of what's left, and letting out a sound that is a mix of sobbing and laughter. The ash swirls, a whisper of wind mixing the burnt pieces, and then the grimoire is again in front of me. Candles flicker as the shadows move closer and closer, the icy chill of them brushing against my skin. I shiver, a puff of white releasing into the air as I exhale into the abyss threatening to swallow me whole.

"Darkness guide me. Gods save me. Darkness guide me. Gods save me." My whispered words do not scare the darkness.

This entity, it fears no celestial, mortal, or god.

It smiles, I can sense it. The thought of stripping me of all light and plunging me into eternal darkness and damnation brings it a sickening joy. It grows closer to taking over completely. My room, once full of warmth and comfort, is now as cold as I have felt my heart become over the past few weeks.

As cold as it has made me. Shadowy tendrils like long, pointed fingers reach for me, pulling me deeper into nothingness, into never-ending isolation and eternal abandonment by my realm. I cannot fight it any longer. I have tried, but it refuses to let me go.

"Please," I whimper to the darkness, and though I see no face I feel it staring back at me. "Please!" I scream, tipping my head back, my ruined, blackened wings open wide, begging for the gods to save me.

The candles in my protective circle flicker out. All the books from my shelves lining the walls violently crash to the floor. Pages are ripped and torn from them by hands or magic I cannot see, one that is angry and hateful and dripping with impatience. The pages swirl around me as I quickly cower away, my belongings crashing against the wall and tumbling to the floor. All that is left is a broken, scattered mess of the life I once had. My light has vanished. It is gone. What I feel coursing through my body now is not the minuscule amount of darkness I once felt there, but a hungry, possessive beast. Only darkness remains. I belong to it now. Curling up on my side, I continue whispering the celestial mantra over and over, even knowing it will bring no relief. Even knowing there is no saving my soul, now, not with what it has taken from me.

"Darkness guide me—" Staring at my wrists, I will the skin to rip open and spill my blood on the floor. "Gods save me."

A puddle of crimson forms around me, and I smile. Dizziness sets in and my heart rate quickens, blood rushing from my body. I strain against my power as my body attempts to force me to live, ripping the wounds open wider and deeper, refusing to let magic heal me. The wounds likely will not end my life, but I have no choice. I must try. I will not be an active participant in these wicked games. I just want to be free before it is too late.

The pages in the grimoire flip on their own, and I open my eyes to watch. It again stops on the page it has forced me to focus on for weeks. *Unlocking the Abyss*. Pushing myself to my knees, my hands slipping and sliding on my own blood, I crawl across the floor and kneel before the book.

No. Gods, no, no no. Glancing down at the spilled blood, I gasp at the way it flows from my body and creeps through the cracks to reach the leathery binding, trickling up the page straight to the center of the dark abyss sketched there in ink. I gave it what it needed. It begged for my blood. The nightmares haunted me for weeks, images of me simply pricking my finger or as horrifying as slicing my own throat, to let the blood drip onto the hollow pit on this page.

It needed this. It pushed me to do this. My blood has somehow opened the Abyss. The darkness haunted and tortured me until I broke, until I was so desperate that I believed this was my only choice. The warmth of my tears matches the warmth of the blood clinging to my fingers and dripping down my arms as I stare at the page in front of me. I tremble as dark flames sway and crackle, rising from the once lifeless pit. The god is free. Because of me. Gazing into the fiery pit, my wrists tingle as the sensitive skin pulls itself together, leaving only faded scars and blood stains where the gaping wounds were. I healed much too quickly, even for an immortal. I should have been found lifeless and barely hanging on due to the extreme loss of blood, and yet I feel stronger and more powerful than ever. The celestials were to find me broken and hopeless on the floor with a desire to save me burning in their hearts. It was a cry for help. My last hope to prove my innocence in all of this. They will not forgive what I have done. There is no redemption for my soul, not after setting free that which the gods worked so hard to imprison.

Blood of my blood, it is time for you to rise.

The whispered words are within my mind, no longer from a corner of darkness in my room. I feel him all around me, tangled within every thought and every breath he allows me to take and every single move I make. Evil is embedded deeply in my soul now, and as its grip on my mind tightens, the power from the Abyss tugs at me, calling me home. I do not belong here. I never did, and I surely never will.

I belong to darkness. I suppose I always have.

As a portal opens, a flash of light is followed by Ananthe stepping through, clad in her white fighting leathers and celestial sword in hand. If the king and queen sent her for me then they are scared. She is the oracle who sees all necessity and inevitability, the one they call upon to deliver justice or punishment if needed in times of war. I have never seen them call upon her before because I have never been alive during a war. Is that what I have started, then, a war between the realms? Gods, what have I done?

"Nyx, King Ourahnus and Queen Gaia are requesting your presence." Dark, cautious eyes follow my every movement as I stand. Her white wings ruffle slightly as she waves a hand, bringing the candles scattered throughout the room back to life. "You should have known better than to let the darkness in. Your careless choices have led to my being here. I had hoped it would never come to this." Her rigid features soften slightly as she swallows, raking her eyes up and down my form.

I roughly wipe at my wrists with my robe to rid myself of the proof of what I have done, panting as I prepare to face the consequences of my actions. She is not taking me to the rulers to speak of how they might save me. They sent her because they would like to be rid of me. I can hear it in her thoughts, though she does her best to try to hide them. It is her who is responsible for approaching the ones who have raised me and asking what shall be done now that I have fallen into darkness, and it is her who I suppose will be my savior in the end.

I favor death over being a slave to such darkness.

I nod in understanding and then pull myself to my feet, running my hands down my robe to smooth out the wrinkles and let my magic wash away the blood stains smeared across it. A bright flash is followed by powerful magic that bites against my wrists like hot iron with sharp teeth, suppressing my power and keeping my hands locked together. Swallowing thickly, I step up next to Ananthe, ready to face my fate. She follows me through the portal, and together we enter the Hall of Justice within the Temple of Light. My retinas burn almost immediately from the celestial lights shining down from the diamond encrusted chandeliers. It is disorienting, the light, after weeks of being engulfed in darkness in my room. Queen Gaia and King Ourahnus sit in their thrones on the raised platform in the center of the room, tight lipped and as still as the celestial carvings made of alabaster stone in the curved corners of the room. I slowly make my way to them.

I bow low, hoping they cannot hear the erratic beating of my heart. I am too afraid to breathe. Too ashamed.

"We are extremely disappointed in you, Nyx." Ourahnus lowers his head, his blonde hair cascading in front of his eyes. He clasps his hands together in his lap, staring at the white and silver marble floor, refusing to look at me. His wings are tucked in tight, and the thick crown made of light around his forehead glows brighter than I have ever seen.

They glow brighter the angrier they are, I have learned, and brighter still when a punishment will be harsh.

"We are more than disappointed. We are ashamed." Gaia stands, making her way to the front of the platform, the clinking of her heels against the floor a thunderous declaration of anger. "You have embarrassed us before the gods for allowing you entrance into the Realm of Light. We trusted you. We treated you as if you were our own daughter. You have destroyed... *everything*. Do you have any idea what you have done!?" The ground rumbles as she yells those last words, her fists clenching as her power soars. Lights flicker and then shatter, cracks forming in the walls like slithering snakes eating through the thick marble. Her dark hair glistens as what lights are left shimmer across it, her lips forming a thin, restrained line.

Her crown shines even brighter than the king's. She is much angrier than him and not at all trying to hide it.

My eyes burn and my throat feels like it has been sliced open with razor blades. My trembling hands hang limply at my sides as I step forward. "Your generosity is something I will be forever grateful for. I am sorry I have brought shame to the two of you. You have been more kind and accepting of me than anyone else." Sniffling quietly, I wipe my tears away. "But darkness called to me, and it does not want me here. It whispers that I belong to it in my dreams. It haunts my thoughts and torments me day and night. I-I could not stop it. I-I tried to remain strong."

"You did no such thing! You welcomed it in. You stole your mother's grimoire and chose to set it free. One day, we might all belong to darkness, and if that day should come, we will have only you to blame, Nyx." Gaia paces back and forth, her power surging around the room in waves, the diamond chandeliers swaying and clinking together and pieces of the walls cracking further and crumbling down. "You have no idea what evil you have unleashed back into the realms. And now, the agony you will now endure because of that mistake." She huffs, slowly shaking her head in disbelief. "You belong to it now, Nyx. We can no longer keep you here because you are a danger to us all. You cannot be saved." A momentary flash of sadness in her eyes is all I see before she turns on her heels and takes a seat back in her velvety chair.

"Why does it want me? We must be able to do something to stop it!" My frantic words rush out in a single breath.

Ourahnus looks at Gaia and then at me. "This happened once before. The gods were at war, and our gods won. The Gods of Light." His golden eyes are soft and kind, though his power is tense and rageful, but mostly I sense that he is scared. "We hoped the darkness would never again be unleashed. We had hoped it would not find a way to come for you. But you share the same blood. And when you bind yourself to darkness the way your mother did, there is no escaping it. You belong to the darkness just as much as your mother did." He takes a seat next to Gaia, his shoulders sagging but his head held high. "The gods are not here to step in this time. We cannot let you stay here and put our people in danger. The celestial prophecies predicted this, but still, we foolishly tried to prevent it." He sighs, closing his eyes and clenching his jaw, his thoughts moving too quickly to keep up with. "The realms will be engulfed in shadows and pain, and we must now let it play out as it will. There is no one coming to save us."

The gods will not save me. Gaia and Ourahnus will not save me. And Hekate is not here because I foolishly pushed her away. I am alone. I am terrified and alone and I wish more than anything that I had never touched that grimoire. Gaia and Ourahnus nod at Ananthe in unison. I feel her step up behind me, her breathing too calm and steady for what they are asking her to do. Unsheathing her swords I hear a faint breath as she lightly blows against the metal, the very air from her lungs igniting the weapon with holy fire. So, they will kill me, then. I was willing to die to rid myself of this misery, but a small part of me hoped for a chance at redemption. Maybe time locked away while they discuss things further and form a plan to save me. I was wrong about them. I was wrong about this realm and the kindness of these people. I did not ask for any of this. I only wanted to fight what I already knew would come for me one day. They gave up on me. Even in death my heart will never forgive them.

Magic that feels too warm and too light and too wrong, suddenly wraps around me, forcing me onto my knees before my king and queen. Time stands still as Ananthe circles me, dragging her long sword across the marble as she smiles just to taunt me. I push and pull against the chains around my wrists, but it is useless. I cannot reach my power. I cannot breathe. Maybe I should thank them. Maybe I should hate them. Right now, I am unsure of what I should feel, but a part of me is relieved that darkness cannot have me.

Darkness will not win.

I only wish the people who I would have been willing to die for were willing to fight for me, but I suppose we are just not the same.

"Spread your wings out, Nyx." Ananthe comes to a stop in front of me, glaring down at me like I am the most despicable creature she has ever encountered. "*Now.*" Her growl is angry and cruel as she touches the tip of her sword to my wings.

I hiss in pain as the flames singe my sensitive wings. A mix of white and black feathers drift to the floor in slow motion. Spreading my wings out as wide as I can, she smiles in approval. I want to spit in her face. I want to conjure my dark power and singe the skin off her bones. In this moment, Ananthe's cruel smile growing, Gaia simply thinking she wishes to move on with her day, and Ourahnus standing to leave but being forced by Gaia to stay, I want to burn the whole fucking temple to the ground. But I know this is the darkness in my mind. It is not me. *It cannot possibly be me.*

The sword is lifted, and I close my eyes, preparing for a quick release from the disappointed glares of the silent rulers. Sharp metal and hellfire slice through my wings and I scream, falling forward and gripping at the marble but finding nothing to grip onto, nothing to help distract from the pain. White and black feathers float all around me, landing in a bloody heap.

I grit my teeth and fight through the shock and the pain, my wings spasming, every nerve ending within them on fire. "Wh-what are you doing!? Why are you doing this!?" My screams are desperate and pained as warm blood flows down my back.

Again, fire lashes into me, somehow burning even hotter this time. I scream louder, tears cascading down my flushed cheeks. This is torture. This is cruel. Our wings are sacred parts of us that should never be stripped away, even in death. This. Is not. Justice. Any celestial would choose death over this.

"Please! Stop this!" I rest my forearms on the ground, steading myself as I turn and look into the eyes of my cruel punisher.

"I will not stop until every feather burns away. It is what the gods and goddesses wish to be done."

I look to them now, the just and fair rulers of my realm, but neither of them meet my gaze. I lower my head, not wanting to see their faces any longer, a blazing hatred igniting in my heart.

Another slice is followed by searing pain, and a scream full of anguish tears its way out of my chest.

My heart shatters to pieces.

"You are no longer one of us, Nyx."

They do not want me.

Another slice, rougher this time, and all that is left is a scream that is weak and barely audible, my mouth hanging open and no sound coming out as I close my eyes and look up to whatever gods might be watching.

"You are no longer welcome in the Realm of Light."

They no longer love me.

I have nothing left. I am broken. Ruined. I belong nowhere and to no one.

I would choose death over this feeling of abandonment and cold heartedness any day.

Leaning forward, I rest my cheek against the cold floor, but I feel nothing. My hands are in a puddle of my own blood but I do not care. Blood splatters are everywhere, and I wonder if they will forget me as quickly as it takes them to clean it up with their power. I gaze at the silky feathers scattered around me, plucking a white one out of the pile and bringing it close to my face. I will miss them. I am nothing without them. What am I if not a celestial?

I am aware of Ananthe lashing and cutting and mutilating me, but I no longer feel it. I refuse to feel anything. Numbness wraps around me as my mind drifts to how much the white feather I hold onto for dear life reminds me of Hekate's hair and how it smelled so deliciously like sunshine and tangerines. She made me feel. She was everything to me. I regret never telling her how much I love her. I smile weakly, comforted by the fact that I know she knew. All she wanted was for me to admit the truth, and I should have.

That will forever be my biggest regret.

My hand drops to the floor, no longer having the energy to hold it up. I am close to death. Maybe it will come for me after all.

The rulers, the ones who are now dead to me whether I survive these wounds, call their sons name, the celestial who lives and breathes to fight darkness. A portal opens and then I am lifted off the floor as he carries me through. The silence and darkness are a comfort after all I have just been through. I am placed on my back on a dirt floor, and with what little energy I have, I smile up at the king and queen's son.

"The darkness is strong here. I can hear it whispering even louder now."

"And what does the darkness tell you, Nyx? You really should not listen." He kneels beside me, his green eyes nearly glowing within the shadows of the cave, his wavy hair just like his father's falling over his eyes.

"It says the gods are lying, Kairos. He says that all of you are lying," I am cut short as a coughing fit silences me, blood seeping out from between my lips.

He stands then, glancing around the cave, sensing the darkness within it coming closer. "I am truly sorry this happened to you, Nyx." A portal flashes to life and then he disappears within it, the glow from the celestial dagger in his hand stealing away the last of the light.

A cold chill creeps across my skin as the skulls scattered around on the dirt floor welcome me. My eyelids begin to droop and my limbs are too heavy to move. Lying here after losing everything and everyone I ever loved, not only Hekate, but the two people who for so long were parents to me, and even Kairos who at times tried to be a friend, the warning from the ancestors that day in the meadow when I first met Hekate pushes its way into my mind.

Do not let your power lead you down a dark, winding path, for you may get lost and never find your way back.

There is no finding my way back from this.

CHAPTER TWENTY-FOUR
FATED TRUTH

NORA

After meeting the Dark Legion three nights ago, I begged Kairos to let me stay inside with my nose in a book. He obliged, bringing me romance novels to choose from without even having to ask while refilling my glass with Saintly Rosé one too many times. The pink, glowing liquid helped to ease my dark thoughts after I gave up on reading, choosing to instead dance and sing on his dining room table, him sitting back and laughing the whole time. He refused to indulge with me, saying he would hate himself if something were to happen and he wasn't at his sharpest to be able to protect me. Him being here is enough. His laughter mingling with my own, the sparkle in those eyes as he watches me make a fool of myself so thoroughly, that is more than enough, too.

Kairos helps suffocate the darkness as it seeps back in, refilling my soul and energy with much needed light.

Now, finally sober from my early day drinking, I'm propped up on my elbows on his bed, kicking my feet as I watch him. I don't bother hiding my roaming eyes as I drink him in like a delicious, forbidden treat. Ere is forever etched into my heart as the one who can get lost in darkness with me, but Kairos has a way of making me believe that I'm more than just my darkness. He brings out the best in me. There's no pretending to be happy or pretending I'm fine with him, I just *am*. I do miss Ere, but I don't regret coming here. After all, he left me. Either way, guilt eats at me when I admit to myself that I have feelings for Kairos. I try not to. I try to resist, but I can't deny that whatever I feel for Kairos is...*special*.

His crooked smile is proof he enjoys it when I watch as he whistles and saunters around the room in just a towel, plucking a black blazer off a hanger in the closet, then raising his eyebrows and winking at me. Yeah, he enjoys my watching a little too much.

"How fancy shmancy is this party? A blazer and slacks? Is this a royal ball? Should I wear my glass slippers so my prince can find me after I turn into a pumpkin at midnight?" I ask, resting my head in my hands.

Water from his recent shower trickles between his folded wings. The muscles in his back flex and tense as he gathers a button up shirt in his arms. For a moment I imagine how nice it would feel to be one of those water droplets, lucky enough to caress the whirls and swirls of his tattooed body.

He laughs and shakes his head. "I don't believe that's how the story goes, but no. Our realm doesn't host many balls these days, not like we used to. There is no royalty here, not really." He pauses, shifting his eyes to me briefly before quickly turning to face the closet. "Not at the moment, at least. My mother, Gaia, runs the realm for now, until proper rulers are ready to take over. She never wanted the position of Queen Regent, but has no choice. It was the gods wishes."

Rolling off the bed, I walk to the small golden vanity in the corner of the room behind him, running my fingers along the cold, smooth edges. "Did there used to be? Kings and queens who ruled the celestial realms?"

I still have much to learn about the celestial realms, but what I have learned over the past couple of days breaks my heart. The wars that divided the celestials raged on for decades. All the blood spilled and lives lost was for nothing. The final battle against Nyx and her demons, where the celestials and even queen Gaia were shunned and banished after their white wings gave way to blackness, Kairos believes that the gods turned their backs on them. All of it because of me. He continues to remind me that it wasn't *because of* me, but *for* me, but it hurts to know I was at the center of all this. It hurts more not to remember.

"Once upon a time, yes, there were kings and queens. That ended here when the division of realms happened. I know nothing of what they choose to do in the Realm of Light. They keep to themselves, and we have no way of entering our old home. We can't portal in like we used to. They won't allow us to." He glances back at me. "My father allowed me in once. Only to tell me his plans on keeping us out. Said it was better that way." He faces me, then his throat bobs and his jaw clenches, and I've learned by now that him doing those things means it's not a subject he likes to discuss. "My parents, Gaia and..." his eyes glaze over and then they snap closed, like saying his father's name hurts too much, "and Ourahnus, were going through a rough patch during the war. They disagreed on many things." He huffs a laugh, meeting my eyes and shaking his head. "But refusing to even let his own son in. Refusing to see *me*. I'm not sure I'll ever be able to forgive him for that. And my mother, well, she pretends to be okay, but she isn't. She has not been herself in a long while. She is just as angry with him as I am, and the loneliness is more than she can bear. It kills me."

In a way, he lost both of his parents because of a war I started against Nyx and the demons to try to escape her control over my mind and power. The list of reasons to feel guilty continues to grow.

"Kairos, I'm so sorry." I fight back tears, staring down at the black and gold marble imagining how happy they might all be if Kairos and the others were still in the Realm of Light. "Things could have been so different. You and your people could still be home with your father if it weren't for me. I hate that things ended this way for you."

And now I must face them. All of them. The entire realm will be at this party to welcome me home. To welcome *Hemera* home. The divine one. Their savior. From what it sounds like, I didn't save anyone. Not even myself.

He tosses his clothes on the dresser and then looks at me. "Nora, *this*, the *Realm of Darkness*, is our home. We accepted it long ago and we're thankful for what you've given us. We would be nothing without your power creating this realm the day we fell." He slowly walks toward me, but I refuse to meet his gaze, then he gently lifts my chin and forces me to look at him. "We would do it all over again if necessary. Her getting to you means we're dead, anyway. She won't stop until we all are. She will use your power to shatter every realm. At least with you we stand a chance of fighting against her."

"I'll only be helpful if I can remember how to wield my power. If I can remember *anything* about my past. I need my memories, Kairos. Without them I won't be any help to you or your people." I pull away, standing and then taking a seat on the edge of the bed facing him. "*Nora* won't be able to help you if Nyx attacks you here. *Nora*—"

Needs to die. I don't say it out loud, but the moment the thought enters my mind I know it's true. I'm human. A helpless, powerless human doesn't belong in a world full of celestials, monsters, and gods with high stakes and lives on the line. Ere could've died that night in the alley when the demons attacked. Olivia might be next. And Kairos? He has lost too much already. He told me death will bring my immortal form, and once immortal, I can go to the Underworld myself and get my memories back. I'll no longer fear Nyx's demons or even her any longer. I can find a way to save us all without dragging anyone down with me.

Kairos sighs quietly and sits beside me, the damp towel still wrapped around his waist pressed against my skin. "You have no idea how badly I want you to have your memories back. Selfishly, it's what I want more than anything. For you to remember me." He looks up as if he's praying to the gods for help, then his shoulders sag. "But for now, keeping you mortal without power for Nyx to control is safest for everyone. Until the gods decide it's your time to go, I'm not letting you die. We'll get your amulet back one day. I'd try to find it myself, but my priority is keeping you safe. I can't leave you. I won't. If I'm away from you, she'll see it as an opportunity to attack and I'll lose you anyway."

He shouldn't be the one who has to go and get it back. He doesn't need to risk his life or anyone else's. It should be me. I need to be the one to do it. I can make all this right.

"I don't want you to leave," I whisper, standing and glancing over my shoulder as I make my way back to the vanity. Taking a seat on the stool, I stare at his reflection in the mirror. "I need you to stay, Kairos. Your realm needs you here. So do I."

It's true. I need him here so I can find a way to Nyx myself. He'll never let me go without him, but I have to find a way. I'm not risking anyone's life except my own, and I don't believe she'll kill me, not once I'm immortal, anyway. She needs me alive if she wants to use my power. If I give myself up willingly, I'll not only protect Kairos, but everyone else I care about too. To me, this is the only option that makes sense anymore. I can't hide forever. With my immortality comes my power and if I'm as powerful as everyone believes I am...maybe I can kill her. I want it done. I want this all to be over.

I busy myself with pulling the vanity drawer open and lining up make-up in a neat row, make-up that unfortunately I have to figure out how to use without Olivia here to help.

Holding his clothes to his chest, he stands, smiling down at me. "All I want is to keep you safe, Nora. I need you to stay, too." His gaze lingers on my back as he steps into the bathroom, the door clicking closed behind him.

As soon as the door shuts, tears force their way out and I cover my mouth with my hands to silence the sobs burning the back of my throat. It's all too much. The pain I left here for Kairos to deal with on his own. The broken realms that have never repaired. The dark queen who refuses to move on from the past. And I haven't had time yet to heal from my mortal ex-boyfriend leaving me or even think about the fact that Olivia is now stuck dealing with wars and immortal beings and monsters for life because we're sisters. I have a fated mate who is heartbroken from so much loss and I'm here with him and can't even remember him, and that has to be torture. It's just...too...much. The realization that I've caused so much chaos for others burns and gnaws and slices through my entire body. I will never let harm come to them. I refuse to let the past repeat itself. I should have handled it on my own last time before everyone lost so much.

My phone lights up as it vibrates, letting me know I received a text from Ere. I wipe the tears off my cheeks, then close my eyes and count to ten, reminding myself to breathe. Everything is fine. When I open my eyes, I force myself not to think about things that hurt any longer, holding my head high and letting myself move on. It'll all be okay soon. Picking up my phone, I swipe my finger across the screen to unlock it, then pull up the text from Ere.

I miss you. I'm sorry. Please come home.

I miss you, too. I promise you'll see me soon.

I'm a fool for walking away from you. Soon cannot come quickly enough.

Once I find a way out of the Realm of Darkness without Kairos following me, I'll go to him to tell him goodbye. Yes, I loved him. I still do. But he's mortal. The truth is, we could never work, not anymore. And as much as I try to fight the undeniable pull I feel toward Kairos, it wouldn't be fair to him if I didn't explore those feelings, eventually. I guess that depends on how things go with Nyx. Whether I live and get the chance or die wondering what could have been.

I groan as I swipe golden eyeshadow across my eyelids and smear red lipstick over my lips, a mix of guilt and a fiery determination settling over me. Then I slip into my dress. I have to go to this ball and smile and wave and pretend everything is fine, while in the back of my mind I'm planning my escape from Kairos, the man whose eyes rarely roam away from me. He's intense in the way he cares for me, the way he cares about my safety more than even his own. He'll be pissed. Maybe he'll never forgive me. I hate that my welcome home party has suddenly turned into goodbye, but I have no choice. I'm doing this for him. For all of them.

As Kairos steps out of the bathroom, wearing black from head to toe and a wide smile, all I want to do is shove my face into the silky pillows on his bed and have a good cry. But I'm good at pretending. *Smile. Laugh. Pretend everything is fine.* Forcing a smile, I step toward him confidently, as if thoughts of failing him aren't scraping at the edges of my mind. I don't like having to pretend with him. I've never had to before, but for what I'm planning, it's necessary. He'd never let me go. I understand his worries, that she'll plunge the realms into darkness as soon as she gets her hands on me, but I won't let her. I have to believe in myself the way everyone here believes in me. The way he does. I was powerful once and I will be again.

Slowly walking toward me, his throat bobs as his smile fades and his eyes rake over me with affection and worry. "Hey," he says softly, running his hand down the back of my head and gently holding the back of my neck. "What is it? What's wrong?"

I sniffle, shaking my head and turning away. "I'm okay."

"You're not," he says, gripping my chin between his fingers and forcing me to look up at him. "Talk to me. Tell me what's going on inside that pretty little head of yours."

"I'm scared. Of so many things all at once." I blink up at him, smiling as white light glows around him and then reaches for me, swirling across my skin and soothing the pain in my heart.

"Here," he says softly, unstrapping one of the daggers from his thigh. "Just in case." His whispered words and his magic still sparkling softly around me calm my racing thoughts, easing every worry. "This belonged to you. I've carried it on me every day since the day I lost you, but I think it's time I return it to its rightful owner." He smiles, stepping in closer.

"It's beautiful," I breathe, running my fingers along the ruby stones along the hilt. "Rubies have always been my favorite. Even in another life, I guess." I beam up at him, another little piece of my past clicking into place.

His eyebrows scrunch up as his eyes search mine. "I gave this to you as a gift once on your birthday," glancing down at the dagger, he smiles, but not the crooked, playful smile I've gotten used to, it's a smile full of affection and a bit of pain. "My birthday is in July." He looks at me. "You wanted a dagger embellished with my birthstone because I had one made using yours. You cherished this blade, said it made you feel safe no matter where you were, because a part of me was with you, always." Taking another step forward, he reaches out with his free hand, gripping the side of my face and caressing my cheek with his thumb.

Those eyes, the green and blue waves are like a riptide, dragging me out into the open sea, but his hand against my skin is a safe haven, the only thing preventing me from being swallowed whole by the raging current.

I have to say something. If he keeps looking at me like this I won't be able to control what happens next.

I clear my throat. "It won't go around my dress. The dagger, I mean." I swallow thickly, unable to look away as he smiles and then kneels before me.

"I know," he tells me. "I'll need you to lift it up."

I'm frozen. I can't move as his eyes go feral in a way I've never seen from him before. He grips my ankle, then slides his palm up my calf, slowly running it along my thigh before pushing the thin fabric to the side. I gasp softly as he straps the holster to my leg, his warm fingers torturing my inner thigh as he slips them through the leather and runs his fingers from the front to the back to make sure it's tight. He lowers the dagger into it. Smiling up at me, he drags his fingertips down to my calf, letting my dress fall with it. He didn't pull his eyes away from mine once. Not even for a second.

Holy hell was that sexy, and probably the only thing I'll be able to think about for the foreseeable future. Gods save me. Breathe in. Breathe out. Everything is just fine.

"They're all staring at us," I whisper into Kairos's shoulder as we make our way down the path lined with bright wildflowers and celestial torches leading up to the platform where queen Gaia sits in the center of the meadow.

"Correction. They're all staring at you," he leans in and tells me, wrapping an arm around my waist tighter. "Love the dress, by the way." His smile is bright and full of approval as his eyes drift down the front of my gown.

I chose a black lacey dress from my closet with red roses and vines that climb all the way up the front and sides, then wrap around my waist and shoulders. Kairos' favorite flower. They've always been my favorite, too. My gold diamond encrusted earrings brush against my neck as we slowly make our way past celestials who smile and bow their heads, whispering 'darkness guide me.' My bare back tingles with the energy surging all around, and as we step closer and closer to the queen, the power sparking in the air only gets stronger. There are thousands of celestials here, all of them deathly still, encircling the platform in their black robes with the hoods drawn up. This is not a ball. The two of us and Gaia are the only ones dressed for one.

I clasp my hands in front of me to hide the tremors. Kairos's arm is warm and safe, making me feel infinitely worse about my decision to leave him. The clouds fade as darkness settles in, and the starlight swallows them whole. Celestial wings glisten as shimmers of light radiate off them.

As Kairos and I step up to the platform, the flowers lining the path begin to glow brighter than the stars. My eyes widen and my hands shoot to my mouth watching them illuminate our path as we ascend the stairs. A huff of laughter escapes, and Kairos loops his arm through mine as we step up to the waiting queen, seated on a velvety chair, wings spread wide, and a black ring of light rimmed in gold illuminated around the crown of her head. She's the most beautiful creature I've ever seen.

Her black dress shimmers like onyx and diamonds, and her dark hair nearly sparkles as she smiles and shakes her head, looking me up and down. "Nora," she stands, reaching out and taking my hands. She bows her head, so I do the same, my smile growing wider as I take in her magnificent form. "We are thrilled to have you home. Welcome to the Realm of Darkness."

She drops my hands, then faces Kairos, her dark eyes swirling with power. "You have done well, my son." Placing her hands on his shoulders, she leans in close and whispers, "Fate shall never fail you." She smiles and it's as if all the light in the realm suddenly pales in comparison to her.

"You've always told me fate and time are on my side. I should listen to you more often, Mother." He leans down and kisses her cheek, his eyes drifting over to me.

The queen waves a hand toward the crowd, and soft, classical music begins playing loudly. The celestials gathered around the platform disperse, heading toward long tables full of food and drinks, most likely Saintly Rosé. Others head to a dance floor covered in endless bright pink and purple glowing flowers. They lower their hoods and they're smiling. They're so happy. All of their eyes dance with excitement as they force their gazes away from us and focus instead on the rest of the party.

Gaia gracefully strides back to her seat. "It is such a shame what happened the last time we were here together in this meadow. Not being able to complete your claiming ceremony. That day still haunts my dreams." She sighs, picking up the golden chalice on the small table beside her and taking a sip.

Kairos steps forward, glancing my way, arms stiff at his sides. "I haven't gotten a chance to speak to Nora about," his eyes shift to me before locking back on her, "many things, Mother. Maybe now is not the best time," he whispers, his crooked smile weak and defeated, eyes begging for the conversation to end.

She dismisses his words with a wave, and I can't help but wonder what else there is to tell me, or what the hell a claiming ceremony is, but I force the thoughts away. I'll ask him later.

"Thank you for having me, queen Gaia. Your realm is beautiful, and you are absolutely stunning." Glancing at Kairos, the tightness in his muscles and the sudden paleness of his face, I loop my hand through his. "Kairos has taken good care of me. I'm only lucky enough to be here tonight because of him. I don't know where I would be without him." I smile up at him, but he doesn't smile back the way he normally does.

I'd be dead without him. I'd be immortal and no longer human because Nyx would have forced me to end my life already. I'd be in the Underworld with her, which I suppose is exactly where I need to be to end her centuries long cat and mouse game.

"We all know what happens when you die, and would it be so bad, really?" She croons, taking my free hand in hers and brushing her palm across the top. "Death is not the end, Nora. It is only the beginning," she whispers, closing her eyes and wrapping me up in her warm, tingly light. I gasp as her magic enters my mind.

A vision appears of a woman with long, flowing red hair and freckles just like me, though her blue eyes glow brilliantly with magic the way Hekate's do. White wings behind her back sparkle with flecks of blue and purple light that look exactly like the stars do here. As she opens her palms, flames made of divine light spark to life, flames that match the light twinkling around her wings. It's Hemera, but somewhere deep within I recognize her as so much more. My soul recognizes her as *me*.

Tears fall from my eyes, but the warmth of Kairos' arm suddenly around my waist and holding me against his side snaps me back to the present.

I smile at him before looking back into Gaia's dark eyes that no longer swim with power or excitement but dim slightly. "Thank you for showing me who I once was. Who I will be again one day if only I can remember how to."

The glowing light across her brow disappears as she takes a deep breath. "I sent celestials to search for your amulet and they could not find it. We assume it is with Nyx in the Underworld." She brings her chalice to her lips. The echoing clink as she sets it on the table announces that she emptied it entirely. "You must remember, Nora, that sometimes we must face great darkness in order to end it. You, my dear, will face more darkness than you know. Nyx is only the beginning. Hold onto your light with everything you have." Her eyes drift to Kairos. "As for you, maybe it is time you speak to Nora more of your future here together. The throne awaits you. She deserves to know the truth." Uncrossing her legs, she stands, giving me one last lingering glance and a nod as she unfurls her wings and leaps into the air, the thundering roar of them as she flies away drawing everyone's attention.

I turn and make my way down the steps and into the party, the laughter and clinking of glasses growing louder now that the queen is gone. I walk over to the drink table where the glasses are piled up in a neat stack with glowing pink wine flowing freely into the cups from a fountain made of gold. Kairos steps up beside me and simply watches and waits patiently as I down one glass and then another.

He clears his throat. "Can I please have this dance, princess?" He bows his head and offers me his hand, peering at me between the wavy locks of blonde hair that fall over his eyes.

I freeze midway through finishing my third glass, slowly lowering it to the table and wiping my lips. Kairos is perfect. He is everything good in this world. The celestial queen said that *I* will face great darkness. Not us. Not her or Kairos or this realm, but *me*. I don't want to involve him. Kairos deserves to be protected at all costs. All the celestials do.

I place my hand in his and we head to the dance floor, the other celestials quickly rushing away to leave it for just the two of us. He spins me once and then pulls me against his chest. My heart flutters as he smiles at me. His hand pressed against my back, the other wrapped around my own, send electrical currents of peace and light into my soul.

I don't speak for a moment, just memorizing every speck of blue within his bright green eyes like it'll be the last time I see them so close. It might be.

After meeting his mother, I have questions I'd like him to answer, but I'm running out of time. I need to ask them now.

Because after this first and last dance I share with Kairos, I need to leave.

CHAPTER TWENTY-FIVE

SLOW DANCING

KAIROS

Her hand is in mine, and my soul feels whole at last. The questions in her eyes as she looks at me send my heart slamming roughly into my ribcage, over and over, a painful reminder that she isn't quite mine yet. I haven't felt this scared in a long time. What if she never falls in love with me again and I'm left to suffer through another century or my entire immortal life without her? No. She will love me again one day.

She will.

"Your realm is beautiful, Kairos. Your people are amazing." She breaks eye contact and lets her gaze wander around the meadow, smiling as she watches the other celestials dance and drink and laugh in a way they haven't in over a century.

We're all thankful she's home. She might not realize now how much she meant to all of us, but one day she will. Their future queen has returned. I have never seen them happier.

"I haven't noticed much else tonight except for how stunning you look in that dress," smiling, I wrap my arm tighter around her waist, pulling her body up against mine.

Her eyes snap back to me, her cheeks turning a soft shade of luscious pink as her lips curve up at the edges in a surprised smile. "I wore it just for you," she whispers, her eyes focusing on only my lips, and gods does it kill me to not be able to kiss her right now. "Why are red roses your favorite? You said they have a special meaning to you."

I wish she could remember that we're fated mates and remember our claiming ceremony on her own along with every other beautiful memory we made together. Gods, do I need her to remember.

Brushing her wavy red hair behind her shoulders, my grip on her waist loosens as I consider my words carefully. "Red roses are important for what's called a claiming ceremony."

She smiles and shakes her head slightly. "What is...a claiming ceremony, exactly? Queen Gaia mentioned it, too." Tilting her head, she lets go of my hand, wrapping her arms around my neck as we continue swaying side to side.

I let my hands slide to her hips, taking a deep breath and closing my eyes to prepare for the pain that barrels into me every time I remember. "The claiming ceremony is for fated mates. All celestials have another they're fated to be with, but not all do the ceremony because if the gods deny your bond, then you can no longer be together. It's by choice if you do it or not." Sliding my hand up her arm, I take her hand in mine, her back arching as I dip her and then lean with her as she grips my neck tighter and giggles. Her eyes go wild as I snap her upright against me, no space selfishly separating our bodies any longer. "The ceremony is a blood bond that links two souls together for eternity. Anything you feel they will feel. Anything they think will become your own thoughts, in a way. It's a bond that cannot be broken. Even death cannot severe it."

Tilting her chin up, her eyebrows crinkle in an adorable way that makes my heart lurch and my stomach drop, because I'd love to kiss all her worries away. I want to bring her lips to mine and let her taste everything she'd be missing if her soul can't remember mine one day.

"So, it's sort of like a mortal wedding, then? And why would the gods deny two fated mates the chance at making their bond even stronger?" As she watches me and waits, I reposition my wings nervously, trying to focus on dancing but wanting nothing more than to escape, to run away from her and everyone else right now, the pain of my broken past finally catching up with me.

I caress her back with my thumb, the feel of her warm skin a reminder that though she doesn't remember it all, that she can't soothe the hurt of losing her, I'm lucky she's here now. "It's much better than a wedding. It's sacred. A literal union of two souls. But it can be slightly... painful." I flash her a crooked smile and her eyebrows do the cute scrunchy thing again. "During the ritual, both parties walk barefoot across a bed of thorns and vines attached to red roses, and the blood they lose is taken into the earth as an offering to the gods." I swallow thickly, memories of the momentary sting and burn of those thorns from the past nothing compared to the constant ache in my heart it causes today.

It haunts me, the thought of being so close to having her heart and soul intwine with mine, so close to having every godsdamn thing I'd ever wanted, and then having it all ripped away by Nyx right before it was done. If my mother hadn't forbidden any of us from returning to the Underworld, I'd have already ripped Nyx's flesh from her bones and happily tossed it into the waiting, open jaws of her demons.

Until the Underworlds sky shines bright. Until celestial wings are neither black nor white. Until the realms are shattered and made anew, you belong to me, and I belong to you.

The promises we made to one another the day we fell to earth as I held her in my arms and watched her slip away...those words, those now forgotten promises, they endlessly fucking haunt me. Our promises were meant to be unbreakable, not even fate or time or death should have been able to tear us apart. Those were things we never thought would see the light of day, impossible to break if not real, so that our love and promises would live on forever.

"Red roses. Your favorite," She breathes.

"I told you they hold a special meaning in my heart." I pull her closer and she smiles. "Red roses are sacred to us. Our history claims that once only white roses existed. During the very first claiming ceremony when the first celestials were created, they were asked to seal their bond and prove their devotion to the gods who created them, and to prove their love to one another." I gently lift her arms and place them around my neck, wrapping my own around her waist. "As they walked to the altar, white roses covered in thorns sprouted from the earth, and they were made to walk across them. The gods told them flying is prohibited during such a sacred ritual. Even to this day, we cannot fly at all on the day of a claiming ceremony." I smile, leaning down and whispering in her ear, "wouldn't want to piss of the gods, now would we?"

"You're right. That sounds awful. It sounds sweet minus the thorns and the...bleeding." She grimaces and we both laugh.

"The gods ask for an offering, and we must abide." I shrug. "As they walked across the roses, their blood leaked onto their petals and spilled into the earth. The gods accepted their union and fated mates were created to continue our lineage. Now, every morning on the day of a claiming ceremony, red roses sprout from the earth, here in this very meadow where the ceremonies take place. We see it as a reminder that love is worth the pain that at times comes with it." Bringing her hand to my lips, I place a soft kiss to the top of it, meeting her awestruck gaze. "Love will *always* be worth it."

"That's beautiful." Tears well up in the corner of her eyes, and I grip her face, using my thumbs to gently brush them away the moment they begin to fall.

"Once upon a time, we were to claim each other that way. We nearly had before it all..."

Before it all went to shit. Before a battle began that we were so unprepared for that many of us died and the rest who fought were tossed out on our asses. My own eyes sting as I watch hers widen in understanding. The calm side-to-side swaying of our bodies stops as she brings our dance to an abrupt end.

She's frozen, her fingers clutching my forearms as her eyes meet mine. "No." She shakes her head. "Fate or gods don't get to choose who I'm with. I do."

"Nora," I try to pull her closer, to bring her back into the moment with me, but she pushes me away. "We belong together. You are to be my queen when I step up as king. My mother doesn't want to be queen, but a celestial king cannot rule without his queen beside him." I sigh quietly, breathing in deep and gazing up at the starlight twinkling above us. Closing the distance she put between us, I take her hands in mine. "The hope of your return is all that has kept me going for a century. I know your soul recognizes me. You are mine and I am yours." I pull my eyes away from hers, gazing down at our hands instead. "Tell me you don't feel it, too. Say you don't want me even a little bit and I'll let it go." A single tear slides down my cheek and her eyes follow the path it traces down my skin.

The thought of losing her all over again because she doesn't choose me in this life, it fucking hurts. My throat burns as I feel the turmoil in her heart, see the hesitation in her eyes, the look beginning to rip and shred any hope I'd been clinging onto.

She shakes her head. "I can't be your queen, Kairos. I can't save your realm or your people because I have no power or light within me. You deserve better." She begins to back away from me, and I step forward.

I refuse to let her run away from me or from the truth.

"You deserve so many things, but I can't be the one to give them to you." Her hands are in fists at her sides, her body trembling. "So no, Kairos, I don't feel it," she takes another step back, shaking her head. "Not even a little bit," her whispered words float through the quiet air, slamming into my heart and letting what little hope I had left crumble to nothing. Tears flow down her cheeks and my heart and soul burn on the inside, dying to reach out and wrap her in light and love and hope or fucking anything, but she doesn't want me.

She.

Does not.

Want me.

I fucked up. I fucked everything up.

She continues taking steps back, glancing at the celestials in the meadow who are all now thoroughly staring, her eyes more sad and empty than I've seen them before. This is hurting her, too. Whether or not she'll admit it, I know it's true.

"Nor, I'm sorry. This is a lot to take in, and I apologize for throwing it all on you at once. Maybe we should leave and speak about this away from the others." I stand still, not wanting to reach for her or push her away even more than I've already managed to. She has to make this decision for herself.

She looks me up and down before speaking. "You talk about fate like I have no choice in any of this, but I do. I make decisions for myself, Kairos. It's not up to you or fate," she spits, turning her back to me and glancing over her shoulder. "I'm leaving. Without you. That's what I'm choosing now."

She heads out of the meadow, rushing quickly toward the woods and away from me. I follow behind her as whispers of giving up and fate being a lie echo from the celestials' lips around me. I don't give a fuck about anything they think or say, all I care about is banishing this soul sucking darkness from her mind and taking her home with me.

She glances over her shoulder one last time and then turns and runs without thinking about how pointless it is to run away from me. Does she truly think she can escape me? No. She just wants this to be over. This conversation and the situation with Nyx, but this is *not* over.

Not. Even. A little bit.

CHAPTER TWENTY-SIX
HE IS EVERYTHING

NORA

A sudden torrential downpour of Kairos' pain and anger blasts from the sky. My dress clings to my skin and my hair sticks to my tear-streaked cheeks as his unrestrained heartbreak drowns me. I don't stop running. I can't face any of this. I can't face him after the hurtful lies I fed him. Mud and rain drip from me as my heels sink into a puddle and I tumble to the ground. I can do nothing but sob as the world around me spins. The look of complete devastation on Kairos' face as I told him I felt nothing plays over and over in my head. I pull myself to my knees just as a twig snaps behind me, and I don't bother turning to look. I don't need to. Of course it's him.

"Great party, huh? Was it everything you'd hoped it would be?" Kairos' voice is somehow calm though the storm raging above us tells me otherwise.

His eyes spark with electricity, the green fading behind the strikes of blue that dance and sway within them. His palms flex at his sides, the same power dancing across his fingertips in waves. The sky lights up in the same moments the power around him does. He's like a bolt of lightning himself right now, and one roar or growl of anger might set the entire world on fire.

I shrug my shoulders and say nothing, because what the hell is there to say? A wild, untamed kind of laughter bursts from my chest and I tip my head back and stare at the sky. The rain pounds against my face as thunder claps overhead, and it burns my cheeks like tiny lashes whipping harder and harder. I can't help but feel like I deserve it. Whatever pain may come is warranted after what I said to him. After how badly I hurt him.

"Oh, it was magnificent." Gathering my now heavy, rain-soaked dress in one hand, I tug off my heals and toss them aside then stand and face him. "My favorite part was discovering you'd been keeping things from me about not only my past, but my future as well. We were basically almost married!? And I'm to be a queen of a realm that I don't feel I even belong to?" I let my false anger soar across the forest and dagger him with guilt, knowing I should stop but that I can't. Not if I want him to let me leave. Not if I want to keep him safe. "You act like you're so perfect but you're not. You're a liar." Shaking my head, I charge toward him, shoving at his chest.

It's cruel what I'm doing to him, and I know it, but I'll deal with the guilt later. I know what I feel for him. Maybe it is fate. Or maybe it's because of the way he looks at me or the kindness he's shown or the way his heart beats only for me. It doesn't matter now. I'm not letting Nyx take anything else from him. He has to believe I'm done. I need my amulet and my memories and to prevent any more harm coming to the ones I love. I need to kill Nyx myself. This is for his sake, and it's the only way I can protect him.

"Nora, please. Calm down. I'm sorry I lied. I understand why you're so angry." He doesn't move, his jaw clenching and unclenching as he tries and fails to force himself to calm down, the storm and rain letting up only slightly.

He's still as a statue as I push him again, unmoving and unbothered as I beat my hands weakly against his chest, sobbing so hard my throat burns. The sobs are real. So is the pain that tears my heart in two for reacting this way, knowing he deserves better. I'm calling him a liar while lying about something that might never be forgiven. I'm telling him I don't want him when the truth is, all I can ever think about anymore is how much I want him. If things were different, if a dark queen who ruined our lives once before wasn't haunting me, Kairos and I could be amazing together. Even without my memories I can feel it.

Wrapping his arms around me, he holds me tight against his chest, running his warm fingers through my tangled, soaking wet hair. The sobs don't quit, pushing out of me in endless waves as I force myself to remember everything I've been through in the past year. All the pain that was caused by Nyx. All the dark nights that would have never happened if it wasn't for her. My parents who would still be alive. I need this to be over.

"I want to go home, Kairos," I whisper against him, pushing off his chest and turning away. "I can't do this anymore."

He grabs my hand and pulls me back to face him, our wet bodies slamming into each other as his eyes burn into mine brighter than the lightning that strikes around him. "You're upset and I get it. I can't imagine how it must feel for others to know things about your life that you can't remember." His hands slide up my arms then he pulls me even closer. "I can't let you leave, Nora. I'd never forgive myself if something happened to you." Tilting my chin up in his gentle, forgiving way, he shakes his head. "It's not an option."

I'm trying to avoid hurting him in the worst way I can think of, avoiding breaking his heart and my own in the process, but this isn't fucking working.

"I can't be with you, Kairos. I won't." I sniffle, gripping his hand and removing it from my chin. "My heart belongs to someone else already and you knew it and still brought me here. I miss him," I whisper, my voice shaking as I fight off another sob. "I love Ere. He loves me. You should just let me go." My eyes are begging, pleading for him to listen, to let it go and let *me* go but still, he refuses to accept that I don't want him.

Shaking his head, he wraps a thick hand around the nape of my neck and the other around my waist, leaning down and pulling me closer. "You're lying," he growls. "Admit it. You've wanted me since the day you met me. Maybe you're too afraid to admit it to yourself, but I feel it, Nora. I will not give up on us, *ever*." Lightning flashes within his eyes as he whispers, "I will not let you go, my flame. We promised. You promised me forever." His lips tremble and his voice cracks, and my heart cracks with it.

As he gazes at me like I'm his everything, his eyes full of tears and pain, the rain shifts to a torrential downpour again and my body is a weightless puddle of need. Gods, I want him. My entire body and soul are crying out for him, screaming at me to let him in, to let him show me why I should stay. I'm frozen, my heart thundering louder than his power that roars above us, and though I know nothing of the promises past me made, all I want is for him to kiss me.

He locks my hair between his fingers, shakes his head and mutters "fuck it," then softly brushes his lips against mine, just a gentle stroke up and nothing else, but it's enough to set my entire soul on fire.

It's all it takes for me to lose control. To forget all about my plan. To not care anymore about anything but feeling his lips on mine again. I grip his neck and pull him to me, our lips crashing together like fire and gasoline meeting for the first time, willing to burn it all down together. His lips taste like promises and hope and forgotten love, all reacquainted after a century apart. His tongue brushes against mine firmly and hungrily like he's been waiting for me his whole life. Like he's been tortured and dying without me, barely fucking hanging on without me.

He savors my mouth on his, refusing to let me go as I grip his hair in my hands tighter to keep myself steady. I should let go. I should push him away. But my heart begs me to hold on just a little longer, to not fight my feelings. Tightening his hold on my hair, he somehow pulls me even closer, deepening our kiss until I can barely breathe, but I don't want to breathe. I don't need oxygen when Kairos is near. I need nothing.

Because Kairos...*He is everything.*

We couldn't have stopped this even if we tried, this kiss feels like fate and destiny pushing us together at last. It was always meant to be. I link my arms tightly around his neck and he grips my thighs, pulling me off the ground. My legs settle around his waist and then we're moving, my back pressed roughly against a tree as his hand shields the back of my head and keeps my lips from leaving his. Rain slides down our faces, soaking our hair and our already slick skin, lightning flashing across the sky in brilliant streaks.

All that matters now is him and I, and darkness or death or anything else that might try to work against us, be damned, because none of it could stand a chance with us together.

He moans softly into my mouth, a deep grumble of satisfaction. I grip him tighter, my thighs trembling as a heated flood of arousal scorches me to my core. Placing his hands on the sides of my face and using the weight of his body to keep me against the tree and to prevent me from falling, the rough strokes of his tongue slow to soft, sensual, somehow even more torturous ones. I completely melt away. I am one with the rain and the storm now, nothing except his lips and mine exist. Slowly pulling his mouth away from mine, he exhales breathlessly as he looks at me and smiles. He kisses me again. This kiss is soft. Gentle. Meaningful. It ends too soon. I need more of him before I combust from the inside out.

I place my hand on his chest, his heart thudding against my palm just as fast as mine beats now. He leans his forehead against mine and closes his eyes. I lean against him, eyes closed too as we enjoy this moment and give our lungs and hearts time to recover. I feel the smile on his lips without having to look, the heat from his mouth brushing against me as his lips part so close to mine. I never want this moment to end. His eyes gleam with happiness, a look of pure peace settling across his features. It's a look I've never seen him give anyone before.

It's a look just for me.

Reaching up, I wipe rain away from his eyes and giggle as he shakes his head back and forth, splashing me with the water that clings to his thick hair. I slap his shoulder playfully and he laughs, wrapping his arms around my waist and laying his head against my chest, squeezing me and holding me against him as if he's the happiest immortal man in the world.

Then he looks at me, all laughter gone and the playfulness drained from his eyes. "Tell me you don't feel what I do. You'd be lying to us both, and you know it. This is fate." His whispered words and the gentle, caring way he brushes rain off my cheeks with the back of his thumbs snaps me back to the truth.

The truth of what I have to do. Now more than I ever, I want to keep him safe. I want him to live. I want him to never have to hurt or suffer again. I unclamp my legs from around him and he helps lower me to the ground. Gripping his arms, I force him to let go of me as I back away, shaking my head.

"This isn't what I want. I'm sorry. This was a mistake." I swallow, my vision blurring as tears make their way back in.

"Why are you doing this?" His pained voice is barely audible and his shoulders droop as lightning strikes the ground behind him. Even the bolt is weak, no energy left to fight.

I think I've broken him. As much as it kills me to see, this is what I wanted. For him to give up, to let me go, to see that we aren't meant to be or that it isn't worth it, no matter how much it hurts us both.

The flutter of wings is followed by Mio dropping to the ground in a crouch behind Kairos, glancing first at me and then at him. He stands upright, tucking his wings in tight behind him. "I wanted to check on you. Everyone is worried. You guys okay?" He smiles nervously, just a quick curve of his lip before stepping up and standing between us.

"No. I want to go home. Can you take me, please?" I avoid looking at Kairos, though I feel his eyes searing into me.

He's pissed and I don't blame him. Our kiss meant something. It was obvious that I felt it, too, but I made my decision and there's no going back. I hate myself for hurting him in the process of trying to save him and his people, but I don't know what else to do. He'd never agree with my plan and it's too risky for him to come with me. This is something I need to do alone this time.

"Kairos, what's going on? Talk to me. Are you okay, man?" Mio puts his hand on his shoulder and Kairos immediately shakes it off.

"I'm not okay. Thank you for asking," he says through clenched teeth, his hands curling into fists at his sides.

"He can't make me stay. I'm not a prisoner or a hostage. I have free-will." I cross my arms over my chest, batting my tear-soaked eyelashes up at Mio.

Mio places his palms out in front of his chest, backing away. "Whoa. What the hell did I just walk into? Of course you're not a prisoner, Nor." He glares in Kairos' direction.

Kairos' eyes widen and his mouth hangs open in shock, but he quickly relaxes his features. "I won't force you to do anything you don't want to do or stay where you don't want to be. You're free to go. Mio will happily take you home, if that's what you want." He nods to his waiting friend and Mio nods back, his eyebrows furrowing deeply as he steps in closer. "Maybe some time away from each other will be good for us both. I realize you're going through a lot, but you have thoroughly destroyed what hope I had left for us. I think I'd rather be alone tonight, anyway."

It hurts seeing the light in his normally bright eyes dim and feeling the raging storm suddenly end. People are wrong about storms. It's not the calm before or the eye of one that's most frightening. The quiet, indifferent silence Kairos' storm leaves behind is what steals my breath away and terrifies me. Nothing could ever be worse than this. His gaze lingers on me with words unspoken before he turns and walks away. He's giving up. He's letting me go. His emotions are no longer in turmoil; he's shutting them off. He doesn't want to force me to stay or force me to choose him. He wants me to make my own decisions so that I'm not angry with him... *because he loves me*.

He loves me. He fucking *loves* me. Oh gods, what have I done?

Mio opens a portal and throws his arm over my shoulder as he leads me through. The blinding swirls of blackness and light don't stop me from turning and looking back, hoping to get one more glimpse of Kairos' bright green eyes before finding my way to Nyx.

All that remains in his realm is the calm wind, the towering trees surrounded by mountain peaks in the distance, and the heavy emptiness floating in the air. My heart breaks as I walk away, knowing if things were different that we could be happy. This isn't the end. I've fought against my feelings for him every single day because of Ere and because I didn't want myself to fall as hard as I knew I would for him, but it's too late. I have officially fallen. One day I'll have to work my ass off to earn his forgiveness, but I will. Then again, maybe none of this matters. I'll be in the Underworld soon and maybe I'll never find my way out of darkness.

I pray to the gods that I will. Though if it's true that the gods have abandoned the celestials, then most likely they've abandoned me, too.

As the portal snaps closed behind us, I close my eyes and take a deep breath, not wanting to see it all without Kairos here beside me. The further we get from him the more broken and alone I feel. I bet he feels it too, the distance I'm forcing between us. I could be wrong. He could feel nothing at all for me anymore.

I hope if nothing else he remembers how it felt to kiss me. How I felt kissing him, too. He has to know I felt everything.

Even in death, I will cherish that moment until the end.

PART THREE

CLAIMED

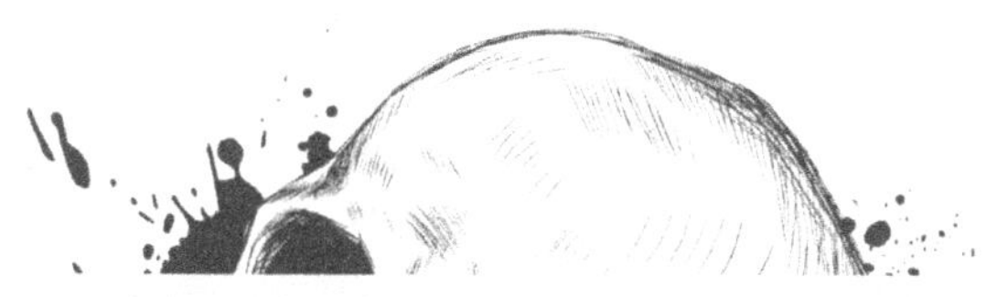

CHAPTER TWENTY-SEVEN

THE BEGINNING OF THE END

NORA

Mio has officially overstayed his welcome. He's worse than Kairos was while he guarded me. I rarely saw him creeping around unless he wanted me to see him, but Mio, on the other hand, his presence is suffocating. I can't do anything without him lurking or hovering beside me. He's not one for hiding in the shadows. I'm dying for an excuse to escape his constant presence, patiently waiting on Ere to have some free time to meet up, but he's been busy the past two days. I'm trying to be patient, but I need to see him. He deserves the truth. Even if he has decided he doesn't want to be with me, I need to explain what's been going on and get the truth off my chest. I kissed Kairos. And worse than that, ever since then, kissing him again is all I can seem to think about. It's driving me crazy.

I lay my book face down and open across my legs, feeling Mio's eyes burning a hole through my forehead. "What is it?"

He leans forward, smiling wide as he sits his mug of coffee on the table between us. "Kairos misses you. Do you miss him, too?"

"What is this, elementary school?" I groan. "No. I don't. He kept things from me, and I don't know how I feel about it." I clutch my book in my hands, burying my face in it to hide the lies written there, then kick my feet up on the coffee table.

I can't tell him the truth. If Kairos knows I'm not upset, he'll come see me himself, and I'm not ready to face him yet. Not after the hurtful things I said and not after that kiss.

Gods, that kiss…

"Someone is lying," his voice starts low and then goes higher in a sing-song, too chipper way, and I want to throw my book at him. I would if it weren't a special edition.

He can never be serious. Everything is a joke to him, and though normally those are my favorite type of people, today I'm not in the mood.

"Kairos is the expert at withholding information. Why don't you ask him if I'm doing a good job of it? He would know." I smile.

He groans. "Look, Nora. I know you care about that guy—"

"Ere. His name is Ere." I correct, rolling my eyes.

"Right. I know you care about… Ere, but is now really a good time to see him with everything you're feeling? The confusion and anger toward Ro, I mean." He tucks his wings in tight, the darkness of them pulling my attention away from the bright wall of white behind him. "You and Kairos had fifty beautiful years together. Your love was like nothing I've ever seen. I think maybe a part of him is so crushed because he'd hoped you'd fall for him like you did before even without your memories." He leans back against the couch, shrugging weakly. "He's a romantic and a true believer in fate. I don't think he realized how difficult this was all going to be for him, and he didn't know how to handle it. He just wanted to wait until the right time to tell you that you're meant to be his queen. He realized that's a big thing to ask of you."

Leaning forward, I snap my book closed and slide it onto the table. "Fifty years, Mio? Why did we wait so long to perform the claiming ceremony? If we were fated to be together, why not make it official sooner?"

Smiling, he shakes his head. "The bastard was scared. He wanted to make it official the moment the bond snapped into place, but he had never been happier. You were all he ever wanted or needed in life." He brushes his dark hair back away from his face, his soft green eyes meeting mine as he leans his elbows on his knees. "Yes, you were fated to be, and yes, it was obvious to everyone that you were perfect together, but it wasn't up to you or him or any of us. The gods, in the end, choose our fates. He was scared they'd choose to take you away from him. To him, making it official wasn't worth the risk. There is nothing that terrifies that man more than the thought of losing you."

"But he did it anyway. Why?" I breathe, tilting my head to the side.

"You wanted it. You wanted to rule beside him as his queen. You had hope that nothing would or could tear the two of you apart, not even the gods themselves could break you, you'd say." He laughs quietly, his head dropping and shaggy hair falling over his eyes, before looking back up at me, all humor gone. "I still believe that, Nora. Not even the gods could break the love you shared. There is no point in fighting what you feel for him. And there is definitely no excuse for you hurting him the way you did, especially when you didn't mean any of what you said. You may be my future queen, but you better believe I'll still be there to tell you both when you've fucked up, just like before. You fucked up, Nor." He stands, shoving his hands into his leather pants pockets, then nods down at me with pain in his eyes and whispers, "fix it, please."

Holy shit. I had no idea how much time Kairos and I had spent together, but several decades was not at all what I'd been thinking. I had six months with Ere, and when he left me, I could barely breathe. This goes beyond the small stinging pain that comes when someone you're just starting to feel things for leaves, what Kairos feels for me runs deep. It's decades of love and then a century of loneliness and blind hope while he waited for me to come back to him. It makes it all hurt so much worse. It makes me wish I had my memories even more. I want to remember. I need to remember him. I can't go on this way, not even knowing who I truly am. Not even knowing the man I'm meant to love.

I stand, heading to the kitchen and grabbing my phone and purse off the counter, slinging the crossbody strap over my head and tossing my phone in the pocket. "I need to go for a walk. I'm starting to feel like I can't breathe in here." I glare at him as I walk past, pretending to be angry at him for pushing me to apologize, or pushing me to care, but I'm not angry.

I'm lost and sad and scared, more than anything else, because as much as I want to believe I'll find a way out of this for all of us, the truth is, Kairos might lose me again. Maybe this time for good. How will he feel if he discovers Nyx has killed me? Will he ever be able to heal? The guilt eats at me, clawing and tearing and ripping my heart in two, but I have to try. I have no choice. I'm not living my life hiding or scared or haunted by her. I refuse to let her win.

"Great. I'll be watching from the sky," he says with feigned excitement, pushing open the sliding glass doors, shoulders slouching as he steps outside.

He looks about as defeated as I do. I know he's only trying to help Kairos and even me, but the only thing he's doing is making me not want to drag this out any longer. I'm done with not remembering anything people tell me about myself and my past. I'm done with it all.

I slip out the sliding glass doors and find Olivia and Hekate lying face first on towels in the sand. "I'm going out. I don't know when I'll be back, but don't wait up for me." I smile as Olivia pulls herself to her knees, tilting her head down and letting her sunglasses fall to her nose, peeking over them at me.

I'll miss her. I can't tell her where I'm going or that there's a chance I might never return, but I believe in my heart that I'll see her again. I wasn't reincarnated just to die for nothing. I'll see them all again. I have to believe that.

"Where are you going? I want to go out!" Her smile is wide as she glances behind me at Mio who wiggles his fingers at her and shows off his dimples. "Especially if you're going with him. Damn. He's hot, right?" She gives him a flirtatious wave, licking her lips as she does.

I roll my eyes. "If you say so. He's like a really buff, immortal child with weapons he probably shouldn't have." Glancing behind me, his mouth hangs open in shock. "I'm only kidding! Shit, I'm sorry. You are so hot, Mio. The hottest, actually, and the best warrior I've ever met, but don't tell Kairos I said that!" I laugh and then Olivia and Mio's laughter follow as I pull my sister in for a hug. "I'll miss you, sis." I quickly blink away the tears beginning to spill over.

Hekate rolls over onto her back. "That is the most accurate description of someone I've ever heard, actually." She laughs, glancing at him and then at me. "Hey. What's wrong?" She wraps her arms around Olivia and me and then pulls back slightly to look at me.

I force a smile. "I'm fine. I promise." I wave it off and shake my head. "Life has just been weird lately. It's a lot. I'm sure I'll feel better soon."

We untangle ourselves and Hekate pins her unwavering gaze on Mio. "Do you want me to come, Nora? I can use my magic to put him in an endless sleep if you're tired of his incessant chatter." She smiles wide, her fingertips sparkling with blue light as she wiggles them toward him dramatically.

Mio simply winks at her. "Try me, little witch. I dare you. You know I love a good challenge." His smile is seductive and taunting, begging her to play.

"Eww, Bromios. You realize I'm not attracted to men, right? I've told you this before. Save what little dignity you have left and let it go." She shudders, pretending to be sickened by his flirting, but both of them laugh.

"Hey, who needs dignity anyway?" With that, he looks to my sister. "Nice seeing you again, Liv. Thank you for being nice to me, unlike these two." Smiling, he walks backward, eyes on her the whole time before spinning on his heels and sauntering away.

What the hell was that?

After Olivia stops staring after him with desire burning behind her eyes, she refocuses on me. "Where are you going, anyway? You sure you don't want us to come?"

"No, I'm okay. I just need to take a walk and clear my head, that's all." I avoid looking directly at my friend and sister, gazing at the foamy, crashing waves behind them instead, afraid they'll pick up on my lie.

"Are you going to see Kairos soon? Mio told me you got into a fight. I'm sorry." Olivia gently grips my forearm and tilts her head. "I know fate says you're meant to be, but if it doesn't feel right then it doesn't feel right. I like Kairos, but I think you should follow your heart. Do what will make you happy, little sis. *Always.*"

I wrap my arms around her one more time, squeezing her tight. "Thanks, Liv. I love you." With my head on her shoulder, I reach out to Hekate and she scoots in closer, wrapping her arms around us both. "I love you too, friend."

I have to leave before the tears turn into full on sobs and then they'll be no hiding that something is truly wrong. I stand, wiping sand off my floral sundress as I turn my back toward them and begin to walk away, not glancing back.

"Love you! Have fun!" Their voices follow me around to the front of the house as I make my way into town.

Where I'm headed isn't a place meant for fun, but at least there's hope I can find myself while I'm there. With my memories I believe I'll feel whole again. I'm tired of feeling so broken.

I glance up, and though Mio is glamouring himself to stay hidden, his positive energy radiates down over me like a warm, gentle rain shower washing away my worries. I breathe it all in, letting the tingly sensation of light remind me of why I'm doing this.

I want them all to live. To be safe and happy for good. I want to be free of her. I want to be me.

The sun on the Earth Realm is too hot against my skin and too blinding after my time in the Realm of Darkness, so I shield my eyes with a hand. The grey clouds of Kairos' realm kept it mostly out of sight and away from my sensitive eyes, and now I find myself missing it. I miss many things about being there.

I pull out my phone and send Ere a text once I'm in town, and he responds back quickly.

We need to talk.

I'm in town. Meet me at Lunar Waves in fifteen minutes.

I'll be there.

How do I explain everything I've learned and how my feelings have changed over the past couple of weeks? How do I confess my feelings for Kairos to the man I loved before? I don't want to hurt Ere. I care about him, too. But this has to be goodbye no matter how I might feel. No matter how *he* feels. This isn't even about Kairos, not really. A mortal and an immortal make no sense together. He and I could never work.

With Mio's positivity and light still stalking me, my worries drift away and suddenly I feel hope that I'll find my way out of this mess. I only need to die and get my memories back so I can remember how to use my power, and then slaughter Nyx so she can no longer live another day to ruin my life. Easy enough.

Mio checks the time on his phone, *again*, and then looks at me. "It has been longer than fifteen minutes. Where is this guy?" He sighs.

I bump my shoulder into his, both of us leaning our backs against the brick wall in the alley outside of the club. There were too many people lingering and too many overly noisy, drunken conversations out front. I needed to escape the chaos.

"You can't really keep forgetting his name. You're doing it on purpose at this point." I pull out my phone and anxiously stare at the clock, hoping he's okay. "Maybe we should walk around back. Maybe something happened."

I push off the wall and head down the alley with him close on my heels. "Nothing happened, Nora. Your boyfriend is just fine. An inconsiderate asshole, yes, but I'd know if..." he freezes, palms shooting out and a shield of white light going up around the both of us. "Walk backward and get behind me. *Now*." He grips my upper arms, nearly dragging me back to him.

Peeking over his wide shoulder, I squint through the darkness, looking for any sign that Nyx might have come for me. "What is it?" I swallow. "Is it...is it a demon?"

"Kairos is going to fucking slaughter me if something happens to you. You should run." He puts his arm out to shield me from whatever is coming, gripping the celestial dagger strapped to his hip with his free hand and pulling it out slowly.

I see and feel nothing except for his power pulsating around us in waves. "What is it, Mio?" I whisper, my eyes focused only on the dim light shining from the street at the end of the long, shadowed alley.

Wings flutter and he pushes me back further as a demon growls and barrels down from the sky, landing on top of him and knocking him to the ground. It lifts its head, and its red eyes meet mine, the dark, familiar venom leaking from its teeth onto Mio. He screams as it repositions its clawed feet on his chest, digging into his skin and pressing down until bones snap. He rolls across the ground, grunting in pain as he pulls himself to his feet and runs toward me. His thick arms wrap around me, feathery wings thundering as we rise off the ground. A growl sounds out behind me and Mio spins to keep the demon away from me, then screams as claws lash and teeth sink into his wings, both of us crumbling in a heap on the ground. Anger floods me as I take in the bloodied feathers on the ground around us, and the gashes, raw and bleeding across his beautiful wings.

"Run, Nora!" He screams and then hisses in pain as he reaches for his celestial dagger, his wings shifting behind him and the thick gashes tearing open further.

I ignore his command, reaching down and grabbing his other celestial dagger from his thigh as he pushes the demon's head away with both hands, struggling to free himself and failing.

I won't run. I wanted this. I need this. She can have me. Whatever it takes to keep everyone else safe.

"Let him go," I spit, holding the point of my dagger against the demon's black, scaly throat. "You can have me. I won't even fight you. Just let. Him. Go."

The demon whips its tail forward and snaps it against the side of Mio's head, and he's no longer awake but he's still breathing.

"There are others who will come if they sense that I'm in danger." I smile as it rises and faces me, picturing Kairos' face. "I promise you won't live if you wait for them to arrive. I'd hurry."

Growls and shrieks from the sky grow closer, and my hands tremble as two more winged, glowing red-eyed demons drop down in front of me. I wanted this, but fuck, now I'm questioning everything.

"I surrender. This is between Nyx and I, and no one else. I don't want anyone else hurt because of me." Fighting against the adrenaline coursing through me and urging me to run, I step closer to them.

Laughter rumbles from their chests. My body trembles and my muscles twitch in fear.

"Our queen does not want you to surrender. She wants your warm blood spilled along the streets of your precious city." The demon's voice is deep and vicious and makes the hair on my neck and arms stand on end as fear rakes its claws down my bones.

"Hemera," another growl, and this time the demon circles around slowly and comes up behind me. Its wet, thick tongue darts out of its mouth, the slimy flesh exploring my ear and the end of it swiping across my flushed cheek before it disappears again.

I snap my eyes closed as the promise of death gets closer. I don't want to look. I just want it to be over.

"We love nothing more than the chase before the kill," it grumbles against my ear, a long, low growl vibrating excitedly against my skin. "Run."

The unearthly, guttural roars of the three demons make the ground beneath us tremble, and as the words sink in and the very real threat of being ripped to shreds hits me, I can no longer ignore the adrenaline pushing me to fight or run away. I run. Keeping my eyes forward and focusing on the light pouring in at the end of the alley and the wooden dock and lake across the street, I run and run and run.

I was naïve for thinking they'd make it quick and painless without turning it into a sickening game. I should have known better. They're demons. Nyx is a cruel monster. It was never going to be easy. My mind races with thoughts of how angry Kairos will be once he finds out I'm gone, not only with me, but with Mio too. I shouldn't have dragged him into this. As I push myself to run faster, thoughts of Ere waiting for me at the club and the possibility that I'll never see him again so I can explain sends new pangs of guilt eating away at me. All I wanted was to be free. I hope one day they can understand.

Glancing behind me, the three scaly, winged demons are quickly closing in, running on all fours, red eyes glowing with excitement. A scream bursts from my chest, and I push my legs to move faster, knowing deep down it's useless. They're huge and strong and so much faster than me. The sunlight taunts me with its rays of light, glinting across their sharp teeth and shining a spotlight on the sickly black substance dripping from them.

These monsters killed my parents. Nyx commanded them to do it and then tried to make me take my own life several times. I want them all dead. I tighten my fingers around Mio's celestial dagger as a searing rage pushes its way in. It's not fear that has me wanting to suddenly tear out their throats, but anger over everything they've destroyed around me. Even as I take my last breath and say goodbye to humanity, I will not go down without a fight. My parents didn't deserve what they did to them. Neither did I.

My feet thud against the wobbly wood as I sprint across the dock, the weathered boards creaking and crying out for help that isn't coming. I'm thankful in a way that no one will be here to watch me bleed out or suffer through hearing my screams of agony. All that'll be left here for the ones I love are the blood stains and the gentle hum of the fading energy my soul leaves behind before the lake washes it all away.

"You cannot escape. You have nowhere left to go." The growling is too close now, and I know running any further is useless.

I stop, inhaling deep as I raise my dagger and turn around to face them. A mix of terror and acceptance wash over me, one wanting to send my heart out of control, and the other trying to keep it calm and steady. They tower over me, the black poison leaking off their bodies and splattering on the ground. The weight of their monstrous bodies leaves cracks in the pavement as they continue running full force toward the dock. How Kairos can so easily kill several of these things at once is not something I can fathom.

"Will you take me to Nyx after you kill me?" My voice may tremble, but my hands do not, as I raise the dagger higher.

Dark laughter spills out of their wide, gaping mouths in unison, their pointy teeth on full display. The glow from my weapon illuminates their faces, and they squint their oval eyes as they creep closer to the light.

"The Queen of Darkness is waiting for you already. It is time you join her," growls the demon in the front, the other two flanking its sides. Their red eyes burn into my soul, branding it with the promise of belonging to her for eternity.

Their spines crack and pop as they step forward, the otherworldly movement of their bodies a thing I'd enjoyed seeing in horror films, but not so much now. Their large heads and pointy ears tower over me as they stop and stare down, constant, quiet growls rumbling in their throats.

"I can't wait to meet her. We have much to discuss." I grip my weapon tighter and point it directly at the heart of the hideous monster standing front and center.

They prowl toward me, eyes slanting as they tilt their heads and stare at my blade. "You are useless to her. She only needs your power. Your death will be what hurts the least. She will have eternity to make you suffer." The words are a quiet, crooning vow, a smooth tone that grates at my skin and sends my stomach spinning. Even through the thick, scaly skin, I can see its lips curve up into a wicked smile.

Darkness guide me. Gods save me. Darkness guide me... shit.

I step back as all three snarling demons advance at once, clawed feet scraping against the wood dock. The first one lunges for my throat, his sharp poison dipped claws burning my skin as it slices it open, a scream shattering from deep in my chest. In one swift movement, I grip the demon's wrist and it howls in pain as I dig my nails into the thick flesh there, then push past him and run back down the dock. The other two demons stand side by side blocking my path. I drag my dagger across one of the large arms that reach out to grab me. Black blood sprays as I jam the blade into the chest of the one who grips my shoulders, trying to keep me still. I scream as the burn of the venom from its claws eats at my skin. The demon with the celestial dagger embedded in his chest shatters and turns to ash at my feet, the weapon landing on the dock with a victorious clunk.

I laugh, even as slimy, scaly arms grip me from behind and trap me in place. One kill is one less demon to do Nyx's bidding, and possibly many lives saved from its evil games.

As the venom sets in, my limbs fall weak, I can feel them there, but it's hard to move. The searing pain rages through my body. Warmth trickles down my cheeks as I try not to scream, the realization that it's almost over hitting me hard. I refuse to let them watch me suffer, though the venom drags its teeth across every nerve in my body, scorching me from the inside out more and more by the second.

I'll be thankful when I'm finally dead.

The demon in front of me steps closer, its black blood dripping down its arm from the wound I gifted it. It leans down and nuzzles into my neck. The sound of flesh ripping apart drowns the constant roaring of the waves as it sinks its pointy teeth into my skin. My back arches and I fall to my knees. I can't breathe. The burn is relentless, a rageful, viscous beast.

Covering the bite mark with my hand, I hiss as the venom clings to my fingers and pushes the poison deeper into my gaping wound. I place my palms flat on the cracked, grainy surface of the dock, my tears dripping helplessly onto my hands. Gods, it burns. It burns worse than any pain I've ever known, or any pain I ever imagined could exist. I want it to be done. I want it to be over, this persistent, growing agony that's burning me alive.

A quick slash of claws across my chest and needlepoints digging into my shoulder send me sprawling backward, blurry eyes on the sky as screams I can no longer contain echo out past the lake and into every realm that exists. Is this the pain my parents felt the night they died? Is this how she made them suffer? It only makes me angrier at Nyx and more desperate to get to her as thoughts of their last moments alive pass through my mind.

"Please," I sob, unable to move at all any longer, the pain and paralysis growing fiercer by the second. "*Please...*"

They laugh at my words thinking I'm begging to live, but I'm not. I'm begging for them to let me die.

Letting myself sink into darkness—into nothingness—into the hope of something better after death. Water splashes as I'm shoved off the dock into the lake. My heartbeat slows as pain is replaced by a comforting numbness. I find peace in it. The world around me is a blur and my thoughts slowly fade. It's better this way. No one will be in danger any longer if my plan succeeds. Maybe this is more of Nyx's mind games, and she forced this plan into my thoughts. If that's the case, then I walked right into her trap. Either way, I'm fading into oblivion and I'm okay with it.

I succumb to the darkness. I gladly let it take and take from me, thoughts of Kairos, Olivia, and Hekate slipping, tucking memories of them away in a hidden corner of my mind until it's safe enough to think of them again. I let all my love for them drown as I drown with it, because I have to. This is only temporary. It's necessary. I become the darkness. The numbness wraps tight around me, until my last breath escapes. One day this will all be worth it because I'll be free.

Finally.

Fucking.

Free.

CHAPTER TWENTY-EIGHT

I AM THE STORM

KAIROS

I should have known. This was her plan all along. It was, wasn't it? She pushed me away, she nearly broke me completely, just to come back here and give Nyx exactly what she wanted. Nora, even without her memories, is more like Mera than she knows. Mera tried to give herself up a million times, she argued that it'd be better for everyone if she did, but we wouldn't allow it. We wanted to fight with her. And now she's alone. Because I let her go. Because I was careless and foolish and so blinded by her anger and confusion that I couldn't stand to be near her and deal with the pain of it all. This is my godsdamn fault. All of it.

I'm certain how I feel now must be how the demons feel when I jam my daggers into their brains, my temples throb and ache and my vision blurs from the torture of knowing I could have prevented this. I stare down at Mio's lifeless body, relieved as his chest rises and falls because at least I know one of them is okay. I kneel beside him, white light sparking to life as I place my palms against his chest, sending my power surging through his body to heal him.

I don't have time to be pissed or angry even if I wanted to be. I just need to find out what the hell happened and how the hell we ended up here.

"Have you heard from her yet?" I ask Hekate, my voice laced with obvious desperation.

"She hasn't responded to my texts. I'll try calling." Her phone lights up and she puts it to her ear, her blue eyes glowing with fear as she paces the alley.

Fuck. I'm scared, too. Not many things send terror lashing at my mind, devouring any hope or promise of safety there, but right now fear is all that's left.

"Kairos? What happened?" Mio groans and gets to his feet, rubbing at his temples. "Nora. Fuck. Where is she!?" His head jerks left and then right before his wide eyes meet mine. "Ro, I-I'm so sorry." He paces back and forth, running his hands through his hair and staring at the ground, his energy chaotic and enraged as it whirls around him.

"Did you see which direction they took her?" I spit, placing my hands on his shoulders to bring him to a standstill, then stealing his swords and daggers before strapping them to myself.

I felt it all. Her pain. Her sadness. And then the numbness she let herself fall into as she gave up hope. I didn't have time to grab my weapons; I had enough time to end training with my soldiers and portal here with only the celestial dagger I held in my palm.

Thanks to Mio, I now have two swords in the sheaths on my back, daggers strapped to both thighs, and knives tucked into each of my boots. I have a feeling I might need them all tonight.

"She told them she wouldn't fight. Said they could have her if they let me go," he breathes, his head falling back and his eyes firmly planted on the realms above. "It's all my fault."

Of course she did. I suspected it already, felt it was true deep in my bones, but I had no idea she'd be willing to throw her life away in an attempt to keep us all safe. This could end so much worse than she probably imagined.

"It's not your fault, Mio. It's *mine*," I growl through clenched teeth, the anger at myself outweighing the rage I feel toward him. "It was me who let this happen. I should have been here."

"Don't worry, Kairos. We'll get her back." Hekate's warm, gentle glittering blue fingertips pressed to my shoulder send calming energy my way, but it's useless.

The shattering heartbreak alongside the void of all-consuming emptiness now that Nora is gone are not things magic could ever possibly heal.

"I can't feel her at all, Hekate. It's as if she has disappeared completely." I close my eyes, focusing again on connecting to her energy or her soul or fucking anything at all, but there's nothing to cling onto, nothing to grasp and pull me toward her the way I'm used to.

My bleeding, mangled heart, the one that has always beat for only her won't heal if something bad has happened to her. Though a part of me knows the truth. She's not here on the Earth Realm any longer. I would feel her. I would feel *something*. She's down with Nyx in The Underworld. It's the only thing that makes sense.

I shake Hekate's hand off my shoulder, disconnected and gazing blankly at the ground, not wanting her comfort or positivity or her bullshit lies of getting Nora back anywhere near me. The fresh, crumbling cracks in the pavement draw my attention, and then I'm running, chasing the demon tracks I was too distracted before to see, the scattered pieces of cement a possible trail leading right to Nora.

How can I live or breathe or fight another day without her? I can't. I'd allow Nyx to slaughter me herself just to end what would be an irrevocable, never-ending life of misery.

The stench of stale evil smacks me in the face as I stall at the edge of the dock, my boots mere inches from the faded, wooden planks, hesitating as if walking across those planks will plummet me into an ocean of endless suffering. Hekate places glowing blue shields around us without even moving as together we take slow, cautious steps forward. Mio and I are made to sense and track evil, but Hekate senses it here, too. She takes my hand in hers and squeezes it tight, pulling me to a stop.

"Kairos, wait." Gripping my forearm with her other hand, she looks at me, her eyes lacking their normal radiant glow and her energy dull and lifeless, a thing I've never felt around her before.

"What do you sense, Hekate?" I whisper, knowing the truth already but not allowing myself to admit it.

We're too late. I sense her absence the way one might sense charged electricity in the air searching for a target to strike, in a way that feels detrimental and permanent. Hekate says nothing. She simply shakes her head and faces forward, Mio's gaze once again shifting up to our realm, refusing to look my way. We continue across the dock until we're standing at the edge, staring out at the waves and the never-ending darkness. The silvery moonlight glinting across the water isn't enough to chase away that darkness; not the kind that has seeped into our hearts. The putrid scent of evil lingers, but even that isn't strong enough to overpower the scent of fresh blood. Nora's blood. It's unmistakable.

Mio and Hekate's eyes are pinned to the boards near my feet, and that's when I notice the black scorch marks from venom, even the wood blistered and raw from the burn of it, and the crimson stains splattered all around us.

Crouching, I drag my fingertips across the blood stains, breathing her in deep within my lungs, letting the truth of what has happened because of me not being here to protect her burn me alive. This is why I no longer feel her soul connected to mine. She's not here. She's not alive. Nyx took her from me.

"Kairos, this is not permanent. She's going to ascend. She'll be a celestial when she wakes up, and we'll go to The Underworld. We'll get her back." Hekate wipes her tear-streaked cheeks, crossing her arms over her chest. "This will not go unpunished."

"I'll go wherever you need me to. I'll kill the queen myself if you order me to." Mio kneels in front of me, his head bowed slightly.

As if I'm a king or a fucking savior or someone who deserves even a modicum of respect.

My hand trembles as I raise it, my fingers twitching as I open a portal to the Realm of Darkness. "Go home, Mio. Inform Queen Gaia of what has happened. She'll want to know." My voice is detached and deadly calm, the sound far away as if I'm not even here, but I need him to tell the others.

"I can stay, Ro. I want to help make this right. Please let me."

I shake my head, still focused only on the blood stains of the one I failed so terribly.

Nora is no longer alive, which means Mera and her power is. Nyx having that power in her possession is a risk to us all. Every realm must be made aware.

Hekate leans forward, speaking softly into Mio's ear and then he nods once and steps through the portal. The darkness and flashes of color swirl in front of me before it snaps closed, but I don't see it, not really. All I see is red.

Her blood might as well be on my own hands. I failed her. I failed at protecting her because the thought of my chance with her slipping away nearly killed me. It was selfish. Stupid. I should have been here to fight for her. She died alone because of me, and now Nyx has exactly what she wanted, the power to control or destroy the realms using a divine being who has no memories of how to use her own power. Nyx will gladly infiltrate herself into her mind and use it for her.

The queen must die. I will shatter every realm if I need to, break every celestial law or defy fate and destiny or each godsdamn prophecy that exists on my own if it's what must be done to bring her home. This is my fault. Only I can fix it.

Nora was innocent and pure. She deserved so much better than all of this. My stomach clenches violently and churns at the thought of what she must have endured, of how desperate and alone she must have felt as her life slipped away. I failed her. Gods, I fucking failed her.

Pushing myself to my feet, anger surges through my core, a wrathful storm bellowing inside that can no longer be contained. Letting my head fall back, I reach for the sky, fingertips dancing with electricity as I let out a scream so deep and pained and rageful that the sky itself trembles before bursting open and sending rain crashing down upon the beach. I surrender at last to the untamed fury of my emotions. A wall of water rises from the lake, higher and higher, as wide and as tall as the island that I've now grown to despise because Nora should have never been here to begin with. Fuck, *Nora* should have never existed to begin with. Mera should have always been with me. Nothing and no one should have ever taken her away and made her start life all over again.

I drop my hands to my sides and the waves thrash and churn, cascading out in all directions, no longer a tower of wrath and fury. I stare blankly as they swirl and pound against each other, time standing still, the waves lashing at each other in slow motion. This is how life would feel every single day if I could never see her or touch her or even speak to her again. Time for me would not move. It would be unsettling and wrong. Lightning ripples across the sky, blue streaks disrupting the darkness as bolts strike the ground, avoiding me even when I wish they wouldn't.

Tonight, I'd like to burn. For failing my fated mate once again, I deserve to. Thunder cracks and rain continues to drench me, my hair stuck to my forehead and covering my eyes as the wind howls and swirls angrily around me. In this moment, I'd give anything for the wind to carry me away, so far from reality that I never have to face what I've done again. I can't face the pain. My unrestrained power surges through town and streetlamps flicker, the sound of shattered glass following closely behind. The absence of light is all that's left here, in the city and within me.

I'm no longer a celestial burning with a desire to be good or moral or bring peace to the world. No. I don't give a shit about any of that right now. I am nothing but the rage inside of me, a storm barreling toward its target. I am the storm Nyx should fear.

My hands are in fists at my sides as I make my way back across the dock and then crumble to my knees along the shore in defeat. I bury my head in my hands and slouch over, my forehead nearly pressed against the sand as tears begin to fall.

Hekate's blue shield glitters brightly beside me as she sits on her heels. "I'm sorry, Kairos. I know how much you love her, but this isn't all on you. I should have stayed with her when she pushed you away. I never should have left her side." She places her hand on my shoulder, and we stare out at the lake as the water stills and the final whispers of wind and thunder fade away.

Neither of us say anything for a while. I sense her pain, as quiet and calm as it might be, and I know damn well she senses mine. Sometimes silence in healing is necessary. That storm has been building up inside of me for days. For decades. For an entire fucking century if I'm being honest. It hurts. Fated mates or not, I won't believe what the prophecies say, that Mera and I together will end darkness, until she is safe in my arms again. Will I have to wait another century?

It didn't matter how long it took for her to return last time, I would have waited forever for her. Doesn't matter this time either. No matter how long it takes for us to find happiness together, no matter how many times she dies and the gods reincarnate her into new bodies with no memory of me, I will always wait for her. I will help her find her way back to me.

"I think you and I should go." Hekate stands, offering me her hand.

"Just the two of us?" My brow crinkles as I reach for her hand and pull myself to my feet. "You haven't fought a demon in a long time, Hekate. Since the war. You sure you're up for that? It could get very messy." I take in her pristine white dress and heels, a shadow of a smile flashing across my face.

To be fair, even in the war she never gave up her dresses. They're just much shorter and more restricting now with how tight she wears them. And as tempting as her offer is, as much as I'd love to go to The Underworld and slaughter every demon who even looks my way, the rulers forbade us from ever entering the realm without their permission. They promised Nyx we'd leave her and her evil minions alone the day Mera was created. My parents might punish us both if they discover we've gone. Then again, she took Nora. One of our own. They'd have to understand that we needed to act quickly.

"I think I'll handle myself just fine. I am a queen after all." She smiles, her magic flickering around her. Daggers and blades appear in holsters and straps, each of them adorned with bright jewels and the hilts wrapped in golden flowers. “I want to see what exactly Nyx has been up to down there. No one knows. It’s time we shine a little light into the darkness.” Without so much as moving or blinking, two large orbs of light appear in front of her, swirling around her waistline and thrumming with power as she turns away.

They hiss and spark with electricity, and I know from experience that if any demon gets within ten feet of her they’ll be blasted to oblivion and left incapacitated until she can slaughter them.

“We have no way in until a portal opens between our realms. Who knows when that might be, but I was planning on going, anyway. I won’t try to stop you if you want to join. I’ll even let you tell my parents I forced you into it.” I smile crookedly, and then it falters the moment she waves a hand and opens a pitch-black portal that reeks of darkness and despair. “How did you...”

“I have special privileges as a queen. I can go anywhere I choose. No one can stop me. Not even Gaia and Ourahnus, who aren’t aware yet that I’m a queen, by the way, so don’t tell them.” She shrugs. “What’s the plan?” Her tone and demeaner are calm, but her eyes betray the worry her voice tries to hide.

I can’t help but wonder if her reasons for going have more to do with her love for Nyx than I’d like. Does she truly believe she can still save her? Even if she could, is there redemption for someone who has caused as much damage and chaos as she has? I hope she understands that my priority is the woman I love and nothing else. If anyone gets in my way, including her, and *especially* Nyx, I won’t hesitate in doing what needs to be done to protect her.

“Kill anything that gets in our way before it can kill us. That’s as far as I got with my plan,” I say.

We stare into the portal, and it whispers our names, calling to us like it’s where we belong. I’d rather die here and now than to ever belong to darkness. I never will.

Mera will never belong to it, either. I’d let it devour me whole if doing so would save her.

CHAPTER TWENTY-NINE

THESE ARE NOT MY THOUGHTS

NYX

OCTOBER 6TH, 1851

Last time I stepped foot in this despicable forest, the river greeted me with visions that destroyed my entire life. The blood and darkness warped my every thought until I no longer knew what was real or imagined. It did not take long for me to come to the realization that everything it showed me was true. My future was doomed, though I tried to fight it. It was useless. Any hope I had crumbled to nothing the moment my wings were burned.

The butterflies light the way as I smile at Queen Gaia and Hekate, letting my sharp teeth peek out from behind my crimson painted lips. They are both dressed in white robes, becoming one with the scenery around us. I thought the fluffy white landscape with its glowing flowers and insects was stunning when I was here before. Now it is a reminder that even the most beautiful things harbor cruelty and darkness within. I wish to burn it all to ash.

Or is this just that *thing* inside of me that lurks, the monster who controls when I speak and what I think and who I love, which is no one now, because it will not allow me to feel anything. It is always here, lingering beneath the surface, waiting to take the reins, and I cannot stop it. I am not strong enough to break free.

"Welcome, Nyx." Gaia greets me with a small, cautious bow, keeping her eyes on me. "Thank you for coming. I appreciate your willingness to listen to what I have to say."

The goddess who calls herself a queen pulls back her white hood, her diamond encrusted robe glistening under the bright lights of the swirling sky. She enjoys wearing beautiful things to hide what a monster she is on the inside. I see through her disguise after witnessing myself what she is capable of, not to mention all the lies she tells the unsuspecting people of her realm. Though her dark eyes dance with light and love, there is not a thing capable of love within her, though I am certain she would say the same of me. She may think that I do not know her but that she knows me. Yet neither of these fools know a thing about who I am, not anymore. They know nothing of the hatred and resentment the thing inside me feels toward them both, how badly it would love to tear them apart limb from limb and simply smile while doing so. I cannot tell them these things. It will not let me, but one day I am certain it will show itself and let it be known.

Someday they will feel my wrath across every realm, and it will be me but not me, because I simply do the monster's bidding. I have no control over what I do or say any longer.

"It's so nice to see you again, Nyx." Hekate smiles even as my lifeless, blood-red eyes burn into hers, showing her how little I care.

She is beautiful in her robe lined with lace. It accentuates all the most delicious parts of her. I want to hate her because it would be easier for me if I did. I want to wish death upon her as the thing inside of me does, but though my heart may be as hard and cold as obsidian, the unwanted memories resurface when she is near. The beating *thing* in my chest forces me to feel what I try hard to forget.

Stupid, wretched heart.

She is a traitor. She never loved me. It was all a lie. There is no forgiving Hekate.

No! Get out of my head! Please...do not make me do this...

The serpents around my neck hiss in response to her voice, the irritation forced onto me from the beast inside passing on to them. "I wish I could say it is lovely to see you, but you both know how much I despise the two of you. You have made it very clear how you feel about me, as well."

Do not listen to the darkness, Hekate. This is not me. These are not my thoughts. These are not my words...

My black dress skates across the ground as I step toward them, the hissing growing louder as the grip around my shoulders and arms tightens, my serpents displaying themselves proudly as accessories which are not only things of beauty, but deadly weapons as well. I reach up and caress their scaly heads as they peek out from behind my shoulders and the hissing ends, my touch assuring them we are safe for now.

The witch sighs, her wide eyes moving up and down my body, stopping at the curved horns on my head. I smile as she stares and shivers involuntarily. Her fear creeps across her skin and goosebumps prickle up on her bare arms. The sight and overwhelming scent of her fear is delightful.

Good. Hate me. Fear me. Kill me, Hekate. I am no longer the one you loved. That woman died long ago...

"My Gods have you changed. It's difficult for me to see you this way." The chilly breeze sends her icy hair flowing around her, and she reaches up to brush it out of her pale, perfectly heart shaped face. "Tell me, Nyx. Are you happy in the Underworld? Are you truly happy now?" She blinks slowly, refusing to take her eyes off me even for a moment. The blue glow of her big, doe eyes reaches for me, sending her power out searching for what might be left of her lover's soul.

Her magic is warm, like a familiar embrace, like a long lost loved one who wishes to call me home, and it makes my stomach churn with disgust. I should kill her.

Don't you dare touch her! Please, take me home, Hekate. I wish to come home to you...

Forcing my gaze away, I lift my hands and focus on shining my sharp, black claw-like nails, imagining how satisfying it might feel to slash them across her jugular and watch her bleed out until she is nothing but a fleshy, empty shell.

I look up at her after the urge to slaughter her passes, letting the red glow within my eyes ignite even brighter. "Someday, perhaps, you will find yourselves in The Underworld with your fate in my hands. Perhaps you could use a friend there more than you know. It is me, after all, the queen of the realm, who chooses your final fate, is it not? Me who can let you pass through to the Elysian Fields where you will be treated as gods, or who can choose to send you to Asphodel Meadows where you will simply exist as ordinary beings and nothing more. Or, better yet," I lift a clawed finger, tapping it thoughtfully against my cheek, "I can toss you into the pit to burn for eternity." Smiling brightly, I drop my hand as the women shift nervously on their feet, considering my words. "To answer your question, Hekate," I spit her name through clenched teeth, hating the way it sounds rolling off my tongue. "I am as happy as one could be after being betrayed by the ones she loved and forced into the waiting arms of darkness. The Underworld is all I have left. I was not given another option, now was I?" I glare first at Gaia and then at Hekate, my face cold and uncaring, though somewhere within my mind the wounds still burn, fresh and raw and not ones time could ever heal.

Hekate's eyes soften, the glow dimming and her normal radiant energy shifting to a pained emptiness.

I hope my words hurt. I hope they cut her so deeply that it burns, eviscerating her soul and leaving a hollowness that can never be filled. I hope the agony of it drives her completely mad one day. She is deserving of any pain I may cause. They are both deserving of much more.

She does not deserve this! She deserves the sun and the moon and every single star in the sky. Please, let me go. Let me speak to her!

Gaia shakes her head, and her face scrunches up in disappointment. "You will forever blame us for your fate. You will never offer up forgiveness, will you? To me or to her or even the Gods. You chose your path, Nyx, whether intentional or not. We played no part in your choices."

"Why should I offer forgiveness when neither of you have apologized for what you have done?" Clenching my hands into fists at my sides, my nails dig into my palms and warmth trickles down. My serpents hiss and writhe in anticipation. "You do not deserve a thing from me. If you look at me now and despise what you see, you have only yourselves to blame. *You* did this to me." My throat tingles as the venom in the back begs to be let into the air, dying for the thrill of watching their lungs bleed.

Their deaths would spare me the never-ending torture of having to look at their vile faces, knowing the abhorrent things they have done.

These are not my thoughts. These are not my words. This is not me.

"Enough." Gaia faces the River Oceanus, her dark hair shining like velvet against the bright lights within the water. "We did not come here for this. We are here to find peace. To bring unity back to our realms. Fate has brought us together, and try as we might, we cannot fight it."

Stepping toward her, my stiletto heels leave dents in the fluffy ground beneath them. "I want your people to leave myself and the demons alone.

Leave us be. Darkness deserves to exist in this world as well as light. Without darkness your realm serves no purpose. You have nothing to fight for. Darkness cannot guide you or anyone else into the light if we no longer exist."

You serve no purpose. Death will reign upon you one day. They will make sure of it. I will make sure of it once I am free of you.

My insides burn as the darkness raging inside me scrapes its claws across my mind, a warning that I am thinking too much. Feeling too much. Those are forbidden things.

Gaia snaps her eyelids shut and hesitates before speaking. "Fine, Nyx. If that is what it takes to make you happy, then consider it done. "She glances over her shoulder, nodding once. "We will no longer send celestials to your realm to eradicate the demons. But we will have no choice but to slaughter the ones who enter the Earth Realm to torment mortals. It is our duty. You know as well as I do that we could not stop even if we wanted to. It is what we were created by the Gods to do."

Hekate's eyes dart to the queen in shock and they stare at each other for a moment, then she nods and returns her gaze to me. "I will also command the witch covens to pull back, if it is truly what you want. I wanted to stay close because I believed I could convince you to come back to me." Her eyes gloss over as a single tear slides down her cheek. "If there is no hope left for us, then I will let you go. I only hoped to one day bring you home."

Home. I should laugh at her words. She took part in ensuring I could never again return home. Gods, how I would love to gouge those pretty eyes out of her skull. The Goddess of witches is dreadfully more pathetic than I realized, begging for someone who makes it perfectly clear they do not want them.

I cannot bear this torture any longer, the lies you are forcing from my lips. Please let me go!

"It would be wise of you to let me go, Hekate. I let you go so long ago that it is like our love never existed. I feel nothing for you. I have a home now, no thanks to you. A place where I belong. I will never come back to you." I hold her gaze as she wipes tears from her cheeks, my lips curving up the moment my words break her, and she turns away.

I miss you. I need you. Please... you promised you would always have hope! You promised it was us against anything!

I note Gaia's protective barrier of white light glimmering around her, and glancing at Hekate, the faint glow of her blue shield still stands. They have summoned me to form a truce, to form an alliance, or so they say, but they cannot let their shields fall in my presence. They will never trust me, nor should they, but for now, I need them to.

"We are not here today to discuss the past. We are here to look ahead to the future. Our future and yours as well, Nyx. Our futures are dim if we cannot find peace. I have seen it myself." Gaia clasps her hands behind her back, letting her shield of protection fade away.

I should kill her now and end this. I should allow myself the vengeance I deserve for the way I was shunned and mutilated by their people, people I trusted with my life.

These are not my thoughts. This is not me.

Hekate's blue shield glimmers and then fades away. "We only want what is best for the realms. What is best for our people. I am truly sorry for what has happened to you, Nyx, but if you have found happiness within The Underworld, then I truly am happy for you." Blinking back tears, she sucks in a deep, trembling breath.

Tipping my head back, laughter pours from my throat in a high-pitched screech. The beastly women step back as the air around me stills, the glowing creatures and insects skittering away behind trees and in bushes. The lights in the river dim, even it having the intuition to be scared, an attempt to hide the divine light held within it. The light which will be mine one day.

I will never be happy without you, Hekate. I will fight this darkness until I take my last breath. I will not let it win.

"I do not want an apology," I croon, gliding toward them on the tips of my toes, my power floating me on air as if I am weightless before settling my heels back on the plush ground. "I do not want acceptance or approval, not from either of you. What I want is for you to see me as I truly am. Who I was always fated to be. A queen. A creator of life. A ruler who has just as much power and authority as the both of you." I run the point of my nail down Hekate's cheek, smiling as she trembles beneath my touch. "My realm thrives because of me but it bleeds because of you. You have taken so much already. We do not need you. *I* do not need you."

Gods, why can't they see this is not me? I need you! Please, can't you see how much I need you!

The poor, pitiful witch turns her back to me, lifting a hand to her face and sniffling quietly. My lips twitch but I force the smile away, wanting to get this over with and not have to look at them any longer. I am the queen of creation, so if a creation is what they want, a creation they shall receive. It will belong to me in the end, anyway.

The queen places a delicate hand on Hekate's shoulder, her brows scrunching together and eyes narrowed on me. "I see there is a lot of pain here still, but we must let it go. The fate of our realms is in our hands, so we must try to work together. We must forget how we have hurt each other and face the path of healing."

There is no such thing as healing. There is only suffering in silence and pretending the pain no longer exists, but it always exists. It only becomes easier to ignore.

"Are you absolutely certain we are making the right choice?" The false hope in Hekate's eyes is gone.

Has she at last come to her senses and given up on her lover?

"A week ago, a new prophecy was written in the book of Gods and Monsters right before my eyes." Gaia smiles as if she has never seen anything like it. "A new being who is connected to each of our realms must be brought to life. Peace will prosper one day thanks to her light." Staring into the river, the water churns, the lights flickering and growing brighter. She kneels before it. "I saw her. I saw who she will become. A queen. A savior. The mate of someone very special to me. This is our destiny." Dark eyes glance my way as the swirling colors in the river pulsate.

It is calling to us. This *is* our destiny. *Mine.*

"Mixing the blood of the Celestial Queen with the blood of the Queen of witches and the Queen of Darkness... well, what could possibly go wrong?" I step closer, unable to peel my eyes away from the pull of the divine light.

Everything will go wrong, and I will delight in the fiery downfall of the realms as I witness it all burn to nothing. If this being is important to Gaia and her realm, in giving her even an ounce of joy or hope, then I will gladly destroy it myself. Anything to make her pay. To make her hurt in ways she can never recover from, as she has done to me. She might foolishly believe this being will bring us together, but in the end, it will only make me stronger. I will have no need to destroy it. Everything I create ultimately bows down to me.

"If you think it is what must be done, then I will gladly offer my assistance." Hekate kneels next to Gaia, two lying, heartless, *goddesses in disguise*, and as I look down upon them, I relish in the glimpse of the future I see of them kneeling at my feet, begging for repentance that will not be granted.

I might feel badly for them if I did not despise them so dearly. If they had not so thoroughly destroyed my entire life.

Lifting the bottom of my dress, I kneel on Gaia's other side, my reflection rippling across the water and sending the light drifting away in fear. A wince of pain is followed by the scent of blood as Gaia drags her dagger across her palm. Hekate uses her own golden dagger wrapped in roses and does the same. Using the tip of my talon-like nail, I slice my skin open, letting the thick, black blood ooze out and drip into the water with theirs, mixing and darkening the crimson that leaks from their veins.

The water swirls and then our power rises, the divine light depleted as it floats above the now ordinary clear blue river. I cannot help but smile as the sound of large, fluttering wings made of flames, of divine light, greet us in the sky.

"Holy Gods," I whisper.

"Holy gods is right." Gaia's words are barely audible over the crackling of flaming colors that somehow seem to outshine the sun.

"Welcome to the Realm of Light. We are thrilled to have you here." Hekate bows her head low, but keeps her eyes locked on our creation, smiling up at the bright cerulean and amethyst wings.

She is beautiful. Her hair sways in the breeze like little sparks of blood orange embers and her eyes glow and gleam as they meet mine. I cannot wait to ruin her, to snuff out every last spark of light in her perfect, pure body. Divine light should not exist in a world that will one day belong to me, and without it, without *her*, the celestial realm will crumble. It is all within her now—my most powerful creation of all. And she, whether she likes it or not, will belong to darkness one day. I will make sure of it.

No...

These are not my thoughts.

These are not my words.

This is not me.

CHAPTER THIRTY

THE AWAKENING

NORA

All I feel is darkness now. Nothing else exists. The icy breath of death caresses my face, but my skin is immune to the chill, and my body doesn't shiver. I am numb. The cold doesn't sting like the snowy winters I'm used to. In this moment, it feels right, as if nothing will ever hurt me again. No fear exists in my mind, just a sense of emptiness within. My soul is lost to me. I'm not sure it exists any longer. Maybe it died as I did.

Death whispers my name, his soothing voice surrounding me like a blanket of velvety shadows, tempting me back to life. I can't face him. The moment I gazed into the darkness and it gazed back, I understood what it meant. I belong to it...to *him*, eternally. Clutching me tight, his tender strokes against my cheek help distract from the thunderous flap of wings. I won't face him. I can't escape and I know it, but I fear what he will look like. I'm afraid I'll like what I see, the darkness that stares back at me.

The still silence goes on and on, my mind eagerly clinging to it, reaching and begging for more. The last few moments of my life I experienced a sense of freedom, as if an awakening I've secretly craved my whole life had arrived. Maybe this is a gift. A dream. A never-ending fucking nightmare. I'm not sure of anything anymore.

I'll need to face him soon. I'll need to open my eyes, but confronting death will be difficult. I haven't gathered the courage just yet. The darkness, the silence, and the chilling numbness are my escape from the pain of living in a nightmare for so long. I'm no longer that girl I used to be, though, the one who was weak and broken. I can feel the shift within myself. As the silent seconds tick by, a separation from who I once was and who I'll now be continues on. I willingly release those old, useless parts of myself. Never again will I be that unbearable, helpless girl.

Darkness and shadows surround me as the cold, gentle hands of sweet death grip me and lift me into his arms. Melting into his touch, I let him take me, content on having an escape from my old life. I prefer being here in the depths of eternal darkness over my mind being forced stuck in a constant loop of trauma and pain.

"Take me sweet death. I belong to you," I whisper, and I feel his smile against my skin.

I am his.

CHAPTER THIRTY-ONE

QUEEN OF DARKNESS

NYX

PRESENT DAY

Adjusting my crown and spreading my wings out wide behind me, I take my place in the throne, casting a venomous smile at the demons bowing at my feet. The cracked, burnt earth greets their faces as my dark power forces their heads down. They do not deserve to look at me. My shimmery gown flashes, defying the absence of light, the black flame torches casting shadows from the deep depths of the River Styx to the rocky mountains encircling those sacred waters. I cross my legs, placing my talons in my lap, my red lips curling into a wicked smile. It gets harder by the day, pretending the urge to destroy them all does not consume me. Pretending the urge to destroy *him* does not. After a century here one would think it might get easier to fight the chains wrapped around me, the crushing boulders weighing me down and shattering my soul to nothing, but it has not. He is not in my head now, not here with his monsters, but still, I am nothing. I am a slave. And all his pitiful lies about my mother persist.

She is not alive. She is gone. The god killed her, just as he will possibly try to slaughter me once he is through with his games. I have not convinced myself there is much hope left for me. There is likely none. Maybe I am dead already.

The demons are all pathetic. Every last one of them. It truly is disappointing how easily they succumb to me, the one he has declared their queen, depriving me the thrill of tormenting and torturing them with my power. Black flames dance along my palms, and I raise them toward the demons. The flickering lights cast eerie shadows on their grotesque forms.

"Where is the girl, my loyal minions? Did I not make it clear what you were to do after killing her?" My voice is lithe and subdued, one of a calculated predator ready to pounce.

I have come to understand the strength in quiet, deadly calm. It brings with it more terror than a raging, thunderous storm.

My lips slit into a vicious grin as the first fool raises its hideous head, fixing its gaze on me. The audacity it has to make eye contact sends my blood boiling. I flick my wrists, directing my dark, vengeful fire toward its face, engulfing it in flames. With a piercing cry of agony, it bows in submission once again. *Good little pet.*

The second demon's brain is at least a bit less of a waste of space than the one I burned. It keeps its eyes where they belong. "We attacked her. We did not take long, just like you asked. Then he..." it mutters, jabbing his scaly, slimy elbow into the third demon. "He pushed her into the lake to watch her drown." His deep growl is a mix of guilt and regret.

"Why did you not watch her bleed out and bring her to me like I asked?" My voice is a dangerous tool, a venomous force that holds the power to unleash upon them whenever I so choose.

With a stifled whimper, the third demon's monstrous voice trembles in fear. "I am s-sorry, Queen Nyx. The mortal girl's life drained too slowly. Her blood seeped out but she lived on. I wanted to bring her to you as quickly as I could."

His huge, trembling body releases a pungent aroma of fear, and I inhale the scent deep into my lungs, reveling in the pleasure it brings. It is a feast to my senses as they hope for a swift and painless end. I delight in the terror others feel when they realize death is near.

Pushing myself up from my chair, my claws dig into the leather, leaving deep lacerations down the curved arms. I loom over the demons, my black serpents emerging from the fiery black pit and slithering smoothly up my legs to wrap themselves around my shoulders and waist. Their glowing red eyes slant as they glare at the three failures in front of us. With just a thought, the serpents do as I say, flicking their tongues menacingly toward the pitiful demons. Their unified hiss echoes to the end of the realm.

"Tell me what happened after you foolishly tossed her into the lake. Why are *you* here and yet *she* is not?" As I unleash my words they drip with venom, corrupting the air and invading their lungs with its sweet promise of death.

My venom is more potent than my serpents, though they are a pleasant weapon to have. The slow, painful demise it brings to those deserving of it is a lovely sight to see. In my experience, I have found that most deserve it. While I take pride in my role as queen, the power it offers here in the Underworld, the demons unwavering obedience cannot quench my constant desire for more. If there is any hope for me left, if I do not die by the hands of my god, the day will come when my darkness envelops the realms. Not His. *Mine.* If I am allowed to live once this is all over, then he will suffer for what he has done to me. I only need to bide my time.

As the effects of my venom slowly set in, the demons gasp and blink up at me in motionless horror. At first, there is partial paralysis.

"He came for her, my queen," the first demon whispers, his raspy voice filled with fear and a desperate understanding that the end is near.

"Who came for her? That pathetic celestial, Kairos?" Kneeling, I laugh, cupping the hellhounds rough, scaly chin between my fingers.

My sharp talons leave a path of destruction as I rake them across his thick skin, leaving searing, gaping wounds to forever mark his wretched face. Thick, black blood oozes out and stains my fingers, and slowly I bring them to my lips and into my mouth, savoring the taste of the panic and fear excreted from its veins.

They know their impending doom awaits.

"No! Not him. H-*He* took her. We never could have stopped him, my queen. Please grant us forgiveness!" The second demon cries, his pleas drowned out by the piercing wails as darkness envelops the three of them completely and they begin to scream.

Blindness. The second gratifying effect of my venom has kicked in.

Each rattling scream is a crescendo of music to my ears, the wails crashing together and forming a hauntingly beautiful melody. They are now condemned to a lifetime of blindness unless I choose to restore their sight. I have no intention of doing such a thing.

I push my shoulders back as I stand, running my fingertips down the slick, smooth skin of my serpents, anger seething within my chest. The calm and deadly approach is getting me nowhere and I am growing bored of looking at them.

"Who took her!?" My shouted words have the demons in the fiery pit clawing at the walls and reaching toward the surface, preparing to barrel out and tear them apart themselves if asked to. "Speak now or prepare for death!" I roar with such intensity that even the celestials in the realms above might hear.

I hope they do. I hope they tremble in fear from the sound of my voice alone. I am but the monster they made me. The villain the gods created to keep secrets buried in the dark and truths from ever seeing the light of day. The fallen orphan daughter who wears the crown and disgraces them still.

The fire blazing in my palms sends the army of demons scattered throughout the realm flinching and covering their faces, fearful of the dark brilliance of its light and the searing intensity of heat that they are aware I have no qualms using against them. The kneeling, blubbering fools at my feet cannot see the flames, but I am certain they feel my inferno of outrage inching closer. Their backs arch, straining against the invisible force of my venom as paralysis embeds itself deeper into their muscles. Useless imbeciles.

The demon who pushed the girl into the lake sobs, his cries grating against my skin. "It was *Him*, my queen. Our god who we must answer to. Your father has taken her. He only left us alive because he wanted you to kill us yourself. He said if you were distracted with killing us," he wheezes, spitting a mouthful of his own vile blood on the dirt, "then it would be too late for you to get to her."

"He is not my father! He is nothing to me!" My body trembles as I prepare for the familiar feel of his power tearing into my thoughts to subdue my truth and fury, or the deep, disappointed tone of his voice warning me to keep quiet if I would like to stay in control of my body. But it never comes.

Relaxing back into my chair, I take a deep breath as the tremors settle and the anger slowly drifts away, focusing again on the three demons in front of me. As much as I despise the creatures, I do find beauty in the way their black tears cascade down their revolting faces. I push my shoulders back and cross my legs, gazing out at the crumbling pillars and temples in the distance, a city once thriving and blessed now fallen and forgotten. I silently contemplate what should be done. He stole the one thing I had left to use against him. Against all of them for that matter. I pull off my crown, the thin metal bending in my palms as I crush it and rip it apart, dropping the broken, jagged pieces at my feet. The power of the crown once excited me. Not any longer. I do not need the crown when my curved horns strike fear into hearts enough alone.

The demons who failed me shake violently with convulsions, dark foamy bubbles spilling over from their lips and sliding down their cheeks. Gurgling sounds fill the air as black blood oozes from their eyes and nostrils, their lungs filling with it rapidly as their internal organs are seared to nothing. Every orifice will drain until there is nothing left. As they turn to dust on the ground, the third effect of my venom has set in...death. Disgusting creatures.

My work for the day is done. There is nothing left to do but wait for our *savior*, our *god*, our *puppeteer* who keeps us all attached to his short strings, to bring her to me. He will if he knows what is good for him. It was part of our deal. I keep quiet. I do as he says. I stop fighting against his control in my head and relinquish myself to him entirely. Therefore, I get the girl, and in turn, my vengeance. I did everything he asked. I slaughtered her parents. I ordered the demons to end her pitiful, sad life. She. Belongs. To me. If my god would like to play dirty, to go back on his word, well then, I suppose I must do the same. I will not play along with his little games any longer. I will get what he has promised me even if he must die in the process. Even if I must. I do not care. I have nothing left to lose. Running my fingers along the amulet around my neck, the one with the swirling colors within a sea of darkness, the necklace the girl cares so much about, I smile. She will come for it eventually. She craves the truth like I crave the use of her power to shatter the current realms and create a new one.

They will all pay for what they have done as I ascend to a realm of my own and watch each of theirs fall.

CHAPTER THIRTY-TWO

SWEET NUMBNESS

NORA

My eyes flutter open, and I squint to see through the blinding darkness. Candles flicker all around the large room, but the black flames hold such a small amount of light within their center that all I see are swaying shadows. It's like the black flames are holding the light within them hostage, refusing to let it shine. Darkness devours it. Sitting upright, the velvety sheets are warm beneath my fingertips as I quickly throw off the covers and try to stand, but there's a heaviness weighing me down. Reaching over my shoulder, my fingertips brush against smooth feathers and thick cartilage, and I gasp. I'm a celestial. No. Something more.

I stand and the hardwood floor groans beneath my bare feet, the chill in the air biting at my skin, and though normally I would curl into myself or shiver from the cold, I don't mind it. Do immortals not feel things the way humans do? I never thought to ask. Here it's like all my senses are on the verge of numbness, even fear in this moment feels far away. I'm not scared. Right now, the only thing that matters is figuring out if I am in fact in The Underworld, which judging by the darkness that has seemed to swallow me whole, I'm pretty damn sure that I am. I died. This is what I wanted. Now I need to figure out how the hell to get to Nyx.

My wings cast a beautiful shadow on the wall as I spread them wide and stare in awe. Gods, shadows really are all that exist here. There's a shadow of a bed, a shadow of a bathroom on the opposite side of the room, and a shadow of a door that I assume leads out of this huge room that's nearly the size of my entire house. I carefully tiptoe across the room to make my way to the door. I need to see what's out there, but I also need to be careful not to let them see me before I want them to. It could be Nyx or more of her demons on the other side of that door. They could be waiting for me to wake up to begin torturing me all over again. Although fear doesn't course through my veins the way it probably should, my heart does beat faster and louder than I'd like it to. Fuck, they're going to hear it.

A shadow moves in my peripheral vision, and I freeze. "Hello?" I call out, peering into the darkness.

Why the hell are there no lights? What I wouldn't give for the hellscape of orange flames humans picture when thinking of this place to be real right now. I just need even one bright flame. The black ones aren't enough.

"Nora," A gentle, low murmur comes from behind me, and I slowly turn around to face the voice. "Please do not panic," the comforting timbre in his voice soothes my anxious mind.

A candle moves closer and closer as if floating on air, but around the dim flickering flame is the shadow of someone stepping toward me. I'm not afraid. Fear will not rule me. First, large wings come into focus, followed by muscular arms and then eyes the color of molten gold. I take two steps back, gasping in shock as the curved black horns demand my attention.

"What are you?" My whispered words aren't really a question.

From the look of the horns and leathery wings, I have my answer already. It's a demon. It has to be. Except this face doesn't look at all like Nyx's demons who murdered me. This face is familiar and kind and so... *beautiful*. This face is one I know all too well.

"Ere, what the fuck are you? Why are you here and why do you look like this?" I take another step back. "Did *she* do this to you?"

"It's okay. I would never hurt you. Please do not be afraid." He brings the candle closer to his face, his gaze calm as he backs away, giving me space.

"Answer my questions," I spit, anger boiling in my chest.

I don't step back this time. I prowl toward him, fists clenched at my sides as fire flickers in my peripheral vision. I can't trust him if he's a demon. If he belongs to her then he should die like the others.

He takes two more steps back. "I will explain everything, I promise. But I need you to stay calm."

"Tell me why you're here and why you look like one of her demons!" It's no longer a question.

Heat surges in my palms and snakes up my arms, flaring within and around my new, heavy wings. My light glows brighter and hotter, nearly devouring the darkness in the room. He's a liar. How long has he been lying to me, and how can I possibly believe anything he says now knowing this?

He sighs, lowering the candle, his eyes pained and gentle as he watches me, slowly taking another step away from the power sparking and shimmering around me. "The Underworld is my home, Nora. It has been for quite some time. We have much to discuss. Why don't we calm down and sit for a moment?" He gestures to the bed.

After all the times we've spent in bed together, and seeing him here as this *thing*, I can't stand the thought of sitting on a bed with him or even being in the same room as him. He lied to me for over six months. Pretended to be mortal and naïve about the things lurking within darkness, even pushed me to accept the darkness that haunted my thoughts. *Why?* Why would he do any of it?

"No. I won't sit here with you, demon. Tell me where Nyx is. Did she send you to kill me for good this time?" I open my palms, the heat there urging me to fight, to use whatever magic I can to put an end to his lies and save myself.

Glancing at my magic, really noticing it for the first time, my eyes widen at the sight of the purple and blue swirls of fire dancing in my palms that grows hotter and angrier by the second. I considered running out the door a moment ago, but if I am who everyone says I am, the divine one with power like no other, then maybe I can still burn him alive even without memories of how to use it.

Raising my hands, I face my palms toward the man or demon or illusion in front of me, smiling as fear briefly flashes behind those golden eyes.

A charming, slow smile flickers across his lips. He tilts his head and gazes into my flames. "Your power is both delightful and terrifying."

I huff a laugh, shaking my head. "I hope you find it just as delightful as it burns you to ash."

His smile vanishes and his eyes now glow like crimson death as tendrils of shadows appear behind his back, stretching and reaching out for me. They wrap around me and caress my body and my mind in a way that brings back the numbness and freedom that enveloped me as I died. The numbness I felt all those times we were together before when I thought I was healing or letting the pain go or learning to be strong and fight the pain of grief and loss that consumed me. It was always his power numbing me and pushing away the pain, wasn't it? It was always him. He's a liar. He never cared about me. He never wanted me to actually heal, he only wanted to control my feelings.

"Nora, I know you are angry. I know you have been through more pain and grief and confusion in the past year than ever before, but you are not angry with me. You are angry with *her*. So am I." His shadows swirl along my arms, and anger races through me, my body trembling and my breathing too fast. The skin where his shadows touch me become bright rageful flames, sending his shadows slithering away as the flames burn hotter.

Smiling, I focus on his chest, the spot where his lying, deceiving heart still beats. His shadows form a wall of protection around him, devouring my flames as they reach for him. There is no light within his power. He belongs to this realm and to Nyx. Light cannot exist around or within him, not when he *is* darkness.

"You don't know a thing about my grief or what I've been through. Demons don't feel. How could you lie to me so easily? How could you pretend to care so damn easily?" My words quiver as I step toward his shadows, flames swirling around me in every direction.

The flames hurt, but his lies scorch my heart in ways fire never could. I want *him* to hurt. I want him to suffer the way Nyx has made me. The way he has.

Sending his shadows out around me, he snuffs out more of my light, the bright blue and purple of my power fading as the burn on my skin subsides. I try to force the flames to return as his shadows engulf me in a darkness that's nearly suffocating, but all I can manage is a flicker before his shadows wrap around me tighter, refusing to let me go.

"You must stay calm. You could easily kill me or anyone else with those flames, but how will you stand a chance against Nyx if I am dead? How will we find the amulet and get your memories back?" He steps toward me, the shadow of his horns menacingly close and the red glow of his eyes enveloping me in numbness until I can't move or feel a thing. "That is what you came here for, is it not? I know truth is what you want. I want that for you, too, more than anything else, Nor. Your truth shall be my salvation."

I should have run from him. I should have made an escape while I had the chance instead of hoping to use a power against him that I can't yet control. Now he might control me for good.

"Let me go!" I push and pull but his shadows only hold me tighter.

His face is close to mine now, and as I stare into his eyes, I feel the warmth of the man I once knew. His jawline is sharper, the muscles along his forearms and chest more pronounced, and he towers over me in a way he hasn't before. He looks much different than he did on the Earth Realm, but as we stand and stare at each other just inches away, I feel him.

Ere. *My* Ere. The man I loved. The man I still care about, though if I'm honest, my feelings for Kairos were beginning to eclipse them. But I love him, still. I can't deny it as he stares down at me, warm golden eyes begging me to calm down and give him a chance to explain. How the hell could my truth be his salvation? I need to know.

He reaches out, caressing my cheek with his fingertips. The charming smile on his lips I've always adored makes my heart flutter. "Please listen to what I have to say, then decide for yourself if you might still like to kill me. I only want to help you. It is all I have ever wanted." His leathery wings shift behind his back as he walks past me, heading to the dark light spilling in from the crack under the door on the far wall.

I swallow, taking a deep, calming breath as his shadows leave with him and I'm able to think and move and feel once again. I reacted harshly and I feel it now, now that the simmering rage of my power has slipped away. But my power reacting was out of my control. It wanted him dead. Not me, the power within. It's beautiful, my power, but hopefully one day I can learn to—or remember how to—control it before someone gets hurt. In a way, Ere and his shadows are quite beautiful as well, but I push the thought away. I cannot trust him. I can listen to what he has to say, but it doesn't mean I have to believe a single word of it just because of our history.

The door is wide open now and he glances over his shoulder as he crosses the threshold. I need the truth. If this will get me closer to it, then I'll follow him wherever I need to. And then I will decide if he deserves to die.

Now that his power has left the room, the numbness it brought goes with him. Fear tries to burrow its way in, but I force it down as I step into the hallway. I follow the sound of noise down a long, dark corridor with candelabras along the walls and chandeliers with more black flames hanging from the high, pointed ceiling. This place looks like an old, gothic castle and I hold my breath as I admire it. It's dark and creepy but it has a beauty of its own, a beauty that I'm sure couldn't be found anywhere else in the world. Stepping into the kitchen, the open area is less shadowed because more flames line the walls and hang high above us from the black diamond chandeliers. The living room has a large, dark stone fireplace with more black flames and bookshelves that line the walls from floor to ceiling, each of them cluttered with old, worn books. No marble or golden swirls or bright celestial light exist here like in the Realm of Darkness. Ere's home is all dark stone and black floors that look like they could have been crafted from obsidian, peaking between dark shadows.

Glancing over his shoulder with a smile, he comes to me, pulling out a chair at the dining room table and gesturing for me to sit. I can't peel my eyes away from his horns. I try, but they're all I can focus on when I look at him despite the huge, almost translucent black wings that take up so much space behind him. Darkness swirls around him as he instantly appears back in front of the stove to finish plating food and setting it up at the table. I've never seen a celestial or witch move the way he does, as if he's tearing through space and time and flittering through motions in fast forward. My head spins watching him.

His eyes don't leave mine as he places food on my plate and then on his, and I can't bring myself to look away from him either. I have so many questions, thoughts, and feelings racing through my mind at once and can't seem to focus on just one. Fear exists, but so does an underlying intrigue and pull toward him that I can't deny, like I've never been able to deny when I'm with him. Hope exists as well, but there's a sense of hopelessness entangled with it, like no matter what he says or what we do it won't matter when it comes to Nyx and what she wants. Pain pushes its way in at the thought of the hurt Olivia, Kairos, and Hekate will feel finding out I'm gone, but then his shadows reach out and brush against me and a layer of numbness wraps around my mind until the thoughts disappear.

A smile briefly flashes across his lips as he takes in my still wide eyes full of shock. "My full name is Erebus, by the way. I only used the name Ere to seem a bit more human for someone who was human at the time. Ask whatever you'd like. I will tell you only the truth."

I place my elbows on the table and lean forward. "What the hell are you? How did you get here? And is this who you've always been?" I swallow, my hands in fists, my nails digging into my palms.

It's not fear that has me angry with him in this moment. I'm not afraid as his icy, numbing energy courses around us to push those feelings away, keeping my heart steady and my mind calm. I'm tired of the lies the people around me keep feeding me in hopes of saving me from any added confusion since I can't remember a damn thing about my past. I just want the truth.

"Yes." His smile I've grown to love, the one full of kindness and charm and dark secrets flitters across his lips. "I have been this way since you met me. Much longer than that, but that is a story for another time." Scooting his chair forward and staring down at the glass in his hand, the one full of a dark liquid that looks like poison, he whispers, "I am the king of The Underworld. Nyx grew tired of ruling her realm alone so she *forced* this transformation on me in hopes that I would follow her blindly and do as she says." He takes a sip, then slams the cup down, his grip on the glass making me worry he'll shatter it to pieces. "She is not just the Queen of Darkness and demons or the queen of this realm. She is one of the forgotten goddesses. If I refused the life she offered me, I could have been slaughtered."

"Nyx is a goddess?" I breathe, leaning back against my chair and gazing up at the ceiling, hopelessness pushing its way in even further. "If she is in fact a goddess, and she did this to you, then how are you able to resist her power? The demons can't. They do exactly as she says when she says to do it, from what I've been told. How are you able to leave and live a pretend happy life with a human she's haunting and hunting for power? Why doesn't she just kill you if you're so disobedient?" I cross my arms over my chest as I wait.

Finally releasing his grip on the glass and pushing it to the side, he tells me, "I have grown good at fooling her over the past century. My power numbs my mind and heart in a way that lets her believe I am under her spell. That I feel nothing. I have also watched Nyx slowly lose her mind down here. The whispering to voices that are not there, and the darkness she claims will not let her go keep her occupied. She has been too distracted falling into madness to notice or even care what I am doing most of the time." Smiling he pushes his chair back to prowl around the table and stop beside me.

Pulling out the chair and facing it in my direction, he takes a seat, his thighs spreading apart slightly as he leans back, raking his eyes over me. I try not to stare at how large he is, or think about how tiny I feel sitting here beside him, or how he looks so much the same as he used to and yet entirely different. I look away.

"Nyx believes what she wants to believe, Nora. She has one goal only and that is to control you and wield your power. My one goal since I met you has been to help you not see yourself as something weak or broken that needs to be fixed. You must be strong to stand against her. The power she possesses will eat at your mind until there is nothing but her thoughts and desires left within you, but," he leans his elbows on his knees, the warmth of his body much too close. "I can help you fight her because as much as she has tried, I have accepted the darkness she forced within me and have learned to use it to my advantage against her. Darkness cannot rule a mind that is numb or drag its claws across a heart that feels nothing. But I fucked up." His eyes meet mine. "You gave me hope while I was stuck here with her. You were always my flame within the darkness. My escape. With you I allowed myself to feel after a century of feeling nothing but emptiness. She sent the demons to attack me that night at the club because she found out I was sneaking away and spending time with you. I was always so damn careful, but my feelings for you could not simply be numbed or forced from my heart." He leans back, crossing his arms over his chest, glaring into the emptiness beside him.

"That's why you let me go. Nyx found out you were spending time with me and neither of us would have been safe any longer. You could no longer protect me." I swallow, my heart lurching at the thought of how easily I allowed it, at how hard it must have been for him to let me leave with Kairos. "So you let *him* protect me."

"It killed me, Nora, to walk out your door that night and pretend I wanted nothing to do with you. If I told the celestials the truth then, they would not have trusted me. Hell, they probably would have killed me. Kairos taking you away was the only thing that made sense. If I lost you, if Nyx got her hands on you, I might as well be dead myself. I'd have no reason to go on living." He stands, making his way back to his original seat and picking up his fork and knife, no longer focused on me. I can't pull my eyes away as I take in everything he's just told me. He has been stuck here for a century with her? A century of forcing only numbness into his heart to avoid any pain she might like to cause. That's torture. It's cruel on so many levels I can't even begin to understand. I hate her. More than anything, more than the lies I've been fed and the pain she has already caused me, making Ere suffer and holding him captive here for an entire fucking century might be the worst thing she has done of all. I want her dead.

"Why you, Ere? What was her interest in you in particular? She could have forced this on anyone if she really wanted to hurt me or get me here. Kairos who is my fated mate or Hekate who was my best friend even in the past.

What is it about you—or was choosing you a random, thoughtless decision by her?"

"It was not random," he says, his eyebrows furrowing as he thinks for a moment. "She loved Hekate and I believe deep down a part of her still does. And *Kairos*," he growls his name like it's the worst sound to ever pass over his lips. "Torturing Kairos, she believed, would have done little to hurt you. If only she knew how you'd fall for him this time around. You see, you never loved him before." He scoffs, his head shaking slightly as he averts his gaze back to his plate of strange, blackened food. He sits his utensils down, sighing loudly and placing his head in his hands.

"What do you mean? Kairos believes we're fated mates and Mio told me we spent fifty years together. The entire realm believes we're meant to be. That we were once together."

Slowly, he raises his head, pushing his shoulders back and tucking his wings in tight behind his shoulders. He takes a deep breath. "Kairos is not your fated mate, Nor. A few heartless, bitter gods have fooled everyone into believing what they want them to believe, but I remember the truth. Nothing happening within the realms is how it should be. It is all a lie. Once we get your memories back, you will remember, too. That is why helping you was so important to me. I need you to remember. I am tired of being king in a realm ruled by her and tired of being a pawn in the gods games. I am sorry for what has happened to you and what led you here to me, but what I am not sorry for is having you by my side now. With me is where you have always belonged."

My light, my flame, open your eyes.

His whispered words within my mind wrap around me like a dark, sweet embrace, and I remember the night of my parents' deaths and how those same words echoed in my mind then. Those words are familiar in a way that my heart can't comprehend, but deep in my subconscious I know they once meant something special to me. This is all too much. I want to run. I want to scream. I feel tears brimming at the edges of my vision, but I force them away. I know I must be strong. Everything will make sense once I retrieve my memories and remember the truth myself.

"So, you can speak into my mind. That's fun." I smile, picking up my fork and cutting into the fluffy, black pancake on my plate. "So what you're saying is that the celestials don't realize they're lying by telling me Kairos and I are fated mates because they don't know the truth themselves. Because the gods are playing some cruel game with us all? I don't know whether or not to believe you," I tell him, taking a tiny nibble of the food on my fork and being thankful when it tastes exactly like the special recipe he used to make for me back home. It's delicious and not at all as poisonous or sickening as it looks. "You said we belong together. Did you mean something to me in the past, then?" I swallow and then poke at another triangular piece of pancake. I shovel it into my mouth, realizing that dying and coming back to life has made me ravenous and empty.

I wipe my lips with the back of my hand, looking up at him as he leans his chin on top of his clasped hands, his elbows firmly placed on the table. "Were we together before? I'm assuming so with how intense and raw your words come out."

My cheeks redden when his eyes sear into me in silent confirmation.

I don't know what to believe anymore. For him to tell me everything I've learned about my past is a lie is hard to take in, but would it really surprise me? I've been gone for a century. A lot could have gone wrong. There are gods and royalty and witches and separate realms and magic and no one seems to be who they say they are. I don't know who to trust anymore or what the hell to believe. He still hasn't told me why he would be forced to stay here with Nyx. Who was Ere to me?

"Nyx forcing me to rule by her side as king was another layer of pain she hoped to cause you. She knows what we are to each other. She knew it would hurt when you found out what she had done to me. Knew it would kill me having a front row seat to her destroying you and breaking you until you become nothing but a shell of magic for her to use as she pleases." Shaking his head, his eyes meet mine, and the fear and heartbreak within them hint at all the pain he has already been through.

You and I are fated mates, my love. Your memories are just as important to me as they are to you. They are our memories.

I freeze midway through taking another bite of the dark, delicious food. I didn't ask why Nyx forced him to rule, I only thought it. Not only can he speak within my mind, but he can read my thoughts, too. A part of me is utterly terrified by this, but another part tingles and blazes with excitement. His power is amazing.

I nod, setting my fork down and gazing across the table at him, really looking at him for the first time. I'm not sure if I'm hoping to see a hint of a lie there, or suspecting that I might, but there's nothing but confident truth as he watches me. It scares me to think Kairos could be wrong, that any feelings we had for each other were a lie, but a part of me knows anything is possible in a world where magic exists. What if what we all know or think we know are lies? I can't look away from Ere and his glowing eyes as they burn through my heart and soul. Here in this moment, a part of me truly believes him. If Ere is my fated mate, then it makes sense that Nyx would use him as a way to hurt me while my soul waited for reincarnation. If she could no longer torture me, then my fated mate would be the next best option to make me suffer. The pieces feel like they're clicking in place, and more than ever I want to know the truth. With everyone else so far away, with no one here to stop me from going after Nyx or my mother's amulet, for the first time I feel like my future and my fate are within reach. I will find my memories, and if what Ere tells me turns out to be the truth, then Nyx will fucking pay for what she has done to him.

On the other hand, if he is lying and deceiving me to get me closer to her... I will burn us and this entire realm to ash.

CHAPTER THIRTY-THREE

SHADOWS AND FAIRYTALES

NORA

The week passed in a shadowy blur. There has been a constant flow of servants entering and exiting Ere's home, some of them I might have thought were mortal if it weren't for the shimmery blue magic I know makes them a witch, or the soft black feathers like Kairos' and mine. Celestials from the Realm of Darkness. Ere explained in detail how and where magical beings end up after death. The Elysian Fields is a paradise the original gods created for themselves and the kings and queens. Or for those who die performing a heroic act to save their people. Asphodel Meadows is where most immortal, magical beings end up. Sometimes they go there to await reincarnation, but usually, it's their final resting place.

Ere lives somewhere between those two places, in a place he calls the Abyss because no light exists here. It's him who decides who stays here and who is thrown into the pit to live out their days being tortured and tormented by Nyx's demons. He's not sure why some end up here instead of Asphodel Meadows, only that they wander around aimlessly until he finds them and gives them a job or a position in his army. Or until he chooses to toss them into the pit. The ones with vile hearts who committed unforgivable crimes are taken to the pit, and the rest stay here with him. The servants seem thrilled to be working for him, each one smiles, bows and praises him, thanking him and referring to him as King Erebus with pride in those words. Each time, Ere's spine stiffens, his words are short and flat, and he quickly orders them away.

The only time this man smiles here is when we're alone and he's looking at me.

He hasn't only been teaching me about Nyx and the Underworld, he's also been trying his best to teach me how to wield my power. I've only almost burned his entire home down once. Luckily his shadows suffocated the flames and saved the day. The thought of escaping to assure Olivia that everything is fine tugs at my mind, but thoughts like those are quickly followed by a numbness that calms my nerves and reminds me how important it is that I stay. I need to learn the truth, and I can't do that with Kairos and Hekate refusing to let me help or keeping me hidden in the Realm of Darkness. I need to stay here and fight, and despite the lack of warmth and sun, the past week of being here with Ere hasn't been all bad.

He finds small ways to infuse joy into my days, bringing me my favorite books when I feel sad or warm coffee when anxiety sets in. He always knows exactly what I'm feeling or thinking, and that fact doesn't scare me anymore, because it makes things so easy between us. I guess it has always been this way with us. *Easy*. I just never let him fully in to notice it before. Even when I tried, I always had walls up. Not anymore. There's no point in trying to shut him out. He'll just break through.

Today he promised we'd go outside to practice magic, and although I'm excited to see what it's like out there, I think it's for his benefit more than it is mine. He'd like to keep his home standing as long as he can, he says, and I haven't learned a thing about how to control my flames. He stalks across the room with two coffee mugs in hand and wears a bright smile.

His horns are on full display and his shadows linger and creep along the floor and flow out behind him as he stops in front of me and offers me one of the mugs. "First coffee, then magic and mayhem." He winks down at me. "I will have to take you to Nyx soon or she will grow suspicious. I am sure she already has, and the last thing I want is for her to send the demons here."

Taking the mug, I sip on the deliciously sweet darkness, drinking it in and letting it warm my restless mind. It might be the coffee, or it could be Ere's shadows as they embrace me in that way that they often do, but I immediately feel calmer. There's something intimate about him doing this, about his power holding me this way, but it doesn't bother me anymore. I've grown to like his shadows holding me close even when he's far away.

"Listen, Ere, I want to stay positive and have hope that I can stand a chance against Nyx, and I'm trying to, but we both know I'm not ready. We have to stall her somehow. I'm really trying to learn how my magic works, but I have no idea how I used it so easily that first night here with you. It felt natural then. It hasn't felt that way since. I don't know what I'm doing wrong." I shrug, sitting my mug down and admiring the way the muscles in his biceps flex as he does the same.

He throws his arm over the back of his leather recliner as his eyebrows slant, and then he gives me a nervous grin. "It was easy then because you were angry with me. A part of you wanted me dead. Anger fuels your power and makes it stronger it seems. Maybe other emotions do too. With Nyx, you have a lot of pent-up anger so I am hopeful that when you do face her you will easily be able to defend yourself. I believe in you, my love." He keeps his eyes on me as he grips his mug and slowly brings it to his mouth, smiling slightly as he licks his lips clean after.

Damn. I shouldn't be looking at him this way or thinking about him this way, but gods he makes it hard not to. I shift in my seat, staring into my mug to avoid the embarrassment of the flush on my cheeks and the wildly inappropriate thoughts and images spinning in my mind, a mind I know he reads too easily. In the past when he called me 'my love,' I thought it was cute or endearing, just a sweet thing a boyfriend might say. Now, with his towering horns and his glowing eyes that flicker from gold to red as he watches me, and that same smile that has always sent my heart racing, "my love," feels a lot like *you're mine.* Wanting Ere or thinking about if I might want him sort of feels dirty. Wrong. *Forbidden.* And gods does it make me want him even more. It's hard to process or accept that I still have feelings for him or that calling me that does things to me I can't explain. *Him*, a dark king. I'd be naïve and stupid to want him now, wouldn't I? Not yet. Not until I know the truth.

"Whether I learn to use my power or not, I'll face her eventually. I can't sit around and hide forever. I've done that enough already." I finish my coffee and head to the kitchen to rinse out my glass.

He follows close behind, and as I turn on the water and submerge my glass beneath it, his shadows gently brush against my shoulders and the sensitive edges of my wings. I close my eyes and lean into the touch. His rigid body is right behind me, and as he reaches out to rinse his glass, he encases me within his arms. I glance up at him, his towering frame still and his smile unwavering as my eyes widen and my heart races. He has tried to keep his distance, giving me the space I need, but now with him so close and his eyes blazing into mine, every part of my body burns with unbridled desire. The crimson color spreads out from the edges of his irises and takes over his eyes completely, and there's a hunger and need within them that sets my soul on fire.

I take a deep breath, in and out, in and out, eyes still held captive by his. It's useless. There's no denying or stopping the passion and heat that scorches us both each time our eyes lock.

"We should go outside and practice."

I need to put distance between us or the sparks that push us closer will ignite into full blown flames.

"Or we could stay." His words are a temptation, a trickle of gasoline that could make those sparks combust and destroy everything.

I shake my head too roughly, more telling myself no than him. Looking away, I concentrate on washing our mugs then quickly dry them and place them in the cabinet. He doesn't move from his place behind me, his arms gripping the edge of the counter beside my hips and keeping me trapped too close to him. I glance up and he tucks my hair behind my ears, caressing my cheeks with his fingertips before stepping backwards out of my way. I head to the door without looking back, but he appears in front of me before I get a chance to reach for the handle.

His eyes narrow and flicker back to their golden, warm hue, all heat blazing within gone. "Give me a minute to send out a message to the soldiers. I need them on the borders so I know you will be safe."

"There are so many here from the Realm of Darkness. They all wear the Dark Legion emblem on their chests. Why are they here?" I watch as his eyes go glossy, and he looks far away for a moment.

The light in his eyes returns and he smiles. "Most of these men were your soldiers. The ones Nyx and her demons slaughtered during the war. Like I've said before, I do not know why some of them end up here with me, but your soldiers did. They despised me at first until they realized it was either stay here with me or suffer in the pit with the demons. They fell in line then rather quickly." His jaw clenches and he forces a tight-lipped smile. "I would never have sent them into the pit with them. I knew you would one day need your army here for you." He stretches past me to open the door, then steps out and offers his hand and I gladly take it.

I'm scared of what's out there, and even with an army of celestials keeping watch, I feel better having Ere with me. I'm beginning to trust him again a little more every day. More than trust him, actually, I'm beginning to feel that Ere would protect me with his life. The way he looks at me is like he'd rather die than ever lose me again, and even though Kairos looked at me the same way, Ere doesn't treat me like I'm fragile or incapable of protecting myself.

He treats me like I'm capable of anything.

We stroll down a stone path, the darkness of the sky swallowing the black, rocky mountain peaks into nothing. I can hear the River Styx, the black water that flows in front of those mountains, the one Ere has shown me through the windows upstairs, but I can't see it from here. I smile, listening to the sounds of the sacred body of water echoing against the elements and floating through the surrounding skeletal, charred forest back to us. It's beautiful. All of it. The whispering of the river and the deathly silence of everything else. The way the trees and mountains hover and yet shrink away to the outskirts of the realm, as if afraid to take up too much space here. Black flame torches line our path and surround a large yard closed in by pointy metal fencing with dark vines climbing up each post, as if even greenery here was consumed and spat out by darkness. The scorched, black earth crumbles under my feet as we walk to the center of his yard and he releases my hand, taking several steps back. He's afraid of my power, he told me, which doesn't offer comfort while I'm learning. I'd never forgive myself if something happened to him because of me not remembering how to use my magic.

"We're safe here?" Glancing around, there's nothing but shadows and darkness for miles, it seems, even with all the torches surrounding us.

There are no stars or a moon here in The Underworld. Only darkness exists. I would be terrified and running in fear if it weren't for Ere's comforting eyes never leaving mine. Those glowing golden orbs keep me calm and steady. They're the only light I need right now.

"The army has been guarding my section of the realm day and night since I brought you here. They'll warn me if any demons or rageful queens get anywhere near us." He offers me a teasing smile. "You are safe. I promise." He nods, and I take that as my cue to start practicing, though I don't actually know where to begin.

I raise my hands, staring into my palms and trying to will them to burn, but only a flicker of blue and purple light dances across them before quickly fading away. "Damnit."

"Concentrate, my little flame," he sighs quietly as he steps up behind me, cupping his hands around mine and facing my palms out toward the inky darkness of the river and the mountains and trees.

I breathe in deep, letting his power calm my mind as I lean back against his chest, the sound of the river flowing in the distance a reminder of the peace I used to feel at the lake back home.

"Understanding how to wield your power could be a matter of life or death for yourself or someone you love." The muscles in his chest tense, his body pressed against me and my wings suddenly feeling in the way as I crave leaning further into his soothing shadows and his calming voice.

"I'm trying, Ere," I whisper.

"Close your eyes," he murmurs against my ear, so I do. "Now, focus on only our breathing. On only our hearts beating as one. Clear your thoughts. What is the thing you want more than anything? Focus on that. Focus on what you need to do in order to have that." He places his hands on my hips, and the reassuring touch sends comforting shivers of hope down my spine.

Freedom. It's the only thing I want in this moment, and what I've been wanting more than anything for the past year, and possibly even in a past life that I can't remember. I focus on only Nyx and my hatred for her, pushing away thoughts of his body and his touch and his silky power wrapped around me. I step forward and he pulls his shadows away, tightly tucking them back within himself and giving me free reign to feel and let the anger and hatred that burns for her in my heart ignite.

As heat engulfs me, I step further away from Ere, focusing only on all the pain and agony and death Nyx has brought into my life. Bright flames swirl around my entire body, the fire vengeful and angry and cruel. I smile as I place my palms out and focus on the already lifeless vines wrapped around the fence in front of me. I imagine her face there as I command my flames to stretch toward them, burning them into a pile of ash on the scorched ground.

Nyx is what motivates me to control my power. Anger and pain help too, but it'll be Nyx who my flames search for in the darkness when the time comes. My power rages within, begging me to find her here now and burn her alive. It speaks to me in a way I understand, and I speak back, urging the flames to die out and save their energy for her lying, evil face. They listen. Slowly, the heat dissipates, the bright light fades, and my flames disappear under my warm, slick skin.

I can control my power. Ere being here with me helped. Him reminding me that I'll need to fight if I want to be free, that helped, too. The sound of his dark laughter echoes off the mountains, his thick arms wrapping me up in a tight embrace. I laugh, locking my arms around his waist as warm, proud tears flow down my cheeks. I did it. I can do this.

"My queen," he purrs against my forehead, placing a gentle kiss there.

I pull away, my eyes wide and my mind immediately racing. "Why did you call me that? I'm not your queen, Ere." Backing away, I shake my head in disbelief, suddenly feeling a sense of déjà vu from my time in the Realm of Darkness.

Why the hell does everyone assume I want to be their queen? What about what I want? What about what I need, which is to first figure out who the hell I even am and who these men are to me.

"With Nyx's death, someone must remain here to rule. I will not be allowed to leave. The gods will not let me out of this so easily. I am trapped whether I like it or not, but without her this realm could be so much more than it is." He takes my hands into his, his eyes a glowing crimson that makes me question every decision I know I must make in the future.

It'll be him or Kairos. Him or the celestials. Him or no one else. If everything he says is true and he is my fated mate, then it'll be only *him*. The celestials and witches will never accept me if I'm a part of this realm. Even Olivia might fear me.

I pull away, shaking my head as I take two steps back. "Dragging me here without my consent doesn't give you the right to control my decisions or dictate my way of life. What if I don't want to stay here with you? What if I..." I swallow thickly, his eyes burning brighter and his wings shifting behind him as he closes the distance between us. "What if I choose to live out my life with the celestials or decide I want to live on the Earth Realm with Olivia? I should be free to choose my own fate. No one chooses for me. I'm so damn tired of everyone treating me like I have no say in my own life. You do not own me!"

I stomp past him, heading for the torch-lit path back to his house, not wanting to look at him or speak to him any longer. I need a break from him and the chaos and confusion of trying to decipher who's telling the truth and who's lying about what they are to me. Two crowns and two men and how do I know which one is meant for me? I can't handle it all anymore.

He follows closely behind but doesn't speak. As I step up to the door, he grips my shoulders, turning me to face him. His eyes are soft, golden pools of sadness as he looks at me. "I know I do not own you, my love." I back away and he prowls closer, closing in on me until my wings are pressed firmly against the stark black door. He places his palms against the doorframe, his arms caging me in as he leans down and whispers, "You own me." The honesty in his eyes sets my heart on fire and my soul sings as if it's been awoken from a deep sleep. Every rational thought goes out the window as his words sink in.

He doesn't smile or look at me as he opens the door and steps past me to go inside. His wings brush against mine and then he's gone, engulfed by swirling shadows. He looks hopeless. He looks scared and hurt and my heart shatters as I consider that maybe he has lost more than I can comprehend. Maybe he loves me more than I will ever know. Maybe he did suffer for a century just waiting for me, haunted here in darkness and misery. What if everything he has told me is true? What if it was never Kairos who was meant for me and Ere really is my fated mate? One of them waited for nothing. Both are waiting still, and it kills me to think of either of them suffering because of me. Because I can't remember. Because I will have to choose.

"Ere, wait. Please." My voice is a soft plea for forgiveness and he freezes before reaching his bedroom door. "I'm sorry. It feels like everyone wants to control me. Nyx. Kairos and Hekate. Now you." I sigh, running my hands through my hair and stepping into the kitchen. "I've always loved how you let me choose who I want to be and how I want to live. I don't want that to change. I want to be me, whoever that might be once I remember. I don't want anyone choosing for me."

"Hate me if you wish, but all I want is to keep you safe and let you find the happiness you deserve. Forgive me if my excitement over the thought of a possible future together was a bit overwhelming, but you are all that matters to me." He leans back against the stone counter, hands gripping the edge as if it's all that's holding him up, his eyes dull and empty for the first time.

"I don't hate you, Ere. Not at all. I just..." I lose my train of thought as he pushes off the counter and steps toward me.

The scent of him is like a midnight breeze tinged with the essence of shadows. It's hard to describe how comforting and calming Ere smells, only that taking a deep breath, breathing him in, makes me feel like I'm back outside in the cool night air and I could live within that scent forever.

'This is hard. I don't know what I feel for you anymore," I whisper, staring at the floor, unable to look at him as I confess the truth.

My love for him still exists, but I can't pretend my feelings for Kairos are non-existent. I fell for him, too. Throw in the magical connection of fated mates and not knowing who I'm meant to be with, and it's hard to know what the hell I'm *supposed* to feel, let alone what I *do* feel.

The soothing touch of his hands as he brushes my hair back and then tilts my chin up, forcing me to look at him, makes my heart flutter. "You only fell for him because I left you, and I am sorry for that. You thought he was all you had. That he was the only man who could keep you safe. You were wrong." His fingertips graze across my cheek bone and he tilts his head slightly. "I think you know exactly how you feel for me and what it is you truly want, my little flame." His smile is brief and small as his gaze lingers on my lips. "I just don't think you are quite ready yet to admit the truth."

"Why do you use that name for me? My little flame. You never called me that until I got here." Lifting my chin, my eyes roam over his face and get distracted by his lips, the perfect curve of them driving me wild as he inches even closer.

"It was a name I gave you in the past. You used to love it. If you hate it now, I can stop." He grips my hands and places them on his chest.

I shake my head. "No. I like it."

I close my eyes as the steady thumping of his heart soothes the ache I feel in my own over the possibility of hurting him if I don't choose him. If he isn't meant for me. But there's something about touching him like this that sends waves of hope and trust rushing through me, a gentle reminder that he has always managed to keep me calm regardless of what I'm going through. His hands hold me captive, the smooth warmth of his skin pressing into me as I feel and listen and get lost in the rhythm of our hearts. I keep my eyes closed, letting his comforting energy wrap around me and remind me to breathe.

"Tell me what you are feeling right now. Do not think, Nora. Just *feel*." His words are a command, but there's a longing laced within his voice, as if begging me to surrender to the sound of him and the feel of his heart and to the moment we're sharing here together.

Everything. I feel *everything* with Ere. As my breath catches in my throat and my heart beats wildly, I'm momentarily stunned to silence over that admission to myself. Every moment is intense and full of passion with Ere, especially when our bodies are so close. It's hard to deny or hide from the truth.

"I'm afraid of what my heart feels for you. It's like there's a depth to it I can't fully grasp," I admit, the words rushing out with no filter.

He sighs, his grip tightening around my hands, refusing to let me go. I open my eyes and his fiery gaze burns into me. "I have so much I would like to say to you, but it is not the right time yet. It kills me every day that you cannot remember our love and the bond we shared for nearly a century. You have the freedom to choose or control whatever you would like. My only hope is that you choose me in the end." He swallows, his grip loosening as he rubs his thumbs across the tops of my hands. "However, there are things about me which you cannot control, either. One is the absolute satisfaction I will feel while mercilessly slaughtering anyone, immortal or otherwise, who dares to stand in the way of me having you by my side. And you will not control the way my anger rips through the entire world if you are taken from me. I will not lose you again." His fingers tremble, flexing slightly as he frees my hands.

I stand frozen for a moment, hands still pressed to his chest, a heated shiver running down my spine as I struggle to grasp the depth of his feelings for me. I knew he loved me, but this possessive, 'I'll burn the world down for you' passion is new, and although his words and the truth they hold should probably scare me, they only make me want him more. His intense gaze flickers away as he turns to leave, and without pausing to reconsider, I grasp his face in my hands and force him to stop. To not leave. To stay here with me. The warmth of his cheeks burn my palms as I kiss him with an intensity that could make the entire realm combust into flames. In this moment, I would burn the world down for him in a heartbeat.

He stands still for a moment, shock written across his features, then in one swift motion he lifts me off the ground and I cling to him. I wrap my arms and legs around his muscular body and hold on for dear life, wishing and praying I'll never have to let him go again. His large hands grip my hips and press me against him harder, pulling me in closer, and a rush of arousal forces its way in and burns me to my core. His mouth against mine is passionate and hungry and urgent as if we may never get the chance to do this again. His kiss and his ravenous tongue are a dangerous mix of desperation and possessiveness that I've learned to crave, a kiss that makes me fearful it'll be the death of me one day. Tendrils of shadows envelop us in a blanket of darkness, dancing and spinning and brushing against my sensitive skin, forcing our bodies closer together. Oxygen escapes my lungs in breathless moans to make room for him deep within every part of me.

As he deepens the kiss, his fingers tighten around my hair, getting lost within the moment. My scalp burns from the pleasure of that small amount of pain, and I melt into his arms. A desperate moan escapes into his mouth, begging for release, for more, for him to never fucking stop. I need him. I think of nothing else as I pull my lips from his, my entire body coiled in tension and burning with a desire I've never known before. This moment with Ere is one that could never be forgotten or stolen or replaced, it's a moment that will forever be etched into my memory.

"I want you," I whimper, squeezing my thighs tightly around his hips, my forehead pressed against his as I close my eyes.

"Not good enough, my little flame," his voice is dark and taunting, and I know he's smiling without even looking. He grips my ass and presses the hard length of his cock against my center, slowly and torturously grinding against my clit again and again, and I writhe back and forth desperately. The bastard.

"Please. I *need* you," I beg, thighs now trembling with desire and need as I force my eyes to meet his. I want to prove that I'm thinking clearly and that I'm sure and that I have no other thought besides him and I.

"I thought you might never ask." His smile is playful and cruel and delicious in a way that makes my insides burn.

His eyes are glowing orbs of hope and his shadows a menacing power that others might fear, but in this moment, I feel lucky that he only has eyes for me. I can't deny there's something special between us. It could all really be true, couldn't it? We might be fated to be. If that's the case, then I will thank the gods for allowing me a chance with such a sexy, terrifying, amazing creature, because Ere is what many women's dreams are made of. I would be lucky to have him.

Once upon a time, I imagined my life would resemble a fairy tale, where a gallant knight would rescue me from the darkness in the world, and we would live happily ever after. Here I am being dragged into the shadows by the King of the Underworld, and enjoying every dark, blissful minute of it. Close enough, right?

CHAPTER THIRTY-FOUR

SURRENDERING TO SHADOWS

NORA

The bedroom is pitch black until Ere waves a hand and starts a chain reaction, one black flame flickering to life after another. He tosses me on the bed, and I squeal as I sink into the plush mattress, biting my bottom lip as his laughter vibrates within my mind, breathing life into neglected corners of my existence.

"Every time I touched you before, it killed me that I could not be myself," he stands before me, slowly unbuttoning his black button-up shirt and slacks, tossing them onto the floor as I lean on my elbows and watch him with no shame. "This time... I will not hold back, Nora."

"Good. I don't want you to," I tell him with a smile, his horns creeping closer and his glowing eyes growing darker by the second as the gold shimmer melts away.

I'm smiling but fear lingers. I'm breathless, but his presence fills the void within me, making me feel complete with no need for air. As my heart pounds out of control, I realize it beats this way only for him.

Always for him.

He crawls across the bed toward me, leaving me no time to consider how easily he could ruin me or to fear the man who looks like a demon in front of me. He roughly grips my face in his hand, the intensity making my cheek ache, but I won't resist or pull away. No. I want this. I run my fingers through his thick hair. He groans, closing his eyes and giving in to the pleasure of my gentle touch. He's as desperate for this as I am. Gripping my shoulders, he pushes me backward onto the bed, a playful, aroused expression flashing across his face that has me wanting to beg for more. Lifting my hips and forcing me back, he positions me comfortably at the top of the bed with my neck nestled on his satin pillow.

His eyes roam across my body and he shakes his head, gripping and tearing at the fabric clinging to my body until I'm completely naked and wide-eyed in shock. My clothes are never safe with him. Arousal burns within his eyes, and I'm both fearful and excited at the thought of him not holding back so I can experience the pleasure he truly desires in that dark, shadowy mind.

His voice, low and cruel, whispers in my ear. "Do you like to play, my love?" His teeth lightly graze the sensitive spot below my ear as he pulls away from me, putting too much distance between us.

I reach out to grab him, to keep him with me, but he moves too quickly and is standing at the foot of the bed before I have a chance to pull him back to me. A dark, charming smile spreads across his face as his gaze rakes over my bare skin. The look he gives me nearly burns me alive. A surge of need mixed with a tingling sense of fear courses through my entire body. I lift my head off the pillow just as he commands his shadows to come out and play, encircling us within them. I don't move, not willing to risk pissing off him or his shadows for fear of what they might do to me.

But those shadows caress my skin so gently, so affectionately, that I can't imagine them hurting me or anyone else. I shiver from their soft, torturous touch just as they retreat back into him. I moan quietly, silently begging with my eyes as I keep them pinned on him. Being denied his touch is a slow death I won't survive, yet he simply smiles, enjoying the sight of me in agony.

The shadows reach out for me again, teasing and tormenting my nipples and clit with an intensity and hunger that surpasses any other experience I've had with him before this. My moans are desperate as I spread my legs wider, grinding my hips against his dark power, fully aware I should appear less needy, but unable to control myself any longer. I need more.

I am completely and hopelessly desperate for him.

Again, the shadows retreat, slithering away then vanishing completely and I throw my head back against the bed with a quiet whimper of frustration. I can't handle the teasing, torturous, cruel man who stands before me. He will be the death of me, I'm sure of it. My flushed cheeks burn as my lust filled eyes meet his, and then my head falls with another needy whimper the moment he licks his lips seductively. He laughs, fully aware that he holds the key to satisfying my insatiable hunger for him.

"Look at you. You love it when we play, don't you?" His wicked, seductive smile only makes me wetter, and I hate him for it. "You are so fucking beautiful when you are desperate for me to fuck you."

"Please, Ere. I don't want to play anymore. I need it," I pant breathlessly, my desire for him raw and unapologetic.

His shadows pour out of him now like they, too, can't take it any longer, stretching out from behind him and reaching for me hungrily. I breathe a heated sigh of relief. *Gods yes.* They swirl around me, the tendrils caressing my skin in gentle strokes and soft lashes. Their tender, ravenous touch electrifies every fiber of my being, and I want more. *More.* He doesn't give me more. Instead, he swiftly draws them back within himself, and my heart stops at the realization that he doesn't plan on giving me what I need easily. He is going to make me suffer. He stands at the edge of the bed, licking his lips and staring down at me with bright, glowing eyes as if I'm the only light he needs in this world. And fuck, I might not need light at all if I have him. I crawl toward him and take his throbbing dick into my hands and then slide my lips down the length of him. I suck and twirl my tongue against each jolt of pleasure I feel coursing through him, taking him in as deep as I can. Swirling my tongue around the tip, I tease and lick and savor the delicious taste of him as his pleasure filled moans add fuel to my own arousal. Keeping my eyes locked to his, I slowly glide my hand down my breasts and torso, his eyes following the movement the entire time, and then I caress my swollen clit, trembling as he growls breathlessly, his eyes widening and his mouth falling open at the sight of me pleasuring us both. I refuse to wait any longer. I'm taking what I need from him.

Clutching my hair in his hands, he slowly tilts my head back, a wide smile on his face as his shadows wrap tightly around my wrists, gripping and pulling my hands away from both of our bodies, refusing to let me touch either of us. His eyes no longer shimmer with liquid gold, the bright crimson glow as he watches me now makes the hair on the back of my neck stand in fear. I fight his power, pushing and pulling against it but his tight grip on my hair keeps me locked in place. I'm not afraid of him or his shadows, but somewhere deep within my mind a part of me screams that I should be.

With a mischievous grin, he leans in close to my face and whispers, "You have two options," he says darkly. "Either you want all of me, exactly as you see me now, or you want the old me who I will no longer give you because he does not exist here." Those bright red eyes search mine. "It is all or nothing with me. Tell me if you do not want this. If you do not want me."

The words spill from his lips with such intensity that I would fall to my knees if I weren't already on them.

He felt my brief moment of fear and my heart aches that he thinks I might not want him. A part of me does fear this version of him, but it also excites me more than I care to admit. Deep down, I believe he's wanting confirmation that I won't deny or reject him, because he's afraid. Even though he's not the mortal Ere I fell for in the past, he knows how I feel. He hears every thought that passes through my mind. I want all of him regardless of what he is. Demon, King of The Underworld, or Hell itself, it doesn't matter to me. Not long ago, I felt like a puzzle missing its pieces, searching for a way to make sense of the emptiness I felt. He was always there to fill those empty spaces. To remind me that I was enough even when I felt like I wasn't. He is the missing piece that completes me in this harsh, chaotic world. The monster in front of me is no monster at all. He's just another lost soul wandering through a world full of darkness and pain that looms nearby ready to consume him entirely. We are alike, him and I. He is as much of a victim to Nyx's games as I am. And he is enough.

His smile as I look back up at him reminds me that he can hear every untamed thought racing through my mind, but I want to tell him how I feel anyway. I want to assure him that I embrace who he is and want him exactly as he is.

His shadows release my wrists, and I place my palm against his cheek, the warmth of him soothing the sting of him believing I wouldn't want him. "You are beautiful, Ere. I thought it the first day I ever met you, but I also thought the same when I first saw you here. Menacing horns and wings and all." I smile, brushing my fingertips along his cheekbone. "I accept you completely in all your forms, and that will never change." Looking up at him, I smile through the tears that now fall from my burning eyes. "I want this. I want you. All of you."

His face lights up in a way I've never seen before as his eyes flicker back to a soft, warm gold. A rush of heat flows through me as they suddenly shift back to the fiery red that drives me crazy.

"Good girl, Nora," he whispers, his fingertips gently trailing up my neck and then stopping at my cheeks to wipe away my tears. "Now, lie back and let's see if I can make your pussy weep for me, too." Keeping his eyes pinned on me, he brings a finger to his mouth, gliding his tongue across it and sucking the saltiness away, savoring the taste of the tears I cried for him.

This king, cruel and naked, stands before me—a smile capable of stopping hearts, eyes the shade of fresh blood, horns that would make a sane person scream, and wings so vast they should instill terror, yet I am unafraid. Right now, my only fear is that he'll refuse to touch me where I need him to most.

This man is going to ruin me, and I can't wait for it.

I lay back on the bed, and beyond the veil of darkness, his shadows come alive and trace a path from my hardened nipples to my aching clit, finally granting me the touch I desperately crave. They crawl up my arms and legs, every touch of them like it's him touching me himself, like twenty or fifty or a hundred of his hands pleasuring me all at once. The silky smoothness of them holding me and feeling me and so damn hungry for me to come is almost too much. They continue rubbing and caressing and grinding against my center, growing needier and more impatient by the second. I lift my head and our eyes meet. I surrender to his shadows, give in to him completely, losing myself in a pleasure filled oblivion as tears flow down my cheeks. As the orgasm crashes into me, I cry out his name and he conceals his predatory, satisfied smile by tucking his bottom lip into his mouth.

He rakes his eyes over me from head to toe as my body trembles and my breath comes out ragged and uneven. "Hearing you scream my name is my favorite sound."

I feel the bed shift as he kneels between my legs, using his fingertips to tease my breasts, pausing at my nipples and giving them a firm pinch that snaps me out of my blissful, orgasmic state.

I whimper and his dark laughter sends a tingle of heat through my body as he gently brings one nipple into his warm mouth, and then does the same to the other, easing the sting.

"Mmm...was that your attempt at begging for me?" He scrapes his teeth across each nipple harder than before, then again brings them into his mouth, lashing his tongue against them one by one to soothe them.

Letting out a moan full of both pleasure and pain, I keep my eyes on him. "Please. Don't stop. I need more."

This time he touches me himself, his shadows snaking up and encircling my wrists and ankles to bind me loosely to the bed. His fingertips slowly trail across my skin, from my breasts down the center of my abdomen, and then he tortures my hips, drawing little circles and swirls lower and lower, but not quite low enough. He knows where I need him to touch me. Then he glides his fingers across the wetness at my clit once and then twice, before plunging a thick finger deep inside of me immediately followed by another. Waves of pleasure wash over me as he thrusts in and out. I grip his shoulders, digging my nails into his skin, and his growl of pleasure nearly tips me over the edge.

His shadows grip and pull tighter, forcing my hands above my head and spreading my legs further apart. "No touching. Not yet," he says firmly, his voice leaving no room for argument.

Like this, I'm completely paralyzed. With each thrust of his fingers, his shadows press into me harder, caress my clit even faster, and he smiles, his eyes dancing and relishing in seeing me vulnerable and desperately begging for him. Although he seems to love this, I think I love it even more. Not being able to touch him is driving me crazy.

"Please, Ere. I can't take anymore. I need your dick," I beg, my voice cracking as I shift my eyes away.

Gazing too deeply into those dangerous red eyes might send me spiraling into another orgasm, and I need him inside me above all else right now.

I've never needed anything more than I need him in this moment.

"Keep your eyes on me, my love." He grips my face, forcing my attention back to him while he rubs my clit with his shadowy touch, swirling gentle circles around it while thrusting his thick fingers in and out of me.

"I can't." My voice trembles, knowing that I truly can't handle much more. "If I look at you," I breathe, barely able to hold it together. "I'll come."

Although he has taken enough and I've given enough, my hunger for more still grows. I want all of it. All of him. I don't care if this wrecks me or if no one ever understands why I feel the way I do about him. This is all I'll ever need. He is undoubtedly all I'll ever want.

As our eyes meet, a flicker of bright purple and blue flames illuminates the darkness, and it's as if we can see into the depths of the other's soul for just a moment. My magic flares in my palms, and his shadows don't run or hide. They mingle and swirl together as one in a silent confirmation that everything will be okay if we stick together. Then his shadows gently swallow the light, and it fades away.

"Come for me. I want to hear you cry out my name until you can no longer speak." He leans down, pressing his tongue firmly against my clit, sucking and devouring it until I'm on the brink of sweet oblivion once again.

"Ere..." my moan is soft and barely audible.

He shakes his head. "Not good enough."

"Ere... *please...*" I beg louder, desperately hopeful he'll give me what I need.

"Try harder," he breathes, slowing the thrust of his fingers as his tongue stills against my clit.

"Ere... please, please, please. I need to come!" I scream his name over and over, pleading with the darkness to either drag me away or let the demons end me if he refuses to give me what I need.

"Good. You are learning," he growls, his voice laced with a mix of satisfaction and dominance as the thrust of his fingers become more demanding and eager, curling and hitting that spot on my inner wall that makes my legs quiver. "You will scream my name until your lungs give out if I ask you to, and in return..." his tongue flicks across my swollen clit, lavishing it with two powerful licks that send me spiraling over the edge.

I scream his name as I come undone around his fingers, my vision exploding into a cosmic burst of stars.

"Thank you. Thank you, thank you..." My whispered words rush out of me like a chant or a prayer or some magical godsdamn incantation, so faint and breathless that I'm not sure he can even hear me.

"You are so sexy," he murmurs, his voice husky and wild. "You have no idea how incredibly sexy you are." He kneels between my legs, using his palms to spread me open wider. His smoldering gaze makes my heart race. "So sexy, in fact, that I am dying to fuck you so hard you forget about the good girl you once were. That you remember who you are truly meant for," he says, before thrusting into me so hard that my eyes roll back.

I can't form coherent words or thoughts any longer. All I can manage are quiet, pleasure filled whimpers and tears that fall freely against my will, tears from a pleasure so great that I can't even begin to comprehend it. My tears spill relentlessly for this dark king, the man I'd willingly give my soul to, consequences be damned. My heart burns with an undeniable passion, my soul is ascending into pure happiness for the first time, and my body... it now belongs entirely to him.

There is no one who can do to me what Ere does.

As his shadows drift down my body and disappear within him, I waste no time pulling his mouth to mine now that they've set me free. I kiss him with the intensity of a wildfire that can't be contained, my hunger so fierce that I can taste the metallic tang of blood on my tongue as I bite his lip, greedily sucking it into my mouth, desperate to consume every part of him. With every thrust, he pushes deeper inside of me causing waves of pain and pleasure to collide in the most beautiful, impossible way.

"Touch yourself. I want to feel you come so hard on my dick that the grip of you around me takes everything I have to give." His voice is guttural and low and his eyes have the intensity within of a sex-crazed god.

He is coming completely undone, and I use that to my advantage, grinding my hips into his, rocking back and forth to push him closer to the edge. I want him to lose himself entirely. He growls impatiently as I slowly drag my hand toward my clit. He grips my wrist and forces my hand between our slick bodies. He keeps his hand on top of mine, the motion of our fingers moving and stimulating me, flooding me with a wave of pure bliss. Then as he grips my waist, pulling me toward him harder with each thrust, a thought lingers in the back of my mind. Ere's invasion of my body with his shadows has forever altered everything. I know in this moment that I've always belonged to him. Call it intuition or fate or whatever the hell else it could be, but I know I'm right. He is mine as much as I am his.

I open my mouth to speak, and he smiles. "I know. Now come for me like the good girl you are. Come for me until you cannot breathe or imagine life without me again." He wraps his hand around my throat, gripping it and pulling me against him with each thrust, his shadows teasing my nipples and sending electrifying surges of pleasure through me. "I will come for you so hard that my darkness consumes us both." A feral smile and glowing crimson eyes peer into mine.

As the intensity of pleasure builds to an unstoppable breaking point, I can't hold back any longer. I give in to his shadows. I give in to every word and every touch, allowing him into my mind and my heart and soul fully for the first time. All the other times with Ere were passionate and full of heat, but this time is something else. This time it means so much more, to finally embrace how much I care for him without fighting it or pushing him away.

Each time I scream his name, his shadows grow denser around us, whispering past my ears, their presence suffocating and blinding, but I welcome it because they're a part of him I refuse to shy away from. I'm surrounded by them as he groans and spills into me, and the darkness following does in fact nearly consume us. The flickering black flames disappear, the only thing left shining within the void are his glowing ruby eyes that gleam as he growls and thrusts, chasing the last delicious peaks of pleasure. His back arches and his wings unfurl and spread out wide as if he can't control them any longer. In this moment it's as if he's lost control of both himself and his power, and I've never seen anything quite as beautiful. He surrendered himself to me just as much as I have to him. I get it now, why he has pushed for me to accept myself, darkness and all since I've known him. He wanted me to one day be able to accept him, darkness and shadows and all, and I do.

"You know, I actually prefer the red eyes," I admit, smiling down at him as he stretches out and leans his head on my chest.

He smiles back in a way that I swear could light up the entire realm. "Whichever you prefer, my love." His eyes flicker back to the beautiful glowing crimson.

"Actually, you know what? You might look really sexy with sparkly blue eyes. You'd have all the ladies in your realm swooning in no time," I tease, laughing as he lifts up to look at me, his eyebrows scrunching together as he shakes his head.

Taking my face in his hands, my laughter stops as a pained expression flashes across his face. "I want no one else swooning over me, but you. You are the only one for me. Now and forever. It has always been you, my little flame. You are my light. My only hope in this dark, cold world I have been trapped in." His voice is raw and tender, and it chips away at the walls I've built around my heart.

I swallow, my gaze lingering on his clenched jaw and the tight line of his lips. "I'm sorry. I don't understand what you've been through or what you lost so long ago." Running my fingers through his dark locks, my mind struggles to find the right words. "I wish I could remember, Ere. *You. Us.* I want to remember everything," I whisper, leaning up and placing a kiss to his soft cheek.

"You will. We will go to Nyx tomorrow." He lifts his head, searching my eyes before he continues. "I only wanted to give you time to trust me." His smile is crooked and small as he takes my hand, his lips brushing against it in a gentle, comforting kiss.

"I trust you and I'm ready. No more running or hiding. I need the truth."

As his eyes flash with pain and he releases my hand, a wave of regret washes through me. He wants me to trust him, and I do, but with the possibility of us being manipulated, trusting him isn't the issue. What if we've both been lied to? What if this is another one of Nyx's cruel games to hurt us, to give us hope just to snatch it away? I won't know for sure until my past is a part of me again. And if what we feel for each other is in fact real and true, then it brings about a whole other slew of questions. Like why the hell Kairos believes with every piece of his heart that we're fated to be. Why the rulers of the realms and the rest of the celestials believe it, too. Deep down, I know getting my memories back won't end with me or us riding off together into the sunset, not right away, at least. Discovering the truth is just the beginning of what's to come, because no matter which way this goes, people are being manipulated and lied to.

All I know for sure, is that with Ere's head on my chest and both of us holding each other tight, my heart melts at the sight of his warm, gold eyes gazing deeply into mine, the soothing numbness of his shadows chasing the pain and darkness away. This is happiness. This is freedom. This is something I'd be willing to fight for a hundred times over. In the depths of my soul, I know I have never and may never again experience such a profound and real sense of happiness like I feel in this moment. Here in the Underworld. Here with Ere. *My* Ere.

I hope he's right. I hope we are fated to be.

CHAPTER THIRTY-FIVE

STARLESS SKY

NORA

I peek over my coffee cup and take a sip. Ere does the same as he watches me watch him. He winks and throws me his most charming smile then sets his mug down. The table is laid out with fresh fruit, pancakes, and bacon, all the color of poison of course, but neither of us have really eaten anything. Some days coffee is enough. There are new strange things at the table, though, things he said will help me heal if I'm hurt and make me stronger if I need to fight today. Ambrosia and Nectar. They even look semi edible, the shadows unable to block out their golden hues. I force down a bite of the sweet fruit and a few sips of the even sweeter drink, but the anxious energy taking up so much space in my stomach leaves no room for much else.

Leaning my chin on my hands, I return his smile as I admire the curve of his black horns and the warmth of his golden eyes. I've learned that when his eyes are this color his mind and power are calm, but the second the red glow sets in, his shadows are dying to come out and play. If you're an enemy of his, it might be smart to run when that crimson glow takes over. But I'm not an enemy. Ere would never hurt me. I can't help but wonder what his shadows might do to enemies after discovering what they're capable of doing to me. Surely there's another use for them than pleasure, though I'm not complaining. Kairos and Mio, I can imagine, would take one look at him and judge him harshly or possibly try to kill him on site. He told me he looks like her. Nyx. The moment she cursed him to a life as her slave in The Underworld, the curved horns and leathery wings appeared. In a way, he looks like the demons, too. But to me, he's anything but terrifying. He's beautiful.

"So, todays the day, then?" My eyes are calm and steady, but my heart thuds loudly against my ribcage, the rush of blood vibrating within my ears like a warning bell screaming within my head.

His smile fades, his eyes darkening as he nods. "It is. We have no choice. The soldiers out guarding are getting restless as they wait. They know she will make a move soon if we do not." He takes another sip from his mug, gripping it tight as his eyes stay on me. "You do not have to do this if you don't want to, Nora. As much as I would love for you to know the truth, it will be risky." His knuckles begin to pale from how tight he grips the mug, but he doesn't release it when he lowers his hands to the table, as if he needs something to keep him grounded.

He's nervous, too. I reach for him and take his hands in mine. "I don't care about the risk. Living a life being haunted by darkness and used in Nyx's games isn't something I'm willing to do any longer. I'm done hiding. I want the truth, and I want her to pay for what she has done to me. And to my parents and you," I spit, releasing his hands as mine begin to tremble. I clench them into tight fists in my lap.

Closing my eyes and taking a deep breath, I lean into his shadows as they embrace me. They caress my skin with that icy scent that only exists in a wintery midnight breeze until sweet numbness takes hold of my mind and then my heart. He's right. For now, I need to remain calm, but when I face her, I'll let my anger and my fire tear into her cold, dead heart. I relax my shoulders and unclench my fists as Ere's soothing touch erases the lingering pain and torment from my scattered mind. I'll save my anger for her.

He leans forward, stretching his arms across the table and opening his hands, so I place mine within them. "In person, Nyx is more vicious and cruel than you can imagine. When she wants something, her voice is innocent and alluring and her deceptive charm naturally sways others into believing she is nothing but a delicate flower." He caresses my hands with his thumbs, staring down at them blankly. "Her power to seduce the mind into giving her what she wants is hard to resist. You must see through her facade and fight it the way I do. You can't let her into your head." He meets my gaze, his features shifting to what I believe is fear. "She is far from a delicate flower. Once she has her claws in you, she's a rose dipped in poison, her fragrance capable of ending you with a single breath."

I should be scared, but I'm not. Not with his shadows holding me tight and enveloping me in a soothing calmness that embeds itself into every part of me. I know he'll do what he can to keep me safe, All I can do is fight for my memories and freedom the best I can, and hope and pray it doesn't end in permanent death. At least he's giving me the chance to try. Better than laying low and staying helpless and human like Kairos and Hekate preferred. She would have become angrier and angrier, and people would have died.

"I appreciate you helping me. I couldn't do this without you. I wouldn't want to." I smile, gazing into his glowing eyes and wishing I never had to look away. "She's not just going to hand over the amulet. She has me right where she wants me. She knows I'll come for it, and she thinks she'll win. We could both be hurt. Or worse, we could be killed. I hate even dragging you into this."

"We will not be asking her for permission to take it back, my love. We are taking what belongs to you whether she likes it or not. She believes I have been under her spell and that soon you will be, too. What she does not know is that I have been training my army for this very moment, an army of powerful celestials and witches who she thinks I tossed into the pit. We will not be alone. And you are not dying today. Neither am I." He stands and grabs our empty mugs, stretching his wings out wide and then tucking them tight behind his back, his shadows staying behind to keep me company as he walks away.

He wants this just as badly as I do. Maybe even more so. I've dealt with her torment and games for a year, and it has been pure hell. I can't imagine going through this for an entire century. If he truly has been stuck down here just waiting for this very moment, then I'm certain he's ready for it to be over. He deserves a new beginning, too. I head down the dark corridor, waving a hand and lighting the black flame candles in the bedroom as I enter, and it brings me comfort that at least today I seem to be able to control my power. I haven't accidentally set anything else aflame *yet*. I need to be in control, at least for today, not only in control of my power, but of my mind. My thoughts have been quiet. I've heard no cryptic whispers or dark thoughts about ending my life, but I know she's still in there. She's just waiting for the most opportune time to try and take over. I cannot, under any circumstances, let her.

I quickly change into black fighting leathers, running my hands down the

Dark Legions wings and sword emblem on my chest. Thoughts of Kairos and what he might be feeling or doing in this very moment crash into me, ricocheting through my mind. My heart aches and my chest feels heavy thinking about the hurt he might have felt after I gave myself over to Nyx's demons. I can't even begin to imagine how much more it will hurt him to find out Ere is my fated mate and the one I'm meant to be with. I collapse to the edge of the bed, putting my head between my knees and forcing myself to breathe. It fucking hurts. If Ere is my fated mate, then Kairos isn't. I place my hands against my chest, trying to hold my heart together, to force it to not think or feel, because guilt eats at me when I do, because I hurt him. I kissed him and then chose to leave him. *Fuck*. If Ere is mine and I am his, then it means someone has lied to Kairos, but not just to him, to an entire realm of people. Why? And how? It doesn't make sense. Maybe he chose to lie to me himself for his own fucked up reasons that I don't understand. No. Kairos loved me, didn't he? *Loves* me. Gods, is this his pain or my own? Him falling apart, or me? It's too hard to tell. I never wanted to hurt him. And I'm going to hurt him again, aren't I?

I'd rather end up broken hearted myself than for either of them to ever feel pain.

Are you ready, my little flame?

Ere's whispered words within my mind are like a velvety, warm blanket wrapping around all the wounded, broken pieces of me, and suddenly I can breathe again.

Yes. I'm ready.

I'm not sure how I force my words to not quiver even within my mind, because no, I am not ready for this. I'm not quite sure I ever could be. Right now, I'm more afraid of finding out the truth than I am of Nyx or her demons, but that fear is fading as I stand and face the shadows trickling into the room from the hall.

The towering horns and enormous wings come into view first, and then he tilts his head up and looks at me, flashing a ghost of a smile. It isn't real. He's trying to keep me calm. To keep me from spiraling. It's what he does best. So, I step toward him, welcoming the slowing of my racing heart and the calm that takes over as I loop my arm through his, heading outside to the darkness that awaits us. Neither of us speak for a while. We silently make our way down the stone path lined with black flame torches, nod at the soldiers who stand and wait, then continue walking as Ere commands them to take off into the sky. We head toward the black waters of the River Styx, the dark, rocky mountains towering over us on both sides as he grips my hand in his.

The river is deathly still. Gazing into it as I walk past the mouth, there's something that tells me it might enjoy devouring the bodies of restless, lost souls and spitting out the useless bones. Like souls are what keep it satiated and content. I shiver over this thought, wrapping an arm around my center. This river, though, it's also...familiar. Like I've seen it up close before or have even stood in this exact spot before, but I wouldn't remember. Maybe that's part of its magic and allure, to make all who pass by feel like they're meant to be here. Like they're home.

"You said this river is sacred. What makes it so special?" Gripping his hand tighter, I bring it to my chest, clasping my free hand around our entwined fingers.

I can't tear my eyes away from the still water. It feels charged and magnetic like it won't let me look away until it's through searching within me.

His fingers twitch slightly in my hand as his head tilts down at me. "If the stories are true, then where we stand is a place gods and goddesses once came to. This very ground is sacred. Gods rarely made oaths with one another, but when they did, it was this water they would drink to seal it for eternity." Looking away, he gets lost staring into the pool of water before us. "Oaths broken would bring both gods here no matter where they were or how long it had been, and punishment would be swift. You do not make a promise before this river that you do not intend to keep with the other party. The magic within the River Styx never forgets. And the one who breaks the oath, well, their life will be changed forever, one way or another. It is up to the river to decide what is taken from them."

"Holy shit," I breathe, finally able to peel my eyes away and look at him. "How did my life go from being so simple to this in just weeks?" I huff a laugh, shaking my head. "Are there other sacred places that exist similar to this?"

Smiling, he shifts his attention to the walls of the mountains, pointing up, his eyes glowing with excitement. "There. That's called the River Lethe. It has magical properties of its own. There is another here named the River Msemosyne, and it does as well. I will take you to see them one day." Releasing my hand, he turns his back to the rivers and begins to walk away.

As I turn with him, I Glance over my shoulder, taking in the highest peak of the mountains where a glimmer catches my eye. A huge waterfall cascades down the side and pours into the open mouth of the sprawling mountain range below, too far away to see where it lands.

He stops and faces me, and I look at him, really seeing him tonight for the first time. I admire his beauty and grace in the black attire, choosing to forgo comfort in order to play the part of a true king. His black slacks and blazer give the impression that we're not at war or that not a single drop of blood might be spilled, and something about it makes him feel even more dangerous and lethal. It's an illusion of calm that I know is a lie, because his shadows, I fear, want to tear the world apart tonight.

"Sit with me for a moment?" Placing a hand on my lower back, he helps me sit as a soft blanket appears on the ground and a black flame fire pit that wasn't there seconds ago flicks to life beside us.

I smile as the warm flames extinguish the chill in the air and Ere sits down next to me. "A date before we meet with death? How romantic." Leaning my head on his shoulder, I curl into him as he wraps an arm around me and then softly runs his fingers through my wavy hair.

"I told you that you are not dying today, and I meant it." His dark locks fall in front of his warm, caramel eyes as he pulls back slightly to look at me, adjusting his wings behind him. "Let's just enjoy this peaceful moment together." Gently gripping my chin between his fingers, he caresses my cheek with his thumb before placing a soft, comforting kiss to my lips.

"Are you afraid?" I whisper, a part of me scared she might hear, that the darkness might always be listening. "That she'll take me from you again, I mean."

"Yes," he says simply, his trembling hand grasping mine. "I fear how I might respond." His voice cracks with vulnerability, his brows furrowing as he looks at me. "I have endured Nyx's darkness for over a century, but the emptiness I have been avoiding will consume me if you are taken away now. It is a darkness, a pain, I could never escape. I will drag anyone who gets in our way into the pit, even if it means surrendering myself to its fiery depths. She will not hurt you again."

I swallow, tears burning my eyes, my throat raw from a slicing anguish that has me gripping his hand tighter. He has endured too much. I can't let her hurt him anymore either.

"I'm sorry you've been hurting. I know I was human when we met, but you knew my struggles, and you were there for me. You helped me more than you know. I wish I would have known that you were hurting, too."

In this moment all I want is to help him find happiness. My memories and my own future are important, but if darkness is all he has known for more than a century, then no one deserves freedom or happiness more than Ere. Anger ignites in my core and threatens to spill out into the world, my power thrumming within with a desire to fix things for him.

"I never wanted to lie to you. To tell you my pain was caused by another would have been absurd when the only one I have ever loved is you." His smile is small, agony showing through, as he shifts on the blanket and faces me. "Every second without you has felt like an eternity. I will set this whole goddamn world on fire and watch it all burn if that is what it takes to get your memories back." His glowing crimson eyes burn into mine, swirling and flickering with deadly promises.

"Your love for me is intense and slightly terrifying." I laugh quietly. "Was the love between us always this way?" Pulling a leg up, I turn to face him, tilting my head and watching as his eyes dance with a darkness and fiery passion that makes my heart melt.

"Yes," he whispers. "Always."

There's no questioning my feelings for Ere. I know my love for him runs deep and that if something were to happen to him, I would do whatever it takes for him, too. Being with him feels like coming home after not knowing where I belonged for too long. I need him to finally break free of Nyx so he can find the happiness he deserves.

"Kiss me," I whisper, my pulse quickening as his heated gaze washes over me. "One last time before everything possibly falls apart." Pulling myself to my knees, I run my fingertips along his jawline before clasping my hands around the nape of his neck.

He grips my waist and pulls me onto his lap, hands sliding up my thighs and then holding firm at the arch in my back. I lock my ankles behind him and he holds me steady. Tucking my hair behind my ear, his hand lingers, thumb caressing my cheek as he wraps his fingers around the side of my neck and brings his lips to mine. Our kiss is slow and gentle at first, unrushed and tender, until the world falls away and it's just him and I and nothing else. Fisting his hair in my hands, his tongue moves against mine now with a newfound passion and desire like I've never felt before. This isn't just a kiss, it's us saying goodbye the only way we can, using lips and tongues to say what he can't bring himself to admit, that one or both of us could die tonight. Hope and love radiate around us as his shadows meet the swirls of my blue and purple divine light, and they flicker and sway, combining as one. Darkness may have succeeded in extinguishing our light for a time, but the love between us reignites blistering flames of hope within both our hearts.

I don't want to let him go, not now or ever. I want to stay here in the darkness with his shadows wrapped around us keeping us protected and hidden from anguish and pain. This feeling, this moment with Ere, this is the kind of love I've been hoping to find my whole life. Nothing will ever compare to what I feel for him. I'm no longer scared to find out the truth because I know the truth already. There's no way he has been feeding me lies with all the nourishment he provides to my heart and soul.

Pulling my lips away from his is difficult. If it were up to me, we'd stay here like this forever. The gentleness of his forehead pressed against mine helps ease my racing heart and cool the fiery need pulsing in my core. I close my eyes and smile as he traces lines up and down my back with his fingertips.

"Our love is written in the stars," he breathes, looking up at the sky with a mesmerizing smile and eyes golden and swirling with hope.

Following his gaze, my eyes widen and my mouth pops open in disbelief. The normally pitch-black sky shimmers with twinkling blue stars bigger and brighter than any I've seen before. An electrifying feeling of shock and awe shoot straight to my heart. I can't deny that it's a little like fate whispering down at me that prophecies and predetermined destinies are real, and that everything is happening as it should. The beauty of the stars, so out of place here in the Underworld, make the glow of them even more brilliant against the backdrop of the shadows and dreary darkness of this realm.

"How is this possible?" I shift in his lap, wrapping my arms around his neck and leaning all the way back to get a better look. "There shouldn't be light here. No stars in the sky."

"You are not one to believe much in fate, but how can you deny what you see with your own eyes? What you feel in your own heart. Fate will always make itself known, whether you choose to believe in it or not." He smiles, brushing hair away from my eyes and tucking it neatly behind my ears. "No amount of darkness or passing of time could ever keep us apart. Our souls will always find their way back to each other."

I shake my head. "I should have learned by now to expect the unexpected." I untangle myself from him, standing and reaching for his hand. "I don't want to wait any longer, Ere. I'm ready for whatever fate will bring." I smile as he reaches for my hand and pulls himself to his feet, leading us away from the river.

We choose to not fly into our fate, not wanting to appear rushed, afraid and hopeless. We aren't those things, not anymore. We choose to instead stroll hand in hand with our heads held high, carrying only hope in our hearts.

CHAPTER THIRTY-SIX

I LOVE YOU'S

KAIROS

Well, coming to the Underworld without a clear plan was a disaster we should have seen coming. If you'd have asked me days ago when Nyx and her hellhounds first captured Hekate and I if I thought we'd be alive four days later, I would have said fuck no. Yet here we are. Alive. Bound and kept near the flaming black pit, the heat of it scorching my neck and making my skin uncomfortably slick as shit, but we're alive. There were too many of them to fight our way out. I can't afford to die when I haven't saved Mera yet. I'm getting her the fuck out of here even if doing so gets me killed. I just have to stay alive long enough to get the chance to. I will not fail her this time.

The demons' growls fill the silence any time one of us moves or speaks, but it's usually only me doing the talking. Hekate has kept mostly silent and dazed since we stopped at the River Mnemosyne before we were captured. She stared at the sign for a moment, mumbled something about the water looking familiar, and she drank from it as I sharpened my blades. She has been strange ever since. Now she's just silently staring up at the queen on the throne like she's someone she knows. But she does not know that *thing* sitting there smiling down at us. With the thick, curved horns, the leathery wings, and the glowing red eyes that make the light within me ache with the need to kill her, she's as evil and demonic as it gets. Not to mention her little pets, the black serpents with beady glowing eyes like hers that she wears like jewelry around her neck. I was right. Hekate was wrong. There is no light left within her.

My knees burn from kneeling on them for so long, the dry, hot, scorched earth forming new blisters on my skin each time I heal the old ones. We tried to be civil with Nyx, or at least Hekate did. I threatened to rip out her heart with my bare hands while Hekate begged her to let Mera come home, for her to come home as well. Talking to her was useless, and Hekate has lost her godsdamned mind if she thinks she's going to convince her to come back or that it'd be safe to do so. She doesn't belong out there in the semi civilized world. This is where she belongs.

Nyx stands and sways her hips as she makes her way across the throne platform, the crumbling stone pillars on its four sides leaning dangerously like they might fall at any second. Her black horns cast eerie shadows across the ground as she gracefully descends the steps and makes her way over to us.

Using her sharp, demon-like claws, she slices through the thick rope tied tightly around our wrists and ankles, setting us both free. "It is time." Her lips curl up into a beautiful but deadly smile, and the serpents around her shoulders hiss as they track my every move, heads weaving side to side.

I glare up at her, rubbing at the raw skin around my wrists and healing the bloody, torn flesh there. Nyx reaches into a hidden pocket on the front of her black, flowy dress, pulls out Mera's amulet, and then dangles it in my face just to taunt me. My future is in there. My heart is in there. Everything I've ever wanted exists within that amulet and she fucking knows it. She lets it sway back and forth, hypnotizing me and reminding me of all that I've lost, of all I might never experience again if she controls Mera's entire life. Taking a slow, cautious step forward, she bends and slips the chain around my neck, the amulet and the magic holding Mera's memories within it humming against my chest like it's home at last. It is. Mera is my home, and I am hers, and these memories belong to both of us.

"I think you should be the one to return Mera's memories, Kairos. After pining over her so pathetically for a century, there is nothing I would love more." Leaning in close, she grips my chin between her fingers, smiling down at me as she whispers, "You deserve this." Turning her back and sauntering away, the demons who were hiding within caves carved into the mountains slowly creep out, eyes locked on Hekate and I, low snarls rumbling from their chests.

Fuck, there are so many of them. Too many. More than I could have ever imagined existed here, and much more than the number I've slaughtered in my time, which is in the thousands. The stench of their venom in the air alone might be lethal. Even biding my time, waiting for whatever fucked up plan Nyx has in store to end, how the hell we're going to make it out of here alive is beyond me. Gods fucking save us all.

Groaning from the pain of my blistered knees, I push myself to my feet and pull Hekate close, a flash of white flickering as I heal both our wounds. She could heal herself if she weren't so lost in gazing after the queen who stares at us with a devilish glint in her eyes.

"For what it is worth, Hekate, I think I did love you once. But the darkness you abandoned me to, it consumed me. Until you were nothing and my realm was nothing, until all I could think about was how badly I wanted to watch it all burn." She shakes her head, meeting my eyes before dragging them back to Hekate. "You could have stopped this. You could have saved me. Now I wonder if the woman I once was exists within me at all. Maybe she tired of screaming for you to save her. Maybe the pain of knowing you would not come made her simply...fade away into oblivion. It has been quite a while since I have heard her in here at all." She taps her temple, her red lips curving up into a smile that makes my skin crawl and my blood run cold. "So, if you are wondering if the woman you love still exists, dear Hekate, the answer is no. She does not. That poor, sad woman you abandoned died long ago."

Hekate pushes away from me and charges toward her, palms out and blue lights flaring in her palms and all around her so bright I have to cover my eyes with my arm as I chase after her. Shit. It was her job to stay calm and rational, to keep the peace and talk me down from using thoughtless violence, especially before having Mera in my arms. I want nothing more than to rip Nyx's head from her body and toss it into the pit, but not yet. Not until I know the woman I love is safe. I wrap my arms around Hekate and hold her back. Nyx crosses her arms over her chest, tilting her head and still smiling, glowing red eyes begging me to tear them from her skull.

"Hekate, she is taunting you. Ignore it." My muscles flex as I hold on to her tighter, her grunting and fighting against me. I lean in, whispering only to her, "We came here for Mera. Let's focus on that. After we know she's safe, if you want Nyx dead, I will happily kill her myself."

She relaxes against me, tilting her head back and meeting my gaze. "That is not Nyx, Kairos. It is not her," she breathes, slumping back against my chest as if all hope or life has been drained away. "I am not who you think I am, either."

All I can do is stare back at her and say nothing, because what the hell am I supposed to say to that? She's seeing what she wants to. Hearing only the words she chooses to. But I've never seen or felt her this way. She's not making sense or even thinking clearly, from what it seems. What the hell does she mean she isn't who I think she is? Maybe there was something off about that water she drank earlier. Her energy shines brighter than anyone else's now that she has shown us the queen she is, but as I look at her now, it's barely palpable at all. The bright glimmer of her soul is just a faint whisper of what it was before, and gods does it kill me to see her so dim and hopeless.

I help steady her and wrap an arm around her waist to keep her upright. "It's okay, Hekate. Everything will be alright. Fate is on our side, remember?" I smile down at her, and though she doesn't return it with one of her own, she nods once, pushing her shoulders back and holding her head up high.

That's good enough for now. Ignoring Nyx, I let my eyes drift across the realm, the hairs on the back of my neck and my arms standing on end. The celestial light in my soul rages with the desire to destroy everything that exists here, but it also curls away as if searching for safety from the ancient, foreign evil that exists here that it's never felt before. This kind of darkness, the kind that has corrupted her soul, it's not the same as the darkness her or Mera were born with in their blood. This kind should be extinguished from our world. Nyx clears her throat and drops her hands to her sides, and my attention immediately snaps back to her.

"King Erebus, I thought you might never arrive. We have all been impatiently waiting for you. I nearly died of boredom with these two." Her words are flat as she clasps her hands behind her back, pacing before the throne platform, snarling, winged demons flanking her sides.

There's a fucking king of the Underworld? Why the hell am I just finding this out now? I search the darkness for any sign of Mera, but I don't see her. The black flame torches around the stone pillars and the shadows that seem to be getting thicker by the second are all I can see. Then the shadows change, they take shape and form and another set of curved horns and leathery wings like the demons come into view. My celestial dagger thrums at my thigh and I carefully slip it out of my holster, the light flashing to life in my hand and allowing us to see what exactly is hidden in the darkness. We both freeze, Hekate clenching my forearm tightly and me keeping my dagger raised as Mera takes slow steps toward us.

"The river did not lie. It's him," Hekate whispers, slowly beginning to back away. "Kairos, there's something you need to know. Many things." She grips my forearm and drags me backward.

I try to pull away from her, but she doesn't let me, shock and horror slamming into me as Ere's face comes into view. "What the fuck is he?" I breathe, leaning into Hekate so no one else will hear.

"He looks so much like Nyx." She shakes her head, her grip on my arm tightening. "It cannot be true."

Hand in hand, the love of my life and Ere, who I'm almost certain is another demon or whatever the hell Nyx is, step up to the queen and my body trembles as rage and pain and confusion threaten to take over. He played the part of the innocent mortal so well, but to what end? What the hell does he want with her? He's smirking as he holds Meras hand as if she belongs to him, and *her*...her bright blue eyes dim as she notices me here, her features shifting to a sadness that shatters my heart and has it crumbling to nothing. She wasn't expecting me to be here. She didn't think I would come for her. And godsdamnit, that hurts.

"Let my fated mate go, demon. Get your fucking hands off of her." Lightning prickles under my skin, then takes life around my hands, wrapping up my forearms, my power and I coming to an understanding that we have no choice but to fight. "I knew my hatred for you ran deeper than just despising you for loving the one I'm fated to be with." I step forward, gripping my dagger tighter as Hekate tries and fails to pull me back, hissing as the bursts of electricity running rampant across my skin shock her. "How did you hide what you are so well? How could a celestial and the queen of witches both be so blind to the truth? It's impossible, unless..." I point my dagger at his heart, waiting for the moment Mera steps away so I can jab it straight through the thick muscle and watch him turn to ash. "Nora... I need you to let go of his hand and come to me." I reach for her with my free hand, forcing my eyes to remain calm and unbothered as I swallow back the fear suddenly clawing its way into my blood stream.

"Go on, Kairos. Finish your thought. It's impossible unless what?" He smiles, his glowing gold eyes swirling as they peer into mine.

Those eyes make me feel like clawing my own out just to avoid him staring into mine ever again. They make me feel nothing. Like my heart doesn't exist and my soul isn't real and the only thing that exists is him. I shiver and look away. Dark gods haven't existed in our world for centuries as far as any of us knew, and yet, I'm almost certain from the power radiating around him that it's exactly what he is. And seeing how easily Hekate hid who she was from me and everyone else, Ere pretending to be an innocent, naïve mortal could likely be done easily if he is one of the forgotten gods.

But why drag Mera into this? What the hell does he want with her? Maybe I'm wrong. Gods, I hope I'm wrong.

Are you starting to realize coming here was a mistake? This will not end the way you wanted it to.

I snap my gaze back to him, eyes widening as he simply smiles innocently as if he wasn't just in my fucking head. Looking to Mera, hand still outstretched and waiting for her to run into my arms, she doesn't move. She stands there, eyebrows scrunching up and that same sadness that lingered in her eyes when she first saw me beginning to grow. Glancing down at my chest, her face lights up as she catches sight of her amulet, and pain tightens my chest and clenches in my stomach, wishing she would have looked even half as happy to see me.

"Kairos," she breathes, a small smile forms on her lips, but concern flashes across her features as she looks at me. "I'm okay. Except for the fact that the two of you followed me here. I wanted to do this alone." She's still holding his fucking hand, eyes drifting back down to the amulet around my neck.

Her head whips to the side to focus on Nyx who now slowly prowls toward her. "You tried to ruin my life over and over. You haunted my thoughts and used my grief as fuel to feed the darkness I have within, hoping it would take over completely." She steps toward her, Ere releasing her hand and letting her advance without him. "I should kill you right now. You deserve to die if it's true what they say—that you've tormented me even in a past life." Shaking her head and looking her up and down, she stops mere inches away from the queen.

Nyx laughs, the sound high-pitched and jarring, a powerful shrill of magic capable of making mortal ears bleed. "I did not torture or torment you for fun." She smiles and the sharp points of her teeth glisten as the black flamed torches flicker and rise higher next to her. "I needed you to see that you belong here. That you always have." She leans forward, her lips brushing against

Mera's ear as she whispers, "I will enjoy using you to destroy the realms, Hemera."

Ere glances my way and smiles, and it's the same damn casual, innocent smile that Mera probably believes is charming and kind, but that I know is sinister and full of secrets. I take a small step forward, trying to sense what kind of power he has within, but it's like a glamour stronger than I've ever felt before exists around him and within his soul that blocks me from feeling anything at all. I force myself to stare into his eyes, to not let whatever darkness lurks there drag me into never-ending despair, but he only allows me a glimpse of what he's capable of. Whatever power he wields is one reminiscent of an empty void where nothing exists.

"I belong to nothing and no one, Nyx. If you think I'm going to stand by and let you use my power to destroy the realms, then you're crazier than I thought you were." Huffing a laugh, Mera rakes her eyes over Nyx, shaking her head. "I won't be used as a weapon for your vengeance. I'm sorry to disappoint you, but my power isn't up for grabs. It's not yours or anyone else's...it is *mine*." Her palms glow with a blue and purple light that's so bright it's hard to look at, her power igniting into little flames that flicker and sway as she raises them toward Nyx.

The queen takes a few steps back, terror and excitement dancing within those crimson eyes.

I forgot how beautiful her power is. Mera holds all the light in the world within her palms, and I don't think she realizes how special that is. How special *she* is. Gods, she is the light of my life. My flame within the darkness.

The demons flanking Nyx growl and snarl, charging toward Mera, so I don't hesitate. I charge back. I race toward her, daggers out and ready to slice their throats open and toss them into the pit, but Eres power reaches them before I get the chance. Dark shadows stretch out from behind his back, tendrils whispering through the air, sharp and viscous and hungry. That distinct scent of foreign darkness, the one that's wrong and makes my light hide within corners of my soul that I can't reach, is overpowering now. He spreads those leathery wings out wide and smiles as his shadows engulf the demons within his dark power. In seconds, those shadows rip the demons apart, sending black blood and small bits of demon chunks flying through the air. A scaly, monstrous head rolls toward my feet, and the shadows follow, still ripping and tearing it to shreds. I watch in unmasked shock and horror as it liquifies in front of me.

Hekate grips my arm, her normally delicate fingers digging into my flesh as she pulls me back and away from Mera. "Kairos, I-I think we should leave. Immediately."

"I'm not leaving her," I spit, glancing at her for only a second before finding Mera next to Ere again. "You know I can't. I won't." Stepping away, I take in her trembling hands and her glowing eyes, her dome of blue light shielding us, unbreakable and unyielding as it hums to life. I've never seen her scared like this before, and after that little display with the shadows, I can't lie and say I'm not scared, too. "What is it Hekate? Tell me."

She swallows, glancing upward and then back at Mera whose flames still rage and crackle within her palms. "None of us are who you believed we were, Kairos. Not me. Not him. Not even you." Her hands tremble as she reaches up and places them against my cheek. "The River showed me the truth. I am not just a queen, Kairos. I am a goddess. And the old gods have spoken. Ere was using his power to block out the truth that sits right above us, but just now, when he used his shadows and was too distracted to care, the gods who rest in the Elysian Fields spoke to me and urged me to look up, and I did." Sadness fills her eyes, tears glistening in the corners. "Look up, Kairos. Mera's fate is out of our hands." Her eyes drift up my face as she tilts her head back, a tear sliding down her pale cheek.

I shouldn't have fucking listened to her. I should have ignored her words. Glancing up at the sky stops my heart, because the divine light twinkling brighter than the stars back home mixed with the swirls of velvety darkness that resembles Eres power, is a clear fucking sign from the gods that I am fucked.

Is love a game to the gods, then? The gods who have abandoned us and choose now to show up and obliterate my entire life. Mera's fate is literally written in the stars and she will not be leaving with me. The gods have chosen for her to stay in the Underworld. Without me.

Faintly, I can hear words being exchanged between Mera and Nyx as I step away from Hekate, shaking my head in disagreement with the truth. It cannot be real. It isn't true. She has always belonged with me. Love is a curse. Fate is a blatant, fucking lie. And prophecies, well, they are nothing but absolute bullshit if it means we don't get to be together. I won't allow it. Fuck the gods or the rulers of the realms or anyone else who'd like to stand in my way.

I am not a fucking pawn in the games gods play.

Running to Mera, I conjure lightning in my palms and focus it on Nyx as she smiles cruelly and sends her black flames spiraling toward my face. I will kill both the demons if I have to. *My* fated mate—and *mine* is exactly what she is—will not be staying here with them. I dive and roll across the steaming, hot ground, ducking just in time for the fire to miss me and go hurling into one of the half-broken pillars near the pit. It groans, roaring across the realm as it tumbles and crashes to the ground. I aim at Nyx and my power jolts from my fingertips, wrapping around her like one of her serpents and she shrieks. Even stunned by the electricity and unable to move, she still fucking smiles, sending out a puff of air from her lungs tainted with her venom. The scent of her dark power makes my stomach churn, and I hold my breath as I force my way through her cloud of death, gripping her by the throat and squeezing as I lift her. Her stilettos kick at my raging wind that swirls around us, rocks and dirt flying past as she dangles helplessly in the air.

"Kairos, enough!" Hekate screams, but I smile up at the demon queen and ignore her completely.

Nyx ruined my life. She took everyone and everything I loved from me. Mera wouldn't be here right now if it weren't for her. She needs to pay. My plan hasn't changed. I was always going to end her pathetic life.

I stumble back as two demons slam their monstrous heads into my sides. My ribs ache as pain slices through me, but I don't fall. The celestial dagger on my right thigh slips free and goes tumbling across the black dirt directly toward Nyx. My lightning dies out as soon as the shooting pain makes me lose focus of my power. Nyx is no longer unable to move. She blows me a kiss, wiggling her fingers in a taunting wave goodbye as more venom leaks from between her puckered lips. Crouching low, she picks up my dagger and spins it in her hand with expert precision as she prowls toward me. Her demons grip my arms and shove me to the ground, holding me down so I can't move. I thrash and pull as I try to stand, but her venom takes hold because I was too distracted to hold my breath, and now my body feels heavy and useless. Fuck.

A flash of red hair steals my attention as Mera runs to me, but Hekate and Ere grab her and pull her back. She screams my name, the sound muffled and on repeat like I've been trapped within an echo chamber in my own mind, her wailing at the top of her lungs as she fights to be set free. All I can do is watch from a distance as she tries and fails to come to me. Tears fall, splashing and sizzling on the scorched ground. Her mouth opens and closes again and again, blood rushing to her cheeks in anger or possible heartbreak, all of it in slow motion. It brings me comfort in death though, to see that a part of her, at least, still cares. Hekate pushes Mera behind her and steps forward. A flash of blue light whirls closer, barreling into one demon and then the other, and they fly back, slamming into the mountain wall. Ere's shadows creep closer, ripping and shredding them until they're nothing but a puddle of thick, black blood at the foot of the mountain. As if he cares whether I live or die. It's an act. A show just for her. A façade, the way it has always been with him.

My blood boils and my internal organs are on fire, hot pain tearing through me. I've felt the demons' venom countless times, but *this*...godsdamn I've never felt anything like it. All I can do is lie here and wait to die as Nyx raises my celestial dagger above her head, light flaring out around us as she prepares for the kill. I still can't move. Her venom races through my system making it harder by the second to even use the muscles of my diaphragm to fucking breathe. I am going to die here. Flames, beautiful blue and purple flames, soar toward Nyx and hit their mark. And fuck, if I could smile right now over how proud I am of Mera, I would. Seeing Nyx slump over in pain, her body curling in on itself and screeching so loud the demons grumble low in surrender, the ground trembling as they run away, offers a small amount of relief.

It all happens so fast after that. One second, I'm paralyzed and watching in slow motion, like an outsider who's not even here, and the next second Nyx is lying on top of me. Warmth spills from my stomach and gushes down my sides as my own celestial dagger tears through muscle and nerves that are already burning from Nyx's venom, so hot that I can't even feel the stab wound. It's a death sentence and she knew it. Her final gift to me.

"Kairos!" Mera screams, and the pounding of feet on the hard dirt is fuzzy and far away as blurry shadows and shapes rush to my side.

Hekate rolls Nyx's motionless body off me, and I can sense her heartbreak, smell her tears in the air, her knee brushing against my arm when she collapses between the two of us. "No!" She screams, her pain ripping through the air, my numb mind and body still feeling the ache of her bleeding heart as my own slowly dies.

"Nora, help me!" Hekate grabs Mera's arms and drags her to the ground in front of her. "Place your hands on my shoulders so I can draw from your power and heal them. I don't know that I'm strong enough to do it alone. They aren't dead yet, but they will be soon." Taking a deep, trembling breath, her eyes snap closed. "We can do this. They will be fine," she whispers, soft shimmers of blue light illuminating the hazy shadows.

Mera doesn't look at her. She only looks at me. At my gaping wound and the blood draining rapidly from my body. I cannot be healed. This wound is deep. Permanent. The way our love once was. Her mouth hangs open in disbelief, a tortured, knowing expression on her face as she takes my hand in hers and squeezes it once before placing her outstretched palms on Hekate's shoulders. She's ignoring the fact that Nyx is going to be healed, and that I cannot be saved, but I can't fucking speak or resist or argue for them to just let us both go. I push the truth away the way Mera does now beside me, not accepting that I'm going to die, because I can't face it. Dying means never getting to spend even one more day with her, and it's not a truth I can fucking bare. Lying to myself is better.

The glowing lights of their magic float above me, and as soothing as their power is, my eyelids are too heavy to hold open. I let them close. I let my mind wander to memories of date nights under the stars followed by *I love you's*. To promises made that could never be broken.

I drift off with only thoughts of her, the way I always do.

CHAPTER THIRTY-SEVEN

FORGOTTEN PROMISES

NORA

Since the day I was killed and woke up as an immortal in the Underworld, fear has been a distant memory most days. In this moment, waiting to see if Kairos somehow survived that wound from his dagger, fear is the only thing I do feel. I've never been this scared in my life. But his heart is still beating. His breathing is slow but steady. He's not dead yet. I don't think I can live with myself if he dies. This is my fault. I sent my power raging toward Nyx so carelessly, and her dagger ended up in his stomach because she fucking fell. Because of me.

Ere doesn't wrap his shadows around me to numb my pain as tears silently stream down my cheeks. He stands behind me just watching and waiting as I hold Kairos' limp hand in mine, softly caressing it with my thumb. I think he knows the numbness, the feeling absolutely nothing, would hurt infinitely more than not suffering through this pain. If Kairos suffers, then so should I, because *gods*, I deserve to.

Hekate sniffles beside me, staring intently at Nyx as if she's counting every single breath, pressing her fingertips against her neck periodically to feel her pulse. "They should be awake by now. Something must be wrong." Her words are quiet but they're laced with panic and heartbreak.

I want to be pissed. I want to yell at her, to ask her what the hell is wrong with her, but I can't gather the energy to do it. It doesn't help that I've never seen her so broken and lost before. She loves my mortal enemy, and as much as I want to hate her for it, I can't. I won't. Because I love her.

"They will wake up any second now. Ere steps around Kairos and kneels beside Nyx. "Though when this one wakes up, we might all want to run. She is not going to be herself for a while." He meets Hekate's eyes, nodding once before he stands and comes back to my side.

"What the hell does that mean? What happened to her?" Hekate glares at Ere, holding Nyx's hand against her heart and gripping it tight within both of her palms.

Her blue shield has been up around her and Nyx since the healing ritual, after she dragged her lifeless body away to a spot near the mountain wall. She hasn't even looked at me since.

Ere's head tilts as he gazes down at Kairos and I, not looking at her as he speaks. "You are asking the wrong questions, little witch."

Kairos jolts upright, gasping for air and clutching his abdomen, his wide, bloodshot eyes darting across the realm. "How the hell—" another gasp for air and he chokes on his words, his heartbeat racing, "Am I alive? It's impossible." He finishes, his bright emerald eyes meeting mine.

"Good, someone who *is* asking the right questions," Ere glances at Hekate and then walks away, taking a seat on the stairs of the raised platform.

"I don't know how you're alive right now, Kairos, but I'm so thankful you are." I throw my arms around his neck and pull him to me, squeezing him tight as he pushes himself up to his knees. "I'm so sorry. I'm so damn sorry I almost got you killed. I don't know what I would have done if you weren't okay." Warm tears fill my eyes, but I'm smiling, too, because a world without Kairos would be a much darker place.

He wraps his arms weakly around my waist, leaning his head on my shoulder and taking a deep breath before pulling back slightly to look at me. Cradling my face between his palms, he whispers just for me, "There are so many things I never got the chance to tell you. Too many things." Glancing over at Ere, he grips my amulet in his palm, running his thumb across the swirling colors within the black stone.

Gods, with everything that has happened, the amulet and my memories were the furthest thing from my mind until now, but it is why I'm here. To find the truth. To find myself. I am so fucking scared. Staring into Kairos' eyes, the hope overpowered by pain that lingers within them, my heart already threatens to crack in two. I don't want to hurt him. Either of them.

"The truth shall set us free," I lie, because the truth no longer feels like freedom, it feels more like a poisonous affliction I'll be granting someone. I take a deep breath, unable to look into his eyes, to face the pain there any longer, so I look at the amulet instead. "I guess it's now or never."

He tilts my chin up, leaning in until his face is just inches from mine. "Please," he breathes, his warm breath brushing against my lips. "I can't take this pain any longer. I need you to remember. I need this nightmare to end." His eyes burn into mine, searching my own for something, as his glaze over and fill with tears.

It hurts. I can't stand the heartbreak that rises and falls like broken, stormy waves within those dim green eyes. He loves me. And looking at him now, the light and adoration that his soul wraps me up in, I'm brave enough to admit the truth to myself for the first time. I love them both. How could I not? Fate brought them both to me for a reason. I just have no idea why.

I push myself to my feet and offer my hand out to Kairos. He sways and then hisses in pain as he stumbles into me. I wrap his arm around my shoulder, looping mine around his waist, until he straightens and steadies himself, then nods down at me. His eyes pin me in place, like he doesn't want to or is afraid to let me go, but I release him and he's able to stand upright on his own.

Hekate gasps, drawing all of our attention, and then she quickly slides away from Nyx as blackness seeps from her skin and settles on the ground around her. Slowly, her curved horns and leathery wings begin to crack, and before I can even blink, they shatter and turn to ash. The black blood trickling out of the burn on her chest, the wound my flames gave her, fades to a bright crimson. That evil I felt wrapped around her before is gone. I sense powerful light and a pure heart that has been buried beneath a century of darkness. The darkness isn't gone. It's still there, coursing through her veins, but it's different. Her celestial blood overpowers it.

"Nyx," Hekate whispers, crawling across the ground and taking both of her hands. "You're free, Nyx. You're finally free."

Her eyelids flutter open and warm brown irises greet me as I meet her gaze. She sits up, looking at all of us with wide, terror-filled eyes as she slides backward on the crumbling dirt. She doesn't stop until her back is pressed firmly against the side of the black, rocky mountain. She doesn't speak. She only screams. She screams and sobs uncontrollably, unconsolably, as Hekate tries to take her into her arms and Nyx forcefully pushes her away. Hekate gives Kairos a dazed and terrified glance as she opens a portal to leave. Ere steps up behind me, placing his palms on my shoulders, thumbs absentmindedly caressing my skin, but I can't look away from Nyx. She seems so...*broken*.

"Please...take me home...these are not my thoughts. I do not belong here." Nyx curls into the fetal position on the ground as Hekate gently brushes hair out of her face and then cradles her head in her lap.. "*You* do not belong here," Nyx spits, eyes pinned in my direction, Ere stiffening behind me.

Hekate blinks and they're gone.

"What the hell just happened?" Kairos steps away, eyes searching the ground where Nyx's darkness disintegrated to ash.

I force my mouth closed as my mind races with thoughts of what it all could mean. "I have no idea," I whisper.

Ere steps up beside me, lifting a hand and running the back of his fingers across my cheek. "You are safe. That's all that matters to me." He smiles, golden eyes warm and comforting. "It's Nyx. Probably a new game she has decided to play."

He's right. I felt light within her, but none of us know what's going through her mind, or what she'd be willing to do to get exactly what she wants. She didn't seem okay. What if this is another game? I hope Hekate is safe.

Kairos, Ere, and I stand in silence for a moment, none of us knowing what the hell to say or do.

Kairos lifts my necklace over his head and takes my hand in his, gently closing my palm around it. "I believe this belongs to you." He smiles at me and then glares in Eres direction.

He backs away but his eyes search mine as I look from him to Ere. I should be happy to be holding this. I should be thrilled that it's finally over. But gods, I'm terrified of what truths I might uncover.

Opening my palms, I hold it in front of me and gaze into the swirling, hypnotizing colors. "What do I do now?" I glance over at Ere.

He steps up behind me, reaching over my shoulders and placing his palms beneath my hands. "Whatever it tells you to do, my love. Close your eyes and feel the power. Listen to the magic within it."

I don't even feel him walk away, too engrossed in listening and feeling and connecting with whatever magic holds onto my memories. In my mind, I'm holding the amulet and filling it with water from a river that glows with lights and colors so vibrant and full of power that it takes my breath away. I seal the bottle closed with a wave of a hand, and slide it onto a dainty, golden chain. I know what I have to do. I open my eyes and hold the bottle upright, waving a hand above the top, hoping and praying my magic works. I've only practiced with my flames. Nothing else. A flash of soft light envelopes it for a moment and then slips away. I feel the power calling to me, whispering my name, my real name, as I bring the bottle to my lips.

I keep my eyes closed tight as I drink the contents down, but then I'm swaying, hands gripping my arms and keeping me on my feet. I gasp as memories come rushing back faster than I was prepared for. I let them all in. Memories of Kairos and I training our soldiers and laughing as we walked home after a long day. Memories of Mio and Kairos and I fighting side by side against Nyx, both right there always, keeping me safe and guarded. Then there are memories of *him*... Erebus. The rush I felt as we slowly fell in love under the stunning backdrop of the stars those nights we'd sneak away to the Earth Realm. All the nights we made love beneath them when we should have been sleeping. The night I told him I loved him for the first time, and he told me he knew from the day we met that our love was written in the stars. He's the one I've always loved. The one I made promises to as I was dying in his arms after we fell from the Realm of Light. The one I willingly walked over roses covered in vines for in the meadow, because I wanted more than anything to bind myself to him for eternity. *He* is my fated mate. I am his and he is mine, always.

Warm tears flow down my cheeks as I open my eyes, my gaze settling first on Kairos and then shifting to Ere. I step toward him, my heart overflowing with more love than I ever thought could exist. His smile brings me back to the nights under the stars and the way he looked at me the day of our claiming ceremony, so much love and passion he was offering all to me. How did I not feel it with such certainty even as a mortal? How could I be so blind? Erebus—he is everything to me. I throw myself into his arms and he lifts me by my waist and wraps me around him, my ankles locking at the small of his back and arms clamping tightly around his neck. I never want to let go of him again. The rest of the world drifts away, there are no sounds or people left who exist, no demons hiding within caves all around us. It is only him and I.

"I remember you. I remember everything." I sob, our lips crashing together as he grips my face and pulls me to him, his tongue and his lips consuming me, claiming me as his. "I'm never leaving you again. I promise."

His warm golden eyes darken, the crimson and feral glow taking over. "I am yours, Mera. I always have been. You are never getting rid of me."

"Our promises. I remember," I whisper.

"Say it." He smiles, his hands sliding down my body and settling at my hips.

"Until the Underworlds sky shines bright." I brush my nose against his the way I used to, closing my eyes and breathing in the sweet reminder of our love.

"Until celestial wings are neither black nor white." His lip twitches, a single tear sliding down his cheek.

"Until the realms are shattered and made anew." I wipe the tear from his cheek as my own cascade down mine.

"You belong to me, and I belong to you," he whispers, his voice cracking with all the emotions and memories and love he has had to live with alone for the past century. The things he had to bury down deep to keep hidden from Nyx so she would continue thinking he was a slave to her manipulation and power.

His lips meet mine and I lose myself again in the moment as everything else fades away. There's only him and I and nothing more, and there's nothing I want more than to stay here in his arms forever. Brushing his lips against my cheek, he glances over my shoulder, slowly lowering me to the ground.

Gods. Kairos. I slowly turn to face him, and the look in his eyes, on his face, it's a look I'll never be able to forget. The agony and discernable heartbreak seep out of him in tumultuous waves, his energy no longer soothing light and hope, but pure, palpable anger and pain.

"What did you do?" He charges forward palms connecting with Ere's chest and pushing against him until he stumbles back. "What the hell did you do to her?"

Ere lets out a huff of laughter and shakes his head. "Mera knows the truth now, Kairos. Memories do not lie. Whatever mind games you and your people were playing with her before can end here and now. It's over. I had to resist my urge to kill you when she could not remember you or even me, but now that she does," he steps forward, shadows snaking across the ground and swirling around them both. "I am done playing nice, Kairos. This ends *now.*"

I swallow back tears and pain and anger that rush through me as I consider the possibility that everything Kairos did for me and told me he felt was all a lie, like Ere seems to believe. But to what end? To keep Ere and I apart? To gain access to my power? I refuse to believe that. Gods, I need time to fucking think.

I wrap an arm around Eres waist, looking Kairos up and down. “I think you should go home, Kairos. I don’t know what to make of all of this, but I need time.” I don’t look away from him, even as his features shift from heartbreak to complete and utter devastation, or when Ere’s shadows slip around his arms and chest, forcing him back when he tries to step toward me. The shadows drift away but stay close as Kairos comes to a standstill.

I don’t look away, but I don’t show how much my heart is breaking looking at him, either.. He’s special to me. He brought so much light into my life when all I felt was darkness. But I need time to process and heal. From the lost, broken look on his face and the tears sliding down his cheeks, I think he does, too. None of this makes sense.

Lightning flashes briefly around his palms, strikes lighting up the dull green within his eyes, but his power flickers out immediately as if he has no energy left to give. “None of this is real. It can’t be. Love is not a curse. Fate is not a lie. *This*...all of this is one huge fucking lie. Mera, please. You have to believe me.” His tears turn to unrestrained sobs, hands trembling and body swaying as he runs his hands through his hair, falling to his knees in front of me. “Please don’t do this. Please,” he whispers through the desperate, heart shattering sobs, eyes snapping closed as he tilts his head back like I’m a god he’s praying to.

I crouch and take his hands in mine and he stills, sniffling and wiping at his cheeks with our intertwined hands and then he opens his eyes. “I hate this. To see you hurting this way.” Keeping his hands in mine, I reach up and brush tear-soaked locks of hair away from his eyes. “Go home, Kairos,” I whisper. “Get some rest. I’m sure you’ll feel better after you do. You’ve been through so much. We all have. We’ll talk soon. I promise.” I give him a small, reassuring smile without giving away how much it truly does kill me to see him this way, because I can’t.

To show him my own pain means showing that I still care, and maybe that would hurt him even more. Seeing him this way breaks me. He has been lied to. Manipulated in the worst possible way, and who the hell would want to hurt him? He deserves so much better. He deserves everything. But these are problems for another time, when wounds aren’t still fresh and bleeding and entirely too fucking confusing. I was right before. The truth that was supposed to set me free, doesn’t feel as freeing now with so many truths still unraveled. I stand and release Kairos' hands as Ere opens a portal to send him home.

Kairos glares at him, lightning sparking at his fingertips and again behind his eyes as he stands and takes an unsteady step toward him. "I will burn this entire fucking realm to the ground one day with you in it. I promise you that. You're wrong. This is not over. This fucking ends when you are dead."

His gaze never leaves me as he steps through the portal, his green eyes piercing through the shadows of the realm. Then he faces forward and doesn't look back, his soul leaving remnants of his pain and heartbreak lingering within my own.

As soon as the portal snaps closed, I collapse in Ere's arms, letting my own heart crumble as he holds me against him. I didn't want to break in front of Kairos. I didn't want to make things harder for him. But gods, does it hurt. Even if he was lying to me the entire time. Even if it was all some fucked up game the celestials or gods were playing. It still. Fucking. Hurts. Ere brushes his thumbs across the tears on my cheeks and then cradles me against his chest, one arm under my knees and the other wrapped around my back. He carries me all the way home this way, me crying, heart in pieces, never questioning why.

I loved Kairos and he knows it. Of course all of this hurts. But none of it matters now, or at least it won't eventually. I have my fated mate. The one who was created just for me. His undying love and soothing kindness will continue to carry me through this and anything else that may come our way.

I am his and he is mine, and this is only the beginning of our forever.

CHAPTER THIRTY-EIGHT

BLOOD AND THORNS

MERA

I raise my hands, bringing life to the black flame torches lining the path leading up to the throne. The curves and sharp edges of the towering altar on the platform are made of dark stone, and vines and crimson roses are wrapped elegantly around the entire thing. Gods, it's like I'm living in a gothic fairytale. It is breathtakingly beautiful. My black dress flares out gracefully behind me, the velvety materiel caressing my skin as I lift the sides to keep it from dragging on the ground. Red waves bounce and sway as I push my shoulders back, smiling out at the shadows and darkness of the realm I now belong to.

This past week was a beautiful disaster. Those are the only words that seem fitting for what I've been through. It was a disaster because I hurt Kairos, and had to stand by and watch as he fell apart, because what else could I do? I can't fix it or heal him. Still, I'd be lying if I said I didn't miss him. I miss Olivia and Hekate, too, but the heart-wrenching pain of looking into Kairos' eyes and being able to feel and sense how deep his agony cut him, that memory haunts me. I keep reminding myself that whatever hurt he might feel is only temporary. Kairos' happiness, his fated mate, she exists somewhere out there. He will find her.

But then comes the beauty of it all. A week ago, I fell in love all over again with my fated mate, and after a century apart we finally get to make it official. It's the day of our claiming ceremony. I finally have everything I've always hoped for. Nyx is out of our lives and we feel peace at last after too long being suffocated by her darkness. We can breathe again. Gods, freedom feels so damn good. Ere says Hekate took Nyx to the Earth Realm and is trying to save her. I hope she does. I hope there's a soul left within her worth saving. My friend deserves to have her happy ending.

The Underworld today doesn't feel dim or dreary at all. Hundreds of flames flicker across the realm, pushing the shadows away a little more than usual as a sweet woman from the Dark Legion plays a melody on the violin, her silky ebony wings peeking out over her slender shoulders. I smile as she meets my gaze, nodding toward the path between the torches, the path I'm choosing to follow toward my destiny. The one leading to him.

I take one more look around the realm, gasping in awe, because not only is the black, scorched earth covered and gleaming with crimson roses and thorns, but the rocky mountains from the bottom to the highest peaks are blanketed in them, too. He did all of this for me. I tilt my head back and gaze up at the newly created starlight twinkling brightly above us, smiling up at fate as it smiles back down at me. Tears fill my eyes as memories of romantic midnight dates, heartfelt confessions, unbroken promises and making love beneath the light of the moon and the stars flash within my mind, my eyes snapping to Ere, because he's pushing those thoughts in to remind me how special our love is. To remind me how much he loves me. We've waited for this day far too long.

All of this beauty is nothing compared to the sight of him smiling down at me. His black suit blends into the shadows, while his glowing red eyes, curved horns, and leathery wings create stunning shadows of their own. He is the most beautiful creature I've ever seen.

Gods, you are stunning.

Heat rises to my cheeks at his words within my mind. I clasp my hands together in front of me and lock eyes with him.

I was just thinking the same of you. You are devastatingly beautiful, and I am so, so lucky.

The whispered words I send back quiver with emotion, tears streaming down my cheeks.

Come, my queen.

His dark, soothing voice sends a shiver of anticipation down my spine.

I glance at my bare feet and then at the roses and thorns I have to make my way across to get to him. It'll be worth it to finally be able to call him mine after a century of my soul being lost without him. The thick, jagged thorns that will tear through my skin, and the blood that will drain to seal our eternal bond is worth any amount of pain.

I take my first step toward him. The prick of thorns burying themselves in my skin leaves me frozen and hissing in pain. I knew it would hurt, but damn, it's much worse than I imagined it would be. A part of me is dying to use my magic to heal the wounds and shield my skin from any more damage, but I know it's forbidden. If I want him, then I must prove to the gods and to him that I will endure through anything. The next step hurts even more, the thorns digging into old wounds and ripping open new ones, the searing pain endless and unforgiving. Warmth drips from my feet and stains the ground with my crimson sacrifice, but through the pain, I persist. I endure. I keep my eyes focused only on him. His smile grows as I step closer and closer, fists clenched at my sides, blood pooling as it drips from me, smiling as I imagine his shadows wrapped around me and offering sweet numbness. It hurts, but I am deserving of him, and this is how I prove it.

Making my way up the steps to the throne, my feet slip and leave bloody imprints on the stone, but my heart melts as the look in Ere's eyes changes to one full of pride, and the scars left on my skin will be worth it. He extends his hand to help steady me, and I grip it tight as I ascend the last two steps and join him on the platform. His glowing eyes wrap me in warmth and numbness, the stinging pain from my fresh wounds fading to just a dull ache.

He takes my hands, eyes on mine as he kisses the top of one and then the other, bowing his head low. "My queen," he says, his horns rising back up and towering over me.

"My king," I whisper with a small smile, bowing low in return.

The energy radiating from both of us is full of more happiness and hope than I've ever felt or known could exist. This is our moment and we deserve this. *He* deserves this.

Releasing one of my hands, he faces the crowd full of the dead he chose to keep safe from the pit, so I do the same. Even the demons are here, though hiding and peering out from behind boulders and pillars across the realm and from within caves on the sides of the mountains. Ere offered them the choice of either death by his shadows or peace, and they chose to submit to him, so they live for now. I'd prefer them all to be dead

Ere closes his eyes. "We offer our blood and our unwavering loyalty to each other and to this realm. Old gods awaken and hear us. Accept our offering and bind us as one."

My eyes widen, arms stiffening at my sides as the blood covering the thorns and roses scattered below us is absorbed into the cracked earth, vanishing before my eyes. The flames from the torches encircling the altar and surrounding the platform shine brighter, the black flames flickering out and then igniting in bright blue and purple flames. Shocked faces in the crowd are no longer enshrouded by darkness and shadows. My divine light flashes to life around the entire realm.

Glancing over at my dark king, I can't help but smile. "What exactly does this mean?"

Dipping his head low, his hot breath tickles my ear as he whispers, "it means you belong to this realm. You belong to me. The gods have accepted our bond." He presses his lips to my cheek, lingering against my skin for a moment.

I press my forehead against his, getting lost within the red swirls of his hypnotizing eyes. "I have always belonged to you. I always will."

His eyes dance with excitement as he pulls away. "There is one more thing we must do to make it official." The mischievous smile that brightens his face makes my heart lurch, but I'm not afraid.

I'm ready to be his. The worst of it is over. The wounds on my feet no longer hurt at all. Magic healed them the moment the gods accepted our bond.

"Anything for you. Whatever it takes." I smile, stepping forward with him as he wraps his hand around mine and leads me to the darkest corner of the platform.

He lets my hand fall as we step up to a table draped with a velvet burgundy cloth with two golden cups and two rings in the center. These aren't the rings I remember from before. Ours were made of pure gold and they were wrapped in beautiful red roses. These rings look like they've been carved from black obsidian, and vines and thorns coil around their curves.

"The rings are different. What happened to the old ones? These are beautiful, but those rings were so special to both of us."

He stares into the cups in front of us, only briefly meeting my eyes. "Those rings hold memories of our past, my love, a past that has been corrupted by Nyx's darkness. I prefer to not have reminders of that day. Losing you. Losing everything I had ever wanted. I would rather we put it all in the past and focus only on the future. On only the good from this day forward."

I nod in agreement. I'd rather we never have to think of Nyx or talk about her ever again, but even so, those golden rings meant a lot to us. A part of my heart aches at the thought of never seeing them on our fingers. But these ones, now that the stars have aligned and the gods have accepted our eternal bond, they will mean much more.

"This is how we become one and how we show our realm and every other that you belong to me," he places his hands on the chalices in front of us, his crimson eyes glowing brighter.

"And that you belong to me, as well," I tell him with a smile.

His lips quirk as he winks and then waves his hands above the cups, his shadows curling out around him and swirling around the table. Mesmerized by the beauty of his power encircling the rings, I reach out to touch them.

Gently stealing my hand, he shakes his head. "Let me, my flame." He smiles and keeps his eyes pinned on me.

I can't breathe or think, everything else falling away as he looks down at me with so much light and love in his eyes that it nearly stops my heart. I get to have him and hold him forever, and I am so damn grateful.

He reaches for the smaller ring, the obsidian glittering under the flames of the torch light. Unbreakable thorns slowly spike out from the inner circle of the ring, thorns that will push their way deep into my skin, binding me to it and to him forever, and gods will it hurt so good knowing he's mine.

Any amount of pain, temporary or endless, will be worth it for him.

"Will you give yourself to me in every way, Hemera, mind, body, and soul?" His eyes burn into mine, waiting for the answer he already knows will come.

"Yes," I tell him without a moment of hesitation.

"Even if it means following me into darkness? Being so consumed by me that there is no light?" A smile flashes as his shadows wrap around me, enshrouding me within a pitch-black void.

"I will follow you wherever you may go. I want your love to consume me." I swallow thickly as the words ring true in my heart and soul.

I know he's all I'll ever want or need. I'd let his love swallow me whole if it meant I could spend the rest of my days hiding within gentle shadows and soothing darkness with him.

His eyes glow brighter as he slides the ring onto my finger. I keep my eyes locked on his, even as my skin tears and blood trickles from the fresh wounds, and he smiles at my refusal to wince in pain or pull away. My vision goes hazy, tears brimming from the corners of my eyes, but it isn't from the pain, it's from the beauty of this moment with him. This is a moment I'll cherish for the rest of my life.

His voice is softer, more gentle than usual as he lifts my hand, placing a soft kiss on my skin right above the ring, crimson still trickling from the sharp thorns embedding themselves in my body. "I claim you, my queen. Today. Tomorrow. Forever."

Holding my hand above the cups, he lets my blood flow into one and then the other. He smiles and pushes his ring toward me.

I don't hesitate. I hold the cold obsidian between my fingers, dying for it to be warmed by his skin, for him to finally belong to me. I know what I want. All I need is him. It will hurt him, pushing the ring into place on his finger, but I know he won't mind. He wants this just as badly as I do. I gaze into his eyes as I place the ring on his finger, warmth spilling from his skin and staining my own as the thorns latch on and refuse to let go. I want it to hurt. I want the thorns to hold onto him forever, to bind me to him and to be a constant reminder of how much worse it'd hurt if we ever let this love go.

I will never let go.

"I claim you, my king. Now and always." My voice echoes off the mountains and into every corner of the realm, my divine light in the torches rising higher and flickering brighter from the strength in my words.

I lift his hand above the golden cups, and his blood drips as the shadows swirl the contents within. He palms the one closest to him, and I do the same. We bring them to our lips and swallow the bittersweet liquid as my heart thuds with triumph and excitement from watching him seal our bond in blood.

"Eternity with you, Ere, is all I've ever wanted." I carefully set my cup down.

Taking my hands within his, he turns and faces me. "Then eternity is what you shall get, Mera. I am never letting you go."

He goes still, eyes widening and a smile full of feral excitement taking over his features. My soul rages within at something foreign and ancient raking its claws down my subconscious. The skin at the crown of my head burns, my eyes and wings scorching hot and wrong, black feathers falling to the ground in a heap in slow motion. I yank my hands out of his and run my palms against my cheeks and then the top of my head, backing away from Ere as I feel the curve of horns sprouting between locks of wavy hair. Every nerve ending in my body prickles, a transformation tacking place that's out of my control and doesn't feel right. I feel sick, my stomach churning and a vile taste coating the back of my throat, threatening to force it's way out. I bite back my disgust, at the wrongness intertwining itself with my soul, curling in on myself and bending at the waist as I'm torn apart from the inside out. Darkness threatens to take over. The curved horns are wrong. Ere knows how much I loved my wings, so why the hell is he smiling as the last feathers fall at his feet. I collapse to my knees and wave a hand, a mirror glistening in front of me, back arching as I scream out in pain from tendons and muscles being shredded and torn apart along my spine. Hunched forward, I gaze into the mirror and my face is no longer the innocent, freckled face of Nora or the face of Mera from the past, but one I don't recognize at all. One I've never seen. My hair slowly darkens, leaving only small sections of red between thick strands of raven silk locks. Nyx's serpents with their crimson eyes slither across the stone platform, taking their place on my shoulders as if it's where they've always belonged. The woman in the mirror looks like she belongs in this realm. She is a mirror image of Ere.

"What is happening? W-why is this happening?" I breathe, staring into my reflection, tilting my head, the woman in the mirror smiling wickedly though my own lips tremble in fear.

Ere pulls me to my feet and grips my face between his palms, lips curving at the corners as he tilts my head back and leans into me. "*Síko, vasílissa mou.*" His voice is dark and commanding and suddenly my eyes roll back as my weightless body goes limp and falls into his waiting arms.

Everything goes black. I'm here but I'm not here. He's touching me but I feel nothing. My eyes snap open but not by choice, fingers trailing down his jawline that I can't feel or control.

"Your sparkly blue eyes were beautiful, but I must say... your red eyes are now my favorite, my love. You are so beautiful," he breathes, shifting my weight and helping me stand upright, fisting my hair and searching the eyes that were once mine but now feel like someone else's. "Tell me your name." He says softly, running his thumbs along my cheeks. "Who are you?".

Brushing loose locks of hair away from eyes that look like they're seconds away from shattering in pain, tortured and haunted and desperate, the voice that isn't my own speaks. "Melinoë. Goddess of nightmares and madness," she says, running her fingertips down his chest.

"And?" He asks, pulling my body in closer, eyes drifting down to my lips.

Running her tongue, *our* tongue, up his lips, she moans softly against his mouth. "Your true fated mate. The one you are now bonded to for life. The only woman your heart has ever yearned for."

He groans quietly against her mouth, eyes crimson and full of so much fucking betrayal that if I could, I'd gouge them from their sockets and shove them down his throat. My heart shatters as he kisses her, so much devotion and passion from them both that it nearly kills me. Her thoughts and feelings and her fucking corrupted, sickening soul are so tightly bound around me that I can't move or act or scream, but I try. I try and I try and no matter how hard I do, I am fucking powerless, chained and locked captive within my own mind.

"I love you, Melinoë. Welcome home. You will make an excellent queen." He stands me upright, his glowing crimson eyes burning with a raw, heated desire that I've never seen from him before.

In this moment, I realize the truth. He gave me as little as he could and I still fell for him. This look, that smile, the happiness radiating from his soul, all of this is real. All that he showed me, gave me, and offered to me were half-ass efforts wrapped in meaningless lies. He doesn't even look like the man I knew as he watches her with gentleness and unwavering loyalty in his eyes. She is his sun and his stars and his entire world. I was only a means to an end to getting his world back. I am nothing to him. I never was. And Kairos, *fuck*...I try to pull away from Ere, tears that I can't cry ripping my heart in two, because Kairos...I remember the truth. It's Kairos who has always been everything to me. Him in all those memories my amulet returned to me. And seeing this man, this monster for who he truly is has unveiled whatever power or control he held over me. He destroyed my entire life. He destroyed the only person in the world I'd give my own life for.

"I love you more," the woman tells Erebus, warmth flowing down our cheeks as my heart and soul ignite from the way he looks at her, and I cannot dwindle the burn or suffocate it until it doesn't exist, though I want to.

I don't want my heart or my soul to burn for him. To crave him. To want anything to do with him, but her soul is too strong. She is in control. I am simply a passenger along for whatever fucked up ride I've been dragged into.

"Are you ready, my love?" He brings my hand to his lips and brushes a soft kiss against it.

"I forgot what a gentle beast you are, Erebus. It is why I will gladly kill everyone who has made us suffer," our lips curve into a grin, a wicked laugh spilling from our lips.

The words she spoke are not a threat but an absolute promise that would make my blood run cold if I had any semblance of control.

"Come. It is time for my queen to rise at last," he whispers against our ear, and my head tilts back to search his eyes, and I am thankful that I at least can't feel his breath against my skin.

I can feel myself fading, being pushed further and further into the background, her power and soul wrapping tighter around me. I cannot fucking breathe. I can't fucking move or think clearly or save myself and I don't know how the hell I ended up here. No one is going to come for me. I am alone. I will be trapped and lost within myself until I don't exist at all. Gods, what the hell do I do?

Please! Someone help me!!

I scream, my voice echoing into nothing, throat burning as the words play on repeat for no one to hear.

"Are you sure I'm ready?" She holds her head up high, pressing her shoulders back."Abso-fucking-lutely." His face shows no doubt that she'll be his perfect queen.

"What if they discover I am not her? What if I fail?"

No! Don't do this! Please! Let me go!

Horns lower as he bends and places a kiss to her forward, her heart racing in response. "Impossible. I will not let you."

"Together?"

"*Always*," he replies as if nothing could be more true.

As if nothing will ever come between them or take them away from each other again. As if he'd kill anyone who dared to try. He will. I pray no one comes for me. I pray Kairos and Hekate leave it alone, thinking I'm exactly where I want to be and blissfully happy. I pray my sweet sister finds a way to move on. I'd rather Kairos believe I never remembered the truth, for all of them to forget about me rather than getting themselves hurt or worse trying to save me.

The goddess whose dark thoughts are impossible to block out, impossible to fight through, presses her palms against his cheeks. "It will be an honor to rule beside you, my savior. My king," she tells him, voice quivering and overflowing with emotion.

Please, let me out! I want to go home! These are not my words!

I fade a bit further as sharp claws scrape down my mind, commanding me to keep quiet, to not think, to not even *be*. It's so dark. Gods, it's so cold and I'm numb and my heart doesn't exist within me anymore. I am nothing. I do not exist.

He wraps his hand tightly around hers and together they face the steps leading down to their realm. None of this belongs to me. It never did and it was never going to. Nyx whispered into my mind once that I belonged to darkness, and she was right. I never had a chance at belonging anywhere else or to anyone else. This was my fate. Erebus' eyes burn into hers and mine as we descend the stairs, their waiting people carving a path for our bodies to make our way through the crowd.

The darkness, the void, the endless abyss, it stares into me, and I stare back, and I am not afraid. I've become familiar with endless darkness. We were friends once, or so I thought, but still, I am comfortable within it. I will not hide. I will not kneel. I will not fucking break. I hope he feels my wrath and hatred for him somewhere within his lover's eyes.

"My queen," he whispers, and as he smiles, the beautiful monster forces one in return, through the many heartfelt tears that fall from our eyes.

"My king," she whispers back, linking our arm through his.

Their hearts are full. To them, this place doesn't feel dark or gloomy any longer. This is their home. Their fortress of hope. To thrive in. To love in. To reign in...

Always together.

But I'm here, too. And the thing about being friends with darkness is that no matter how hard it tries, it cannot steal your soul or break you entirely unless you let it, because you know all of its little tricks. It will not win. I will be here in the background, watching and waiting to tear them apart from the inside out however I can. I will not go quietly. I will fight.

Fear will not rule me.

Maybe I'm too far gone already. Her thoughts are mine and mine are hers, and deciphering where she begins and I end is growing harder by the minute. Are these even thoughts of my own? Gods, is this even me?

Kairos...

My love...
I am so sorry.

CHAPTER THIRTY-NINE

THE BIRTH OF A QUEEN

NYX

OCTOBER 6TH, 1848

Waking up on the cold, wet floor, the sound of rain smacks against the cave walls outside as I pull myself up, wrapping my arms around my knees, trembling in fear. The scent of wet earth, rot, and death crawls down my throat and steals the oxygen straight from my lungs. I press my hands to my chest, gasping for air, tears sliding down my cheeks from both the heartbreak of losing my wings and my home, and from the thick, rancid air making it impossible to breathe. I snap my eyes closed and press my forehead against my knees, praying for the gods to just end me. The chilly midnight air prickles across my cheeks, the icy numbness wrapping me up in a blanket that steals my heartbreak and fear away.

When the realm leaders, the two people who had been like parents to me, cast me down to earth, I felt the edges of my soul begin to rip and then my heart shattered, soul splintering and cracking into hundreds of tiny little pieces. They do not love me. Hekate did not save me. The gods have abandoned me. No celestial has ever been cast out of the Realm of Light, and certainly has never had their wings burned to nothing by Ananthe's holy fire. I will never forgive any of them. I will never forgive myself for losing my soul to such darkness.

Hekate once told me the Earth Realm is where darkness roams free. It is why she believed I did not belong here. As much as the celestials and witches have tried to stop it, it always lingers, bringing chaos and death with it. The mortals are their own sort of monsters, in a way, some of them more wicked and cruel than the demons who feast on mortal bones. Some are consumed by a sickening amount of hatred toward their own kind over trivial things that should not matter. Some power hungry to the point of never doing right by the people here, so long as they are thriving and have people kneeling at their feet. And for some reason I will never understand, they love to see others fail. This hellscape cannot be where I die, but I believe it will be. I will fade out of existence here, alone and broken, forgotten and despised, and feared by those who once loved me.

I am surrounded by cracked, faded skulls and bones of others who found their resting place within the darkness of these cave walls. I try not to think about who they could have been. Maybe other celestials or witches the rulers and gods banished from existence. Digging my nails into the dirt by my feet, I push away old bones to clear a spot to rest my spiraling, tormented mind.

The whispers from the dark followed me here, even stronger now amongst the mortals with the celestials and their light so far away. King Ourahnus and Queen Gaia knew it was too late to save my corrupted soul, that there is no hope left for me. With darkness is where I belong. As it whispers my name and reaches its tendrils of numbness and icy emptiness toward my soul, I know they were right.

I am his already.

I have tried to fight this, to hide from the truth and bury it deep within until it could not reach me, but the harder I fought, the more it took from me.

It took *everything* from me.

Faint sounds, a soft gliding movement across wet dirt, and loud hissing from the back corner of the cave get closer and I jolt upright. I scoot away as quickly as I can, pressing my still throbbing, aching back firmly against the cold wall. Billowing plumes of darkness emerge, filling the space and closing in on me. The scent of death burns my nostrils as thick tendrils and clouds of shadows gets closer. Numbness and nothingness wrap around me like a vice, refusing to let me escape its clutches this time.

"Please. No," I whimper, my lips trembling as I close my eyes to avoid facing the darkness.

A velvety, dark laugh cuts through the silence and I freeze, paralyzed by fear. I cannot face him. I will not.

"You cannot fight this any longer, Nyx. You will do as I command you to do." The voice is like a comforting embrace, but the shadows creeping closer are more like a void that would enjoy swallowing me whole. "Open your eyes," it commands, and my eyes flutter open, though not by choice. His power buries itself deep within my mind, taking full control over my body.

That power now owns me. There is no escaping this. The hissing grows louder as rough scales wrap around my legs and slither up my body until resting around my shoulders. Three black serpents with eyes like blood rubies, glowing within the shadows, stretch their heads out from behind my back. They taunt me, eyes burning into my soul as their tongues shoot in and out of their mouths, their sharp teeth glistening with a thick, black substance. The venom leaks from their mouths, and I sense that they are smiling, welcoming me home. They do not want to hurt me.

Your fate was sealed long ago. You felt it. You knew this day would come.

The darkness whispers the words within my mind, not speaking out loud, but a face does not yet appear.

Clouds of ancient, dark power pour into the cave from every direction and the air grows thick with the smothering presence of evil.

"Leave me be!" I yell into the void, my shaky voice echoing off the curved, rocky walls of the cave.

Shadows of darkness stretch toward me, raking its claws across my mind and swirling across my skin, healing every broken part of me that remains. The power mends the wounds from the mutilation of my wings, and a raging, gnawing emptiness takes over as new wings push out of my back, the feel of them leathery and slippery like the snakes perched around my neck. The dark power embeds itself in every part of me, flowing within the blood in my veins now, and I scream so loud the walls shake and rocks crumble and fall, the burn from the transformation much worse than that of holy fire. Claws bite at the sensitive skin along my fingers, forcing their way out, pointy and as sharp as daggers. A screech like nothing I have ever heard climbs from my throat, whatever hope I had left of light existing within fading away.

"W-what are you doing to me!? I do not want this! Just kill me, please!" I lash out at the darkness, my claws slicing through the air.

The darkness persists. It laughs and does not stop as it wraps my heart in a veil of blackness as hard and unbreakable as obsidian, and I no longer feel it beating at all. Pain tears through the skin on the top of my head, a scream bursting from my chest that is what mortal nightmares are made of. Reaching up, my hands shake as I run my fingers along the hard, thick curves of the horns on top of my head.

"No! No! Stop this!" I still fight though I feel the dark power letting me, allowing me a moment of horrified outrage before the tendrils of shadows take over once again, burying themselves in every fiber of my being and silencing my cries.

My soul is broken. I am corrupted. My heart is dead and gone. I feel it. My celestial form is gone entirely, and I am a monster on the inside and out. Darkness has ruined me. Is this the fate the celestials knew would one day come for me? The destiny no one should have to bear? How dare they cast me out and abandon me this way when they knew the truth. They should have ended me while they had the chance to.

Curled up on the floor, numb and shattered and unable to move, darkness whispers my new name, titles I have never been called before.

Goddess of the Night. Daughter of Gods. Heir to The Underworld. You have not fallen. Rise.

I do as it says. Like hearing the names reminded me who I truly am, that the past I have lived has been nothing but lies. I rise to my feet to face the darkness, and it faces me at last, golden eyes glowing and then fading as he turns toward the opening of the cave. He leads me out into the moonlight, the brightness of it breaking my heart, serving as a harsh, unavoidable reminder of all the light I once had that is now lost for good. I follow him knowing I have no choice, or maybe I am not in control. It is hard to decipher the difference now. His power lives and breathes within me. He smiles down at me, the beautiful curve of his lips capable of either stopping women's hearts or devouring them whole, and I smile back, my sharp teeth brushing softly against my tongue. I taste the bitter venom on my lips as I breathe it out into the air, and my serpents, my only companions now, coil tighter around my shoulders and arms, brushing their faces softly against my cheeks. Their hissing grows louder as the rain ends, and the storm dissipates.

"My king," I bow low before darkness, keeping my eyes on him as his crimson stare rakes over my body.

"Rise, dear daughter. I am no king to you. My blood is yours and yours is mine, and we bow to no one." As the words leave his lips, my body instantly does what he says, but I do not fight it. It is easier not to fight. "Call me father." He stands up straighter, hands clasped in front of him as shadows disappear. His horns rise higher and his leathery wings open fully behind him.

Some moments our minds are one, his thoughts are my own, and my actions are what he chooses them to be. For those moments I no longer exist, and I feel nothing. He is everything. Then his power releases my mind and body, and I am free. It's like a twisted game as he demonstrates his power over me.

Taking advantage of the moment I hold the reigns, I slowly back away. "If you are my father, then I want nothing to do with you," I spit, venom leaking into the air, his shadows instantly swirling and pushing it away. "You killed my mother. Murdered your own fated mate like she was nothing! You are dead to me!"

His dark hair falls into his eyes as he tilts his head to the side. "Everything you have been told is a lie, my sweet daughter," he says, circling me like a predator about to devour its prey. "You see, I brought you here to help me in getting your mother back." He stops in front of me, too close, too much vulnerability in his energy for his words to be anything but truth.

"My mother is dead," I whisper, gazing up at him but no longer wanting to back away, because as much as I hate to admit it, I would do whatever it takes to meet her, especially after losing everyone else.

He gazes up at the moon, and as his shadows pour from him, the moon is swallowed whole for a moment. Then he reels his power in and allows the light to return.

"Your mother is not dead. Her soul is trapped in the pit of The Underworld, and we can bring her back." Placing his hands on my shoulders, the hard lines of his face, the one shaped exactly like my own, soften. "The realms need a villain, dear daughter, and that is where you come in." The softness fades, the crimson glow of his eyes swirling and stealing my attention.

"Why is she trapped in the pit? There has to be another way. I will not be your villain." I curl my hands into fists at my sides, planting my feet firmly in the dirt, refusing to let him make me the monster he wants me to be.

He clicks his tongue and shakes his head. "I was afraid you might say that, so let us make a bargain, then. Accept it now if you care for your lover, because I will not offer it again." Backing away, he clasps his hands behind his back. "Be the villain, Nyx. Be the monster I need you to be while I pull the strings in the background. The ones who call themselves royalty, the ones lying to their realms about their true identities might I add, cannot know I am free. Erebus is dead to them and shall stay that way. Knowing I am alive means knowing I seek revenge for their heinous acts against myself and the one I love, and I would rather their downfall be a delightful surprise." He swallows, eyes shifting above my head to the twinkling stars visible now that the storm clouds have faded away.

"What the hell did they do to you? What happens if I refuse?" The serpents hiss in my ear, unhinging their jaws and then snapping their mouths closed near my face, a threat or a warning, I am not sure. "If you want revenge so badly, why not go after them yourself? You do not need me."

"I offer you the bargain out of the kindness of my heart because you are my flesh and blood, but if you refuse, then Hekate will die right along with everyone else who destroyed my life and my home." Eyes pinned on me, his jawline clenches, his fingers flexing at his sides. "I would love nothing more than to watch the witch who betrayed me burn with the others, but I will let her live for *you*. My daughter."

Anger surges through me, flames igniting in my palms and crackling with fury. They are no longer bright and beautiful, but fully black now and icy like the feel of my father's power. I stare down at them, considering his words. No matter the cost to my soul, the stains left on my withered heart, I would do anything to keep Hekate safe. If being the villain is the price I must pay, then I will pay it gladly for her.

"Who betrayed you so, *father*, that you feel the need to use your own daughter in your diabolical plan for revenge? Tell me everything." My flames flicker out, and I swallow back the fear, the absolute terror of accepting my fate. "I accept your bargain. Just please, let her live."

He nods once and then steps in closer. "My dear old mother and father destroyed my life, Nyx. And my brother," he huffs a laugh, shaking his head. "Well, it was him who destroyed my heart by siding with them over me, stealing away the last bit of hope I clung to. He is who must suffer worst of all. I will smile as I watch his world fall apart, helpless to do anything to stop it." Shadows emerge, tendrils whispering in the air, searching for a target, his brother I assume, who is not here.

"What are your parents' names?" I ask, and my muscles stiffen in fear, mind racing to put pieces together, clues or signs or anything to point to who it could possibly be.

"You know them well, or at least you believed you did." His head tilts and he takes another step forward. "My mother is queen Gaia and my father is king Ourahnus. The betraying fools who have now also betrayed their own granddaughter. I should not be surprised." His fingers twitch and then clamp into tight fists at his sides near the hilts of curved three-pointed weapons strapped there.

"That is impossible," I breathe, more to myself than to him. "We would know of another son."

"You know of the only son they accept as their own. The one who they believe is the perfect example of what a celestial should be. The one they chose to rule one day when it was always meant to be me." Shadows skate across the grass, reaching the tree line and smashing into the large trunks of them, snaking around them until they splinter and creak and come tumbling to the ground.

"No. I do not believe it. It cannot be true. It has always only been..."

"Kairos," he spits through clenched teeth, his dark power searching my mind and pulling the word out the moment I think it. "My brother and my betrayer. The saint. The son of gods who will one day be crowned king. The forgotten god of fate and time who fucked me over eternally." His power surges, the twinkle of the stars dimming as small clusters of them are ripped from the sky by his shadows.

Kairos abandoned me in the cave, bleeding and scared after his parents commanded him to do so, and though I hate him for it, I do not wish for him to die. He was kind to me even when others were not. He trained me to fight when others were too fearful to come anywhere near me. Oh gods, I cannot let him do this. I fear his wrath, his vengeance, will not only destroy the three of them, but will likely destroy them all.

"Your thoughts are not wrong. I wish to slowly, and painfully, destroy them all." His shadows retreat, the darkness wrapping around me, numbness again replacing anything I might feel or think. "I see you are having second thoughts. Your heart is too gentle, dear daughter, and unfortunately, mine has no room for gentleness or compassion for any of them any longer." Warm eyes darken to crimson, his lips curving up into a smile that one should not wear while breaking their own daughter.

But that is what he has done. What he will do. He will break me.

"Please," I beg, fighting against the power that is much too strong, too foreign to know how to begin to fight it.

I cannot move now unless he allows me to. Cannot breathe without his power within letting me. I am a weapon to him, and he will use me as he pleases. I never had a fucking choice.

"I am not just your father, Nyx. I am the beginning and the end." Golden eyes meet mine and his charming, deceitful smile flashes briefly. "I am not only king of The Underworld, but the God of Shadows and Darkness. The devourer of light. And you, Nyx, will do as I say and say as I do until I release you. Fight it if you wish, but it will only hurt more to hold onto the past. I can help you forget."

Images flash in my mind, ones of Hekate and I together and happy, her face slowly fading from each memory and ceasing to exist in them as if she were never there at all.

No! Please, do not take her from me. I need her to exist! I cannot exist in a world where she does not!

Screaming does not work. The words do not leave my lips like I intended them to, instead they echo back to me, crashing against a thick wall of darkness where I am trapped within my own mind. I am nothing. Non-existent unless I play by his rules, and dead like the others, if I disobey or betray him.

The memories of her return and I thank the gods above for not letting her fade away, the same gods who do not care about what happens to me now and the ones who will one day be victims of my fathers' wrath. I do not dare to speak in my mind or fight against his power, too afraid to lose her for any amount of time ever again. I stay silent as he offers me his hand, dark magic releasing its tight grip on my mind, a test to see if I will play by his rules or risk it all to fight or flee.

He waves a hand and opens a portal, the inky black swirl of it hypnotizing in a way. What lies within it seems to call me home. He raises a hand, gesturing toward it with a graceful elegance that looks strange on a man like him. He is the most beautiful yet powerful and terrifying creature I have ever encountered, and I know even if I wanted to, I could not escape him. Nothing could compete or banish or extinguish an immortal who possesses the kind of dark, cruel power that radiates off him, let alone one who is a god.

"To your new realm, daughter, where you will now be queen in the eyes of every realm. They will all fear you and I will be proud. Your mother will be even prouder."

Though my old self fully exists when his power does not consume me, I do what feels entirely wrong and let her fade away. That woman cannot be here. This is not the time to fight. For now, I must survive. I tell myself anything I can to push the old me away, to bury her down so deep until I cannot feel her at all. The celestials did not want me. My realm abandoned me. At least here, I am wanted. I tell myself anything to survive. I take a deep breath and step through the portal, groups of demons stopping and lowering themselves to the ground, bowing their heads against the cracked, dry earth.

Here, I will be a queen, and I suppose for now that is better than dead.

Erebus enters the realm and closes the portal behind him. With only black flames flickering from torches lining the path up to the throne, he is even more frightening. His power not only creates the darkness but controls it in his surroundings, too. The shadows part as he steps forward with only a slight twitch of his finger. What little light exists from the flames of the pit and torches focuses only on lighting the way for the two of us.

I follow him up the stone steps and come to a stop beside him as he gazes down at the velvety chair and the spiked, obsidian adorned crown sitting on a cloth beside it. He waves me forward and I do not hesitate. I sit, crossing my legs and holding my head high, eyes burning into the demons gathered below us, commanding their attention and submission. If he wants me to play the part of the villainous queen, then I shall.

"You are no longer the celestial called Nyx, but a queen to be feared by all. You can hide no thought from me so do not waste your time plotting. I know you do not want this. I can feel the hatred seeping out of you." He picks up the crown, running his fingers along the glistening obsidian stones. "I am only doing what is necessary to save your mother. You *will* forgive me one day. She did not deserve what happened to her. Neither did I." Placing the crown upon my head, he smiles and then brushes the backs of his fingers across my cheeks. "Your mother and I are not the villains, here. Everyone you believed to be innocent and pure; they are the true villains. You shall be free to do whatever you please once I have my fated mate back in my arms. I only hope you choose her and I over the monsters who hide in plain sight, pretending to be the heroes." His crimson eyes swirl and I feel myself fading into oblivion, my ability to think and speak for myself slowly slipping away.

"What will we do to your parents and Kairos? To the celestials?" I force out, grinding my teeth and fighting against the dark power, because I need to know how far gone my soul will be after it is all said and done.

"Your soul is too pure, dear daughter." His head tilts, eyes shifting from gold to bright crimson. "I truly hope one day you will forgive me. After all I have been through, there is nothing pure or good within me. All life in this world, save for yours, Melinoë's and mine are meaningless to me. I will take all they find beautiful and let it rot. Every precious thing they hold dear—I will drain the life away slowly until it is nothing. They will endlessly suffer until they beg for death to take them. Their realms will crumble to the ground after I am through, and it will be exactly what they deserve, and nothing less." His gaze shifts away from me and focuses on two rings he pulls out of his pocket, his shadows whispering to life and swirling around us. "Destroying my brother, taking everything away from the traitorous bastard, that will be my favorite part of all." He smiles, lifting the rings toward the light of the torches before gently sliding them back into his pocket.

I stand, shaking my head as the realization slams into me that having my wings burned with holy fire was not my true punishment. This is. "It cannot just be us who exists. Light must exist. Mortals, witches, and celestials must exist. The balance of light and darkness cannot be broken or else we all fall."

He laughs, tipping his head back and spreading his wings wide. "Look around, my queen." He bows his head slightly, waving a hand out to the realm for emphasis. "I have fallen long ago. Your realm let you fall. We cannot get much lower than this." He turns his back to me, one foot on the top stair, hesitating there. "Light has existed for long enough. Let them all fade into oblivion as they deserve to. It is time for shadows and darkness to reign. You are the Goddess of the Night. You were born to live amongst only darkness. You will thrive in it."

He makes his way down the stairs, the demons growling and snarling and running to his side like little children thrilled to have their father's attention. As I follow after him, the scent of decay and death and emptiness seeps into my soul, numbness slipping in stealthily and clamping down tight, refusing to let me fight it any longer. My thoughts are not my own. I feel nothing. All that exists now is him. The only thing that matters is making those who have wronged us pay dearly. My father smiles and I smile back, suddenly knowing this is where I have always belonged.

After all, I was born of darkness. In the end, into darkness I shall return...

Thank you for reading! Did you enjoy? Please add your review because nothing helps an author more and encourages readers to take a chance on a book than a review.

And don't miss more from S.R. Hartley coming soon. Be sure to visit srhartleyauthor.com to stay in the know!

Next, discover THE BOUNTY OF BLOOD AND NAILS, by City Owl Author, N K Brown. Turn the page for a sneak peek!

You can also sign up for the City Owl Press newsletter to receive notice of all book releases!

SNEAK PEEK THE BOUNTY OF BLOOD AND NAILS

BY N K BROWN

It was almost time.

The final night, the crescendo, the climax. The other charlatans would be turning up the fires, pouring out the charm, increasing the danger, the difficulty, the disbelief. I had to remain stoic. Isolated, yet approachable. Alluring, yet aloof. They didn't *need* to know what I could see, yet I appealed to them, like a whispering siren. A craving. An urge. An itch.

There was only one I needed to satisfy tonight.

I shivered as night rose around me. The air thinned, laced with a refreshing chill as the last of the sun's color bleached from the sky. One by one, fairy lights popped to life. Green, amber, purple, silver, all small fiery splotches of color suspended from spindly wires looping between the stalls. A gentle breeze rumpled the cloth in front of me, evoking the small tinkling of bells that hung weighted at the edges of my table.

The gentle twang of a harp filtered through the calm night. A few isolated notes of a violin chased after it, attempting to warm the pre-magical atmosphere. The wooden sign suspended above my stall creaked in the breeze.

A low whistle snagged my attention. I placed the tarot deck upon the velvet cloth and brushed the deep hood from my face, allowing a glimpse of the stall across the aisle to the left. The candy man grinned, dimples puckering his cheeks. I didn't know his name, nor age—somewhere in his mid-twenties surely, but the high-waisted tan trousers and star-studded suspenders made him appear twice that age. Or perhaps transported in time from a century ago.

I wasn't doing anything to subvert the stereotype either. Black cloak with scarlet trimmed hood. Sleeves that dripped down past my hands allowing only a flash of red nail polish and multiple silver rings to emerge as I tapped confidently upon the chosen card, eager to bestow my knowledge of the future upon the lucky client.

Candyman ran his hand around the gold-rimmed edge of the floss machine. Cotton candy swirled around his finger, interlacing like a fat pink chrysalis. He slowly brought his finger to his lips, maintaining eye contact, sucking the chrysalis into his mouth. I knew what he would taste like later. Sugar and caramel and a hint of rum—kept in a not-so-secret bottle under his stall. I swear that when I looked away, he would dab himself with the candy floss like sticky cologne, knowing that it would make me kiss him harder, that it would entice my tongue to caress his skin, my teeth to nip in all the right places.

Though tonight, there would be no fun for either of us.

I let the hood fall back across my face. The music picked up, a thrum of excitement charging the air from a crowd of people I couldn't yet see. If I was successful, there would be no time to lose myself amongst the bags of sugar, the mounds of sweets, the warm, roving hands of Candyman. If she came and it worked, I would have to dissolve into the dawn, putting as much distance between myself and the Collectors as possible.

Sweat prickled my palms, threatening to slide down my skin and pool upon the velvet tablecloth. I forced my breathing to deepen, my lungs to expand past the point of recoil.

From under the peak of my hood, I caught sight of the first eager footsteps rushing the aisle. The grass lay trampled, blades permanently bowed from the weight of passersby this past week. Yet, for the last six days, she had not come.

She must tonight.

My heart ticked like a bomb, speeding toward the deadline. Sixty days it had taken me to find this one. She was reclusive, a shadow. I didn't know what she'd done, but I wasn't surprised they'd ordered me to track her down. Her bounty was impressive. If I could be as stealthy as her, we'd both disappear into the ether, no tracts, no guilt, transformed into legacy.

Candyman handed a large paper bag stuffed with toffees to a small girl. He bent over the stall, deftly flicking the top cube into the air and snapped his teeth shut around it. He winked as the girl giggled, her mother affectionately patting her braided hair.

So that is what he would taste of later. Cinders and treacle. I swallowed, holding his gaze which had floated not-so-innocently to mine until he turned to the next customer, a broad grin lapping at his cheeks.

The music hung thick now in the air, twined with shouts and laughter. From my right, the swoosh of a lit torch rippled a wave of heat toward me. Marianne didn't only eat fire, she commanded it, molding it into shapes like smoke rings from a cigar. Some of the magic here was real, parlor tricks, really. Just enough to make people part with their money, but not enough to be arrested.

Sweat trickled down my spine. At least now I could blame it on the heat in the air.

Once the first rush of visitors subsided—those who instinctively knew where they wanted to go or were dragged by small children—the timid arrived next. These were innocents, virgins to the fayre. They'd come for a specific reason. Perhaps to catch the eye of one of the performers, eagerly hoping to be chosen as a volunteer to levitate ten feet into the air before being caught by the toned biceps of the magician. His shirt sleeves rolled up, winding ink crisscrossing his flesh.

On more than one occasion I'd seen his tattoos morph into the mirror image of the person he wanted to tempt backstage. How could one resist when your face was clearly visible etched permanently upon his body? It was fate of course, and so one did not resist.

My first client was here. It wasn't who I needed to see, but I doubted I'd be lucky enough to escape so early. She was a young woman of nineteen or twenty. Her cheeks were flushed, and she gripped the arm of a young man, tugging him toward me. She would never have ventured this far by herself, and yet, the eagerness in her eyes told me I was who she'd come to see.

Shame I was a fraud.

I gestured silently to the bench in front. She sat carefully, scooping her long skirt beneath her, the bells tinkling seductively as she rustled the tablecloth. The man stood behind, one hand on her shoulder. The sinews popped from his hand; his fingers almost clawed, but he stopped short of releasing that pressure onto the bare skin of her neck.

I riffled the tarot cards in my hand. The deck was pristine, the pattern on the back that of a simple silver skull upon black, the kind you could purchase anywhere. The satin cloth and silver ribbon binding them also looked new, like I'd exchanged them for a handful of pennies a week ago when the fayre opened.

A trained eye would see the con, could smell the treachery a mile away. I could scrunch the deck, bend the edges and yet wasn't this whole place one large trick? A parallel realm an ordinary being could wander into for only seven nights per year and be transported into a land of magic and fun and frivolity. One where they could step out of their ordinary, meagre lives and succumb to their dreams. Or so the proprietors would have you believe.

"Are you sure, my dear?" The man's face stretched tight. His mouth was obscured beneath a manicured moustache. "We have talked about your disposition toward the supernatural at length. Have you forgotten?"

I flattened my palm and raised my hand toward him. My nails wanted to extend, the gift coursing through my bloodstream like poison.

"Oh yes, honey," she answered. "It's only a bit of fun. I won't take any of it to heart, I promise." Her mouth curved downwards as she spoke, her dark eyes beseeching.

They all wanted the same reading from me this week, *will I marry the crown prince?* No one was so bold as to outright say it, but it was written in the singe of heat on their cheeks, in the coil of hair they twined nervously around a finger. But not this one. She needed something else.

The man tutted and fumbled in his waistcoat for coins. He withdrew two coppers and dropped them into my open palm, returning the pounds and gideons that were ostentatiously brandished amongst them back to the pocket.

I nodded, tipping the coins into my cloak and returned my hand to the tarot. I tapped the skull on the uppermost card as my thigh knocked against the table leg, silently cracking a vial of incense. The perfume seeped out, infusing the air with a faint shimmer. The young woman's eyes widened, her chin lifting as she inhaled deeply.

"That's my nana's smell," she whispered. "Roses."

The man above her said nothing, everything he wanted to utter explained in the twitch of his mouth and the tightening of his hand upon her shoulder. If she wasn't so enraptured by the aura, she would be able to feel the bruises pooling beneath his fingertips, blemishing the smooth skin beneath.

I turned the first card over. The Grim Reaper. It was my favorite to start with. Everyone knew someone who had died or was dying. That was life.

"You have lost someone whose wisdom meant a lot to you." The crack in my voice was not intentional. I needed to get a grip on my emotions.

Another pulse ricocheted through my veins as the magic struggled to escape.

She inhaled sharply. Her hand pressed to her breast, but not over her heart. Her fingers rested on a gold brooch shaped like a butterfly pinned to her green dress.

I turned the next card face up revealing two entwined skeletons with empty sockets gazing at one another, bony arms encircling barren ribcages. The Lovers.

Her face faltered. She stared at the card, her knuckles blanching as she gripped the brooch.

"You see," the man interrupted, pulling her back from the table, "it's us. Now, let's go."

I turned over the next card, pushing it in front of the others and toward her. A man dangled upside down from a spiral pillar, his legs entangled with a serpent, a crown of thorns encircling his head.

"What's that one?" He lowered his head, squinting at the table.

"The Hanged Man."

He choked, jerking backward. He grabbed the woman's shoulder again to half-drag her from her seat. "Come on, we're leaving."

When he released her and turned to straighten his waistcoat, I slipped the final card across the table. The woman took it, glancing quickly at the picture and the inscription before slipping it back face down.

"You know what she would have said," I whispered. "Because that's what you believe as well. Trust your instincts."

She swallowed, her eyes wide, cheeks drained of color. She bestowed a small smile upon the man as she delicately took his arm, as if suddenly repulsed by the thought of touching even his clothing. As they walked away, she turned back to me and nodded. My chest tightened as my breath paused on the inhale. Good. No one should be trapped by another.

I reined in my emotions, crushing them beneath years of well-trained lies. The air thinned again as the cool breeze drained the incense.

Perhaps there would be time to linger when the fayre closed, and the patrons had departed. We could all finally be ourselves. I did love toffee, probably more than the small caramel droplets Candyman kept in a bowl for melting. Maybe tonight I would line the small candies down his chest, arranging them like stars, before using my tongue to trace swirls and patterns and galaxies as they melted from his body heat...

There she was.

Everything stopped. The dragon of fire Marianne shot into the air paused, a great tongue of jade flame cauterized from its mouth. The jaunty spring from the bow of the violin froze on the strings. The clouds of pink candy floss strangled the white stick.

Then the breath whooshed from my lungs, adrenaline igniting my body as the world revolved once again.

She was here.

I'd studied every inch of the small portrait I had been given when assigned this task. Ingrained the details onto the corrugations of my mind while traveling through wood and dale, skirting cities and plowing through barren countryside.

As I closed in and navigated the labyrinthine streets of this town, I imagined every conceivable change of hair color, added wrinkles or frown lines, each blend of fabric she could opt to wear. I had questioned the baker, the tailor, the midwife, all in a roundabout, casual tone, painting an amicable smile on my face while secretly probing their answers for the minutiae.

Dully, she was as expected. Mid-forties, brown hair streaked with gray, thick glasses perched upon a straight nose. Her clothes were average—well-pressed, but clean. She hid her wealth in the diamond necklace that peeked out of her frilled collar and the pointed shoes inlaid with golden thread and satin bindings which serpentined up her ankles.

What had she done? And, more importantly to whom? Maybe it was better not knowing. Then I was just doing a social service—for a hefty fee. The chase had been fun, the funneling of the hunt heart-pounding. But the kill? I may not be directly slitting her throat, but I was handing over the knife. My stomach flipped, the sweat beading upon my palms.

I flicked the top card at her. It fluttered on the breeze, dying at her feet.

She stooped to pick it up, turning toward me with a cock of her head as she considered what I could deign to offer her. I raised my face, allowing the color from the fairy lights to fall upon me as the hood lifted, unmasking the shadows. I gestured toward the empty bench.

Don't run. Don't flee. I don't want to have to chase you.

She moved closer, a smirk stretching her lips. "That was a silly little trick." Her voice stretched, the sarcasm snagging the attention of passersby. "Is this my likeness?" She twirled the Death card in her fingers.

"A warning," I said.

She didn't believe in the power of the deck, for her fortunes were not told in fables and fairytales. She would sit just to prove a point. To prove how ridiculous this was.

The crowd grew steadily around her, magnetized by her scorn.

My heart hammered and my mouth dried. The hood flapped back over my face as she settled herself, elbows planted upon the velvet cloth, the bells cackling wildly with the movement.

Don't leave.

Don't hate me.

"I don't need a fortune read," she said. "What else do you have?"

I pulled the tarot toward me and positioned them perfectly square at the edge of the table. I held out my palm hoping she wouldn't notice the sheen of congealing sweat.

She extracted a dainty coin purse from the depths of her outfit and handed over one copper. "You can have more if these fine folk are impressed." She waved her hand, inviting the hovering people closer.

A small throng had gathered. It wasn't surprising. She was well known, respected, and feared. It had been difficult getting anyone to talk about her, to reveal even the smallest morsel of information. Once they sniffed where the conversation was going, they rapidly scurried away. Being tantalizingly close for such a long time had been half the fun. They were as curious as I was about the woman underneath.

I reached under the table and pulled up a velvet-draped divider. It was a foot high and the same width with an ebony cloth attached. She watched me intently as I reached across and gently lowered her left arm. I moved it to the side, palm down, fingers splayed. I slid the board along the table and into the crook of her arm, arranging the cloth over her left shoulder so she seemed to melt seamlessly into the fabric.

Next, I flopped out a doll's arm. Stuffed, pink and plump, perfectly proportioned to her own body size. I slid the severed end under the cloth, positioning the hand and unpainted nails exactly like her real one.

Candyman's eyes lingered on mine through the packed bodies as they jostled for a better vantage point, but the flirtation had gone. His brow furrowed, a fleeting look of worry marring his features until my view of him was engulfed by the crowd again.

If this went wrong, I would need access to all his hidden rum. Gorging on sugar and drinking myself into a stupor would be a good swan song for my life thus far.

I tugged the two strands of silver ribbon out from under the tarot. I ran each length along the fake arm and her real one simultaneously. Her brow furrowed, a small crinkle of disgust burrowing into the skin above her nose.

"Do you feel this?" I asked.

She huffed, her eyes darting to those closest before answering, "Of course I do."

I stopped stroking her real arm but continued to slide the ribbon up the doll's arm. "And now?"

She scoffed again. "Yes."

A small murmur arose from those watching. The woman stilled, her blue eyes narrowing on me.

I nodded. "Very well."

Returning the ribbons to the corner of the table, I scooped up a handful of fire jacks from an alcove underneath. Marianne had kindly lent me a few dozen at the beginning of the fayre, in return for a doctored reading of ill omens when her ex-wife visited.

I cracked one of the jacks between my fingers, tossing it quickly into the air as a small ball of white-hot fire cracked into life. It hovered for a split second before sizzling into ash and drifting toward the table. I shifted in my seat, pressing my thigh into the table leg where another aroma waited. This would release the charred scent of burning flesh, raising the air temperature by a few degrees with it.

I took another jack between my fingers and squeezed, dropping it quickly onto the doll's arm. As it landed, I cracked the vial with my leg, the noise lost amongst the woman's shriek.

She gaped at the fake arm and the charred circle marring its pink wrist. The crowd tittered. Whispers of, "Did you really feel that?" and "She's part of the act." I waited until they quieted and took another jack to her real arm. She couldn't see over the screen, hadn't even noticed my arm move to the side as she stared transfixed at the black stain on the doll's arm.

I cracked another and rested it on her real hand. It ignited, a brief ripple of heat firing into the crowd. They drew back, some gasping, a few honks of nervous laughter, but the woman did not move.

She frowned at me, then swiveled to assess the crowd. I reached out to tug on the fake arm. "Sit still please." As if I'd pulled her physically, she turned back and settled. The crowd gasped again.

I pushed the remaining jacks aside, willing the tremble in my fingers to cease and pointed toward an elderly lady to the right of the woman. She wore an elaborate jewel-spattered hat, braided with ribbons and flowers.

"A pin, please." She extracted one, a fine specimen, two inches long with a diamond head.

I started on the woman's real hand. Gently, the pin sunk into the flesh between her fingers, skewering her to the velvet table as if she were a butterfly. She made no sound, nor even flinched. The crowd was silent, sensing the finale, their eyes wide, muscles tensed as they hung on every little movement.

I pulled the pin out slowly, a smear of blood coating the barb. Moving toward the fake arm, I gently prodded the flesh of the forearm. The woman jumped. I did it again, and she flinched. Hovering the pin just above the fake skin, my eyes locked with hers beneath the hood.

My right hand crept toward her real arm, nails silently extending. Power coursed through my body, pooling with a tingle in my fingertips as I dragged my nails down her arm, the jagged ends biting into her flesh.

She didn't move an inch.

I fought to stop an exhale of relief as the magic rushed out, my body yearning to lay limp as if exsanguinated.

A young boy popped up beside the woman and crammed himself next to her on the bench. "What's going on, Ma?" He shoved a pink and green swirled lollipop into his mouth and stared at the fake arm with my pin hovering over it, before peering past the barrier.

My stomach twisted. She had a child?

It was too late, but the real question was, would it have stopped me?

I smoothed the blood away using the velvet tablecloth and tugged down her long sleeve. Unfolding the cloth from her shoulder, I returned the barrier beneath the table and lowered my head. The audience broke into applause.

In a daze, the woman cautiously wound her arm in as if the nerves had all come loose. Coppers rained onto the table, bouncing off one another until the excited voices turned away to see what other wonders the fayre held.

Midnight had barely struck, but I was done.

When I pushed the remaining fire jacks toward the boy, he pocketed them gleefully. I waited until his mother had fully roused herself and shepherded the boy away before tugging down the wooden sign above my stall. Candyman was obscured again in the rush of customers who had left my performance, blocking my last view of him. I scooped up the coppers, left the tarot and other equipment, and headed toward the far end of the field.

Once the grass began to tickle my knees and the colorful glow from the fayre had dimmed to an ashy firelight, I doubled over and retched.

When there was nothing left in my stomach, I straightened, wiping my mouth on my sleeve. The woods bordering the field were thick and almost impenetrable, but I had scoped out my retreat already. Picking my feet high along a narrow game trail, I made for the other side, a distance of only a few miles if I stayed true.

I didn't know how much time I had before the Collectors came. They wouldn't snatch the woman at the fayre, it would be too public. On her way home, perhaps? Maybe they had a shred of decency left and would wait until she'd tucked her child into bed, sparing him the eternal nightmares. It would be better to wake and find her vanished than the alternative.

This, I knew firsthand.

The wood pressed in around me, brambles snagging on my cloak and razor-thin spiderwebs caressing my face. Where were the night creatures? The hooting owl, the mouse rustling through the fallen leaves? Even the bats were not silhouetted against the dark clouds.

I ignored the acid roiling in my stomach, the ever-deafening roar in my ears to turn back and spend the night in the warm embrace of Candyman. Safely tucked up amongst people and far away from the darkness that lurked everywhere else.

A twig snapped like bone from just ahead.

Is that why the animals had fled? The Collectors were already waiting?

Crunch.

I tried to submerge the screaming of my subconscious mind, the instinct for self-preservation and pushed through toward a small clearing.

A figure emerged from the shadows on the other side.

Don't miss more from S.R. Hartley coming soon, and find out more at srhartleyauthor.com

Until then, discover THE BOUNTY OF BLOOD AND NAILS, by City Owl Author, N K Brown

Tam is a heartless, ruthless bounty hunter—or so her handler would have you believe.

With her ability to use forbidden blood magic, Tam tracks and captures her prey. The same blood magic that curses her to a life of servitude under a cruel handler—one wrong move and not only her life, but her family's will be at stake. But when she's sent to a remote, superstitious northern town where even a glimmer of magic will send you to the gallows, she's forced to confront the darker consequences of her work.

After the murder of her bounty, innocent townspeople are blamed—and Tam's conscience begins to stir. But there's no turning back. Her handler raises the stakes, and her next mission is even more dangerous: infiltrate the royal castle and capture the enigmatic Prince Bellinor. Disguised as a maid, Tam is drawn into a world of deadly secrets, where her words are whispered into the prince's ears through an ancient magic she's never faced before.

To get close to the prince, she befriends his loyal bodyguard, Clement, but the deeper she digs, the more she realizes that Clement's destiny is tied to the prince. With time running out and the castle tightening, Tam is forced to watch the trial of the people blamed for her own prior actions. But will she complete the mission—or risk it all as she falls in love with the person whose life she must destroy?

In this fast-paced, thrilling tale of magic, betrayal, and forbidden love, Tam will have to decide if being the bad guy is worth losing everything.

Please sign up for the City Owl Press newsletter for chances to win special subscriber-only contests and giveaways as well as receiving information on upcoming releases and special excerpts.

All reviews are **welcome** and **appreciated**. Please consider leaving one on your favorite social media and book buying sites.

Escape Your World. Get Lost in Ours! City Owl Press at www.cityowlpress.com.

ACKNOWLEDGMENTS

Thank you to my fiancé Stephen for supporting and encouraging me when I decided randomly one day that I wanted to chase this author dream. You've been my biggest supporter and number one fan since the beginning, and I appreciate you so much for it. I also want to thank Ellie and Brennen, my two amazing kiddos for listening to me yap about book deals and editing and things they don't understand, but being there to listen anyway. Thank you all for being patient and understanding now that my life is much busier and I talk endlessly about books and writing. I love you all so much.

Thank you to Lisa Green from City Owl Press for reading my book and loving it enough to offer me a book deal. You've helped make the dream I've had since I was a little girl of becoming a published author come true, and working with you is something I'll always be thankful for. You've taught me so much about not only the craft of writing, but about myself, and I've gained more confidence in my stories while working with you than I ever thought could be possible. You are amazing! Thanks to everyone else from City Owl Press for working in the background and helping bring this book to life. I appreciate each and every one of you so much.

To my critique partner Lauren who was there cheering me on and offering advice and suggestions while I queried this book and edited it to perfection, your help and support meant everything to me. This book became what it is today thanks to you, and I'll always be grateful for meeting you. Thank you.

To anyone else I might have missed, friends, readers, or otherwise, if you're reading this now, then thank you for being here and showing your support.

Last, but certainly not least, to any ex-boyfriend, fake friend, or secret hater who thought my dream of becoming an author one day was a joke because "how could I ever be good enough for that," or anyone who told me I'd be wasting my time even trying. How does it feel knowing you were wrong and that I've succeeded? Thank you for teaching me that I can do anything with dedication, a dream, and a little spite running through my veins. I hope it annoys the hell out of you watching me succeed, and I'm sure it does, so you're welcome.

ABOUT THE AUTHOR

When S.R. HARTLEY is not fantasizing about make-believe worlds full of morally gray characters and magic, she's working as a night shift nurse. She spends her free time at home (will always be a homebody) with her amazing boyfriend, her two crazy kids, and her black cat, Romeo. She's a huge lover of wine and books! She resides outside of Columbus, OH.

srhartleyauthor.com

instagram.com/s.r.hartley
x.com/srhartleyauthor
facebook.com/author.sheena.hamm

ABOUT THE PUBLISHER

City Owl Press is a cutting edge indie publishing company, bringing the world of romance and speculative fiction to discerning readers.

Escape Your World. Get Lost in Ours!

www.cityowlpress.com

facebook.com/CityOwlPress
x.com/cityowlpress
instagram.com/cityowlbooks
pinterest.com/cityowlpress
tiktok.com/@cityowlpress

www.ingramcontent.com/pod-product-compliance
Lightning Source LLC
Jackson TN
JSHW070729100326
98939JS00001B/1610

9781648985348